Dreams
of the Fae

TRANSCENDENCE

Dreams of the Fae

Transcendence

ANNA PATRICK PAIGE

Acknowledgments

First, to my granny, who made me believe fairy tales exist, all girls are princesses, and Prince Charming may be waiting around the next corner. The beautiful moments at the Lake House where you channeled my imaginative childhood into a creative muse will always be a part of me.

Greg, my supportive asshole, thank you for believing in my writing and listening for hours as I blabbered about plot ideas until you tuned me out to keep your sanity. Without you these pages would have remained blank. Thank you for giving me the resources to chase my dreams. Someday I'll figure out a way to make it up to you.

Dad, I am eternally grateful for everything, and I miss you every day.

Bug, thanks for always sticking around during the times I lost my mind.

Axle, because of you I finally turned the story in my head into computer print babble. I love you.

Ayla, my very own little Fae princess, chase your dreams, because it's possible.

Chris, thank you for keeping your promises to my father with shining colors. It has meant everything to me.

Mom, thank you for telling people I was an amazing author even when you had never read a single word I'd written. It was an odd form of encouragement, but I think it worked.

Cammy, thank you for a childhood filled with imagination and fairy tales.

Wendy, my alpha, thank you for letting me use your brilliant mind and giving me everything I needed, even when it was hard. This story would not be what it is without you. Thank you—Thank you—Thank you.

Janie, the influence you had over a child by sending her books every year for her birthday was colossal. You shaped my love of literature. Thanks for that.

Sam, you have been such a wonderful friend during this entire process. I doubt I would have made it this far without your encouragement. Thanks for helping me keep the lights on.

Lastly, my incredible Beta Team!!! Just when I was ready to give up, you put hope back into me and this series. Thank you for the hours of witty banter and shop talk, for loving my characters as much as I do, and for helping me finish the enormous task of writing this monster. I love you all.

For Granny,
whose weekends in the Florida sun shaped
my imagination and sung me a fairy tale.

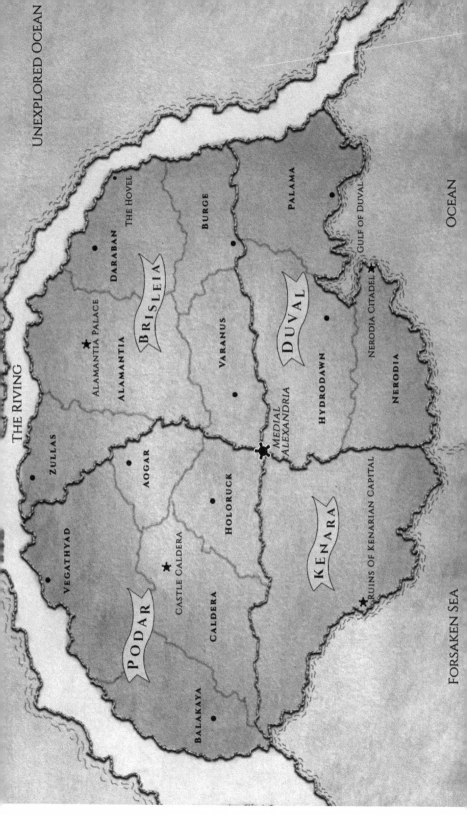

Prologue

We called it the Riving. The crack in the foundation of the planet that split the crust to the core and stole our dreams.

The Riving forced us to form peace by the punishment of a bleeding wound—a method to save the planet from our destruction. And to save us, a new power rose to the surface, called by the planet to accept the burden of human corruption.

Four mortal men, marked by the power of the Riving, became the *Divine* and split our world.

The black soil and volcanic fire of Podar.

The snow-capped stone mountains of Brisleia.

The windswept grassy plains of Kenara.

The waterfalls and lush tropical forest of Duval.

Four distinctly different lands—two bordering the sea, two bordering the Riving.

With Divine lifeblood sustaining the continent, the world of Athera would forever flourish, but if the bloodline died, then so too would their country, and all life therein would cease to exist.

It was the duty of the Divine to govern, to protect, to love the land and its people above all else until the Riving sealed.

Though it would seem the planet left no clues to discern how to unify her, and if there ever was instruction, it had long since been lost to time.

Chapter 1

I started dreaming the day I turned thirteen. An affliction that would get me killed if anyone discovered the secret.

The ruling Senate at Medial Alexandria explained "dreams" as symptomatic of a disorder called *Fae*, with onset in early childhood. The Senate had warned the continent of Athera about these criminally insane children since the Riving appeared four thousand years ago, but no one knew exactly why they had been deemed too formidable for society.

Parents were instructed to watch for signs of the impairment. If affected, the child would claim to see visions in their sleep before the age of ten. The Senate were to be contacted immediately to detain the dangerous individual. Knowingly abetting or harboring a Fae was punishable by death from the Sights of the Onyx Guard.

So, apparently, I was insane.

Impaired, criminal, symptomatic.

Developing the hazardous anomaly past the assumed age.

Whenever I slept, my mind became a paintable canvas, and the dark, slumbering peace that abided for everyone else in Athera came to life.

Weightless, I moved through a black abyss abundant with twinkling stars, the curls of my hair hovering about my face. Blue rays of hazy light twisted through the darkness. Mesmerized by the supernatural blank slate, I fixated on the stars until they faded, then drifted through the smoky haze to find the ground. Little plants grew out of the cold, wet soil and tickled my toes. The scent of flowers hung thick in the warm air. I longed to return to the world above, a place where life poured out of me in a fantasy too similar to reality. Who knew dreams felt like a second life?

How could I be insane? I didn't feel insane. No one would dare hint at such an atrocity or attempt to condemn the King's daughter and ignite a futile battle to declare me unfit for society. The Divine were critical to the planet's survival. Still, I guarded my secret, believing the Fae to be deranged and dangerous.

The Senate and their Onyx Guard were inescapable, and yet they never came for me. Even so, a prison is still a prison, whether it's Medial Alexandria or the stone walls of Alamantia Palace.

Prior to my thirteenth birthday, life was stagnant. Nothing significant or changing. The memories look young and pretty, faded and fogged images of simplicity. I spent days isolated in my apartments, wondering if anything would ever happen to me—until by some twisted miracle, "different" occurred.

When the dreams started, my excitement over having something new to engage my mind warred with my terror over the situation. Eventually, fear triumphed. I began to avoid nightly slumber altogether—and discovered an alarming new phenomenon accompanied my secret: I didn't suffer from the lack of sleep. Weeks would pass before I finally grew tired and faced the visions.

I hid the affliction well. Hiding in plain sight was the only way to exist as a Divine royal. The hours I spent forcing myself to be numb to the cunning dukes and eager maids roaming every hallway fueled an intransigent part of my personality. Trusting no one and loving few wasn't a life, and I ceased to live at all.

The Onyx Guard kidnapped Dreamers and imprisoned them in Medial Alexandria, but not the daughter of a king who knew how to hold her mystery. After all, dreaming was impossible.

I opened my eyes to the knock at my chamber door and pulled the heavy fur-lined covers farther up my chest, twisting my fingers into the creamy embroidered satin. It was spring, April. The cold still lingered, but the frost had finally left the ground. The absence of snow didn't change the frigid Brisleian air that never completely disappeared, even in the summer months.

I rubbed my fists into my eyes. *Eighteen.* I was eighteen today and legally an adult under Atheran law.

"Good evening, Your Highness." Elizabetta appeared in the arched double doors. She carried a large silver dinner tray, and her delicate arms strained under the weight. The cooks must have sent extra items on this ridiculous holiday.

She lowered the tray onto the nightstand and uncovered the variety of food. A chicken, leg of lamb, warm bread with butter, cheese pastries, small cakes topped with cherries, strawberries dipped in sugar, and other exotic delicacies covered the platter.

"You've missed the King's supper." She shook her head in disapproval, and a strand of burgundy hair fell from her white bonnet. "You don't sleep for weeks, then choose today to snooze the hours away." She eased the damask canopy back to the bedpost, leaving the sheer silken veil in place. The gemstones sewn into the lace fabric flittered in the candlelight.

I narrowed my eyes at her for hinting at my *condition*. I'd purposefully missed the day's earlier festivities: dawn's lantern-releasing ceremony, breakfast, dinner, the parade, supper with the lords of Brisleia.

"His Divine Majesty will not be pleased." Raising one eyebrow at my subdued smile, she pushed the tray closer to the edge of the table. "Eat."

I grabbed only a strawberry and popped the end into my mouth, sucking the sweet nectar through my teeth and licking sugar from my lips. The late-afternoon sun peeked through the heavy blue velvet curtains. I threw off the fur covers and hopped onto the marble floor. "When are the fireworks?"

"Tonight, during the ball," she replied. "I've been instructed to ensure that you are at court this evening for the celebration, on pain of excommunication." She pulled aside the drapery on the behemoth arch that led to the balcony, and I shivered as a flood of chilly air froze the russet marble under my feet.

I quirked an amused eyebrow. "Well, we can't have that now, can we? Besides, what's a party without the guest of honor?"

Elizabetta had been part of my household since the day I was born. She had arrived in Alamantia shortly before my birth and insisted on serving as nurse to the newly born Divine heir. Oddly entranced, my parents had trusted the strange woman with deep amber eyes and burgundy hair, and she had scooped me into her tender arms and refused to put me down for the majority of my elementary years.

Long after I outgrew the need for a nurse, she had remained as something even more essential. Beyond a trusted friend, she was a steadfast companion. Constant. Strong. Unstoppable. I had never lived a day without her—a cause for concern when guarding a dangerous secret.

When the dreams began, her attention to me bordered on alarming. Yet, despite my reluctance to sleep, she never questioned me beyond the occasional banter—"Why don't you get some rest?"—always followed by a logical explanation: "A

Divine Princess should never look tired." If anyone was going to discover my *condition*, it would be her.

The evening sun painted the sky purple and orange over the half-circle balcony jutting into my private garden. Below, cobblestone pathways and minimal flora led to a stone fountain in the garden's center, which was flowing for the first time in months now that the ice had thawed. A thick layer of roses covered the garden's marble privacy walls. The faint sound of music and cheering floated in from the city as the citizens of Alamantia celebrated my birthday.

I tossed the strawberry aside, eyeing a little blue bird making her home inside the willow tree in the back corner. She disappeared into the low-hanging branches that feathered and swayed in the chilly breeze.

"*Spring. Spring.*"

I sunk my head into my hands, trying to suffocate my mind. For the last month, I'd started hiding a bizarre new symptom: hearing voices. Medial Alexandria's records of the Dreamers never mentioned this one.

Failing to shut out the clamor, I crossed my arms over my chest.

"*Cold water. Spring.*"

Annoying chatter.

Elizabetta slipped my heaviest fur robe around my shoulders, smoothing the fabric and easing my arms into the ample sleeves. As she finished, she smacked a blue bird flitting relentlessly around our heads. The poor thing lost the wind and almost hit the ground before finding its wings and flying away.

"Elizabetta!" I scolded.

"Pesky things." She pushed me back into the security of my bedchamber.

Elizabetta hated animals. She shooed away birds, cats, and mice and kept me away from horses. She tolerated only the King's hunting dogs. Sometimes it seemed as if she had made it her life's work to keep me isolated.

Inside, my three ladies had returned. The girls, all wearing matching champagne-colored gowns, giggled while straightening my bed covers.

First, Camille Lamare, the daughter of the duke of Daraban. Much to our father's dismay, my brother and I favored the Lamare family, and Camille fancied Prince Luken, but so did most girls at court.

Next, Daphne Wallington, the little sister of the Unity Knight of Justice. She had been placed in my household a year ago by the King. One consequence of keeping a small household— it left positions open for His Majesty's enjoyment. Daphne's family was the embodiment of everything I despised about court. The Wallingtons were ambitious wolves, ready to devour any competition standing between them and their close connection to the Divine.

Lastly, Melody Hothburg, the daughter of the duke of Varanus. I found her nonthreatening.

My apartments consisted of five rooms in the eastern wing of the palace. Carved rose reliefs, detailed in pearl and glass, decorated the marble floor, and ornate gold trim gilded every arch and curve of the white quartz walls. Extravagant lace inlaid with tiny diamonds curtained around chairs, pillars, and doorframes. Bear rugs lined the floor in a plush half-circle seating area by the alabaster fireplace.

I spent most of my time in these apartments. Unlike my older brother, I would never rule a country. Forming alliances and becoming knowledgeable in the laws of the land were not my roles. My duty was to display happiness to the people of Brisleia, stay beautiful and desirable, and above all maintain a standard of modesty for young women. Yet I performed these roles poorly, or so I was told. I wore my emotions too openly. It was easier to stay asocial, locked away with my books.

Elizabetta pushed me down onto the tiny gilded stool in front of my vanity and vigorously combed the mess of almond curls extending past my waist. She snagged a stubborn strand and yanked my head back from the force of her pull. A mildly painful *pop* sounded when the curl snapped.

I slapped the comb. "That hurts!"

"Your Highness." Camille's reflection appeared in the mirror. "Your gifts from the King and queen have arrived."

I pushed the comb from my head. Elizabetta grunted in defeat as I trotted through the aureate double doors leading into the receiving room.

One immense window, stretching all the way to the carved walnut ceiling, let plenty of light into the room. Today it was open, allowing the spring breeze to eradicate the stale winter air. The vast chamber contained a curved staircase ascending to a second floor, which housed an extraordinary collection of books. Fancily decorated gift boxes crowded the pitcher of wine and fruit bowls on the lace-covered table, and layers of lavish dress fabrics were draped over the blue-upholstered chairs.

My ladies looked anxiously upon the many trinkets. I nodded my permission, and they scattered around the room, squealing with delight, opening each box and admiring its contents.

The gifts emerged in the form of chocolates and candies, fine white cotton, dress dyes, shoes, and jewels.

"There is nothing here from Podar, Your Highness," Daphne noted with a disapproving twist of her lips. "How appalling."

I ignored her, and Melody captured my attention with a new book of dress patterns.

Elizabetta plucked the booklet from my hands. "Your father waits for no man," she tutted.

"It's convenient I'm a woman," I replied.

She frowned, unamused, and rushed me back to my vanity. An eighteen-year-old Princess stared back at me from the mirror.

Fair skin. No marring. No blemishes. No distinguishing marks, except one—the Mandala.

The symbol of my Divinity stretched over my skin like a scar, shimmering with a muted glow. The silvery-white pattern of filigree spirals began at the edge of my forehead and covered my temple. It receded under my hairline and wrapped around my ear to spread down the side of my neck and spill over my shoulder. The intricate design glared at me—a reminder of what I meant to the people of Athera.

The Mandala connected us to the Riving and tied the life of each Divine to the continent. As long as the Divine lived, the country would flourish, but if a nation's bloodline died, so would everything else. Many gave their lives in defense of the Divine, but there were always those who sought to destroy us. For these reasons, royal families stayed locked behind palace walls.

Divine. Royalty. Deity. No matter what title we were given, it didn't change the fact that even luxury could be a prison.

I shut my eyes for a moment, trying to forget the small girl in the mirror who wanted anything but the lot she was given.

Elizabetta's comb ran along my scalp, pulling each strand of my hair. Daphne set a bathing dish on the vanity and gingerly washed my hands, then repeated the process with my feet. Camille brought a hot curling iron from the hearth and handed it to Elizabetta, who wrapped each lock into a tighter spiral. *Ridiculous.*

Elizabetta slid the heavy robe from my shoulders. I firmly held the bedpost for stability as she cinched a silk boned corset around my waist. The laces crushed my lungs, my intake of air cut in half. Before I could catch my breath, an elaborate blue silk gown with silver embroidery was thrown over my head, and my arms were quickly fed into the sleeves. Daphne attached the dress train to the back of my shoulders and smoothed the fabric.

The crown jewels of Brisleia were the final ornament for a public appearance. Elizabetta placed the tiara on my head.

The heavy crown was so encrusted with diamonds—arranged to hide little flowers within the pattern, to mimic the Brisleian Mandala—that the silvery base vanished beneath the gemstones. By the end of the night, my neck would be sore.

She clipped matching diamond earrings to my lobes, then turned me to face the mirror. The flickering candlelight sent reflected sparkles dancing across the walls.

The Divine Royal Highness Ayleth Rose of Alamantia. The words echoed through my head with all the emptiness and loneliness that accompanied them. I projected an image to the outside world: Brisleian perfection. A valuable piece of the Divine King's property. The Princess whose quiet demeanor was as renowned as her tenacity.

Another performer in the inescapable choreography of fate.

A certain sadness accompanied the life of a Divine, a sorrowful inevitability I wasn't sure I'd ever learn to accept. I would forever be owned by a king and obligated by one royal duty or another.

Lost in my reverie, I almost missed the faint knock from within the walls, to the right of the fireplace. Elizabetta dismissed my ladies, and I rushed to my only glimmer of happiness.

Rarely dismissed, Elizabetta knew the most intimate details of my life, including the secret way my brother and I communicated within the palace. When Luken and I were children, she introduced us to the intricate web of stone tunnels within the walls of Alamantia. Once used for safe passage during the War, they had long since been forgotten. To our knowledge, Luken, Elizabetta, and I were the only people who knew they existed.

The embellished gilding gave way to reveal a little hidden door, which opened into a dark corridor. My elder brother, the Divine Royal Majesty Luken Rose of Alamantia, Crowned Heir to the Throne of Brisleia, stood in the dark, a gleaming smile across his handsome face. He entered the room and kissed my cheek, a little too close to my mouth, and handed me a shiny rectangular black box. "A gift for Princess Ayleth on the evening of her eighteenth birthday, from her loving and charming older brother," he proclaimed, stifling a laugh.

"Charming?" I scoffed. "Don't flatter yourself. They may celebrate you most days, but today I dare overshadow you. Jealous?"

"Completely," he teased, closing the door behind him. It melted into the wall as if it had never been there. "So, how does it feel to come of age?"

I raised an eyebrow, then set the box on my bed to embrace him.

"Supper was awkward without you," he said. "Father was . . . displeased, to say the least."

I let out a short burst of laughter. "I was tired."

"You? Tired? Never." He winked with eyes the same shade of pewter as mine and nudged the parcel towards me.

I lifted the pristine lid off the birthday gift.

"It's very fine," he bragged. "Fit for a king."

Inside rested a purple satin purse. I untied the gold drawstring and emptied a dagger into my hand.

"Exquisite, isn't it?" He plucked the weapon from my grasp and ran his fingers up the black leather scabbard. The grip was crafted from a solid piece of ebony bog-wood, with a rounded black diamond pommel. The small guard had the insignia of Medial Alexandria carved into the grain: a circular geometric pattern comprising elements of all four Atheran Mandalas.

"This is an Onyx Guard weapon," I observed, amazed. "How did you get this?"

"It was given to me by the Senate master during my last visit to Medial Alexandria. Knowing your birthday was approaching, I thought it would make the perfect gift for you. It will hold in place around your ankle, if you wish. Medial weapons are the best in Athera. It's a shame the Senate won't distribute them." He tapped the diamond pommel.

I took the dagger and examined the most unusual gift I had ever received; a dagger was typically a present for a boy. "What would make you think a dagger would be a suitable gift for me?"

"I have a theory you may need it someday. Better you be protected than outnumbered," he confessed.

Elizabetta laughed, stirring the fire.

My brother always saw me as more than a perfect Divine Princess. He knew the things I wanted, unusual as they were for a Divine. One day he would rule as King of Brisleia, and I would at last be allowed to live a life I could only imagine. Dress how I wished. Marry whom I wished. Come to court if it pleased me instead of when I was ordered.

Maybe the dagger was proof of this promise. I couldn't help but love Luken as much as the rest of Brisleia.

I dropped the blade back into its purse and placed it within the gift box.

"Are you not pleased?" he asked.

"It's beautiful."

"By your expression one might think it's the worst thing you've ever received," he drawled.

"I'm used to jewelry and fabrics. I don't know how to accept a gift I truly am going to treasure."

Luken pulled me back to his chest and squeezed, crushing my arms to my sides. "Eighteen is a rite of passage. I hope you remain open to the changes lying before you." He kissed my forehead.

Be open to change? My heart fluttered with the possibilities.

He eased me out of his arms, and his face fell, as if there was more he wanted to say. The expression quickly passed, replaced by his glorious smile. "So, what do you think, Elizabetta?" He turned to my nurse.

"You're foolish to give her a weapon," she chided. "She will commit bloodshed."

"Don't be so dramatic." I rolled my eyes. "It's just a knife. Besides, Luken promised to teach me swords someday."

"The King will have me jailed if he sees her wielding a sword." Elizabetta shook her head. "And she will ruin every dress I've made her."

Luken chuckled, squeezing my shoulder. "I have to leave for Daraban in the morning."

"What? Why?"

His eyes landed on the remaining food next to my bed, and he strolled to the nightstand. "Business."

I rested my hands on my hips, waiting for a more thorough answer.

"Curtus Lamare and I have something we need to attend to in Duval." Luken tore away a chunk of chicken breast and crammed it into his mouth.

"Duval?" I tried to make my disapproval clear. "For how long?"

He shrugged. "Three weeks."

I scoffed. "The last time you said three weeks, it became three months."

"I have to visit Nerodia Citadel to meet with Prince Tydous," he mumbled, swallowing. "Politics, Ayleth, it wouldn't interest you."

"And you have to leave tomorrow? You just came back from Medial Alexandria."

"I heard a rumor going around the Senate that Prince Marcus of Podar is trying to convince the Duvali heir to turn sides when he claims the throne. King O'dern is growing feeble. It won't be long before Prince Tydous is the Divine King of Duval. Marcus's influence could destroy the peace we've grown accustomed to. He's just . . . too radical." He disappeared into thought. "I don't want to imagine a world where Duval becomes combative or, worse, joins forces with those damn Podarians. Divinity won't help us if that occurs, and another war can never be in Athera's future. The duke of Daraban will be accompanying us. We need to keep the Divine of Duval in our good graces."

I sank onto the mattress. "You seem worried. It's unusual."

He rubbed his palms together. "Preventing hostile activity on a continental scale."

"Traveling the world to do so."

"Being constantly homesick and missing my little sister."

"Influencing people."

"Would it be absurd to say how, through it all, I envy you." He sat on the opposite end of the bed.

"Envy me, trapped here every day with a few maids to keep me company?"

"You are Divine royalty with no expectation. If it suited you to do so, you could do nothing all day but wear pretty dresses and dance."

"Is that what you think I do all day?" I asked, offended. "You talk as if I'm no different than my maids, who only care about finding a man of stature to marry. Dresses and dancing? Honestly, Luken?"

"If you followed the protocol the King and queen wanted, then marriage and stature would be all you cared about as well." His eyes fell, and he poked one of the white crystals sewn into the bedspread. "Still, marriage . . . it might do you some good to start considering the possibility."

I jumped off the bed, and my stomach did a sick twist. Luken never talked this way. "Prince Luken Rose! Where have you gone and who has replaced you?"

He rolled his eyes. "I need you to promise me something."

I petulantly folded my arms over my chest.

"Promise me you will always remember I have your best interest at heart. If I were King, I swear, I'd make sure you were always well kept. Happy. Free. Or you could run around in trousers, if it pleased you. I wouldn't care. You would have privilege beyond measure. But . . ." He paused for several long seconds, then swallowed hard. "I am not King, and there are things not even my influence can change."

Chapter 2

The blue paisley rug flew beneath my feet as Elizabetta and I sped down the hall towards the ballroom. She held an armful of my gown while adjusting stray curls around my face. Instead of her daily indigo satin dress and crisp cotton apron, she wore a black taffeta gown with trumpet sleeves, laced up the back with maroon cording that matched her hair. Her beauty and graceful manner resembled royalty.

My ladies struggled to keep pace with us as we hurried past the doors of the dining hall. The servants inside busily carted away dirty dishes. Startled by my unexpected appearance, they dropped to their knees. The crash of porcelain echoed through the corridors.

We turned the corner and came to a halt, my heels skidding across the marble. I smoothed the front of my dress and straightened my back, folding my hands in front.

Proud and tall, Luken stood by the colossal stained-glass doors leading into the Rose Court. His silvery crown perched atop his head. The diamonds garnishing the metal flickered in the candlelit hallway. He wore a white silk tunic cinched at the waist with a blue belt, and the deep purple sash strung across his chest was embellished with the pattern of the Mandala. His sword hung at his side, half-hidden by the velvety eggplant cloak brushing his boots. A fine chain around his neck and his most opulent black trousers completed the affluent ensemble.

A familiar cheerful smile spread across his face. "Always late."

"Your Majesty," I huffed, trying to catch my breath, and bowed. My ladies mirrored the movement.

Luken bowed in response. "May I escort you, Your Highness?"

I offered my hand. He kissed it before slipping my arm around his elbow.

"Are you wearing the dagger?" he whispered with a devious smirk.

I scowled. "No, of course not."

"You should. All the time. It suits you." He led me to the arched doors, our entourage of attendants following behind.

"As grateful as I am, it isn't proper."

"When did you start paying heed to what is proper? Would you have worn it if I had told you that you look like the type of woman who is secretly armed?" he teased, suppressing a grin.

"You're ridiculous," I grumbled.

The guards opened the doors, bowing their heads and reciting a polite chorus of *Your Majesties*. Inside, the Rose Court lay before us.

Rays from the evening sun pierced the immense gilded windows, causing the air to glitter. Numerous blooms of white and pink roses budded over the pillars and across the lavish stained-glass ceilings. The flowers grew year-round, and petals constantly littered the gray marble floor, filling the court with the most luscious aroma in Athera.

Down a massive alabaster staircase, a festal reception of couples danced in unison to the enchanting music.

"Happy birthday, Ayleth." Luken kissed my temple, then turned to his adoring lords and ladies.

Fanfare drowned the music as he stepped into the light at the top of the stairs. The crier's voice boomed above the trumpeting. "Presenting His Divine Royal Majesty Prince Luken Rose of Alamantia, Crowned Heir to the Throne of Brisleia."

The crowd of noblemen fell to their knees, bowing their heads to welcome the beloved Divine Prince. Luken didn't miss a step gliding across the blue-and-gold runner and down the stairs, his two personal attendants—Curtus Lamare and Aaron Rolf— following behind in a magnificent display of Brisleia's future leaders.

Unlike me, my brother luxuriated in his role as a Divine. I envied his ability to find happiness in a world I had always known as bleak and shallow.

At the far end of the ballroom, three prodigious oval windows illuminated a round raised platform, where five satiny blue chairs created the Divine throne. The rest of my royal family stood there in adoration.

Leaving his attendants behind, Luken climbed the stairs of the dais and fell to his knees in front of our parents. The Divine King nodded in approval, and the Prince took his seat at our father's right hand.

As I'd done many times before, I crept into the light at the top of the stairs following my brother's glorious entrance. The heir not quite as important. *The Spare.* The fanfare replayed. The trumpeting made my eardrums throb. "Presenting Her Divine Royal Highness Ayleth Rose of Alamantia," the crier yelled. The crowd touched the floor, and I descended the stairs.

Different from Luken in political power, I was equal in grace and poise. Back straight. Head high. My ladies striding in perfect unison with me. Like the flowers inside a garden, we were the decorations complementing the beauty of the Rose Court.

The walk to the platform felt endless. Noble eyes glanced up to admire the charade. Judging. Waiting for my perfect Divine image to falter. It was enough to turn a person insane.

After an eternity of silent ridicule, I reached the stairs and bowed before the King and his queen. King Hugo sighed in disappointment, placing his hands on my shoulders and pulling me from the floor. He was tall and wide, with thick gray hair that still held threads of black from his youth. A full beard, crafted from the same pewter color as his eyes, covered his chin. "I'm glad you are well," he said skeptically, taking my chin between his fingers. "We will be discussing your behavior in the days to come."

I lowered my eyes and nodded meekly.

The King released his light but forbidding hold on me. "Happy eighteenth birthday, Daughter. You become more beautiful every time I see you." I hadn't seen him in two weeks.

"Thank you for my gifts," I said with a quiet sweetness that did little to hide the fraudulency in my voice. "As always, Your Majesty has been more than generous."

My mother gently kissed my forehead, her puffy, pouted lips identical to mine. "Happy birthday, Ayleth," she whispered against my skin. I'd inherited her large eyes, petite features, almond curls, and sour expression.

My father escorted me to my chair. Instead of retaking his seat, he took my mother's hand, and they promenaded to the ballroom floor.

"You're late," my grandmother, the Divine Queen Mother Ambrosia, said without looking in my direction. She scanned the crowd from her elegant throne next to Luken.

Two generations ago, Brisleia had fallen into chaos when my grandmother became the only living Divine tied to the country after her brother died. Parliament forced her into marriage to produce Divine children. I'd heard she didn't mourn upon her husband's death and rejoiced when my father, her only son, took the throne. My grandmother's scandalous youth was a popular topic of gossip. Many still talked about how she had run from the palace, frequently disobeyed the King's orders, and publicly disagreed to her arranged marriage. Defiance seemed to run in the family.

"I didn't spoil the party," I observed, watching my parents glide across the dance floor.

"No." The glowing shimmer of her Mandala caught the light. "People at court are far too self-absorbed to notice. You made your brother late. I see he waited for you."

"With no regrets." Luken flashed a proud smile.

"Punctuality was never your strength," she added, "even if the tardiness does infuriate your father."

I would be at the mercy of a severe lecture from the King tomorrow. "I've been distracted."

Luken chuckled. "Distracted."

I glared at his mocking tone, but he already had his eyes on Lady Camille.

"Excuse me, ladies," he said as he left the platform.

Ambrosia waited for Luken to interrupt a conversation between my lady and one of the Sloan brothers before continuing. "He's worried about your welfare. Whatever ails you has him bothered."

"I don't know what you're talking about," I fibbed, suppressing the concern that Luken's strange behavior this evening was linked to his bizarre birthday gift.

"I've recently learned that Luken had a concerning disagreement with the King about a subject in Parliament. It has become a heated debate in the Senate."

"Luken?" I questioned, finding him in the crowd. Lady Camille blushed, enamored by his royal charm. "Luken never disagrees with the King's decisions."

Fanfare stopped our conversation, leaving me to wonder why Luken would dare contradict Parliament. As heir to the throne, it was his duty to adhere to the King's ideals.

"Presenting the Unity Knights of Brisleia," the crier announced.

Speaking of ideals.

The Unity Knights acted as the personal guard to the Brisleian Divine and often came from gentry families, only to become the desire of many young women at court. The King collected men that best described his virtues and offered them the world in return for loyalty to the crown. Divided into two groups, Counsel and Combat, they served in Parliament and lived in luxury at court.

The Unity Knights had seating on a second-floor balcony that overlooked the ballroom, allowing them to be vigilant over the crowd of wealthy landowners and giving eyes and ears to the King where his grasp exceeded him.

In addition to celebrating my birthday, this ball was meant to welcome home the knights, who had been absent from the palace for several weeks. They marched into court in two lines, and each one took a knee before the royal family to proclaim the virtue he served. The Counsel Knights: Honor, Honesty, Justice, Trust, Wisdom. The Combat Knights: Patience, Loyalty, Strength, Peace, Valor.

As the knights filtered through the room, some heading to their perch and the others flirting with noblemen's daughters, my brother appeared before me.

"Would you do me the honor of a dance, dear sister?"

Luken knew I didn't dance unless forced. It was often impossible to decline an invitation, especially from a member of the family—though the persistence of dukes and knights could be equally impossible to escape. I'd danced with Sir Gregory Owens of Loyalty more times than I cared to acknowledge.

Luken extended his hand. Faking a smile for my father's sake, I accepted.

The crowd parted as he led me to the dance floor. "Are you enjoying yourself?" he asked.

"That's a leading question," I quipped.

I held up my gown, and he took my waist, twisting me around him, my dress flowing in riverlike waves behind us.

"You're hiding something from me," he said.

"I could say the same thing about you," I countered, wrinkling my nose. "One thing was different this year. I didn't receive a gift from Podar." The heavily volcanic western country usually sent the most elaborate presents. Once I'd received a magnificent bed carved from pumice rock. Having no use for it, I gave it to the palace to be used in one of the guest rooms.

"Perhaps"—his eyes wandered to the stairs and back to me— "I do know something you do not." He twirled me, flaring my gown. "And maybe it's about Podar, and maybe it is why I haven't been completely myself."

A sense of oncoming turmoil tightened my chest. "So, tell me," I pressed.

His expression hardened. "I promised the King I wouldn't. It will be up to you to decide what to make of it."

"That isn't fair. I would tell you." Yet, I had not spoken a word of my dreaming.

"Something is about to happen, and you are at the center of it."

Before I could continue my interrogation, fanfare blared, and Luken escorted me back to the dais. I eyed the rest of my family, all smiling and thrilled by some new arrival.

"Presenting His Divine Royal Majesty Prince Marcus Ember of Caldera, Crowned Heir to the Throne of Podar," the crier proclaimed.

My stomach jumped into my throat. Why had I not been informed of a foreign Divine Prince visiting Alamantia Palace? I shot Luken a disgruntled stare while he faked the happiest smile to welcome our Divine guest.

I had never met Prince Marcus, but I knew a little about him and his vague history. Sick for most of his childhood, he had only recently entered the political world of the Divine. Though the Podarian King still reigned, he was seriously unwell, and Marcus had taken over the ruling of Castle Caldera and all Podar, with praise heaped upon him. Under his direction, Podar was coming out of the violent darkness that had so long consumed her.

Prince Marcus started down the stairs with fifty attendants following him, each carrying a box or tray. At only nineteen, he was grand in stature and appearance, tall and broad for his age, with silky black hair and smooth olive skin. Flecks of loose black locks framed his dark brow. Ambition and control edged his deep basil-green eyes. The Podarian Mandala wrapped around his features in the same manner as the Brisleian, but it lacked the floral filigree pattern. Instead, the sharp design had few curved edges and glowed a deep blood red. Intimidating, yet still beautiful.

He wore a silken ebony tunic enhanced with black diamond threading, and the matching pants were tucked into the top of shiny onyx boots. A heavy chartreuse cloak was slung over his right shoulder, and the black diamond hilt of a sword peeked out from under the resplendent fabric. The spectacular entourage that followed were dressed in all black, with glistening platinum chains decorating their shoulders.

My father's court bowed as he walked through the center of the ballroom, each young girl excited to glimpse a Prince they could only admire from afar. He stopped at the base of the steps and dipped his head, his attendants following suit.

"Your Majesty, King Hugo." His deeply determined voice flowed bold and rich yet seemed to hold an ongoing internal power struggle. I swallowed nervously.

King Hugo opened his arms, inviting the foreigner to join us on the platform. "Prince Marcus, welcome to my court." The two embraced. "I am pleased to hear of your safe travels through Brisleia."

"The convoy you sent to assist mine made for an impervious journey. Your Unity Knights were of fine service."

The King smiled pleasantly. "You remember my son and heir, Prince Luken Rose." The two Princes bowed to each other. I blinked rapidly, stunned by the tension tightening my brother's mouth. "And may I introduce to you my wife, Queen Helena."

Marcus respectfully kissed my mother's hand. "Your Highness, your husband has hardly done your beauty justice in his descriptions of you."

My mother blushed. She *actually blushed*. "I hope you find your visit meets all your expectations."

"Alamantia could never disappoint me. Your kingdom holds the most beautiful city in Athera, and I have every intention of enjoying its splendors." Marcus's smoldering eyes darted to me.

"May I also present to you my daughter, the Princess Ayleth, to whom we owe this joyous occasion," King Hugo continued.

Marcus's gaze bored directly into my eyes, and his mouth spread into a slow, satisfied smile. "Princess Ayleth." He paused for a long moment, examining me. "I hope that during my stay I may get to know you better. I am sure we will have much in common." He took my hand and kissed it. A strange rousing sensation eased through my fingers and up my arm. I forced myself not to pull away. I did not need to insult a foreign Prince. "I've brought many gifts in honor of your birthday. I hope you enjoy them." He gestured to the fifty men standing behind him, presenting me with the most outlandish gift ceremony I had ever received.

"Your Majesty . . ." I hesitated, uncertain I could still speak. "Surely you do not mean all these gifts for me."

"Indeed. I have also brought you a Podarian mare, as well as pumice rock to have crafted into anything of your choosing."

Instead of the proper appreciation, rage boiled through my insides. I did not need a mare, and I highly doubted I needed anything else in his fifty parcels. What game was he playing? Not even the King of Alamantia had ever received so much from a Podarian Prince. Something was amiss and I could see it in Luken's fake smile.

A lifetime of royal training dictated I conceal my anger. I dipped my head. "Thank you, Your Majesty," I said through clenched teeth.

Marcus smirked, his countenance accusing me of naivety. A wave of his hand dismissed the entourage. "Have these gifts delivered to the Princess's apartments, where she can enjoy them to their fullest this evening."

My head began to spin, and a clammy sweat took over my palms.

"Princess Ayleth"—he closed in on me—"would you do me the honor of a dance? With your father's permission, of course."

King Hugo smiled. "Splendid."

Every ridiculous eye in the room watched me, waiting for my answer with grins or anticipation.

"It would be my pleasure," I accepted reluctantly.

Prince Marcus towered over me. I felt meek standing next to him, the way a finch might feel sharing a branch with an eagle. A bizarre silence fell over the guests as he led me to the center of the ballroom.

He turned me to face him. I craned my neck back to meet his gaze and instantly regretted it. He was extremely attractive—almost unnaturally handsome—with high cheekbones, full pink lips, and every bit of the bravado of a man overflowing with power, yet his presence still held something of the young boy trying to fill his father's place in history. A chess piece that didn't match the others, in use only so the game could continue.

The music began. He took my waist and glided me across the floor, our steps in perfect sync.

"I hate this ostentatious nonsense," he said after we had circled the ballroom. His voice didn't seem to belong to him. "People will always expect Divine royalty to put on an exhibition."

I gave a small nod. "Seeing a Divine royal is a once-in-a-lifetime experience for most. You should know, despite falling into duty for appearances, I despise dancing." Unwilling to let fear control me, I met his gaze, hoping the terror wouldn't show in my expression.

"Your footwork is exquisite, despite your resistance."

"It's not the steps I dislike. It's touching someone I find repulsive."

He suppressed a laugh. "Someone of your beauty *should* be repulsed by those of lesser value. I suspect you only associate with those you find befitting to your station."

I frowned. "No one would dare accuse me of being so shallow."

"I meant it as a compliment."

"Does my father know how you mock me? Do you assume this backward flattery is charming?" Handsome, yes, but his arrogance and pompous behavior overshadowed his regal appearance.

The edges of his mouth twitched. "As it happens, I have spoken a great deal with your father. I aim to take a wife in the near future."

"I suppose it would be prudent for a country with only one Divine heir to secure its bloodline," I cautioned.

"My interests differ from the majority currently ruling the Senate." He paused, and though he continued to pull me along, my steps noticeably began to drag. "Podar and Duval both have their share of beauties."

"I cannot agree nor disagree with you, as I have never been to either," I said, attempting to steer the conversation away from marriage.

"Beauties none as fine as Brisleian royalty." He gave the same deceitful grin.

In that moment I began to realize Luken's secret, because it wasn't just Luken hiding it. My eyes darted from face to face around the ballroom; each one stared with an expectant luster. I furrowed my brows. "Why are you here?"

"My desires for a wife have fallen upon you."

My feet came to an abrupt halt. "Your Majesty, you don't even know me, nor should you desire me."

He sighed, annoyed by my reaction. "I didn't need to know anything more than your beauty, but I am indeed finding your obstinance equally attractive. Despite your brother's concern, you will make a fine Podarian Queen. Like the beautiful mare I brought for you, stunning and wild, you too will need to be trained—I can't have your tenacity hindering my throne—but a long engagement should fix that snag."

"Trained? You mean, as in breaking a *horse*?" I ripped my hands away from him.

A hush fell over the court. This was not a conversation for the middle of a ballroom with noble onlookers.

I charged onto the court balcony. The large glass doors swung open, leading onto a massive alabaster terrace three hundred feet above Alamantia City. The immense pearlescent pillars glittered as the last memories of daylight faded into the stars and the first of the celebratory fireworks exploded over the palace.

Prince Marcus followed on my heels, giving a nod to the King, who urged the music to continue. The nobles commenced dancing in awkward steps, each head still turned towards the Podarian Prince and me.

"How dare you proclaim such affection. Compare me to a mare!" I shrilled. "A Prince you may be, sire, but a gentleman you are not. Surely you have not forgotten that I am as Divine as you. Divines do not marry other Divines. It's forbidden."

After the Riving appeared and the Divine became critical to the continent's survival, the Senate believed crossing country bloodlines would bring disaster to Athera. Others dismissed that idea as paranoia. In any case, I did not want to be the first to test the theory.

"The prospect of a cross-continental Divine marriage has been under discussion in the Senate for some time," Marcus said casually, crossing to the railing and scanning the city. "It has been prudent in the past for the Divine to marry outside the circle, but with fewer of us born each century, we must consider alternative means to keep Athera alive. I believe crossing bloodlines could create a hybrid whose life is tied to both Podar and Brisleia. It may be the only way to ensure Athera's lifeblood. My proposition is beneficial to your brother's reign and will keep Brisleia under the safe protection of Podar. The blood of mixed children will ensure both countries' survival into the future."

I couldn't believe my ears. "I won't do it."

He raked his nails over the marble, making faint scratches in the stone. "You lack the faculties to make this decision. The Senate, Parliament, and your father have decided what is best."

"My father would never approve a marital taboo."

He fingered the indentation he had created before turning his back to it, as though to hide the destruction. "The purpose of the Divine is to ensure the life of their given country. Kenara no longer exists, and Brisleia already came close to disaster when your grandmother was the only surviving heir two generations ago. Your father fears the same outcome. Only a Divine male heir should ever rule as sovereign."

"Kenara no longer exists because a Podarian King thought the ruling Queen too weak to command her country and, just as you propose, offered *protection*. Podarians, your people, killed the life of Kenara, and it would seem Podar is about to repeat history. Tell me, Prince Marcus, is Brisleia in need of protection?"

"The royalty of my country has not always done what is best for Athera, but we have learned from our mistakes. Keeping the last branches of the continent alive are of upmost importance to Podar. I assure you, with you as my wife, Brisleia will always remain."

"What makes you think I would ignore a taboo and accept marriage into a country with your history?" I glanced into the ballroom. The nobles had fallen back into normality, but my family still actively watched us.

"It is no secret that when Prince Tydous ascends the throne, the Duvali monarchy will be swayed. It is likely that whoever remains in the Prince's good favor will become Duval's ally. If Podar and Brisleia partner now, it will isolate the south, essentially forcing them to fall under the new bloodline's command."

"This is absurd." I buried my nails into my scalp, dislodging my crown from its pins.

"It's politics."

I pulled my fingers out of my hair and balled my hands into little, nonthreatening fists. "Politics or not, I refuse to be a pawn for your sexual experiments and political gain. Take your gifts and leave. I want nothing to do with you."

Marcus narrowed his eyes, and the once hint of a smile disappeared into the darkness of his tone. "Your opinion in the matter is irrelevant. If you care for your country, you will do what is commanded of you. That is your only concern." His smile reappeared, but this time his teeth looked pointed.

"My father has consented to this?" I questioned.

He nodded. "The unity of our nations will be a magnificent turning point in the fusion of the entire continent. I will see to it that you are happy and have all the riches you desire. As the Divine Queen of Podar, you will have everything you can imagine. I will prove to be a fine husband."

"Why ask me?" I took a deep breath, trying to keep my emotions under control. "If my father has consented and it is not my choice, then why does my answer matter?"

"It would please me to hear you accept my proposal of your own accord," he admitted.

"It would please you?" I hissed. "Of course, how could I not have taken your pleasure into consideration?"

His eyes gleamed at my sarcasm. "I aim for you to love me in the future, as I am certain to grow very fond of you"—he ran his fingers along my cheek—"and your vivacious spirit."

I slapped his hand. "Love you? How could I ever love you after being forced into this. I'll hate you. I hate you now, and I'll hate you then." I stomped my foot against the stone.

"As much as I had hoped for your willingness"—he stepped closer, his voice low—"forcing you to submit to me will be just as invigorating."

My shoulders sank in defeat; the Divine Royal Highness Ayleth Rose of Alamantia diminished into a nameless political tool.

"I must remain in Podar over the course of our engagement. I shall visit you and write to you often. I am speaking with your father of the possibility of moving your household to the Ember Court." He took my hand, ignoring my previous refusal of affection, and another charged wave pulsed up my arm. I pulled back so forcefully my skin stung. He breathed out in a growl, trying to control something boiling deep within him. "After you have spent time with me in Podar, you *will* grow to love me. Or at the very least you will have learned respect."

"I have no intention of moving my household. Nor do I desire to marry you or any man who would seek to buy me because of my status. Furthermore, if you were the Prince you claim to be, you would respect my decision and turn your interest elsewhere."

"You would do well to remember that your happiness means nothing to the people of Athera. You serve a purpose to the world, and if you exhaust that means, your King will have no use for you."

"I would rather exhaust every option I've ever had and fall out of the King's favor than live in that sunless volcanic nation with you."

He nodded indifferently. "Unfortunately for you, my mind is made up." He closed the gap between us. "I know there is more to you—things you don't know about yourself. I can help you. Hold you in your darkest moments while you discover who you really are free from Brisleian rule. Together we would be unstoppable, with power beyond your wildest imagination. But if you still refuse me," he murmured on a throaty hiss, "I will have no choice but to bind you into submission until my plans become your only desire."

"First you force me into marriage, and now you threaten me with some sick version of slavery," I whispered.

"Yes, Princess, if that's what it takes, then that's what I am willing to do."

Chapter 3

I ran from the ballroom in a desperate flight, the clank of my heels on the stone floor sending furious echoes down the hall to my chambers.

Elizabetta followed. My ladies lost their grace and stumbled to keep up. They whispered to each other, ready to spread any rumor detailing the evening's events.

I violently shoved my chamber doors before the guards could open them, and they swung on their hinges, hitting the walls with a defiant thud. The guards shut them behind me and sent worried glances to my ladies.

The rage that had been building since the moment Prince Marcus entered the Rose Court burst to the surface. I let out a harsh scream, allowing all my fury to roar through my throat. Startled, my ladies scurried to the bedchamber.

My cheeks burned hot. My pulse throbbed. I trembled, wringing my hands. Such fervent anger was immodest and improper, but I couldn't bring myself to care.

"Why!" I shrieked, throwing a silver goblet from the center table across the room. The base stuck into the wall like a knife, piercing the quartz with ease. I tilted my head, examining the oddity of it.

"Ayleth, calm down." Elizabetta sank into a chair at the dining table and folded her hands in her lap.

I paced from wall to wall. I felt abandoned. Consumed by a sea of red that turned each thought into a lightning strike to the brain. "I will not be shipped to Podar like cargo. I will not be an object for them to trade. A marriage proposal? I won't do it! I won't!" Each asinine word Prince Marcus had spoken echoed in my head, driving me to madness. I let out another scream.

Daphne dropped a fire iron in the next room. It clanged loudly on the floor, and my raging shrills went up an octave. "Get out!" My throat burned. "Get out!"

The girls instantly ran from my apartments in a disorderly fashion.

I snatched a glass of red wine sitting next to Elizabetta and downed it in one gulp. She plucked the empty goblet from my grasp and stole the pitcher, dumping the remaining wine into the water basin.

"He wants to break the marriage taboo!"

She returned to the table and refolded her hands.

"He wants to move my household to Podar. To live with him! So that we may know each other better! I do not wish to know him at all! And I certainly do not wish to know him better."

She sighed. "You must relax. Take a deep breath. It will help."

I ignored her. "And if I refuse him, he says he will break me into submission!"

"Ayleth—"

"And my parents have agreed to this insanity!" I slammed my fist on the table.

"Someone will hear you," she warned.

"I don't care who hears me! Perhaps they will reconsider this ridiculous prospect." I turned to the door and projected my voice so any palace ear within range would know my discontent. "I am the crowned Princess of Brisleia!"

Elizabetta put her elbows on the table and massaged her temples.

The chamber doors exploded open. Unannounced, my grandmother barged into the receiving room. She gripped my shoulder and shoved me into the chair beside my nurse. "Do you have any idea what they are saying about you in court as we speak?" Ambrosia grabbed my chin and forced me to look at her. "Honestly, Ayleth, is this the behavior of a Divine Princess? You are doing nothing but reinforcing the belief that you are an unruly child who needs to be sold into marital control. Immature. Selfish. Incapable of making her own decisions. Do you truly believe this is going to change the outcome? Stop your screaming and complaining this instant."

I jerked my chin away, but the sting of her hand lingered. Shoving past her, I stormed into my bedroom. The room had been bombarded by the gifts from Prince Marcus. Gold boxes and trays invaded every free table and chair. I dug my nails into my scalp. I couldn't escape him.

"Royalty does not behave so despicably towards a decision made by Parliament, especially when it is endorsed by the Senate," Ambrosia said to my back.

I nabbed one of the parcels and hurled it into the fire. The box came apart with a smash and sizzled as the small intricate cakes inside turned to char.

Ambrosia's anger began to wane. "I understand how you feel. More so than anyone in this family. I know how unpleasant it is to be forced into an unloving precontracted marriage. But this has been the way of Divine women for thousands of years."

"Betrothals and contracts, yes, but never to another Divine."

"It is your duty to do your part for Athera," she said steadily.

"How is this advantageous to Brisleia—or Podar? They have less Divine than we do. It's taboo for a reason, isn't it?"

Ambrosia moved several packages to sit on the couch in front of the fire. "No one knows for certain what will happen if two Divines attempt to create a child. No one has ever dared risk an entire generation. When the King told me his plans, I can't say I agreed with him. But neither of us have the authority to disagree."

My knees buckled, and I landed on the cushions. "He could have gone after anyone else. Why me?"

"If Prince Marcus desires to marry a fellow Divine, from a political standpoint it makes sense to pair with you." She set her hand on my shoulder. "Ayleth, you have been born to a rare privilege. Your existence is tied to Brisleia. Because of that, you have obligations. Responsibilities."

"So, because my life is tied, the King can send me to Podar for that Prince's sick ambitions?"

"Yes," she said firmly. "I wish it were different. I too tried to escape it. But, like me, you will come to realize you are bound to that which is expected of you." My heart withered at her words. "The world means more than your happiness. The people come first. The land comes first. That is what it is to be Divine. Our honor and our burden."

My vision blurred from the first burn of tears.

"He is handsome, isn't he?" she said, as if to soothe the bitter realization coming over me.

"Yes," I shakily admitted.

Marcus was beautiful. Tall and elegant. His poise was remarkable. His basil-green eyes were dark and mysterious. Perfection that not even I could match.

"A nice smile, graceful," she added, nearly taking the words from my head. "I was surprised by his appearance. I wasn't expecting someone so powerful to be so young. A Prince playing the role of a King. It makes him more influential than your brother or Prince Tydous. Being the Queen of Podar will give you more influence than you could ever have had as a leftover princess."

"Being a leftover princess is enough." I hated that I found him attractive. It made me as dimwitted as the other swooning girls. The idea made me nauseated, and I pressed my fingertips to my temples, trying to force it out of my head.

"The two of you will be the first foreign Divine marriage in all history. A wedding so extravagant it will be remembered for all time. Not even your brother can contribute to Athera so magnanimously."

It was easy to listen to Ambrosia knowing she empathized with my situation. I took a deep breath, but before I could respond, the guards entered the room.

"Her Royal Highness the Queen."

"Oh, no." I groaned and buried my face in my hands.

My mother floated into the room, disappointment and antipathy already written in her expression. "Ambrosia, do not coddle her." She shooed my grandmother from my side. "Never in all my years at court have I seen royalty treated in such a shameful fashion by a Divine Princess." I could almost see my mother's blood boiling beneath her skin. "Ayleth, you are to publicly accept the engagement from Prince Marcus. The King will decide if you will move your household to Podar, though after tonight, do not expect to be greeted with kindness from him. Podar is a fine country. You shall be a proud Podarian citizen and its Divine Queen, provided the Prince will still have you after such an embarrassing display." Queen Helena placed her hands on her hips and waited for me to beg for forgiveness.

The rage flared back with a vengeance. I stood to look her directly in the eyes. "I will not go to Podar!" I screamed, close enough for her to feel my heated breath on her face. "If you hold volcanoes in such high regard, then you go live there."

My mother's petite hand flew from her side and struck me across the face. My neck cracked from the sudden blow. The impact stung more than pained me. She cradled her hand, a hint of regret passing over her features. "You will go where your King commands!" she screeched, followed by a wince.

Elizabetta was by my side in an instant, checking my cheek for damage.

I sank onto the couch and allowed the tears to take me. I wanted to seem meek and too young for marriage. "How can I mean so little to you? How can the happiness of your only daughter be of no consequence to you?"

"I am thinking of you." She shook her sore hand and placed it back on her hip. "Prince Marcus is a magnificent match."

"You don't know him. And I don't love him."

"Love!" she shrilled in disbelief. "This isn't about love! It's about your country! You will not destroy this opportunity for something so nonsensical."

"But Luken . . ." I sniffled. "He promised things would be different for me."

"Luken is not your lord and master. You obey the Divine King of Brisleia." Frustration hardened her jaw. "Any woman alive would be thrilled to marry Prince Marcus."

"I refuse his offer." I crossed my arms over my chest and leaned back into the cushions.

"You cannot refuse, Ayleth. The King and I have accepted the proposal on your behalf."

I gasped in horror.

"Prince Marcus simply wished to go through the formality of asking you himself. For a foolish girl who wishes to find love before marriage, you would do well to remember that he is offering you a chance to know him through the Ember Court so you are not strangers on your wedding day. What more could you ask for?"

"Forcing me to do something against my will and hoping I become used to it with time is not love."

Queen Helena threw her hands in the air and stepped away, moving for the doorway.

"I won't marry him, Mother." I stood, wiping tears from my cheeks. "You won't change my mind. I'm not going to Podar. You will have to carry me kicking and screaming to a marriage ceremony, and once there, I will not say I do."

"Ayleth." She stepped back into the bedchamber. "I hereby banish you and your ladies from court. I also remove your maids from your service. Until you willingly accept the engagement to Prince Marcus, you will not be welcome in the King's presence, nor mine. I advise you against any further protest to this marriage, or you may anger the King beyond the point of reconciliation." How could she do this to me? "Keep your head on your shoulders, Daughter. It is a pretty head, after all."

I held my ground until the doors closed behind her, then collapsed into a puddle on the bear rug.

I could just make out the queen's voice from outside. "Place additional security at her door. She isn't to leave these apartments, and no one is to enter."

I stared at the fur, unable to move. "Am I under arrest?"

"Of course not," Ambrosia drawled, moving onto the floor next to me. She gripped my arms and pulled me up from the fetal position I'd curled into. "The queen is merely hoping a few days in isolation will make you see things her way."

"I'll never see things her way."

My grandmother struggled to sit comfortably. Her old bones creaked inside her red taffeta gown. "Who then, if not Prince Marcus? Did you have someone else in mind?"

"No, I just hoped since I wasn't heir to the crown that I might be allowed the freedom Luken was offering."

"The amount of time you and your brother sit around talking about frivolous fantasies is beyond me."

"How could Luken allow this to happen?" I moaned.

"You will not blame your brother for this. Not even he can control the will of the King."

A door guard entered the chamber and cleared his throat. "Excuse me, Your Highnesses," he began, "His Divine Majesty the King requests the Queen Mother return to her quarters for the remainder of the evening to give the Princess time for contemplation and reflection."

"Blast that son of mine," Ambrosia grumbled and shifted her legs to stand. I immediately rose to my feet to help her. I met her pale blue eyes with desperation, and she placed a hand on my cheek. "Try to get some rest," she advised, kissed my forehead, and was escorted from my apartments.

The doors closed, and the lock clicked from the outside.

The room felt unnervingly silent, except for the crackle of the fire and the delicate pop from Elizabetta pulling the lacing of my dress back through the eyelets. I breathed in deeply when my corset loosened and exhaled the panic that had caused my chest to tighten.

Elizabetta draped a robe over my shoulders. "I'll draw you a bath with rose oil. It will help you relax."

"No, I'm fine."

She nodded and wandered about the room to remove each golden parcel. I wasn't sure where she was taking them, nor did I care.

Resting on my bed, hidden among the clutter, was the beautiful onyx box containing Luken's gift.

I slid the dagger out of the purple velvet bag. He had known this was going to happen to me upon choosing this present. He had known all along. Why had he acted as though I had the option to decide my own happiness when something this heinous was in my future? I wanted to sleep and shut out the world, but closing my eyes meant visiting the dreams.

"You can leave me, Elizabetta." I never ordered her away, but I didn't want anyone near me.

She smiled sweetly. "Ayleth, this isn't the end. Deep down you know that."

She closed my bedchamber door, leaving me alone with my thoughts. She wouldn't go far, likely remaining in the receiving room until I called for her.

I eased the dagger from its inky scabbard and surveyed the blade. I had never held a weapon before or touched anything deadlier than a butter knife. The blade was heavier than I expected and innately beautiful, with the crest of Medial Alexandria etched into the metal. Luken wouldn't have parted with such a prized item easily, especially considering it was impossible to obtain any weapon from Medial Alexandria's stock. It hinted at something disturbing.

Luken had spent a great deal of time listening to Prince Marcus during meetings with the Senate. He might have armed me for protection against a man who would force himself upon me. This dagger could be the only method to save my dignity after they sent me to live in Castle Caldera.

The King of Podar was old and ill; he would never produce another heir if Marcus died. Was my modesty and pride worth so much that I could be capable of murder—and thereby the destruction of an entire quarter of Athera by my own hand?

I shivered.

Despite the blazing fireplace, the bedchamber had gone cold as night set in. In the garden, the fountain had slowed to a trickle, choked by frost, and lingering traces of winter chill crept past the open curtains. I moved to close them to further isolate myself.

As the drapes fell away from the wall, a knock came from the hidden door in the corner. I shot an evil glare at the passageway. I did not want to see Luken.

The door cracked just enough for his fingers to curl around the opening. "Are you decent?" he asked.

"Get out!" I slammed the door, smashing his fingers in the gap.

"Ow! Ayleth!" He pushed the door open and stepped into the room, cradling his mashed hand.

"I don't want to talk to you."

"Just listen to me—"

"You knew!" I swallowed my tears before they made an appearance. I could stand up to the queen and Ambrosia, but my brother's deception broke my heart.

His proud stance crumbled. "Yes, I knew."

"You didn't tell me. How could you not tell me?"

"Believe me, I wanted to. I wanted to so much," he expressed.

"I would have protested this engagement before it was too late," I said, my voice unsteady.

"Yes, you would have panicked without giving Marcus the opportunity to propose. That is why you needed to hear it from him, and I had to give him the respect he deserved as a fellow Divine Prince."

"In case you missed the obvious fact, it doesn't matter what answer I give. The lot of you have decided this marriage is taking place regardless of my opinion." Luken blurred as I lost the struggle against my tears.

"I explained to father how much you would detest this idea before the treaty was drawn."

"How little that did," I snapped.

"I've been fighting Parliament and the Senate for the last year. There is no budging the decision."

"You've known for a year?" I yelled, astonished, and clutched the dagger tighter. I felt stronger with it in my hand. Safer, as if no one could touch me as long as I had it.

Luken put his hands up to shush me.

"I'm to be isolated," I choked out. "My attendants have been stripped and banished until I come to my senses."

"I know." He grabbed my wrist and twisted the dagger from my hand, which felt suddenly bereft. "I'm not supposed to be in here," Luken continued. "The King has forbidden anyone except Elizabetta and Sir Jonathan Helms to be near you."

I jerked away from him and stared through the half-open curtains.

"Maybe it was the wrong day to give you a weapon." He grimaced, placing the blade on the bedside table.

"You promised me freedom," I said, barely above a whisper.

"And you promised you would remember I always have your best interest at heart. I tried everything to change their minds. Father has somehow become terrified he will end up with only a single daughter as an heir. He is desperate to secure the lifeline of Brisleia, even if it means including Podar."

"You seem to be in good health, Luken," I quipped.

"I don't plan on dying." His face fell. "Ayleth, this proposal . . . the thought of you not being with me when I ascend to the throne . . . my sister permanently hundreds of miles away . . . I don't want to let you go. I need you."

I shook my head. "Get out."

"Please, I'm doing everything I can for you."

"Are you looking for my sympathy? Do you want my praise for your failed effort? For me to bow down to you like everyone else?"

"You mean everything to me," he said softly.

"Do you know what Prince Marcus plans to do with me? He intends to bind me into a slave form if I do not submit to his demands." I crossed my arms over my chest. I felt violated just hearing the words rush out of my mouth. "I don't care if he convinced the lot of you of admirable intentions with his ranting in the Senate. Once I am in Podar, once I am his, he is never going to let me go, whether I produce an heir for him or not."

Luken frowned and began to grind his teeth. "Maybe you heard him wrong."

"His intentions were clear."

He took a seat on my bed. "It's worse than I thought," he grumbled, anger shooting through his eyes. He punched the mattress, then rested his elbows on his knees, cradling his head in his hands. "I'm so sorry, Ayleth. I've failed you. I failed to protect you from this marriage, and my attempts to persuade the Senate were useless. What kind of weak King am I going to be?"

I sat beside him and placed a hand on his shoulder. Had I judged him too harshly? He looked so helpless. Luken was used to having things go well for him. He was used to having exactly what he wanted whenever he willed it. For the first time, he was powerless.

"Earlier today, when I told you I was leaving in the morning, I wasn't completely honest with you." He lowered his voice to a whisper. "I am not the only Divine Prince worried about Marcus's intentions. His actions feel like a Senate-appointed kidnapping. Curtus Lamare and I are gathering a following. We plan to overthrow Brisleian Parliament in an attempt to convince Prince Tydous and the Duvali King to veto the marriage."

"Luken!" I shrieked, jumping to my feet. Treason. The word slammed into my mind like an axe to the brain. If his plan went awry, it would mean severe punishment for Luken and death for all those brave enough to oppose the King. "You can't take that kind of risk."

"It is a risk those of us against this decree are willing to take. Father knows nothing, and with luck we can convince the Duvali royals to insist the Senate rescind the approval. Remind them of the dangers associated with a cross-continental marriage. Fix this disaster before it destroys us all. I am not going to lie down and give up. Not yet. I will not hand you over to Podar without a fight."

"I can't let you do this for me."

"This is bigger than just you. We must stop whatever Marcus is planning. People are blindly praising his movements, but if he is left unchecked . . . I fear the outcome."

"Luken . . ." Guilt flooded my chest over my earlier harsh words.

"Consider it already done. I need you to trust me until I either free you or fail you." Luken retrieved the dagger from the table and wrapped my hand around the grip. He gingerly kissed each of my fingers, his mouth lingering close to my skin. Despite his request, I wasn't sure I could continue waiting for everyone else to decide my future.

Chapter 4

A hazy gray encased the sky, with the sun barely visible in the east. I stood in my private garden watching the scene below, gripping the stone ramparts so tightly my knuckles turned white.

In the palace courtyard, Luken gave orders to his attendants as they loaded caravans and readied the horses for a journey south. He had assembled a frighteningly small group of soldiers to escort him through open country, scarcely enough to fend off a gang of bandits. How had the King ever agreed to such a venture? Perhaps, like Luken's objective, he was also ignorant about the Prince's ludicrously inadequate travel arrangements.

Luken's entourage departed through the Alamantia City gates as the rising sun peeked above the mountains and filled the sky with an ominous red glow. The world felt altered—cold and quiet—as he embarked on the most perilous journey of his life.

Before leaving, he had kissed my cheek, hugged me tighter than I ever thought possible, and taught me how to fasten his elaborate birthday present around my ankle. The blade rested snugly against my skin, under the layers of silk and taffeta. As long as I had it with me, Luken remained. A minuscule comfort, but comfort nonetheless.

Elizabetta had turned a blind eye to the dagger when she had dressed me that morning. She had chosen a yellow gown embellished with pink embroidered flowers—simple, elegant, refined—tossed my mess of curls into a hairnet, and braided a strand across my head like a band.

"Ayleth," she called from the balcony, "Sir Jonathan Helms has arrived."

Sir Johnathan Helms, the Unity Knight of Wisdom, was my tutor. He fascinated me with tales of traveling Athera and often brought books from abroad. Much to the queen's dismay, he embraced my love of literature instead of shunning it in favor of sewing, singing, dancing, and music—skills to please a future husband. I was a poor pianist but had read every book in my library.

Breakfast covered the table in the receiving room, and nestled in the seat closest to the fire, drinking a steaming cup of tea, sat Sir Jonathan Helms. He was handsome for an elderly man, tall and muscular in the arms and shoulders, with a striking set of pewter eyes.

"Your Highness." He stood when I entered the room and gave a slow bow. "Congratulations on your engagement."

Any flicker of happiness I'd had upon seeing him was extinguished. I ground my teeth. "Thank you. I am . . . overjoyed."

Jonathan laughed. "Don't sound so convincing. You might actually make someone believe you don't detest the idea."

"Your sarcasm is unappreciated this morning, sir."

"You have never been a good liar." He shook his head and reseated himself. "You seem to be more accepting of the situation this morning."

Elizabetta scoffed, pulling a chair to the window and settling in with her sewing.

"Please." He gestured to the seat beside him. "I would love to hear more about this tantrum you threw last night, for anything that makes the King and queen as furious as they were this morning is well worth me lending an ear to." He held back a smile but couldn't hide the twinkle in his eyes.

I breathed deeply before joining him. He poured me a cup of tea and stirred in a cube of sugar.

"I have to get out of this engagement. Can you talk to the King? You're a Counsel Knight. He trusts your opinions, and you have a seat in Parliament. There must be something that can be said on my behalf."

"I'm afraid I could no sooner get you out of this engagement than I could make you sprout wings and fly. Your brother has been outspoken, and the King is furious at his opposition. I have no intention of doing anything to further enrage him."

My fingers trembled around my teacup, and my chest tightened.

He placed a hand on my shoulder, his brows furrowing in concern. "Breathe, Ayleth."

I inhaled sharply and hiccupped. "The queen has banished me from court until I acknowledge this engagement," I said in a rush.

"Well, of course she has. She will expect you to have a certain love towards Prince Marcus in public, and currently you are not fulfilling your mother's expectations for her Divine daughter. She can't have the newly engaged couple not acting newly engaged. It's easier to hide your actions than admit to Athera that you oppose the union. The people don't want the truth. They want the fantasy of two strangers falling instantly and madly in love."

I needed air. I left the table and joined Elizabetta by the window. The city below bustled with activity. From six hundred feet up the mountain, everyone looked so small—merchants selling wares and servants arriving for duties at the palace. *What must it feel like to look up from the streets of Alamantia in hopes of seeing the figure of a Divine?* "Wear perfection like a second skin, the image of Divine purity. No matter the cost. No matter what you truly feel on the inside," I mumbled.

"Can the Divine and those they choose as their partners be anything less?" Jonathan bit into a cheese pastry. "The Divine are Athera's treasure, and we all must play our part."

"They think they are protecting us by locking us in palaces, giving us riches, as if that were all it took to make a person happy. I'd rather rot than continue this hollow life in Podar." I watched a group of children run through the noble district, kites trailing in the air behind them.

Jonathan put down his pastry and rubbed his palms together. "Be careful with your words, Ayleth. Your father is on the verge of making that happen."

"I've heard the air in Podar is so thick with ash that you can't see the stars. I've heard the smoke burns your eyes and the sun never breaks through the clouds."

"Some of that's true." He sighed, running his finger along the edge of his discarded pastry. "The sun appears as a glowing yellow ball behind the haze. Red skies are always on the horizon. As for the stars . . ." He gave a defeated shrug.

"I would miss the mountains."

"Volcanoes are a kind of mountain." He winked, his lips curving into a halfhearted smile.

"Hardly—"

The chamber doors swung open, and Ambrosia stepped into the room.

"Your Highness, I must insist—"

"Insist what?" she snapped at the door guard. "That I not see my granddaughter due to some doltish rule placed by my son? Be on your way."

The guard's mouth formed a hard line as she glared at him. Yielding, he closed the chamber doors.

Ambrosia's flushed complexion complemented her peach satin gown. Jonathan looked at her warmly, and his mouth twitched into a grin as her cheeks took on an even deeper red.

"Good morning, Grandmother." I bowed my head to her. "Come to join us for breakfast?"

"If there is enough to go around," she teased.

"And if the King pays it no mind," I added.

Jonathan pulled out a chair for her. "My son has no right to tell me I cannot comfort my granddaughter in the weeks before her wedding," she asserted, taking a seat.

Jonathan pushed in her chair, discreetly trailing a gentle touch along the back of her neck before sitting beside her. I raised a suspicious brow at Elizabetta. She shook her head and returned to her sewing. In all the years Sir Jonathan Helms had been my tutor, Ambrosia had never missed a lesson.

"You are always welcome, Grandmother." My voice disrupted the lingering stare they were giving each other.

"That will be enough, Ayleth," Ambrosia said sharply, putting a stop to my questionable smirk.

"Might I make an observation?" Jonathan said, changing the subject as he poured Ambrosia a cup of tea. "In the past, you had spoken fondly of leaving the palace. Traveling with your brother. Seeing the world before another bloodline becomes extinct. The beaches of Duval. The volcanoes of Podar. I remember a young girl who became quite distraught when the King put a firm end to any talk of her leaving the palace. Now, as fate has it, you get the chance to see a different setting."

"Crossing the border to stay indefinitely in Podar is hardly seeing the bulk of Athera," I argued.

"Do you think it implausible that Prince Marcus would take you with him when he visits foreign dignitaries and the Senate?" he asked.

I shut my eyes, trying to squash the image of the Queen of Podar from my head. Jonathan Helms was obviously unaware of how the Prince planned to treat me. I could voice the horror once to my brother in private, but uttering the words again was impossible. "Don't presume that the King means to tell Parliament and the Unity Knights everything about Prince Marcus's arrangements, or what happens in the Senate." The words came out with more acid than I intended. I didn't mean to offend Jonathan, but the growing silence in the room suggested I'd done precisely that.

Jonathan cleared his throat. "Prince Marcus's caravan made a detour to Medial Alexandria during our journey to Alamantia. I had the opportunity to visit the public libraries."

My interest piqued, and I slid back into my chair.

"Prince Marcus spends much of his time at Medial Alexandria. According to the library scholars, he has a specific interest in the Divine bloodlines and the function of the Mandala. Your brother has been anxious to examine the same texts to search for any information proving the bloodlines cannot interbreed. It appears, despite the treaty being authorized by the Senate, Prince Luken has not given up his attempts to prevent this marriage. Unfortunately, I was unable to deliver the information he requested before his departure this morning."

I ignored the churn in my stomach to remain straight-faced. "What information were you giving to him?"

"It seems that along with all information regarding the Riving, the documents on Divinity and the Mandala have also been lost to history. There are absolutely no texts on the subject. Careless of the senators to misplace such critical data, don't you think?"

"Are you suggesting the senators just erase from history anything they don't want made public?"

"That would be an intriguing concept." He tilted his head and clicked his tongue. "My theory is the lost scrolls are not truly lost, especially considering Prince Marcus has such an expansive knowledge on the subject. Such accusations are denied, but I suspect the Senate has removed the information from public access."

"Why?"

He hesitated, his eyes wandering to Ambrosia, who quietly sipped her tea. "I can't be certain, but I do know that Prince Marcus—" He stopped abruptly when she squeezed his wrist, and he patted her fingers to reassure her. "He has become instrumental in the research of the *dreaming* children the Senate has locked in their prison. He seems to also be involved with the Onyx Guard, but I found no information to confirm his role."

I went rigid and leaned back against my chair, trying to hide my alarm. A lump grew in my throat, and my palms started to sweat.

"In any case, Prince Marcus did not propose such a controversial idea to the Senate without having some unknown factor backing the decision."

"Ayleth? Are you all right? You've gone as pale as the moon." Ambrosia set her teacup on the table.

Of all the people Prince Marcus could have asked to be his Queen, he had chosen not only another Divine but a Divine who *dreams*. Dreams the same as Medial Alexandria's prisoners, the poor children renounced by their parents and forsaken by all others. I had never breathed a word of my insanity. He couldn't possibly know I was a Fae.

I swallowed hard. "I'm fine. I believe I am . . . still in shock. I would have thought this marriage was too large a risk for Podar, being that Prince Marcus is the last living Divine heir to their throne. He must be confident to mortgage his country's future on an experiment."

"So it would seem," Jonathan confirmed.

"It's Podar repeating history, is it not?" I continued. "The last time the Podarians sought to obtain domination over Athera, it ended in the destruction of Kenara. They cannot openly declare control over Brisleia. In order for Prince Marcus to establish any sort of new world order, he must do it without a war. What better means than by mixing the bloodlines and claiming a true blood pact over all Brisleian Divinity?"

A slow grin tugged at Jonathan's mouth. "You should have been in politics, Your Highness."

I took a deep breath, and my chest rattled. "You are oddly quiet this morning, Grandmother."

Ambrosia folded her hands on the edge of the table. "I cannot help but wonder what my son has to gain from all this. The King cannot possibly be in such fear of losing his heirs that he would allow Podar such a strong hold on Brisleia's future. His recent actions are puzzling."

The receiving chamber doors opened, and my guard trotted nervously into the room. "His Divine Royal Majesty the King," he announced.

Surprised, Ambrosia spilled her cup, splashing brown liquid across the floor. My father had not visited my apartments in years. My heart sank knowing what it meant.

The four of us fell to our knees as the King of Brisleia entered the room. He strolled with purpose, taking his time with each deliberate step. His hands were folded behind his back, and his inflated chest and grand posture reminded me of Luken, only heavier and more cunning, older and wiser.

"Mother, nice to see you here," King Hugo said pleasantly, but an underlying irritation rebuked her presence. She bowed her head lower in submission. "Good morning to you, Sir Helms," he added.

"It certainly is, Your Majesty," Jonathan replied.

"If you would excuse us, I need to have a word alone with my daughter."

I shuddered. Ambrosia looked at me longingly before the guard escorted her and Jonathan from the room, taking my nurse as well.

Alone with my father. This was serious. The queen had already banished me from court. I hated to think what the King was here to do. "I wasn't expecting to see you today, Your Majesty," I said softly and sweetly, mustering as much of the wellborn lady within me as I could.

King Hugo's silver brows narrowed. His mouth quivered and his body went stiff. "Where did you ever learn to speak before your lord and master instructed you to do so?" he hissed and shook his head. "Of all traits for a Divine Princess to have developed . . ." Composing his voice, he continued, "You had every reason to expect counsel with me today. Foolish of you to think otherwise. I am beginning to suspect Sir Helms isn't teaching you a single aspect of respect and manners." He surveyed the room, his eyes sweeping over the stacks of books on the tables and the untouched piano in the corner. "Your actions last night were disgraceful. Prince Marcus has proclaimed love for you, which he has honored by a proposal of marriage. This is a grand occasion—"

"Marcus is presumptuous. As for love, he can't love me any more than he must love his kitchen cat, and I certainly do not love him."

Astonishment contorted my father's face. No one dared interrupt a King. He paused to subdue his frustration. "Luken warned me you are a freer spirit than what is suitable for a Divine Princess. Your brother has always made excuses for your lack of social graces and arrogant character. Yet, despite these inadequacies, I am content to inform you that His Majesty Prince Marcus will still have you as a wife."

"Have me?" I scowled, looking up from the floor to meet his gaze.

The King immediately grabbed my shoulders and pulled me up from my knees, his hands digging painfully into the meat of my arms. I craned my neck back and stared defiantly into his eyes. What else could he do to me? This King, related to me by nothing more than blood, had failed me in every measurable way.

"You have such beauty," he said, his voice calm but his body radiating anger. "Do not make me destroy it." He released me, and my bones fell back into place. "I am true to my political agreements. You represent a lineage of royalty that exists for one purpose. We are privileged as we are burdened. Hated as we are loved. These are crimes for which Athera will forever punish us. Be thankful to me for providing a future to you."

"Ugh!" I turned my back to him and leaned on the window frame.

"I hope your attitude improves by this afternoon, as Prince Marcus will be coming to your chambers to visit with you. Elizabetta will be instructed to have you dressed and well prepared for the occasion."

"I have no interest in entertaining Marcus. Ever!" I slammed my fist into the glass, causing the frame to rattle.

"You will give him the respect he deserves as a fellow Divine royal. You will not speak to him so informally, or you will have my wrath to answer to. I will not hesitate to take action against you if you insult a foreign Divine Prince a second time."

I spun around to face him, crossing my arms over my belly. "The consequences?" I inquired petulantly.

"I will imprison you for a duration of my choosing. All this"—he gestured to the room around him—"will not be going with you. A Divine Princess living in squalor will be your existence until Prince Marcus comes for you on your wedding day. You will marry no matter your actions, so I suggest you take the respectful path and remain in my favor."

It was everything I expected. My father planned to dispose of me if I didn't capitulate. My mother could not carry out the order herself. Banishing me from court and taking my ladies had been the only punishment she could manage.

As always, my choices were clear—prison in luxury or prison in chains.

Shortly after the King's departure, Elizabetta dressed me in an emerald taffeta gown fitting for a royal interlude. She curled my hair and searched among the birthday gifts for jewelry to match the attire. At first, I refused to wear the Podarian beaded jade necklace and earrings she discovered, but having no strength left to argue, I soon conceded. I spent the day agitated, and my resolve wavered with each passing hour. I never wanted to see Marcus again. How long would he be in Brisleia? When did they expect this wedding to take place? How was I supposed to love someone I hated? How could I pretend such an emotion?

The clock tower in the center of town struck four, and His Divine Royal Majesty Prince Marcus Ember of Caldera stood in my receiving room with two attendants behind him, each holding a parcel. With a nod, he instructed them to place the additional gifts on the table.

"You look strikingly beautiful this afternoon." Starting at my feet, his eyes worked up to my neck, and he smiled at seeing one of the many presents he had bestowed upon me. Did he have to gawk as if he was imagining our future wedding night?

"Your Majesty, if I may ask, would you please stop staring at me in such a tasteless manner?"

He smiled fully and my core twisted; I was right, his incredibly straight white teeth were slightly pointed. "There is no need to address me so formally. Marcus will do."

I hid my amazement and gulped. "I may be your fiancée"— my pulse spiked at the word—"but that doesn't mean you can look at me so immodestly."

"Forgive me if my glances give away my desire. I'd heard tales of your beauty, but it appears not even stories can capture one so fair. However, as you are now my property, I will look at you as I see fit."

He took my hand in his. I jumped when he touched me, his skin soft, cold, and smooth, almost reptilian. I had expected him to be coarse and full of heat. An undeniable fluid wave moved through my hand and along my arm, causing my spine to tingle.

He dipped his free hand into his cloak pocket and removed a black velveteen box. *More gifts.* "I must apologize for last night. I acted brazen. You angered me in a manner I did not expect." He opened the box by flicking the lid with his thumb. Resting on a piece of red silk was a shining platinum ring. Its twisted band sparkled with inlaid crystals, and at its center was an obscenely large rectangular diamond haloed by small white pearls. He pinched the ring between his fingers and slid it effortlessly onto the third finger of my left hand. "Let me not be your enemy," he whispered in a rumble that made the hair on the back of my neck stand on end.

"What's this for?" I dreaded the answer.

"I would think someone as opposed to marriage as you would know an engagement ring when presented with one."

The extravagant jewel weighed down my hand. It fit with precision, claiming me as Marcus's property. I hated it.

He wiped a tear from my cheek I hadn't known was there. "I know this is all overwhelming."

"I do not oppose marriage," I hissed. "I oppose marrying someone I don't love so I can be used as an experiment. Please, release me from this engagement. Do not force me into something I don't want."

He dropped my hand, and the fluid wave vanished. He stood straighter, his brow dropping to shade his malicious eyes. "And what of what I want?" He touched the jade beads clinging to my collarbone, lifting the necklace slightly off my neck.

Despite my father's warning, I jerked away. "The King has forbidden me to be impudent to you during your stay. Because I have decided to remain in my apartments rather than a dungeon to await our wedding day, I will speak to you no further to spare myself the indignity. Please, leave, and refrain from further forcing your company upon me."

Prince Marcus gave a dark laugh. "I had thought to spend the evening with you." The same lewd gleam flashed in his basil eyes. "I have many plans for our future. Upon hearing them you may have been more charitable towards me. But since you have chosen for us to be strangers on our wedding night, I will honor your request. It makes no difference to me. Instead, I shall depart for Caldera in the morning. I am needed elsewhere, and it would have been a sacrifice on my part to stay in Brisleia for your benefit. During our next meeting I expect to find you matured, obedient, and prepared to become my wife. The King of Alamantia grants you many allowances that I simply will not tolerate."

"You will find I am harder to break than you assume."

"For your sake, best that not be true. Dungeons are a humane and *uncreative* way to punish disrespectful future Queens."

Chapter 5

At three in the morning, I paced the balcony, unable to rest or even be still. The night air rushed through me, freezing my skin, and an icy burn sped up my legs each time my feet met marble.

Elizabetta offered me my fur robe several times, but I refused her. I was numb. A robe wouldn't make a difference. She bustled uneasily within the bedchamber, stirring the fire and repeatedly heating the kettle with fresh tea.

I scanned the sparse stars, searching for answers. The twinkling sparks of light seemed lost among the cold blackness. Luken was out there somewhere, risking his King's love and the lives of his closest friends for my sake. The guilt slowly devastated any claim I had against Prince Marcus's proposal. I couldn't refuse this engagement if it meant bringing harm to my brother.

When we were children and summer had thawed the frost, Luken and I would play in the palace gardens and let the smell of blooming roses fill our lungs. The gardens of Alamantia

Palace reached up the side of the mountain, where willow trees shaded patches of green meadows and small streams flowed down stretches of exposed granite. Luken used to weave rose crowns for me. We would pretend he was King and I was a simple peasant who had come from afar to be presented to him. My brother loved that game. Childhood imagination would run away with us, and often I believed the fantasy.

Time forgets. As Luken aged, our father's demands weighed heavier on him. Parliament and the Senate took priority, and Divine obligation became his pressing concern. He was being trained to one day take our father's crown and rule Brisleia. It was his rightful place in the world. His destiny. One he was proud to undertake. I fell to the wayside, his beloved sister now second to royal duty.

I stopped pacing. Elizabetta stood behind me, holding a robe, her persistence amazing. "Ayleth, standing in the bitter cold is not going to change anything. It isn't going to bring your brother back any sooner or make Prince Marcus rescind his proposal, and you are far too used to Brisleian temperatures to freeze to death."

I picked at the layer of frost accumulating on the marble railing.

"It's time to come inside." She took my hand to warm it between her palms. "You feel like ice."

At last, I followed her back into my apartments. The hearth was in full blaze. Flames as tall as me spanned the length of the fireplace. A fresh pot of tea rested on the low table in the seating area, next to a carafe of red wine—something that had been carefully kept out of my reach since the proposal. Elizabetta poured a cup of tea and a goblet of wine and sat me down in front of the choices.

"You are not as miserable as you are pretending to be," she said.

I took a sip of the wine. My entire body shivered.

She knelt before me to put her hand on my heart and silently counted the beats. "Nope, not even close."

"Well, I feel dead *inside*, even if my heart disagrees." I took the teacup and poured its contents into the goblet filled with wine.

"Feel dead all you want. Your heart is still ticking." She left me to wallow in self-pity and closed the curtains over the balcony.

I curled into the feather pillows. The bizarre combination of wine and tea soothed my nerves for the first time since meeting Marcus, and I pulled my sleeves over my hands to form a barrier between the steaming goblet and my fingers.

When the little hidden door in the corner gave way, I jumped in absolute fright, and Elizabetta froze.

Ambrosia appeared in the dark passageway.

"Good night, Ayleth," she grumbled as she crawled out of the corridor, tripping on her silk nightgown. Dark circles puffed under her eyes, and her immense silver hair tumbled chaotically about her shoulders.

"Grandmother!" I leaped to my feet to assist her as she struggled to pull her gown out from under her heels. Beneath her arm, she carried a bundle wrapped in purple cloth and tied together with twine. I caught her waist before she completely lost balance.

"Thank you." She breathed a sigh of relief, tossing her hair away from her face. "Those passages are far more treacherous than I remember."

"But I thought—"

"You thought only Luken and you knew about them." She placed the parcel on the bed. "I discovered the system when I was a child. These very rooms used to be my apartments when I was young. Long before I married . . ." Her voice trailed away, as if the memory pained her. ". . . your grandfather."

"Why did you never tell me about this?"

"Naturally after the stir I caused all those years ago, I chose to hide their existence. Only today did it become critical that I use them again. They are not kind to old bones." Her spine made a faint crack when she stretched.

"The King reprimanded you for being with me this morning, didn't he?"

"No need to pry if you already know the answer." She approached my nurse, greeting her with a pleasant nod. "Lady Elizabetta, might I ask you to allow me some time alone with my granddaughter tonight? I feel it is my duty to prepare her for the unpleasantries of being a wife."

Elizabetta flashed a quick glance in my direction, moving only her amber eyes. "Certainly, Your Highness." Dragging her feet, she closed the doors behind her.

Once we were alone, Ambrosia scanned the bedchamber, then went to the receiving room and bolted the front door. She peeked into my privy chamber and closet, but it wasn't until she poked her head through the curtains and peered onto the balcony that I questioned her.

"Looking for something?" I awkwardly balanced the last of my tea-wine between my fingers.

"Anything. Anyone. We must be absolutely alone."

"We have to be alone for you to talk to me about sex with Marcus?" I put down my drink in disgust.

"If you truly believe *that* is what I've come here to discuss, then you really are as naive as everyone expects. Jonathan allows you to read contraband." She grimaced. "I am confident you have a well-rounded grasp on sex."

I crossed my arms over my chest. "Then why are you here?"

"Ayleth, no one can hear you except me." She placed her hands on my shoulders. "I need you to understand how imperative it is that you tell me the unadulterated truth." She paused and took a calming breath. "Has this abhorrence towards marriage been a facade?"

"Grandmother!" Appalled, I jerked out of her grasp.

"Answer the question!"

"Are you completely daft?" I yelled.

"Is there positively no chance you could grow to love him? Are his gifts meaningless? Does being his Queen hold nothing for you?"

I threaded my fingers into my hair and gripped my scalp. "You all astound me! I cannot believe I am having this argument again!"

"I asked you for the truth. If there is even the smallest part of you that regrets how you've acted and wants to reconcile with the Podarian Prince, you must admit it to me now." She had never been more serious, as if life and death balanced on my answer.

"I will never love him. I will never want to be his Queen," I declared, wearied of making the same argument to people who refused to listen.

"Very well then." She took my wrists and pulled my hands from my hair. "I have a gift for you." She nodded at the purple parcel on my bed.

I groaned. "I've had enough gifts." I didn't want a family heirloom passed down before marriage. I didn't want a veil or fabric from her own wedding gown to be woven into mine or a jewel belonging to Divine ancestry.

She clenched her teeth. "Open. It."

Relenting, I loosened the humble twine. Ambrosia glared at the wrappings as if they were going to explode.

I pulled back the fabric to reveal a bundle of worn tawny wool. Confused, I took the thing off the bed. It unraveled into a simple woolen dress with long, tight sleeves. The bodice laced up with leather cording, and the crude fabric was badly frayed at the hem. It was out of fashion and ugly. Not even servants wore something so poor. This was a dress that belonged to a peasant living far from the palace, someone working in the fields every day and barely surviving on what she had. Where had Ambrosia acquired such a horrid thing, and moreover, why would she think I would want it?

"This dress belonged to me," she began. "I've kept it as a memory."

I tried to grasp the significance of keeping an awful bit of tattered wool. My grandmother had never been poor. She was born at the palace. A Divine heir. "I don't understand," I said, mulling over the dress with skepticism.

"I was just like you as a young girl. The idea of sacrifice to my country, my elder brother owning me, marriage to someone I didn't love simply for continuation of the bloodline—it wasn't the life I wanted. So I stole some wool from a maid in the kitchen, and I made this dress. I escaped the palace for the first time at thirteen."

My mouth fell open and my throat stiffened.

"I disappeared for weeks at a time but never stayed long enough for my absence to be noticed. I saw villages and met many people, some that altered me forever. But the palace always beckoned me. I always returned. I thought I would find myself deep in the mountains of Brisleia, but as the years passed, I learned that my place was here."

My arms started to shake as I gripped the fabric; the rattles traveled all the way down into my feet.

"Ayleth, I offer you a choice. Stay at the palace, give in to your father, marry, and fall into the history of the Divine . . . or run. Find what you are searching for. Return if you wish, or disappear into Brisleia. I did not have the courage to leave this behind, but I suspect you do."

I dropped the dress as if it were on fire and covered my mouth to stop myself from screaming. My trembling legs turned to jelly, and I collapsed on the floor.

She knelt beside me. "You do not have time to deliberate. Dawn is approaching, and you must be out of Alamantia before sunrise."

"Luken . . ." My voice cracked. "He—"

"I know exactly what Luken is up to. There is nothing he could find, no miraculous information he could retrieve, that would break this treaty. He is on a fool's quest. You cannot rely on your brother to change your fate. If you stay in Alamantia, you will become the Queen of Podar. It is as certain as the rising of the sun."

"How? How could I leave? I'm marked. If I step one foot outside this palace, I will be recognized by the Mandala."

Ambrosia pulled me to my feet, holding my arms as my legs wobbled. "Jonathan spoke of the texts on the Mandala and its function being lost to history. It's true. The documents were removed by the Senate, and I am to blame. The act of removing your own Mandala was forbidden unless in a life-or-death situation, and yet I abused the privilege so I could roam free. It's shameful to want to be anything but Divine, and many royals believed we should never hide who we truly are—that it disgraces us to remove the mark." Her fingers grazed the glowing pattern on her temple. "This is supposed to be an honor." She shook her head. "When I was found out, my brother petitioned the Senate. He feared it would become public knowledge. The Senate agreed: the people need not know the Divine can willingly remove their mark. Since then it has been taboo to teach the new generation of Divine that if we so will it, we can look just like everyone else. Your father has no idea such a thing is possible. Nor your mother, nor Luken, nor the Divine of Podar or Duval. King O'dern was young when the Senate wrote the new law. He and I remain the only living Divine who know the truth. The Senate master believes the knowledge will die with us."

I blinked furiously, trying to comprehend her words. "I've read every book in the palace. Nothing ever mentioned or even hinted—"

"Erased from Atheran record. Only the Senate master holds the exact instructions on how to remove it. As Jonathan believes, the documents are not truly lost."

"I can't believe it." I turned away from her. It was easier to conclude Ambrosia's age was warping her mind than accept that an escape was within reach.

"Let me show you. Close your eyes," she urged.

I hesitated, then shut my eyes.

"What do people see when they look at you? The details of who you are to the world are never the same as what you perceive yourself. How do others know you? Find that woman inside your head."

I knew the image well: The Divine Princess of Alamantia looked into the mirror of her vanity, adorned in jewels and silk, a crown resting atop her head. Almond curls covered her shoulders and cascaded down her back. Sad pewter eyes stared blankly into the nothing of her own existence. The Mandala curved around her temple and flowed down her neck, glowing with a soft silver sparkle.

Oh, how she pained me.

"Somewhere rooted deep inside of you is the person you want to be. She is foreign to you—someone you have never known but desperately want. Who is she? Envision yourself without the Mandala. Who have you become?"

I attempted to follow her instruction, but the vision was difficult to imagine. Each time the Mandala disappeared, it reemerged.

"Fight against it," she commanded. "The Mandala wants to be seen. The Divine part of you will not be forgotten easily."

The image shook, rattling the edges of my brain. The mirror trembled in its frame, and the once vibrant silks and jewels lost their color, flashing from black to white and back again. Somewhere amid the fit of my mind, a new person began to take over my consciousness. She wore Ambrosia's woolen dress. Her hands were dirty, but in her eyes was a contentment I had never felt.

"It's not enough to envision yourself without the mark. You have to want to be rid of it. You have to know, with certainty, that you are more than the Divinity that defines you."

The vision steadied. The Mandala faded, the skin closing over it as it would over a wound. This new girl touched the side of her face, brushing her fingers across where the Mandala should have been, only to find smooth skin.

My eyes shot open and I stumbled backwards. Ambrosia caught me by the nightgown.

"It takes practice, but you seem to be a natural. You must sincerely detest being born Divine."

She dragged me to the mirror, my feet jumbling across the floor, and tossed me at the vanity. A peculiar feeling tinged with nausea swirled in my core, and I gripped the table to hold myself upright. A warm trickle ran down the side of my face and dripped over my neck.

My reflection came into focus, and I screamed. Ambrosia instantly flung her hand over my mouth, but I shook free and leaned close to the mirror. The Mandala was gone—*gone!*— replaced by a thin coating of blood. I moved my hair away from my face and smeared the red, trying to find the mark, but nothing was visible, not even a wound to reveal where the blood had originated.

"It bleeds," I murmured, aghast.

"The first time, yes." Ambrosia took a cloth from the vanity and wiped my skin clean. She tried several times to turn my head to her, but I was too transfixed by my reflection. By a version of myself I had never seen.

"It went away . . ." I continued, amazed. "How can it go away?"

The slightest grin upturned her lips. "I've always believed we were never meant to be birds in a cage but rather to live like everyone else, as a precious Atheran secret."

I pushed the skin on my neck, still trying to force evidence of the mark. "Do you think Prince Marcus learned about this in his research at Medial Alexandria?"

"It's possible, but seeing as the Senate enforces Atheran law, it's doubtful they would have allowed him near the correct information."

I leaned even closer to the mirror and smiled gleefully. I was normal, and it was exceedingly amazing. Who cared if it was illegal? I threw myself at Ambrosia, wrapping my arms around her in the tightest embrace I could manage.

She hastily pushed me off and plucked the wool dress from the floor. "Do you have an older chemise? One that might be too small or too worn?"

Before I could answer, she disappeared into the closet and reemerged with a cotton chemise I hadn't seen in years. The thin fabric had been a gift from Duval, but the cotton was too sheer to be of much use in the Brisleian cold. The majority had been made into aprons for my maids, and the remainder had become an unimpressive chemise, lacking lace or high-quality threading.

"This will do." Ambrosia lifted my nightgown over my head, leaving me half-freezing in the middle of the room, naked except for Luken's dagger attached to my ankle. She quickly fed my arms into the cotton sleeves and pulled the soft chemise over my body.

Next, she unlaced the leather cords from her wool abomination and helped me into the dress. The wool itched even through the cotton barrier, but the fit was exceptional. She carefully did up the front of the bodice, tying a small bow just above my breasts, then removed two more items from the parcel wrappings. The first was a set of worn brown leather boots that laced up the sides with more leather cording; the second, a hooded walnut-colored wool cloak, which she threw over my shoulders and tied around my neck.

I removed Luken's dagger to slide into the unimpressive shoes.

Ambrosia snatched the weapon. "How in all of Athera did you get this?"

"A birthday gift from Luken."

She squeezed her eyes shut. "Young lady, under normal circumstances I would take this from you immediately. What was he thinking?"

Protection from Prince Marcus.

She glared at the blade. "But these are not normal circumstances," she murmured to herself, then refastened the gift over my boot. "At least now we won't have to steal one from the armory on our way out."

The clock tower tolled four.

"We need to go," she insisted.

"I have to tell Elizabetta." I ran for the chamber doors.

"No, Ayleth!" She caught my elbow, and I skidded on my heels. "You can tell no one."

"But . . . I must," I stammered. "After everything she has done for me, I can't leave without telling her goodbye."

"We cannot risk Elizabetta knowing you have gone. It will make you vulnerable."

"She'll be crushed," I pleaded, trying to tug free, but Ambrosia's grip held firm.

"You can trust no one. I'm sorry, but this is how it has to be."

My heart sank and I stopped struggling.

"Follow me."

Into the dark passage we crept. I had to feel my way down the ebony cobblestone until my eyes adjusted. Despite the thick layer of decomposing hay and dirt deadening the noise of our footfalls, we proceeded with cautious steps and didn't speak a word; sound would carry easily to anyone standing on the other side of the stone.

The narrow path was only wide enough for one person to fit through at a time, and Ambrosia led the way, taking turn after turn as we descended into the belly of the palace. I had never been this deep. Strange vines grew up the walls, and the air smelled stale and moldy. Cobwebs lined the tunnel's ceiling, and water dripped down the stone, making the floor slick.

The walk went on for an eternity, then finally stopped at what appeared to be a dead end. Ambrosia pushed hard on the stone, and the wall gave way with a creak of hinges and the sound of stone raking against stone.

A layer of dirt skittered down from the ceiling as Ambrosia ushered me through the newly revealed opening, and I found myself in a place I didn't expect: the Divine tombs. Carved into the mountain rock deep under the palace, the interior remained coarse and unfinished. Old torches had left black soot on the walls, and dripping water echoed through the vast, otherwise eerily silent space.

Every Brisleian royal who bore a Mandala was laid to rest in this underground chamber. People feared the Divine would be subject to grave robbery, and so they were never buried where the public had access to their bodies. Instead, they were stored. A Divine royal had not died in my lifetime, so I had never seen the tombs. I could imagine the room glowing orange with the torches blazing—the cobwebs cleaned and flowers placed. Now, all that remained of past mournful occasions were wet lanterns and remnants of floral ornamentation, long since scattered by vermin and left to decay.

I looked over the stone caskets. I could only see the ones directly in front of me, but there would be hundreds spread throughout the dark, each carved lid depicting the regal image of the Divine lying just beneath it. After a lifetime of splendor, we all ended up in the same place to rot.

"We have to keep moving." Ambrosia took my hand. We crossed the tomb and once again came to a seeming dead end. She leaned into the wall, but the new door stopped before opening completely. "It's jammed."

Thick roots dangled just inside the doorway. I pulled Luken's dagger from my ankle.

"Quickly," Ambrosia pleaded.

One at a time I sawed through the roots blocking our path. Again she pushed hard on the stone, and the remaining tendrils snapped. The door swung open, slamming against the wall with a loud, echoing *boom*. We both froze and waited out the reverberations—waited to hear someone, waited to be caught.

A lifetime later, the noise subsided, and we found ourselves still alone.

Ambrosia grabbed my arm and shoved me into the corridor, closing the door behind us. The white light of the moon shone through a grate in the ceiling that led up to the streets of Alamantia City.

She stared longingly at the splintered moonlight. "This is the path I used to escape. When I was discovered, I told them I'd been leaving in countryman caravans after they had delivered goods to the palace. If I had not lied, the way would have been sealed."

Freedom existed on the other side of the bars above my head. The moon seemed bigger and more brilliant than ever before.

Ambrosia touched my chin, turning my face to look at her. "You must leave the memories of the Rose Court behind you. If you are to survive, you must forget the name *Ayleth*. Never reveal, never hint, never tell anyone who you are or where you came from, or you shall be at their mercy. Do not put yourself in a precarious position. Stay close to the roads and avoid the deep woods, as the most heinous of men make their homes there. There are dangers that not even I can prepare you for. The world outside these walls is a vastly different place."

I wrapped my arms around her and buried my face in her shoulder. "Thank you."

"Return when you are ready." She stroked my hair. "Always remember, the Mandala can be brought back effortlessly by closing your eyes and reimagining yourself bearing the mark. Be mindful of your thoughts, or it may appear without warning. The Mandala wants to show itself, and it will fight to be a present part of you."

I nodded, and my loving grandmother released me. She stepped onto a square stone placed under the grate and slid the metal bars to the side. Easing me onto the stone beside her, she helped me jump up to grip the edge. My arms were weak. All the days spent reading books on feathered pillows were apparent in my soft muscles. I took a deep breath and let out a groan, using every ounce of strength I had to pull myself up to the dank streets. At last I rolled onto the ground, collecting the road's filth all over my dress.

Ambrosia reached through the opening, and I crawled on my belly to grasp her hand one last time.

"I love you, Ayleth," she mouthed, touching my cheek. She grasped Prince Marcus's diamond engagement ring and removed it from my finger. A weight lifted. I could breathe again.

Her hand disappeared into the blackness, and the grate slid back into place.

"Grandmother, wait!" I exclaimed. "What will happen when the King finds out I'm missing?" There was no answer. "Ambrosia?"

I was alone.

Chapter 6

I lay panting over the slimy grate, my dress quickly growing damp in the muddy city streets. Immediate panic overthrew my senses.

What was Ambrosia thinking? I knew nothing of life outside the palace. I glared through the bars trying to find her, but she had disappeared. I might never see her again. If I died out here . . .

How could she do this to me?

This was senseless. A decision made on a whim. I was no readier to commit to leaving than I was ready for marriage. I had given up my status, riches, luxurious comforts and glamour for woolen rags.

Fear pulsed through my veins like lightning strikes to the muscle. Alone, lying paralyzed on the filthy cobblestone, I considered pulling at the grate and falling back into the corridor. The urge to run to the safety of my room and ease the panic screamed at my feet.

Luken and Elizabetta would never forgive me for abandoning them.

But I couldn't go back. Not if it meant a life with Prince Marcus, lost in the Caldera smoke.

I had to forget. Forever. My Divine life must fade into history, just as the Mandala had vanished into my flesh. But could I really ask that of myself? A part of me would always belong to Brisleia. Hidden or visible, the mark remained beneath my skin, carved into bone.

I tried to remember how to move. My ankles wobbled when I found my footing.

The alley was far darker than I'd anticipated from inside the passage, where the moon had illuminated my escape. To the left, it opened onto a wider street in the noble district. The faint glow of lanterns hanging on ornate metal posts along the thoroughfare beckoned me forwards.

The sun had not yet risen, and I needed to move quickly. Dawn would fill the streets with lords and ladies visiting the palace. I lifted the hood of my cloak over my head and pulled the fabric down to cover my eyes. With the Mandala hidden, the general population wouldn't know my face—I wasn't a future monarch or traveling heir visiting her provinces—but I refused to risk being recognized. Besides, the disappearance of the Mandala still felt unreal, impossible. How was I supposed to forget something that had been part of me since birth?

I scurried through the narrow streets, attempting to navigate the maze of lace-curtained windows and gleaming brass knockers. Every opulent stone building looked the same. I tried to remember the city from above. I had spent a lifetime looking down, but now it was endless confusion.

I hardened my ankles and kept walking, creeping around corners like a criminal. The riches of the noble district grew sparse as the early morning sky lightened to indigo.

When I crossed into the poor district, the atmosphere changed. The cobblestone streets gradually flattened to packed dirt and mud, and the smell of excrement and horse feed hung heavy in the air, with the faintest hint of bread baking in the distance.

After passing row upon row of wood-thatched buildings with clouded glass windows, I reached the market square in the center of the city. The abundant stalls were all empty, due to the early hour, but clumps of dirty, impoverished citizens lingered in the soon-to-be-active emporium. Most sat in dim corners or by the giant oak tree in the center of the square.

The horizon began to glow pink. I could no longer lurk in the shadows if I intended to reach the gates before daybreak. I gripped my hood, the harsh wool rubbing against the skin of my neck. In Ambrosia's dress, I looked as destitute as the rest of these displaced citizens.

I quickened my pace, wary of the darkened eyes glancing at me as I passed. I expected one to follow, but none did. Some even turned away to ignore my shadow rushing through the remnants of night. Relief washed over me when I once again found a secluded alley.

The clock tower struck six. The window of time before daylight narrowed.

Alamantia City extended out from the mountainside in a giant wedge, widening towards the city gates. If I could find one of the two walls leading away from the palace, it would direct me to the outskirts of the city, and I could escape the endless maze.

I hurried past wagons of hay and rats drinking from muddy puddles. I passed emaciated stray dogs eating rubbish in crumbling buildings and the vague outline of street cats moving in the gloom.

As the climbing sun sharpened the morning shadows, the vast wall protecting Alamantia finally appeared before me. The palace towered to my right, so I snapped left and traveled through the steadily brightening streets. Simple servants emerged from all directions, and I tucked my head into my cloak. Mandala or not, palace servants knew a Divine royal when they saw one.

Minutes felt like hours. Each step took an eternity. The smell of unappetizing breakfasts filled my nose, and I narrowly avoided an avalanche of excrement from a piss-pot being emptied out of a window. The sun seemed to laugh at me as the clock ticked away the morning, each second counting down the last moments I would spend in Alamantia.

As I tripped into another side street to avoid a man selling apples from a basket, I found the corner of the outermost rim of the city. Now to reach the exit.

What would I do when I reached the gates? Continue on foot? Ambrosia had said to stay near the road and avoid wandering. But where would I go? I longed for Elizabetta's company, her hands on my shoulders to offer comfort. A deep ache tugged at my chest.

Ahead, the gates loomed over the city entrance. The thirty-foot-tall elaborately molded iron portcullis had just been opened by the guards. I hid behind a large hay bale and waited. Would it be odd for a single *peasant* girl to leave the city alone?

Horse-drawn caravans carrying wares from other towns came through the gates, followed by groups of people on foot holding baskets of goods. Discreetly, I gathered an armful of hay and held it anxiously to my body, waiting for a carriage on its way out of the city. As one approached, I slipped into the small group of merchants following the wheels and passed through the iron gates without anyone taking notice.

Outside the city, I eased away from the caravan and tucked myself behind a pile of sacks filled with horse grain. Chickens busily pecked the ground for loose feed.

The Alamantia breeding stables were a short walk west from the portcullis. At this time of the morning, the stable boys would be feeding and watering the herd. Sneaking in undetected would be no small task, and successfully stealing a horse would be a miracle. Perhaps this was too bold a decision, but I felt illogically confident as I crept into the barn and peered around for anyone working in the area.

Amazingly, the grounds were empty. The fifty stalls were filled only with horses noisily munching their breakfast.

I scanned the stables, looking for one to steal. These were not the grand steeds ridden by the wealthy but workhorses and animals being boarded for traveling merchants. The first stall to my left contained a hefty palomino. The pens across from him housed Podarian stallions. Unlike Brisleia's stocky animals, used to pull heavy loads over hills and mountains, the foreign horses were leaner and taller, bred for elegance and speed. The prestige of the distinguished Podarian mounts would draw attention— not to mention the idea of escaping this life on any form of transportation associated with my heinous fiancé was grotesque. I would not be stealing those.

I unlatched the gate of the palomino's stall. He continued chewing his grain and sweetly nudged my shoulder while I wrapped a bridle around his nose. Saddling him would take too much time. Opting for only reins, I hoped not to fall to my death.

I pulled the horse out of his stall and towards the open door. *"Where are we going?"*

I froze at the deep voice. I'd been caught. My crime would be reported. I would be taken away in chains and forced to reveal my identity. This short-lived adventure had come to an end, my small taste of independence over before it began.

"I'm sorry." I lowered my head in disgrace. "I was just trying to—"

Astonishingly, no one was in the stables. I spun around, trying to find the voice. I looked under the horse. Inside his stall. Behind the hay bales and stacked crates. Nothing. I took a long breath and remembered: *You dream and hear voices.*

I really was insane, and being on the outskirts of the city proved it. Foolishly, I'd hoped the Fae symptoms were the result of the palace's stone walls bearing down on me. Though escaping meant I was ultimately done with the Divine, my deranged mind was here to stay, and without the protection of Alamantia, I would have to be wary of Medial Alexandria's Onyx Guard.

I shuddered.

Composing my jitters, I led the horse out of the stables. I stood on a crate by the corral and climbed onto his bare back. Holding the reins in one hand, I grabbed a fistful of his mane with the other and kicked his belly. The horse jolted forwards, immediately responding to the hard blow from my boots. The hood of my cloak fell off my head, and clouds of dust rose behind us while the dirt and grass flew by under his hooves.

Alamantia receded into the distance. I glanced back, unconvinced. I had never seen the outside of the palace. The mountain loomed high and protective around the glistening gray-and-white marble towers. The ramparts shimmered as the sun rose over the chiseled stone that could control me no longer. The stories were true; my prison was the most beautiful structure in Athera. *Goodbye. Forever.*

We accelerated down the road, racing past the caravan I'd used to escape and out beyond the lines of delivery wagons. Eventually the road wound into the forest, where a canopy of evergreen trees allowed only a few scattered rays of morning light to pierce the gloom.

I squealed with satisfaction and swallowed tears of joy. I was free. Free from ridicule and judgment. Free from Prince Marcus. Free in ways the Divine Princess Ayleth Rose of Alamantia had never known.

I breathed in the intoxicating mountain air: pine, spruce, and the first flowers of early spring.

Finally, I wasn't thinking about my posture or forcing a smile. I wasn't owned by a king or being traded to a foreign Prince. I was never meant to be royalty. This was my true nature—to run wild with the wind straightening my curls and a secret dagger attached to my ankle.

I was never going back, and I welcomed the draw to this new world.

The horse galloped from left to right without reason. We could have been going in circles, but I didn't care. The path had long since vanished. As my horse clumsily wove through the tree trunks, I realized my fantasizing had taken us far off the road and deep into the forest.

I pulled back on the reins, but the beast raced onwards at his own will. The loud clomping of his hooves on hard soil overpowered the songs of the morning birds. Before long, he would run too close to a tree, and I would be knocked to the ground.

"Stop!" I demanded.

The steed came to an abrupt halt. I lunged forwards, hitting my chest on the back of his neck. He stomped and pranced impatiently. Something inside me hinted that he had enjoyed running free with the same unrestrained exuberance as his rider.

I searched the trees, trying to spot the road through the greenery, but all that caught my eyes was the fluttering wings of birds and the wind gently swishing the leaves. The horse tossed his head, eager to resume our run. I combed the canopy for the sun to redirect me, but I knew nothing of navigation. *Am I lost already? I have been away from the palace mere hours . . . I think?*

It was best to turn back, but I couldn't make sense of what direction I'd emerged from.

A sudden rustle in the bushes brought my heart slamming into my ribcage. A blur burst from the brush like cannon fire and landed directly in our path. *A cat.* I sighed, relieved it wasn't an ill-tempered criminal.

The tiny feline's coat was a beautiful, shimmering burgundy, and her warm amber eyes held a familiar sweetness that would have comforted me had not a hideous look of disdain also been warping her brow. My horse promptly backed away from the vicious feline when she began hissing and pacing. I pulled the reins to start in a new direction, but the cat leaped in front of us once again to block our path.

"Get out of here! Go! Shoo!" I shouted. The cat's hissing turned to savage, spitting cries. "If you refuse to move, then I'm going to ride through you!"

The palomino nickered anxiously as the cat bared her silvery claws, ready to strike his legs. Undeterred, I kicked the horse's sides. The beast bounded over the feline in one excited leap and ran through the woods at unprecedented speed, dodging trees and rocks with inches to spare. Yet something ran next to us, matching our pace and darting in and out of the shrubbery in brilliant flashes of burgundy fur.

I hooked the reins to the right. The horse's hooves dug into the permafrost as we swiftly altered directions. Still, the cat pursued us. I kicked harder. We gathered speed. I changed directions, but the cat moved as though she knew what I planned to do. The poor nag was sweating beneath me. I could hear his heavy, exhausted blows as he gasped for air. I would have to rest him soon.

The forest opened into a clearing with a large pond. Defeated, I pulled back on the reins and dismounted to walk the horse to the water's edge, where he rapidly commenced drinking.

The burgundy cat crawled out of the brush. She sauntered to the muddy bank and dipped her head to the water.

"Relentless, aren't you?" I said as she plopped onto a patch of freshly fallen leaves, her pink tongue drooping out of her mouth. She seemed to be silently scolding me for wearing her to such fatigue. "Satisfied? Now that you have chased me well into oblivion?"

I surveyed the area. The horse's hoofprints came out of the brush in a place too thick for us to have broken through. They vanished just inside the tree line, leaving no trace of their origin. After the many directional changes, I had absolutely no idea where I was. For all I knew, we were miles from the nearest town or village, and I certainly was a great distance from Alamantia City.

"I wasn't supposed to go this far from the road." I glanced at the cat, who had stopped panting to watch my every move.

The late-afternoon sunlight reflected over the pond, making the water glisten when fish broke the surface. By now, Elizabetta would know I'd left. Would she notify the King? It would be unlike her to immediately drag my parents into this. She would search the palace or question Ambrosia first. Once my father realized I had disappeared, he would send soldiers to scour the country. Prince Marcus would aid in the search. How long would that take? Would they trace my desertion to Ambrosia? My grandmother seemed to think that after a romp in the woods, I would return and embrace life as a Divine royal. *What a ridiculous concept.*

I slid down a tree trunk and settled onto the leafy ground. I urgently needed to find a mountain village for safety, but with the sun dipping lower in the sky, I'd be lucky to locate the road before sundown. I had not anticipated failing to find a suitable place to spend the night.

"*When you work the day from dawn to dusk, it's fine to have a nag.*"

I scrambled across the ground and darted away from the trees, frantically spinning up on the balls of my feet. Someone was singing. A man. An older man. The road? Was it nearby? I rushed up and down the tree line, peering into the forest to find the mysterious traveler, but there were no signs of human life. Nothing moved through the brush. The road had not magically appeared.

"*Who will ease your cares and pull your wares for the price of one grain bag.*"

I turned on my heels. The singing was close. "Hello?" I said nervously and jumped when the cat gently rubbed my ankle. "We should keep moving . . ."

I patted the horse's mane and reached for the reins.

"*Ladies are few and whores are many, but a mare will see you through.*"

My legs went rigid. My eyes widened. The horse raked his hoof over the dirt to the beat of the song, bouncing his head, and I remembered the tune. It was a common folk ditty the stable boys sang while they cleaned the stalls and fed the herd. *No, this is not possible.*

"*So keep your cows and pull your plows with a stallion brave and true.*"

My sanity cracked. The frightful scream that left my lungs echoed through the forest, and I slapped my hands over my mouth.

The horse panicked, rearing onto his hind legs and kicking his hooves. I could feel his fear. He was frantically searching for the source of my dismay and scaring himself senseless in the process. One thousand pounds of Alamantia steed shook the ground and crushed sticks to a pulp. The cat dived into the tree line for cover, and I followed to escape the onslaught of the terrified beast's power exploding in the small clearing.

When the horse found his bearings, he leaped into the brush at full speed.

"No!" I threw myself back into the clearing, hoping to latch on to his reins, but the forest swallowed him faster than I could process.

I stood frozen in a desolate state of shock. Had I really heard him? Had he really been singing? Or did I imagine it? *The voices.* What if they had never been in my head? What if they were real?

I hunted for the cat and found her hiding under a broken pine branch, her tiny face sneering. "And what about you? Do you sing? Can you talk?" I asked acidly.

The cat's third eyelid moved halfway up her amber iris. She scooted out from her hiding place and shook her body free of the leaves stuck to her fur.

"Ugh, this can't be happening." Emotion slammed into me like a stone wall. I didn't know whether to cry or scream. I wanted to crumble into the dirt and allow every ounce of defeat to drown me. Without a horse I wouldn't make it out of the woods before nightfall, and the thought of traveling back to the palace caused the pit of my stomach to churn with nausea.

The temperature had dropped, yet I felt hot and clammy. I crawled to the pond before the taste of vomit could well up in my throat.

The cat gave a harsh, scolding screech just as my hands dunked into the water. The entire pond vibrated, creating a percussive noise like thunder rattling flimsy metal.

I fell back onto my elbows and gaped at the churning water. White caps smashed together, and waves rolled over the bank. I waited for it to calm. Something massive must have fallen into it. There was no other logical explanation for the disturbance.

The cat smashed her face reassuringly into my arm. I leaned forwards to quench my overwhelming thirst and dipped my fingers into the water once more. I cupped the cool liquid with one hand and brought it to my lips, slurping several mouthfuls before noticing something inhumanly wrong with the hand I was using for support; it wasn't in the water where it should have been, inches deep in the pond and half-buried by clay. Instead, it rested like a spider on top of the surface, creating tiny dimples as if it were pressing into jelly, and my entire hand was outlined in a strange glittering blue.

My mouth fell open, and water dribbled down my chin.

I pushed more weight onto the resistant liquid. My hand popped through the threshold and landed in the mud. I blinked rapidly, certain I was hallucinating. Deciding to prove my theory, I pressed with both hands and balanced over the water. The puffs of unusual blue sparkles drifted away from my fingers. The horse must have knocked me unconscious when he had spooked. *Fine time to be dreaming.*

I stood up and placed my foot on the water; it sank to the bottom. I tried with the other, finding the same outcome. The cat rubbed her face against my shoe and tapped the leather cording in a playful swat. I nudged her away and removed Luken's dagger to untie the boot lacing. Throwing the shoes and weapon aside, I tried with my bare foot. It rested above the water, slipping over the liquid as though on a hardened gelatinous surface.

An odd hysterical laugh tumbled out of me. I took another step, followed by another, then another. The water below me waved unevenly and felt as slick and unpredictable as ice.

When I reached the center of the pond, I looked back to see the cat sitting wide-eyed on the shore, her nose wrinkling and making her whiskers flare. "Can't chase me out here, can you?" I mocked her.

The break in concentration caused me to lose my balance. My legs flew out from under me. I splashed into the water and sank beneath the ripples. My dress dragged me down. I kicked desperately upwards, fighting against the heavy wool, and gasped when I broke the surface. My lungs expanded until I felt my chest would rupture.

I clawed at the surface tension that acted like solid ground and emerged to lie flat on the slippery pond. I stared into the tree canopy, catching my breath. The water churned under me, yet I remained fixed, perched on a liquid mattress with the waves lapping up the sides of my face.

The sky turned ethereal shades of purple and orange, and in the air hung tiny sparkling flecks of blue, like settling dust slowly falling around me. I extended a shaking hand to catch one, but it flickered out of existence.

I sat up and tested the jelly in various locations, looking for any spot I might break through, but this time it held my weight.

Walking back to shore was a more difficult undertaking, as I had to hold on to my sopping dress and couldn't use my arms for balance.

I tumbled onto the bank, shivering and wet, as the last rays of the sun disappeared behind the mountains. The night air settled into the forest, and I curled into the leaves, searching for the dissipating warmth. If I was going to wake up, this would be an exceptional time.

Unfortunately, I did not awaken. Being alone, in the middle of the woods, lost, and soaking wet after accomplishing the impossible was no insanity-originated Fae dream. This was real.

Chapter 7

I could still see the trees and shrubbery in the obscuring darkness, though night had painted the trunks black and turned the shine of fresh leaves into an endless sea of forest shapes. Everything simply looked the same.

I needed to stay calm. I kept looking over my shoulder, thinking something moved—a phantom hiding in the shadows waiting for the right moment.

A glacial wind chilled my core. The ground was near frozen; I could feel the cold through my shoes. My toes had gone numb and moved like ice blocks. Despite growing up in the Brisleian cold, I was woefully unprepared to handle anything like this.

The temperature continued to plummet with each passing hour. With the moon absent from the sky, the only visible light came from the twinkling of stars.

I didn't know which direction I had come from, and I didn't know which way to continue. The reality of being lost terrified me. Though I tried not to panic, adrenaline flooded my brain and my heart pumped with horror. I spun in frantic circles, searching for a familiar point of reference.

If only I had light. If only I knew how to make a fire. I was useless.

I took the deepest breath I could manage, filling my lungs with frozen air.

The cat sat beside my foot, watching me with glowing amber eyes. The luminescent gleam was eerie, but at least I could see her. She made me feel less alone.

I headed towards what seemed like the brightest part of the woods, an area that didn't have quite as much overgrowth as the rest. The cat gave a cautioning meow and pressed her body into my shins to stop me.

"Move." I stepped over her. "This is difficult enough without tripping over you."

She expelled a deafening shriek and leaped into the tree branches, perching on a limb like an owl. She hissed and arched her back—just as something crept over my foot and tightened around my ankle.

In a flash, a violent tug jerked my feet out from under me. The air evacuated my lungs as I landed hard on the permafrost. My chin smacked on the ground, knocking my teeth together and sending shocks of pain through my jaw as my incisors cut into my bottom lip. The sticky, iron-rich flow of blood filled my mouth. I curled onto my side with a groan. I had never felt such a blow.

The brush came to life with black figures, and the forest went ablaze with lit torches. Dozens of crude men ran towards me, approaching so rapidly I didn't have time to think of a way to escape.

I pushed myself up, whipping my head from left to right in search of a break in the bodies. Every possible path was blocked by repulsive men with long hair and frazzled beards. I spun around, finding one grisly face after another. Most held crude weapons high above their heads; others drew rusted daggers from their leather belts. My blood curdled at the sight of their missing teeth and clothes covered in grime. The man coming directly at me had only one eye, and I stared, mystified, at the fleshy socket.

Something rough brushed against my ankle. With the forest illuminated, I glanced down to see a rope. As quickly as I came to the realization, my feet were once more ripped out from under me. Again, I crashed to the hard, frigid dirt. I knew somewhere deep in my consciousness the impact had been extremely painful, but such terror coursed through my body that all I perceived was the throbbing of blood rushing in my ears.

I screamed until the flesh in my throat tore, kicking and thrashing, but my frenzy did nothing to stop them from closing in on me. My fight lasted mere seconds before large, rough hands pinned me to the ground. They bound my legs with the rope already wrapped around my ankle, rendering all my efforts futile. I was small and fragile against brute force and infinite black night. The bitter cold soaked into my dress, stealing the last bits of warmth I had managed to cling to.

My relentless screaming morphed into uncontrollable sobs as my wrists were bound as well. The rope cut into my skin, and my fingers throbbed in agony. I gasped for air but took in nothing but a mouthful of dirt and ice.

"Gag her!" one rasped. "She'll draw attention. That damn rogue is in the area. Do you all want to die?"

A cloth was shoved in my mouth and tied around the back of my head. It tasted of salt and mud, dampened with a substance I didn't want to contemplate. Disgusted, I pushed against it with my tongue, attempting to relieve the awful discomfort that successfully ceased my screaming. Saliva filled my mouth in response. The foul mix of sweat and filth trickled down my throat.

The silencing of my bellows brought my attention to the enraged cat. She spat and hissed. Flickers of burgundy fur shimmered past me as she scaled up one man's back and dug her teeth into his neck. He cried out, and she jumped from shoulder to shoulder among the group of enemies—sinking her fangs into their ears and tearing their skin with her silvery claws. Several men clumsily swiped at her, but she easily avoided their blundering swings.

"What are you doing, you idiots?" another scolded. "Get moving! The rogue heard her screams. I'm sure of it."

The cat continued her bombardment, jumping from tree branch to tree branch and swatting at their heads. The whistle of arrows pierced the night. Each projectile narrowly missed the ferocious feline. She hissed, diving into the brush.

The men crowded over the spot where she landed, lopping at the underbrush with their swords. She exploded from hiding with incredible speed. I barely saw the sudden flash of strange fur as she dashed into the darkness.

"Enough with the damn cat!" one yelled. Giving up their pursuit, the men unsuccessfully wiped their bloody brows, smearing crimson farther onto their gaunt, dirty cheeks.

Defeated, bound, and gagged, I relaxed my tongue from the labored push to keep the rag out of my mouth and swallowed salty dirt down a scorched throat. The muscles around my tongue ached. I blinked several times, attempting to clear away the blinding burn of tears.

This was it. The end. I closed my eyes and prepared to accept my fate. I had wanted freedom and foolishly believed somewhere, outside the walls of Alamantia Palace, I'd find an answer. I had utterly failed. Always so ungrateful for the life I had been given, I'd naively wandered into the unknown—miles away from home— and destroyed myself.

As I waited on the verge of death, I thought of Ambrosia and her fondness for me even in my insolent moments. She loved the worst of me in hopes of bringing out the best. She had risked everything for my escape, trusting I would make a mature decision, appreciate life at court and accept what was needed of me for my country.

The King and queen of Brisleia would lose an heir, their invaluable Divine Princess vanished into thin air, never to be heard from again. Would they forget about me? Would Luken allow them to forget?

Luken . . .

I loved him more than anyone else, and I left him to never know what had become of me. I would never again laugh with my brother nor see his sparkling smile. I would never feed off his enthusiasm or wear his rose crowns in my hair. I wanted to hear his voice more than any other sound in existence. It would have brought me the strength to endure this outcome. But Luken was far away, searching for an answer to break my engagement. And I was here. Alone.

Mortality lingered over me as I came to terms with dying before I had a chance to live. The symptoms of the Fae did not stop at dreaming. I carried something extraordinary—hearing the thoughts of animals and walking across water. I would never know the extent of those forbidden anomalies. Maybe I could return to the dreams so I wouldn't be conscious during the pain of death. I would rather die floating in a black abyss than on the ice-cold ground.

Had Elizabetta known I was dreaming?

My stomach twisted at the memory of her sweet amber eyes. She had never left my side. I had never been without her—until now.

I glanced through the forest and saw the flash of burgundy hiding deep within the brush. The little feline waited patiently, out of sight. She hadn't left me alone in these wretched woods.

"Silence," a shrill old voice commanded, and my captors hushed.

My eyes darted to a short ancient woman with a hunchback that forcefully jutted her head forwards. The hood of her moth-eaten brown cloak covered a mane of long white hair that fell over her round belly and canvased much of her middle. Her nose crooked to the side, and wrinkles surrounded her bloodshot black eyes. She looked well over one hundred, with tapered bony fingers bearing nails so long they curled at the ends.

The men parted for her. When her eyes landed on me, an evil grin grew across her face, revealing chipped brown teeth. A shiver went up my spine. She grabbed the front of my dress and forced me to look at her. "It can't be," she murmured, her dead eyes peering deeply into mine. "Unbelievable." She dropped my dress.

The old hag turned quicker than I would have expected and snatched the collar of the burly man standing over us. "I want her. She's coming with us," she said, then pushed him away by smashing her hand against the side of his face. A delighted smile pulled at her thin lips, and she let out a heinous cackle. "I knew I'd eventually find one. Stupid, pompous dark riders."

My heart jumped into my throat. She couldn't possibly know of my Divinity. The Mandala was still absent.

Footsteps neared my head. I was yanked up from the ground and thrown over an extraordinarily large shoulder, my body dangling upside down like a doll over the icy dirt.

They carried me through the woods. I could see only the ground as it passed under my head, the tips of my almond curls dragging behind my captor's dirty leather boots. I couldn't get enough air into my lungs, and the pressure of balancing on the man's sweaty shoulder made my stomach ache. As the adrenaline faded, every pain my body had endured roared into agonizing focus.

The journey lasted forever into the night—endless rocks, soil, and frost. Sporadically, I would glance to the side and catch the faintest glimpse of burgundy following out of enemy reach. The cat was being cautious, trailing as close as she could while avoiding detection.

I had almost become used to the gag and steadied my breathing when we entered a cave. The narrow tunnel grew brighter the deeper we advanced into the underground. Torches hung at various points along the stone walls, and only one man could pass through at a time without burning themselves.

After a short walk, the tunnel opened into a low cavern, its ceiling studded with stalactites. A sluggish stream flowed along its edge, and additional black tunnels led deeper into the cave. One wide fire burned in the cavern's center, and with no outlet for the smoke, soot hung in the air as ominous charcoal clouds. Ash covered every surface and sprinkled the men loitering in the area with gray cinders. Some practiced sword techniques while a few cheered and laughed at the messy squabbling. Others were too drunk to stand, and one man was vomiting profusely into the stream. They drank from tin steins and chewed on handfuls of pork that dried on racks lining the walls. Most seemed cheery, but a foul smell of death and evil lingered in the air.

The support of my captor's shoulder went out from under me. Still bound, I dropped to the ground with nothing to break my fall. Instant pain. I didn't have a voice left to whimper.

To my right, a forbidding black hole led away from the main chamber, but this tunnel was different. A heavy gate covered the opening, and a colossal metal lock shut away whatever lay inside. I screamed when I saw it, and my ragged throat caught fire.

Two men grabbed me, needing little effort to restrain my body in its weakened state. One took a handful of my hair and jerked my head back so far my neck cracked. He removed the gag and pried open my lower jaw. Insane with fear, I inhaled to let loose a screech of absolute dread, but the second man hovered over me and stopped my scream by pouring a foul liquid into my mouth. I'd have thought any moisture would have soothed the inferno raging in my throat, but the thick, bitter substance burned far more than it cooled. I tried to gargle it out, but the first man arched my neck in such a way that I had no choice but to swallow to keep breathing. My stomach immediately felt unsettled.

"Remove her binds," the second man said, tossing away the small cup. With a large key attached to his belt, he unlocked the heavy gate. The first man drew a knife from his boot and scraped the blade against my skin as he cut through the ropes at my ankles, then my wrists. Before any thought of escape could fully form, I was thrown across the floor towards the iron bars and skidded to a halt just inside. The door slammed shut, and the lock clanked into place.

I scanned the many ghastly individuals until one winked at me. "She's pretty," he murmured to his companions.

"Mother said we have to leave her alone," another informed him.

The first scoffed. "I'll take what I want." He stared at me with a toothless grin.

I jumped away from the gate and slid across the floor, attempting to hide deeper in the darkness. The smell of death filled my nose, and I turned to meet a rotting corpse, flies and maggots falling through dripping holes in the colorless skin. I jerked back and smacked into the stone wall on the other side. Pulling my legs into my chest, I tucked my head in my hands.

Slowly, my eyes adjusted to the dark. The cell was small, only a few feet wide, and full of human excrement and vomit. Roaches and spiders crawled along the filthy floor. I covered my nose with my cloak but couldn't get the scent of rotting flesh out of my lungs.

"It's not so bad once you get used to it."

I flinched at the small feminine voice. My first thought was to look for a mouse, but the figure of a young girl huddling in the darkest part of the cell came into view.

"My name is Abbey, and this is my sister, Mary." She gestured to another girl curled into a fetal position in the corner. Both girls had matted brown hair, skeletal faces with heavy slate bags under their eyes, and green drool drying on their chins.

"What is this place?" I choked out.

"Death." Abbey coughed, and a new glop of thick ooze fell from her mouth. "They will kill you, eventually. They kill everyone."

I grimaced at the filth caked to her skin and clothes. "How long have you been here?" I asked, trying to gauge how much time I had left.

"I . . ." she stuttered. "I don't know." A pause. "They collect people. Then they take them away. They scream. I wish they would take me." She lovingly stroked her sister's hair. The girl breathed but otherwise looked every bit dead. "I want to go home."

"Where is home?" I shouldn't have continued to pry.

She shrugged. "Morgan takes care of us. Sometimes Morgan will tell us stories."

"Who is Morgan?" I asked warily as the strange little girl began to terrify me.

She cocked her head to the side and gave me an odd stare, as if she didn't completely understand the question. She turned to the corpse and studied it. "Oh . . ." Her body shuddered with a sob, but her eyes remained dry. "He died. I wish he would stop talking to me." The sobbing abruptly ceased, and she grinned. "Will you talk to me after you die?"

A sense of impending doom filled the cell. Whatever had happened to this child had caused her to lose her mind.

A loud snort from the main chamber drew my attention. The room had gone quiet; most of the men slept, draped over various objects or curled onto animal skins.

"They'll sleep now," Abbey murmured.

"I have to get out of here." I let the wool fall from my face, and the stench crashed into me.

"There is no way out. No one ever gets out." Her eyes momentarily rolled into the back of her skull, and her head bobbed, becoming too heavy for her thin neck. "We can't leave our home."

I crawled to the gate and eyed the heavy lock. The bars were too close together for me to reach an arm through and fiddle with it. But if I didn't get out of this cell, I would end up just like Abbey and Mary, slowly losing my mind until I disintegrated. Tentatively, I curled a foolish finger around the lock to check its strength.

"I don't care if you've poisoned her. Get rid of the Fae."

I stopped abruptly.

Across the room, the hag stood before a brute of a man, his guttural voice filled with worry as he scolded the ancient woman. "I can't sleep at night thinking of what the Onyx Guard will do to us if they find her here."

"You're a fool if you think I'm letting her go. I do not fear those shadows. Just look at her." The hag's black eyes landed on me, and her withered mouth curled in a corrupt smile. "She's at least sixteen. The tonic will keep her pacified. I choose to keep her."

"This is on you, Mother." The brute groaned and disappeared down one of the many black tunnels.

The old woman's feet scuffled along the rock to the prison gate. "Planning an escape?" She leaned close to the bars and touched the greasy iron. Sticky droplets of drool gathered in the corners of her crusty lips. "It would be in the eve of my long years I would finally cage a Dreamer of my very own."

My heart leaped into my throat. This had nothing to do with my being Divine, but something else entirely. Something hunted by the Onyx Guard in the dead of night to be locked away in Medial Alexandria.

"Let me go," I demanded, wrapping my hands around the bars. "Do you have any idea who I am?"

"Who? Bah!" She spat on the ground. She smelled nearly as bad as the rotting corpse. "Who doesn't matter. Some peasant girl lost in the woods, no doubt. Looking for a lost sheep, were you? Well, who doesn't matter, but *what* . . . yes. Yes, that matters."

"You're mistaken."

"Don't lie to me. I know well what you are, girl, and you are worth your weight in coin." She pointed a bony finger between my eyes. "No one, save Medial Alexandria, holds a Fae captive, and I have never seen a Dreamer as old as you. How you managed to survive this long away from the hands of the Senate is beyond me."

Tired of the torture, I kicked the gate, rattling my cage.

The hag took a step back and gave a deranged cackle, tossing her head joyfully. "You were too easy to capture. If you knew the true extent of your power, there would be no iron bars that could hold you. You are lucky I found you before those cloaked men on horseback. They will not have you. Do you suspect I would turn you over to them so easily? No, dear girl, you belong to me."

I glared at her, ignoring my fear.

"I know what fate awaits you if you keep chasing lost sheep. These days true Sights are fewer and fewer. Others may be blind, but the Onyx Guard will know you when they see you." She turned and made her way towards the nearest black tunnel. "You should thank me for protecting you."

I shook the gate. It didn't budge. The hag's laughter echoed as she disappeared into the aphotic passage.

I wanted to scream. I wanted to wake every single one of them and cause such a fuss they would have to open the cell to keep me from injuring myself. If I was that valuable to her, then she would have to stop me if I chose to act insane.

However, the way these men treated me, their cruelty, the thought of their disgusting hands touching me, silenced my outrage. I glanced at the little girls. Abbey's head rested against the wall, her eyes shut and her chest moving slowly. I did not wish to wake her. Why bring her out of the darkness? In sleep, she had peace.

I found a spot equally far from the corpse and the girls, pulled my legs into my chest, and buried my head in my knees.

Time passed at a crawl. The cave grew darker as the fire died, and soon nothing lit the room except the last smoldering embers. The air turned cold. My dress had dried, but a chill entered my core that iced my bones. My muscles ached in all the places I had been abused.

What would happen to me when dawn came? During my capture, I had thought in rushed bursts about death, fearing I only had minutes to live. I had come to peace with a quick and merciless end. But that would not be my privilege. In this hateful prison, my execution would be labored, painful, and lonely. A Divine Princess would rot away, faceless, nameless, like the corpse melting in the gloom next to me.

It was then.

When everything seemed lost.

And the outside world was a place of the past.

That I heard the faintest clank of metal at the gate.

Chapter 8

I turned my head so fast the joints in my neck popped.

A cloaked silhouette stood at the gate.

I stopped breathing, my heartbeats racing in loud, ominous thumps that might break through my chest. Tears streamed down my petrified cheeks as I remembered the wicked criminal's claim that he could take what he wanted.

I huddled into a fetal position, hoping for a quick death. The faint metallic clicking continued, and I briefly lifted my eyes to see the figure picking the lock. He was tall and rugged, not unlike my captors. I buried my head farther in my arms to block out the stealth rattling.

A stir from a sleeping criminal stopped the locksmith. He paused until the cave dweller resettled and drifted back to sleep. The silhouetted figure waited a second longer before slowly opening the gate.

The iron hinges clanked. The noise seemed loud enough to wake everyone in the silent room.

I peeked out from under my arms as the cloaked man took one half step into the jail and waved his arm, beckoning me out of the cell. I refused to follow his instruction. If he wanted to hurt me, he could come get me himself. I buried my head farther into my knees and kept my breathing shallow. I was short on air and my heart spasmed against my ribs. I wasn't sure how much longer I could last on so little oxygen.

Something hard hit the back of my head. I uncurled from my tight ball just in time to see a rock roll away from me. My skull started throbbing, but the total pain violating my stiff muscles overshadowed the lump growing under my hair.

Again, the figure gestured for me to come out of the cell. Increasing the urgency, he waved twice more. I glanced at Abbey still peacefully sleeping. Mary no longer breathed. She lay in her sister's lap, her chest frozen and her eyelids slightly cracked, revealing a sliver of the dry, fogged pupils associated with death.

I turned back to the silhouette. What was the worst that could happen to me now? Mary was dead, and if I stayed here, I would be too.

I crawled towards Abbey to wake her. A sharp, intense pain hit my stomach, and I stifled a groan. I felt as if I was out of my body, floating in a haze where nothing was quite real. I shook her shoulder. Instead of opening her eyes, she projectile vomited over her sister's body, then slumped, still asleep, over Mary's chest.

I jerked away, the sour stench agitating the growing ache in my stomach, and I inattentively fell into the shadow figure's reach. He grabbed the nape of my dress to yank me to my feet. I stumbled, weakly catching his forearm, and gripped a thick leather bracer housing a set of knives tucked into the binding.

I craned my neck to see his face, but the hood of his cloak shaded his brow. He was taller than me by a head, lean, and round in the shoulders. He shook his arm loose of my hands and grabbed my bicep to pull me through the gate. The roughness of his hand penetrated the wool of my dress, and the force of his grasp was strong enough to bruise bone. My feet dragged across the ground, struggling to keep up with the rest of me. The old hag and these violent men were forbidding, but this dark new figure curdled my blood.

At least I wasn't bound and could scream, if I remembered how to work my lungs. Though something told me he wouldn't need rope to restrain me.

My head ached from dehydration, and another wave of nausea swept through my core. The taste of bile welled in the back of my throat—I swallowed it down.

He held tight to my arm as we sneaked through the entrance tunnel, past the smoking embers of the dying torches. In the distance, starry twinkles illuminated the cave's circular opening, giving the tunnel its only light.

The rock changed to permafrost beneath my feet, and the woods, having seemed so gloomy before, welcomed me. I breathed deeply of the fresh mountain air until I felt lightheaded, pushing the smell of rotting flesh and vomit out of my lungs.

As I anticipated, my new captor did not release me once outside the cave. He continued to drag me through the forest until the sparse starlight disappeared behind the tree canopy.

The cat exploded from the brush like lightning, racing towards us in a spitting, hissing frenzy. Thrilled to see her, my heart fluttered with renewed excitement and the lingering hope of freedom.

The strange hooded figure drew a sword from beneath his cloak, an alarmingly dangerous weapon I had missed. The metal sang upon being released from its sheath, and the shining blade scattered bits of light into the leaves.

The cat pushed all four paws forwards, coming to a sliding halt, and dirt piled up in front of her. With a snap to her right, she put a stop to her attack and ran into the brush. Shimmering burgundy fur disappeared as rapidly as she had arrived.

Sheer panic replaced my small fortune of relief. After fighting so fiercely against my previous captors, she abandoned me to just one man? Ran away at the sight of a sword?

The stranger recommenced pulling me through the woods, now cutting the brush with his blade. We continued for a time I couldn't measure. I didn't realize how heavily I'd been leaning on him until the sudden disappearance of support sent me crashing to the ground. I landed on the frozen dirt, and my pain quickly turned to rage. I was not going through this again. I would not allow myself to be this pathetic and weak. "What do you want?" I demanded, slamming my fist into the ground. My lungs collapsed into a fit of dry coughs from the lack of moisture in my throat.

The stranger returned his sword to the scabbard and knelt beside me. "Shut up. You'll get us killed."

His voiced sounded familiar, like a comfort I should remember from childhood but had forgotten. *Beautiful.* My mind instantly cleared, and fear released its icy grip. Entranced, I waited intently for him to speak again. The features of his face were still indecipherable beneath the hood of his cloak, which kept his eyes and nose in constant shadow—as if he needed to hide his identity from more than just a lost prisoner.

He removed a pouch from a gray haversack slung over his shoulder and thrust it into my hands. "Water," he said, cautiously looking around the woods. "Drink quickly. We can't stay here. This is a dangerous part of the forest."

I stared into the mouthpiece. It had to be poison, but my obsessive thirst overruled reluctance. I guzzled the entire receptacle. The cooling liquid eased my burning throat and washed away the bitterness that still lingered in my mouth. The water was fresh and sweet and gone too fast.

As soon as I'd wiped my lips on my sleeve, the stranger grabbed my bicep and lifted me to my feet. I wobbled on sore ankles and ground my teeth, trying not to show the pain stiffening my body.

"Let's go."

"No!" I shouted. The shriek sent a flock of black birds squawking from their evening nests and out into the night. I ducked, tearing my arm from his grasp, and covered my head with my hands.

Annoyance spread across the statuesque figure standing over me. He waited for the forest to return to silence, until only the occasional bird screech could be heard somewhere in the distance.

He snatched my wrist, gripping so tightly my heartbeat throbbed in my palm. "Quiet!" he scolded through clenched teeth.

"Where are you taking me?" I choked out, saliva gargling in my newly moist throat.

"I'm not taking you anywhere." His voice, once so beautiful, was now tainted by irritation bordering on rage. "The road is just ahead. Take the left to Alamantia and the right to Daraban City. Stay off the path in the daylight or someone else will capture you."

"I'm not going to Alamantia!" I violently shook my arm, trying to free myself from his grip.

He released me. "Fine, stay here then. I'm sure the wolves are hungry. I have no time for idiots who would rather die than help themselves." He backed away, tossing the empty water pouch at me. It hit the front of my dress and fell on my toes.

He turned and sank deeply into the woods.

Everything went dark.

Every tree and shrub had a face watching me. Alone. No horse. No cat. No stranger. Free from the hands of evil men, but at what cost?

My stomach churned. I had been rescued by a mysterious man who seemed formidable but showed meager kindness. Had he really meant to simply free me and send me on the path towards the nearest city?

The wind blew, and the forest howled. The trees creaked, and a black bird chirped above me. My brain played tricks with my senses. Even the faintest branch cracking became an enemy lurking out of view.

Ahead, the road pierced through the woods like a reflective gray river leading back to Alamantia, but going home wasn't the option I wanted to pursue. Even if it meant bringing more danger to myself. Even if it meant facing death all over again. I would take the peril over returning to those stone palace walls.

I could still see the back of the stranger's wool cloak as he faded through the thick greenery. If I hurried and ignored my ongoing nausea, I could catch up and follow him wherever he may be heading.

I quickened my pace. I couldn't lose him. My feet became tangled in the roots of overgrown shrubs, as if the woods had come alive and grew thicker to keep me away from him. I yanked my feet free, but he moved faster, trying to escape.

"Please!" I let out a desperate cry when I couldn't break through the dense branches. "Don't leave me here." I struggled to control my voice. I didn't want to disturb the night any further or give him more reason to abandon me. "I'm lost. I'm frightened." Admitting my fear was as difficult as feeling it.

The branches gave way. I broke free and closed the distance between us—panting and groaning with each painful step—until he was walking mere feet in front of me. Roots and stones repeatedly tripped me. Limbs bent and came back to smack me vengefully in the face. Cobwebs, spiders, and other small creatures lurking in the night crawled up my body. I swatted at them and shook my hair, trying to fling the critters off my dress.

The stranger never stopped. He never turned to see if I was hurt or still relentlessly pursuing him.

The trek turned ever more perilous as the ground began to slope upwards. My muscles screamed, and the rocks and thorny vines split my once delicate hands. The minor relief I'd received from the water had long since disappeared, and heavy open-mouthed breaths rekindled the burn in my throat.

There was no rest. There was no end. Each dragging step up the mountain was more difficult than the last. Each strain pushed my body further to exhaustion.

I was questioning how much farther I could go without collapsing when the sun appeared over the treetops, revealing the exquisite mountain countryside. The snow-capped peaks stretched far into the distance and shimmered in the morning light. As we steadily gained altitude, the forest thinned, transitioning to a maze of jagged boulders and sparse vegetation.

I had never known Brisleia was so beautiful. Distracted, I lost my balance. My feet went out from under me, and I stumbled forwards, sending loose pebbles trickling down the steep slope. Echoes of clings and clanks rang through the mountains.

The stranger turned and grabbed my wrist, catching me before I hit the ground. I stared into the flexing muscle of his arm, then up to his face, hoping to finally glimpse my rescuer, but his hood continued to obscure his features.

"Thank you," I breathed. He said nothing in response but waited until I'd regained my footing before dropping my wrist and starting off again.

Finally, the ground leveled. High in the mountains, a light layer of clouds floated around us. The air thinned, and the frozen dirt grew a thick layer of emerald grass partially hidden beneath sporadic patches of snow. A tiny glen on the edge of a precipice overlooked the massive evergreen forests, and a large willow tree at its center glittered with a dusting of frost .

All at once I felt homesick. I adored my own weeping willow in my private garden.

The stranger walked to the willow trunk and set his haversack among the roots. Sweeping his hand over his head, he pushed the hood of his cloak away from his face, revealing golden-blond hair growing in a series of haphazard directions—uneven and chaotic. His piercing eyes were a brilliant shade of steel blue set among a slightly square jawline and rough, tanned skin. Built broad in the shoulders, he tapered into a triangular torso full of lean hardened muscle. I was shocked to discover he wasn't much older than me, easily under twenty.

When his engaging eyes landed directly on mine, his expression morphed into something like disbelief. His peach-colored lips parted, and his hands formed two clenched fists, as if what he saw disturbed him beyond measure.

After a moment, the stranger lowered his gaze and shook his head, grinning devilishly at some secret personal amusement. My cheeks flushed at his innately charming smile.

He wore a sleeveless white shirt made of light, fraying cotton and leather bracers bound to his forearms that holstered a variety of knives. Around his left arm, a tightly wrapped linen bandage was secured under his elbow. His slack leather boots each housed a hunting blade tucked into the side, and his brown leather pants hung dangerously low on his hips. Attached to the rim of his trousers was a black leather belt holding the scabbard containing the magnificent sword I'd seen during the night, and his long wool cloak swayed over the glistening onyx hilt.

It might have been the altitude, or simply exhaustion, but I started to feel dizzy. My stomach did a flip not associated with nausea, and I couldn't explain the giant knot growing in my chest as I looked at him. The man standing before me was incredibly handsome, with a rugged authority unlike anything I had ever seen. I wasn't breathing. And I hadn't noticed I'd stopped until my chest screamed for air.

"Why are you following me?" he asked, breaking whatever enchantment momentarily rendered me immobile.

I sucked in a breath to replenish my frozen lungs. "You saved my life," I exhaled.

"And that constitutes a reason to follow me?" He crossed his arms over his chest and leaned back against the willow trunk.

"I don't have anywhere else to go."

The stranger raised an eyebrow, losing his smile. "You still don't." He waved his hand dismissively.

"Please, take me with you. At least to a village," I begged.

"I showed you the main road to the cities." He pulled a hunting knife from his boot.

Instinctively, I took a step back. "You don't understand, I can't go near any major city."

"Oh, I understand perfectly. But I'm not going to have you around." He pointed the blade at me. "You're trouble."

"I'm not trouble, really. I'll be quiet. You can ignore that I'm with you." I tried to sound convincing.

The stranger scoffed. "Hardly." He dug the tip of his blade into the willow trunk and filleted the bark, cutting away a large square of the inner white flesh, and stuffed the chunk into his haversack.

I started to feel foolish. I should have taken the road as he directed instead of mindlessly following some mysterious nomad who clearly didn't appreciate my company.

I walked to the opposite side of the willow and slid down the trunk, landing on the soft grass. The stranger glared at me using only his eyes. His gaze lingered for a moment, then he took a deep breath, muttering something unintelligible, and lightly punched his fist against the bark. I swallowed hard.

Movement in the bushes demanded my attention—burgundy fur. I squeaked with glee and slapped my hand over my mouth. The cat looked long overdue for a decent rest. She blinked wearily several times, and my heart warmed, making my rescuer's foul attitude a little more bearable.

I squinted at her, trying to form a connection that might allow me to hear her thoughts, but received only silence.

The stranger tucked his knife back into his boot and took a seat on the other side of the tree. He leaned into the bark and closed his eyes.

"Where are we?" I asked, listening to the morning birds chirping in the branches above us.

"Western Daraban," he answered dryly.

My eyes widened. *Daraban?* How had I managed to travel this far in such a short time?

"It's disturbing that you have no idea where you are . . . considering . . ." He rested a wrist on his bent knee.

Considering? Considering what? That I was the Divine Princess Ayleth Rose of Alamantia and shouldn't be in the forest alone? Or something else entirely? Something I was beginning to realize was more hazardous than being a wandering Divine. "Are you from Daraban City? Or a village? Are we going there?"

The stranger turned to me and furrowed his brows at the bombardment of questions. "We?" He chuckled at the word. "*We* aren't going anywhere, and where *I* am heading is not your concern. I'm not getting involved."

"Involved?" I twisted around to face him. "Involved with what?"

"You." He waved his hand to gesture to me in general. "This."

I frowned. "Excuse me, sir, but didn't you involve yourself in *this* when you opened that prison gate and jerked me out like some sort of kidnapping?"

"Sure, except most people disappear into the woods to be eaten afterwards," he explained, perturbed.

"Well, if you're not some sort of kidnapper or criminal, then for what reason would you rescue people from the likes of that place only to leave them stranded in the woods?"

"Who said I wasn't a criminal? And I didn't leave you stranded. I led you to the road. That's as far as I'm willing to go. The rest is up to them." He returned to his side of the trunk.

"Them? So, you've made a habit of this?"

"Ah . . ." He rubbed his hands over his face, as if I was the most irritating creature he had ever come across. "Salted pork, okay? Damnit, their victims are never this annoying."

I retreated to my side of the tree.

"They're bandits." He sighed, softening his tone. "That particular group makes the best salted pork this side of Medial Alexandria."

Bandits. I cringed at the word. Merciless killers who stole without reason. I was lucky to be alive.

"The point is," he continued, "I've got my own history of thieving, and since I can't tolerate suffering anymore, I free any healthy prisoners they have accumulated. Convenient for you."

I tucked my legs into my chest. "And yet you left behind the other two girls in the cell."

"One," he corrected, "and the other girl is dead by now too. Most of their captives are too far gone to help themselves."

"That is so cruel of you," I whispered.

The stranger spun around, his blue eyes burning with an intimidating brilliance. "I'm not out to be heroic. I just happen to be in the right place at the right time to help a few of them. I'm not wasting effort trying to fix something that cannot be changed. Now shut the hell up, or I'll finish what they started."

My jaw dropped. "You wouldn't." If he knew my true identity, he would never dare make such a threat against me.

He turned back to his side of the willow. "Keep following me and we'll see what happens."

I narrowed my eyes. "You're lying."

"Don't be so trusting." He readjusted his shoulders against the bark and went still.

I knew I ought to leave the conversation there, but curiosity overruled my common sense. Though perhaps dangerous and certainly armed, this stranger had yet to bring me any real harm. "What's your name?"

"I'm done answering questions. And you really need to stop following me."

"And you have the audacity to call *me* annoying." I curled back into my knees, deciding not to push him any further.

I was beyond thirsty, and dehydration cramped my muscles. I reached for a clump of snow and popped it into my mouth. It hurt to swallow, but the freezing powder helped numb the pain. My stranger had not drunk water, eaten, or exposed the slightest hint of discomfort.

I spent the morning sucking on more handfuls of snow, trying to forget the intense figure sitting behind me. By noon I had consumed so much I was shivering and longing for the warmth of my bedroom hearth. As I reached for the last clump I could eat before freezing, the stranger turned his head just enough to see me out of the corner of his eye. "I'd offer you some water, but you drank it all. Don't eat any more snow, or you will die." He went back to ignoring me.

I buried my forehead in my knees at the thought of those piercing eyes spying on me. *How he must view this impuissant woman trailing after him . . .*

I felt faint, weak, pitiful, and more nauseated than I ever had in my entire life. Sleep was impossible, and my body was breaking down. My bottom lip throbbed, and I tongued the deep split where my teeth had bit into the tender flesh.

Crusted blood and dirt darkened my swollen hands, with gashes and blisters separating one blemish from the next. My fingernails were ripped and jagged, and picking at them only made the irritation worse. Instead, I buried my sore hands under a layer of snow.

I watched the mountains for hours, mesmerized by the grandeur of my own country. Perfect gray-and-blue peaks stretched as far as I could see, each capped with a white layer of snow. Puffs of low clouds made it difficult to tell where one summit ended and another began.

This was the land of my ancestors, generations born under the Rose Court burdened to rule these stone ridges. My life kept this beauty alive. My blood. My Mandala. For the first time I understood the critical nature of the Divine. Everyone knew the consequences if a line failed.

Kenara had been the land of great plains, a western nation south of Podar. Once endless grasslands covered the landscape and abundant spring-fed lakes reflected a warm, cloudless sky.

One thousand years ago, the Senate had determined that a woman was too weak to govern alone. That an independent, unwed Queen threatened the survival of the Kenarian Divine. Podar invaded with the intention of forcing Kenara into submission. They swore to protect the land under a male sovereign. The misogynism of Divine men is embedded deeply within their veins.

After three thousand years of Divine power ruling Athera, few in that time truly believed the legends of tied bloodlines. Backed by the Senate, the Podarian King tested the boundaries of Divine command. Being a sea-bordering nation has benefits, and Podar was determined to seize a portion of Kenarian coastline.

The only war Athera ever knew began when the Divine Queen of Kenara attempted to stand against Podar and the Senate. Duval secured its borders, swearing to remain neutral. Brisleia ran to Kenarian aid, but they were too late.

The death of Kenara commenced the instant the Divine Queen's heart stopped. The planet howled in pain. Kenarian trees wilted and died. Clouds blocked the sun, and the ground turned to ash. The animals fled the land and faded into myth. One quarter of all life in Athera vanished, never to return.

Now, the country is a void and barren wasteland. No breeze. No life. No sun. No water. Nothing grows. Nothing lives. Even the bordering sea turned to acid.

Podar took responsibility for their actions by issuing a continental apology. As if that would compensate for the lives lost.

Divinity and the Senate have since vowed to keep the bloodlines protected at all costs. It took death to know the importance of the Mandala. Those who bear the mark truly are Athera's most precious possession.

I shook my head to banish the history lesson I'd heard one hundred times from Sir Jonathan Helms.

The sun began to fall behind the horizon. The sky turned red and purple, the last rays of dying light enveloping the mountains in an ethereal glow.

My stranger took to his feet in a slow, methodical stretch, as if it ached him to move. He rolled his shoulders twice on each side and scanned the surrounding forest before using both hands to lift his hood back into place.

Then he was gone, disappearing into the brush as if he had never existed at all.

Chapter 9

I jumped to my feet and leaped into the brush where he had disappeared.

Smack!

I collided into his back.

The impact knocked me senseless, making my eyes roll around in their sockets. If I hadn't felt the wool of his cloak slam into my face, I would have thought I'd run into a tree.

I fell backwards. The stranger turned faster than I'd ever seen anyone move and swept his arm under my lower back before I could hit the ground. He cradled me in the crook of his elbow until I came out of the daze.

I opened my eyes to find him peering at me. Now that I knew his face, I could distinguish his gorgeous features under the shadow of his hood. One side of his mouth twitched into a snide smirk as he helped me steady myself. As soon as my legs stopped wobbling, he let me go and continued through the woods.

Traveling down the mountain strained me as much as going up. Instead of a strenuous climb, I embarked on a chaotic slide. To make matters worse, the stranger increased his speed. My flimsy ankles repeatedly buckled and sent me skidding into the backs of his legs. After I hit his calves for the third time, he cursed viciously and shoved me away in frustration.

The stranger seemed to travel on air. Never missing a step. Knowing the placement of every stone and stump.

Late into the evening, I finally found a rhythm to the downhill excursion. I learned to avoid rocks and roots, but my feet had bruised to the bone.

Once again, the forest grew thick, and the tree canopy hid the misty blue glow of the moon. I stumbled through the darkness. The onslaught of brush reopened the rips on my hands, making me doubt my sanity for following my stranger back into this hell, yet I kept moving.

Every minute of the long night lasted an hour until the woods cleared. The terrain shifted to mountain ridges where one misstep would send me tumbling over the edge. We dived back into the forest. It continued like this throughout the day and into the next night—a painful crawl up the steep slopes only to slide down the other side.

I began to doubt my resolve. He was inhuman. We covered a distance that no man alive should have been able to traverse in the time given. Ready to admit defeat, I prepared to lie down on the mountain ridge and watch him run into the distance—accept my death or allow fate to decide the future.

As I reasoned with myself, he abruptly stopped. I couldn't halt my steps quick enough, and my feet slipped over the edge of a cliff.

My stomach lurched into my chest, and a sharp tingle shot through my legs. My stranger snatched my wrist. I dangled in midair, legs flailing in search of a stable surface. He pulled me up far enough that I could latch my free arm around his neck, and he spun me back onto solid ground.

"Do you have a death wish?" he scolded, pushing me out of his arms.

I collapsed. Sick to the core, panting and shaking, I replayed the furiously fast events in my mind. The stranger glared at me, taking a firm hold of the roots dangling over the cliff's edge, and down he went.

I groaned, rubbing my fists into my eyes. I couldn't do this. Down the side of a precipice? Was he serious? I had to stop pursuing him. I looked back in the direction we had come. The nonexistent path led nowhere up a nearly vertical climb.

I leaned forwards to peer over the cliff. The treetops were covered with beautiful purple, pink, and white blossoms. I felt dizzy.

The acrobatic stranger quickly descended using the small ledges and roots. A few feet from the ground, he let go of the rock and landed with a thud on the grass. Pulling his hood from his head, he looked up at me, and blond wisps of hair brushed across his forehead. Even from afar, he was stunningly handsome. Seeing him at the bottom made the distance seem shorter than I originally anticipated.

Unnerved, I eased myself to the ledge. A concerned meow came from behind me. The little cat sat on a nearby branch, awaiting my decision. She gave me more confidence—a reminder of the hard journey I had traveled and a physical manifestation of my own strength.

I dangled my feet over the side and took hold of the same branch the stranger had used to lower himself onto the rock face. My arms ached from the weight of my own body. The smooth stone was easier to grip than expected, but finding places to plant my feet increased the challenge. Each time I lowered my foot, I feared not finding the next step. Each time panic seared my brain until I found a solid surface.

The stranger paced, watching and, to my surprise, waiting. His insistent gaze made me feel rushed and unsteady. I looked down to gauge the remaining distance: higher than I was tall. He stopped in my periphery and crossed his arms over his chest.

I shut my eyes. I held my breath. And let go.

The soles of my shoes slammed into the ground. The blow radiated up my legs and into my hips. I toppled over and fell flat on the grass, my ragged breaths reassuring me I was still alive.

My stranger-turned-escort stared at me with a raised eyebrow. The cat broke his gaze when she dropped on all fours next to me. He grabbed the hilt of his sword and prepared to draw, but the feline didn't linger. She rushed past us and disappeared, kicking up fallen petals in her wake. My stranger gave me a quizzical look and recommended walking.

I lifted myself from the ground and brushed colored blossoms from my dress. Thick emerald grass sprouted through a maze of caramel-colored trees twisted and bent over each other in a lovely dance that created intertwined systems. No brush or shrubs crowded the forest floor, and a plethora of white, pink, and purple petals floated through the air. I looked up, and my breath hitched. Hundreds of thousands of flowers hung from the tree canopy. Rays of early morning sunlight pierced the blossoming branches, illuminating the woods in a warm orange glow. The sweetest floral scent filled my lungs. I had never seen anything more spectacular. Even the roses growing throughout Alamantia Palace couldn't compare to the beautiful splendor of this forest.

My intuition on the cliff had been correct. It was time to stop pursuing him. Ambrosia told me to find safety, and here among the sunlight and petals, I felt inviolable and serene. This was where I wanted to stay. This was where my journey would end.

The wind shook the trees, sending detached flowers falling to the ground like snowflakes. I held out my hand and caught several silky blooms on my palm.

The stranger stopped and turned to face me. He stood a moment, waiting for me to follow. When I didn't continue, he walked back to my side. My heart responded by thumping against my ribs.

He took my hand and brushed the petals from my palm. "It's wisteria." His voice held the same heady tone from the first time I'd heard it. Then he did something I never expected; his calloused grip wrapped around my bruised and battered hand. He weaved our fingers together and tugged me with him. Distracted, I kept staring at the enchanting way our fingers looked while interlaced. So much of him exuded a hard and foreboding nature, yet he was capable of this gentle touch.

He kept me beside him through the miraculous forest, walking at a slow pace comfortable for my sore feet. Why wouldn't he leave me behind? Had he taken pity on the lost waif chasing him with such vigor?

I shook my head, trying to clear a sudden fog taking over my brain. He led me to a crag in the corner of the forest. We rounded the rock and stepped into a lush valley completely surrounded by steep mountains. The stranger plucked a pink petal out of my hair. I knocked several more from my shoulders before he smiled and released my hand.

I looked behind me to capture one last glimpse of the wisteria forest, but it was gone, hidden somewhere behind the crag.

The valley opened into a paradise with long jade blades of grass and a river babbling through a rocky bed. In the distance, a midsized lake at the base of a tall rock formation received a cascading waterfall. Mist wafting into the air shrouded the mossy green boulders bordering the bank.

A herd of Brisleian horses gathered by the still thawing river. One colossal white stallion stood guard. He watched us intently as we proceeded across the valley, seeming to take special interest in my stranger.

Rabbits bounced in the grass and nibbled on the abundant wildflowers and lupines. The untouched beauty, so full of life, rendered me speechless. I wanted to stay here forever. I wished to make a home for myself and live isolated among the trees. It was a perfect place for a hidden Divine to take refuge.

I plucked a yellow peony from the grass and twirled the stem between my fingers. My steps slowed; the desire to keep up with my stranger faded. Twisting the little flower, I weighed the odds of survival on my own. The delicate petals broke under the ministrations of my overly eager hands.

My stranger was several paces in front of me, but it didn't matter anymore. He looked back only once and smirked, seeing my idiotic smile at the broken bloom. I trailed him for the entire length of the valley, taking in the beauty and watching the sparkle of sunlight dance over the river.

The feeling of bliss was cut short when I realized he was heading for the entrance of a cave. A huge cave. A cavern. The opening was taller than the gates of Alamantia City. I dug my feet into the dirt. I was not going back into the gloom to be tortured by a new group of perverted, evil men. *Why didn't you listen to Ambrosia?* This man had never taken pity on me. It had always been something more sinister.

I prepared to run.

Sensing my terror, the stranger spun around and rapidly returned to my side. He put his hand on the small of my back and leaned close to my ear. "It's not what you think." His warm breath sent a strange tickle down my spine. I savagely glared at him. He raised a questioning eyebrow and shrugged. "You've followed me this far."

My spirits weakened. He disappeared into the entrance before I could make sense of what I wanted. At least he had given me a choice.

The fear of losing him overrode all rational thought, and I stepped into the cavern.

My eyes adjusted to the dim light. This was no cramped tunnel leading into a rotten room full of bandits; the ceiling rose even higher than the arched entrance. Moss grew up the rock walls, and a spring of crystalline water bubbled in the back of the cavern. Near the pool, a little square home was built against the stone. Green vines grew readily over the dwelling, and a thick layer of moss clung to the thatched roof, where sparse wildflowers miraculously grew without sunlight. The rest of the building was crafted from wooden planks with the bark still attached, and support beams braced a wall that seemed to be weakening. There were no windows, only a single point of access covered by a heavy brown fur. A round metal chimney jutted from the center of the roof, and gray smoke billowed towards the cave ceiling. Stacks of firewood lined the side of the home, along with piles of woven baskets full of vegetables.

In the center of the cavern, a fire crackled, and a cauldron hung from a spit just above the flames. A creamy liquid, filled with chunks of carrots and potatoes, simmered inside the pot, and the lovely smell filled the room. Three cut tree trunks formed a seating area around the fire, and a set of carved wooden bowls rested on the bark. My heart warmed at the sight.

My stranger dropped his haversack next to a seating log, then walked to the dwelling, pulled back the fur door, and went inside. I waited by the cavern entrance, unsure if I was meant to follow. Someone lived here, and they might not appreciate me walking into their house as though I owned it.

I continued to absorb my surroundings. The entire left side of the cavern housed crude wooden racks, most with animal hides stretched across the frames and held tightly in place with twine. A second wave of new smells hit my nose—a sour musky stench from baskets of smoked meat and fish, and piles of dried furs: rabbit, wolf, fox, and deer. It was an incredible amount of contraband. Under Brisleian law it was illegal to hunt the King's game. The Divine are charged with keeping their country safe and alive, so everything belongs to royalty. This was as great a crime as bandits killing lost peasants in the woods.

I heard voices coming from inside the house. They started pleasant but quickly escalated into a heated argument. Absorbed by the muffled bickering, I cried out in fright when the unmistakable brush of a feline body rubbed my leg. I moved my foot to hide her behind my cloak. She gave a disagreeable meow but seemed to understand my instruction to stay out of sight.

"Are you out of your damn mind!!?"

The fur door was flung aside. Out scurried a second man, who froze, mouth agape, when he laid eyes on me. Husky and as tall as my stranger, he had sweet walnut-colored eyes under thick brows, a full curly brown beard, and dark hair visible beneath a tan cap. He wore a pair of brown woolen trousers tucked into the top of his black boots with a long-sleeved tan tunic. The leather belt tied under his round tummy held a variety of different-sized wooden spoons. A small button nose and plump rosy cheeks made him appear as if smiling came easy, but currently he couldn't rid himself of the astonishment of seeing me in the cavern.

My stranger followed behind him. His cloak had disappeared, revealing many scars marring his shoulders and arms. He gave a small chuckle as he sat on the ground by the fire, casually leaning his back against the seating log.

The chubby man rubbed his fingers into his eyes and mumbled something under his breath. "What do you expect me to do about it?"

"She followed me." My stranger shrugged, giving a devious smirk.

"She followed you?" the new man repeated incredulously. "Right." He turned to me with a sigh, clearly trying to swallow a horrid situation. "Good morning." He smiled pleasantly.

"Good morning," I cautiously replied.

"My name is Bromly Keene." He dipped his head to meet my downcast gaze. "And your . . . escort? . . . whom you *followed*"—

he rolled his eyes at my stranger—"I'm sure hasn't introduced himself to you. This is my brother, Darric Ursygh."

Darric Ursygh.

I looked at him, pleased to finally have the name of my rescuer, but the ability to form coherent words eluded me. I started to tremble from a combination of nerves and exhaustion and clenched my jaw to keep my teeth from chattering.

Darric inquisitively tilted his head to the side. "Generally, introductions call for reciprocation."

"Don't make this worse by being you!" Bromly snapped. "What he means is, what's your name?"

"Ay—" I slammed my mouth shut. I had not considered the possibility of anyone asking personal information. Ayleth was the Divine Princess of Alamantia. Everyone knew that, even nomadic peasants. The name was mine and mine alone, an appellation that could not be given to another Atheran child until after my death. Ambrosia warned me I would have to forget the Rose Court. Could I really pretend to be someone else? Take on a completely different identity? But I wasn't Ayleth anymore. Ayleth was the girl I'd left behind in silk dresses, jewels, and a corset, inside stone walls. She didn't belong here. "Uh . . ." I stammered.

"Ay-uh?" Bromly repeated, confused.

The new name left his mouth and settled in my brain in the final instant before I would be considered mentally incompetent. "Aya." The alias rolled off my tongue with ease. It felt right. Simple and pretty. "My name is Aya."

The cat leaned into my leg, purring wildly.

"Aya. Okay. Lovely. And where are you from, Aya?"

"Um . . ." My mind went blank. What should I say? How was I supposed to act? What were the five provinces of Brisleia? Where did it make sense for me to live?

"Amusing," Darric said. "She wasn't nearly so speechless before."

Bromly let out a frustrated breath. "You see, Aya, we don't kindly greet visitors."

"In other words, you are not welcome here," Darric interjected.

Bromly glowered at his brother.

I was having trouble making sense of the change in my stranger. The man who had been reluctant to leave me behind in the final stages of our journey. The one who had saved me from falling to my death and led me by the hand to this cavern.

"I didn't intend to disturb you. I tried to stop earlier, but he—" Darric glared at me with such malice that my voice locked itself in my throat. The wisteria forest had captured my heart. It was miles away, but even that might not be far enough from these mysterious men. "There was an isolated forest before—"

"Clearly there were many places you could have chosen to stop following me," Darric interrupted. "Yet, here you are." His stare intensified. The message was clear: stop talking or face the consequences.

"Yes, she is here," Bromly reluctantly acknowledged. "And she knows we're here too."

"That's a problem all its own," Darric added.

"Agreed. Yet, I have to wonder why this problem ever occurred in the first place." Bromly frowned at Darric. "Are you hungry, Aya? I made breakfast."

"Bromly," Darric began, "don't feed her."

Ignoring my stranger, Bromly plucked a wooden bowl from the seating log, detached a spoon from his belt, and ladled a large helping of creamy soup into the dish. After handing it to me, he sat by the fire and proceeded to make a bowl of his own. "Please." He gestured for me to join them.

I wobbled on stiff ankles, cradling the dish against my belly until the heat became unbearable. I dropped onto the last empty log and nestled the bowl in my lap.

Without my dress to hide behind, the cat darted out of the cavern and dived into the brush.

"And she has a damn cat." Darric pointed at the feline.

"She's not *my* cat. I don't know where she came from. Or why she's been following me." I turned the soup over with my spoon, watching the steam rise.

"You can't be serious?" Darric said in a tone that questioned my sanity.

Bromly gave a discreet chortle that rounded his rosy cheeks. He spooned stew into his mouth as if he was ready to enjoy the morning's entertainment.

"Then you won't mind me disposing of her for you." Darric pulled the hunting knife from his boot.

"No!" I squealed, horrified, then quickly recoiled. "I mean, yes, I mind."

He brandished the weapon and shoved the blade back into his boot. The longer I sat near him, the more menacing he seemed.

"I'd rather you leave her alone." I couldn't help but glance at the piles of fur stacked behind me.

I spooned the first bite of soup into my mouth, trying to ignore the penetrating stare of steely blue eyes. Despite not having eaten for days, I wasn't hungry, but not wanting to be rude, I let the warm liquid slide down my throat. A sharp pain hit my stomach with the second unnecessary bite, and the nausea grew evermore severe.

"All right, now that we've decided to keep the cat . . ." Bromly finished the last of his soup and wiped his mouth on his sleeve. "What village are you from? If you're lost, we can help you get back. Darric knows the landscape."

"That won't be necessary," Darric stated dryly, transferring his gaze to my soup bowl.

"It doesn't matter where I'm from. I can't go back, and I have no intention of ever doing so." And I did not want to disappear back into the hellacious woods with *Darric*.

Intrigued, Bromly set his bowl down and rubbed his hands on his knees. "So, you decided to follow a heavily armed nomad?" He pointed at his brother. "How the hell does he seem like a friendly travel companion?"

I forced a small grin at Bromly's sarcasm.

"Well, this is just fascinating." He smacked his hands on his thighs and beamed at Darric.

"I know what you're insinuating," Darric growled.

The cat stuck her head out from the brush and gave an angry hiss, then quickly went back into hiding.

Darric gripped the hilt of his sword to taunt the feline. "And the cat is enough reason to make me take her back to that cave tonight."

Bromly's face filled with trepidation. "Which cave?"

"That cat is beautiful," I argued, though I had not liked her either upon our first meeting.

"All the more reason to skin her," Darric threatened.

"Every thieves' cave is over thirty miles from here," Bromly said. "You mean to tell me you kept up with his endless trekking? He doesn't stop."

"It was annoying," Darric groused.

I narrowed my eyes. "I'm not so easily dismissed."

"Clearly," he stated, a poisoned edge to his voice.

Bromly tossed a stick in the fire. "You'll have to stay here with us for now."

"No," Darric argued simply.

"Hey, Darric." A third man folded the fur door closed behind him. "You're alive. An' in one piece. Goooood." He rubbed his eyes. "If ya two are gonna yell at each other this early, do me a favor an' go outside. My sleepin' time is important."

This third inhabitant was the tallest of the three but much thinner, almost frail when compared to the toned appearance of my stranger and the brawn of Bromly's frame. He had pointed features, and his nose tapered into a sharp end. Rust-orange hair covered his head, and he didn't seem to care that a brown leaf was caught in the strands. He wore a faded green tunic and oversized gray wool pants, but he lacked shoes, and the same orange fur that grew on his head sprouted from his bare feet.

I tightened my grip on the soup bowl, the increasing male presence making me apprehensive.

The redhead gave a sleepy yawn and stretched his arms out to resemble a scarecrow, with each finger extending like a twig. His bulbous emerald eyes landed on Darric's haversack.

"Pork!" he enthused, running to the satchel. He dug in with both hands and shoved two fistfuls of dried meat into his mouth. Bits flew from his noisy chops and sizzled on the edge of the fire.

Disgusted, Darric kicked him away from the pack and casually tossed the bag behind his resting log.

"Flint?" Bromly drawled.

"Yeah?" The man's cheeks bulged as he looked up and finally noticed the female addition sitting by the fire. He gaped, revealing a mound of brown mash. "Whoa . . ." A cascade of chewed pork fell from his mouth, and he quickly closed his lips and swallowed. "You're a girl."

"You're observant." Darric sighed, exasperated.

The redhead slid onto my log and scooted so close that his thigh brushed my leg. He extended a hand that glistened with a wet layer of saliva. "I'm Flint Keene. Nice to meet ya."

I stared at his moist skin. "Aya," I said, trying not to wrinkle my nose.

"Ya came with Darric?" He flashed a smile, baring every tooth in his wide mouth. "Are ya from Burge?"

"Darric is trying to claim that she followed him here," Bromly provided, amused.

Flint let out a derisive laugh. "Yeah, right." He picked a pork shard out of his tooth and flicked it into the flames.

The smell of burning meat hit my nose, and the nausea ripped through my core like a knife. The bowl fell from my grasp as I doubled over, clutching my stomach and groaning in sheer agony. The soup burned as it rose back up my throat. I tried to stop it, but the pressure increased, and I vomited onto the ground. Flint jumped back to avoid the onslaught.

My entire body went limp from the bewildering pain. I fell from my seat, and hard muscular arms encased me when Darric caught my trembling body inches before it hit the stone. I sank into his chest.

A bombardment of swearing erupted from Bromly. "Darric, which cave?"

"The one on the west ridge, south of the city." My stranger's serene voice echoed in my head, so beautiful when he wasn't angry.

"Why didn't you tell me the second you got here?" Bromly shrieked in alarm. "Why did you let me feed her? You know what they do to people. Aya! Aya! Can you hear me?"

I wanted to respond, but I couldn't. The cavern spun as I convulsed.

"I'm aware of what they do to people," Darric said. "I was hoping this would happen before we reached the Hovel."

"Why? She could die!" Bromly yelled.

"It's the easiest way to handle this."

Bromly's soft hands wrapped around my shoulders. He started to shake me, trying to bring me back to the surface. I flapped around like a rag doll. "Aya, did they make you drink anything? Aya! Answer me! Damn it, Darric! How could you do this?"

Their voices faded. I could no longer comprehend my surroundings, and the darkness took me.

Chapter 10

The Senate ordered the Onyx Guard to take every Dreamer to Medial Alexandria. Most Fae were too young to understand the consequences. They blurted their secret in public or told their families, who became terrified and turned them over to the Senate. Others risked everything to hide their damaged child, defying the law. The Onyx Guard always found them. They could sense them. They knew them when they saw them, though it was not public knowledge how the dark-cloaked Sights detected the Fae.

I started dreaming the day I turned thirteen, but I was not so sure anymore that was factual. Maybe I'd always suppressed the reality. I did not want to be a Fae any more than I wanted to be Divine.

The darkness transitioned into the dreaming abyss. Flowers grew around my bare feet: wisteria. They sprouted in the wrong direction, gravity acting backwards so the dangling pink and purple petals pointed skywards. I breathed in the intoxicating smell, and a chill made me wrap my arms around myself.

The entity that had tried to kill me crept back into the shadows.

My last memories awake were of an inconceivable place with three men whose intentions remained unknown. I pressed my fingers into my temples. *Wake up, Ayleth. Wake. Up. Now.*

The plush fur I lay on tangled between my legs and wrapped around my waist, making me hot. Soft. I smashed my face into it. The strong scent of musk, mold, and burning leaves, followed by a floral undertone, filled my nose. A sleeve of rabbit fur covered the down pillow. I sank deeper into the lumpy, uncomfortable mattress and pulled the sheet over my head. It was the wrong time to be dreaming. Why couldn't I be like the rest of the world and see only blackness when I slept? Experience the peaceful meditation of a blank mind?

I rubbed my hands over my face; the mark of the Divine still lay hidden beneath my skin.

"This changes everythin'." I recognized Flint Keene's voice coming from somewhere nearby.

"There is no guarantee the girl will be coherent," answered Darric Ursygh, "if she wakes up at all. I need you to think rationally. Her brain could be severely damaged after a poisoning of this magnitude."

"Whadda ya suggestin'? Killin' her?" Flint asked in alarm.

"We have disposed of people before," Darric said calmly. He could have been talking about something as simple as breakfast instead of murder.

A hard slam sounded against a wooden surface. "No, *you* changed the rules. *You* brought someone here. Ya can't do this to me. How could ya live with yourself?" Flint asked, his tone accusatory.

"You are already too emotionally involved."

"Ya promised me. Ya gave me your word. I deserve to be happy, like Bromly. *You* made the decision to drag us out here. To hell with the rules now. Next trip to Burge, Hazel should return with us," Flint insisted. "Bromly, wouldn't ya love to have Hazel here with ya? Ya could marry an' be with her all the time."

"I gave you my word predicated on the girl's healthy survival. Don't drag Bromly and Hazel into this," Darric rebuked.

"You can't control their lives too." Flint's grating voice shook me further out of the sleepy haze. "Answer the question, Bromly!"

"Why would I want Hazel here?" Bromly Keene said, his voice quieter than the others'. "She has a fine life in Burge. Her mother needs her. I would never ask her to give that up to live isolated in a pig sty in the mountains. She deserves more."

Pig sty?

"Ya risk losin' her," said Flint. "Every time we go back, ya risk that she's married someone else. Gone forever. Sick of waitin' for ya."

"I would rather she marry a good man she loved in my absence, one who could provide for her amply, than risk her safety by bringing her to a place where she could be hurt, or worse," Bromly explained.

"Darric put those ideas in your head. He's gonna ruin your chances. He changes anythin' he wants, when he wants."

"The girl is a temporary situation." Darric's composure remained unaffected by Flint's belligerent tone. "You would do well to remember that."

"Aya! Her name is Aya!" Flint snapped.

Aya?

"You don't know what you are getting yourself into. This girl is a calamity," Darric continued, "and you are too blinded by your own ambition."

"I am not!" Flint yelled, and my eyes flew open to see a dark room. "I say she stays. Bromly wants her here too."

"Don't put me in the middle of all this," Bromly interjected. "If you two are making stupid pacts about some girl, then I want nothing to do with any of it."

"Even if I allow her to stay—"

"She's stayin'!" Flint interrupted, his shout followed by a metallic slam.

"And what plan have you devised to ensure this doesn't go awry? Seduction?" Darric's voice dripped sarcasm.

"Uh . . ." Flint's confidence flattened. "I haven't decided yet."

"By all means, take your time," Darric taunted.

"Darric, Flint has a genuine argument. You brought an outsider to the Hovel—"

"I did not bring her here on purpose—"

"Yes, we've heard you every time you've said it, though the evidence is to the contrary," Bromly countered. "Anyway, it doesn't matter what events led to this. She's here, and we all need to come to an agreement on how to handle the situation. I hate to admit it, but I agree with Flint this time. Even if his motives are absurd."

Darric let out a long groan.

Soft paws pressed into my back, followed by a gentle tug on a strand of my hair. The cat pulled harder until the ringlet broke.

I flipped over, and she jumped to the ground. In her mouth, she held the stem of a flower with a small cerulean bud crushed at the end. She dropped the bloom and commenced licking her paw.

"What are you doing to my hair?" I squeaked, sitting up.

Torn petals fell from my head. I ran my hands through my hair, scattering more crumbled foliage across the bedding. I scanned the dark room for a vase but found nothing. The cat stopped licking to watch me, holding her arm in midair as if waiting for a response. My mouth hung open as I searched for words to fit her peculiar behavior. "You remind me of someone I used to know," I muttered.

"Aya?" A hanging fur door at the end of the bed cracked open. "Are you awake?" Bromly peeked inside, holding a steaming wooden cup and a thin stick burning red with an ember. He pushed the fur aside just enough to slide into the room. "Oh, sorry." He grimaced. "I should have asked if you were decent before coming in."

"Is she awake?" The top of Flint's red head bounced behind Bromly's husky frame. "Aya! We've been waitin' for ya to wake up. Come out! There's food!"

"Go sit down and wait," Bromly sternly instructed and closed the fur. "You'll have to excuse him. Flint is thrilled to have a girl here. We don't get a lot of women around these parts . . . none actually."

He used the ember to light a single candle on a simple wooden nightstand next to the bed. The room dimly illuminated, revealing a rectangular space only wide enough for two people to stand comfortably. I was lying in a crude narrow bed made from unstripped wood, pushed against the log-paneled wall. The plush covers were sewn from various patches of rabbit fur and tan cotton sheets. Several carved hooks on the left wall held articles of clothing, and above the nightstand hung a sword inside a pristine tawny scabbard.

"I brought you some tea." Bromly sat on the end of the bed, as far away from me as he could manage. He had to stretch to hand me the cup. "It's strong, but it's good for you. Darric brought me the recipe years ago. It's a detox, but don't ask what's in it. You wouldn't want to know."

I gently blew the steam. It smelled herbal, with strong accents of clover and mint. Bits of tea leaves floated across the surface. I was apprehensive of accepting anything since bandits had forced a foul liquid down my throat. "I don't think I should—"

"You've already had a lot of it," he said before I could argue. "We had to do something to counteract the poison. Otherwise, you'd be dead."

My lips parted. *Poisoned?*

"Darric found you in a cave of thieves who use a slow-acting toxin to pacify their prisoners. It usually metastasizes when food or water hits the system. It weakens the brain, causing insanity and hallucinations. Then it rots the body from the inside out. It's a cruel and disgusting way to die. You're lucky."

Abbey's brain had been brutally warped, and the putrid smell of decay had permeated the bandit jail cell. I remembered the intense nausea sweeping over me and weakening every muscle.

"I'm shocked you followed Darric all this way while intoxicated with it. It's impressive . . . to say the least." He shifted awkwardly. "I'm angry he allowed such a thing knowing which cave he released you from."

Unsure how to respond, I sipped the tea and waited for the persistent sickness to resurface. The soothingly sweet liquid traveled through my throat, filling my belly and warming my limbs. Relieved to feel no pain, I wanted to gulp down the delicious brew quicker than it would cool. "Thank you," I muttered, humbled and grateful they had not let their unwelcome guest die. "Thank you for taking care of me."

"You're welcome, but really, I just brewed the tea." He waved his hand dismissively. "Darric held up your head and made sure you consumed it. It was tedious. He said you would be dead by morning, but he said that every day."

"Every day?" I questioned, confused.

"You've been out three days." He scratched his beard with his thumb.

My jaw dropped. Would there be soldiers searching the countryside for me? What if they came here? What would they do to these men?

"You had to sleep off the effects."

"I should be lying dead in a river somewhere." I set the cup on the nightstand. "I have to get out of here before Darric decides to kill me." *Or Alamantia soldiers find this valley.* "I don't want to cause more fighting between the three of you."

"Ha!" His brown eyes lit up with a friendly smile. "You heard that, huh?"

"Some of it . . ."

"Don't worry about any of that. We're brothers . . . well, brothers in theory. We're made to argue. Empty threats. Hostility. It wouldn't be like home otherwise, especially when Darric is around."

"I shouldn't have followed him." Ashamed, I buried my face in my hands.

"Well, if you hadn't, you *would* be dead in a river somewhere. Look, no one is going to take your life. Darric comes off brash, but he means well. He kept Flint out of his room long enough to let you heal. That was a challenge."

"His room?" I looked around a second time and recognized several airy white shirts on the hooks. Darric's gray wool cloak hung closest to the door, and nestled in the corner sat his haversack.

I yanked the covers off my legs, struggling to untangle myself from the binding furs and my own dress. I wanted out. I had been curled up for three days in the bed of a man I never should have pursued.

"Take it easy." Bromly held up his hands, and I kicked the covers into his lap. "You're not completely well. Darric has the least use for his room. He put you in here."

"I have invaded his personal space enough." I twisted over the mattress and set my feet on the floor, scattering flower bits onto the pelt rug. My shoes were missing.

Bromly plucked a handful of petal pieces from the bed and examined them suspiciously. "Your cat is strange. She cried and screamed when we refused to let her into the Hovel. Eventually she snuck in. I guess she brought you some flowers."

The little burgundy feline jumped onto the nightstand and purred. I rubbed my fists into my eyes. "I'm sorry, what is the Hovel?"

"Oh, our house," he explained with pride. "We call it the Hovel. Unoriginal name, but none of us are poets."

The longer I sat up, the cloudier my head became. "You've been so kind, offering me food and a bed. This was more than I deserved after forcing my company upon you. I cannot stay here any longer."

"Flint wants you to stay, and Darric . . . well, he's already forfeited his room. You're welcome here for the time being. If you want to leave, Darric will travel again soon. You can accompany him."

"I am lost beyond recognition. The minute I disappear with him, how can you guarantee he won't kill me? I'm not sure I want to be alone with him. Ever. It's better I head out on my own." The cat leaped onto the mattress and, for the first time, allowed me to touch the top of her head. She pushed into my palm, accepting the gentle scratch. Her sublime fur felt like baby rabbit fuzz. "I don't want to test my boundaries with him."

"It's dangerous out there, and you can't expect to just walk out of here after being unconscious for three days. If you really want to thank us for the hospitality, then you won't leave until my brother can escort you."

I breathed out wearily. Bromly had a point. Leaving meant facing the woods during nightfall. I could end up back in the same situation that brought me here.

"Anyway, you have an invitation to stay. There's at least one of us who would be thrilled if you chose to accept it. I assure you that it won't put us out. This room sits empty most of the time, so it'll be yours until Darric decides otherwise." He bent down and tossed over my shoes.

My boots couldn't have been removed without detaching Luken's dagger. Discreetly, I brushed my ankle against the side of the bed and felt the clank of metal against wood. Whoever had taken off my shoes had reapplied the blade. Idiotic that throughout my entire deadly experience with the bandits, I had not once thought to use the weapon. It defeated the purpose if I meant to treat it as an accessory.

"Well"—he slapped his hands on his thighs and stood—"you have to be hungry. I have a piglet cooking on the spit, but for now there's rabbit stew and roasted potatoes." He pulled the fur door to the side and tied it to the frame with a rope. Warm orange firelight filled the small bedroom. "I'm glad you made it through, Aya," he said and left me to put on my shoes.

Outside Darric's bedroom was a square living space. A wooden workbench against the right paneled wall was cluttered with knives and tools, whittled scraps, bowls, flatware, and vegetables. Several woven baskets overflowing with a variety of spices and dried meat hung above it. The opposite wall consisted of cavern rock decorated with dozens of animal skulls. At the far end of the room, the entrance door turned out to be two large bear furs sewn back to back, creating a thick layer to hold in heat.

In the center of the quaint house, a three-foot-wide firepit lined with smooth gray stones warmed a kettle filled with Bromly's lovely detox tea. Three benches circled the fire, but unlike the rough logs outside, these had been stripped and sanded smooth for indoor living. The low ceiling and rafters were darkened from soot, as not all the smoke escaped through the hole that tapered into a metal chimney.

A thick layer of dead leaves on the stone floor crunched under my feet. Rugs sewn from a multitude of animal skins spread underneath the benches and at the entrance of every doorway. To my immediate left, two more fur doors led into other bedrooms identical in size to Darric's. I assumed these belonged to Bromly and Flint.

The charming Hovel smelled like burning pork, a surprisingly mouthwatering aroma despite the underlying scent of sour animal flesh. A musk also lingered in the air—similar to mold but less unpleasant—coming from the piles of furs in the corners of the room.

This was a massive operation, and impressive. How could such criminal activity occur without the King's knowledge? Now I understood why the three were so concerned about me knowing their location. Everything here was death-sentence illegal.

I glanced into the bedroom I now shared with my stranger (*how odd*), and a sense of contentment washed over me. A smile grew across my cheeks. I felt home, as if there was no other place in Athera I belonged.

The cat arched her back and yawned. She rubbed against my leg, and the vibration of her purr went up my thigh. My serenity flowed into her, as did my fear and distress. For whatever reason, the little feline was here to stay.

The idea of walking out of the Hovel filled me with nervous jitters. The three men would be waiting. I had paraded into court and crowded rooms all my life with hundreds of eyes watching my every step, yet this personal introduction was maddeningly unnerving.

Swallowing my anxiety, I stepped into the open cavern. The fire crisped the skin of a piglet, while Bromly used a hatchet to turn potatoes buried in the coals.

Flint sat upon a log eating an apple, the juice dribbling down his pointed chin. When he saw me, his emerald eyes widened to show nearly their full circumference, and he jumped to his feet with glee. "Aya!" He spat bits of fruit into the air, choked momentarily, and cleared his throat. "Welcome to the Hovel."

I hesitated. "Thank you."

"I see you're not dead. Not sure how I feel about that." Darric walked around from the back of the house, holding a knife in one hand and the carcass of a rabbit in the other. His bracers were coated in spattered blood, and tousled strands of hair stuck to his forehead. He shamelessly looked me up and down, as if he had not been talking about murdering me moments ago.

I wrinkled my nose. I hated him. He had known about the poison and done nothing, even hoped I would die before reaching our destination

Darric handed the fresh rabbit to Bromly, who smelled it and flipped it over several times, examining the poor lifeless creature.

"You don't feel the way the rest of us do, Darric." Flint shoved the remainder of the apple into his mouth.

"I agree." Darric sat down on the end of the seating log. He dipped his hands into a metal bucket of dreggy water and washed his bloody forearms, not bothering to remove his bracers. After a moment, he stopped abruptly to scan the woods, as if he heard something troubling. It caught the attention of the others, who didn't relax until he went back to washing. "Now that you are awake, we can get you out of here." He glanced up with only his eyes, narrowed to a sliver of steely blue. "You tumbled through the woods well enough while poisoned, so it should not be too strenuous for you to do it again. We'll leave tomorrow before sunrise."

"What? No!" Flint's cheeks went red with anger. "She's not well. Ya can't leave now. An' besides, bear season's gonna start."

Darric raised a skeptical eyebrow. "In a month." He plopped his knife into the bucket and rubbed dried blood from the blade. "All right, then when you are not looking, I'll just kill her."

I forgot how to take in air. Flint's hair blended into the fiery color of his face; Darric seemed to be purposefully antagonizing him.

"Sick or not, I'm perfectly capable of traveling through any terrain you choose." *Maybe.* I crossed my arms over my chest, trying to hide from Darric's penetrative eyes. "But you have to ensure my safety. If you did not want me trailing behind you, then you should have stopped me. I certainly did not release myself from that prison, or have you forgotten?"

He smiled peevishly and ran wet hands through his hair before shaking off the remaining water. "I liked your perseverance."

"At least I meet your approval in some approximation." My chest rattled. "What was the point of it all, if in the end you wanted me dead?"

He slid down the log and leaned his back against the bark. "You are still here because of my brothers' decision, not mine."

A second noise outside the cavern caused him to turn around. He shoved his blade back in his boot, and his mouth formed a hard line at the mountains. After several seconds, he recomposed himself and stood to approach me. The muscles in my arms tightened in distress as he towered over my head and peered directly into my eyes. His lethal stare cut into each vital organ, no knife needed.

"Stay then," he said, his voice deepening to match his threatening posture. He slipped the tips of his toughened fingers down the side of my neck, moving curls off my shoulder to expose my throat, and leaned down beside my ear, his lips grazing my skin. "But I would keep looking over my shoulder. I'm not opposed to stabbing someone in the back, and this lovely skin of yours would look beautiful dripping in blood."

A cold shiver went up my spine. He walked past me, his solid arm hitting my shoulder. "And breathing helps regulate the heart rate," he added.

My enormous gasp echoed through the chamber as I pulled a gigantic breath into my lungs.

Darric slipped into the Hovel and returned with his cloak around his shoulders. "I'm leaving," he muttered, exiting the cavern.

"Bloody hell." Bromly shook his head in disapproval. "Are you happy?" he asked Flint. "Is this what you wanted?"

Flint's wide smile took over most of his face. "He's good at it."

"I'm going to let him take me to a town when he gets back."
Concern frayed the edges of my voice.

"Never mind it," Bromly reassured me. "Darric is just being
defiant. Give him a couple days."

"He's ticked that he's been outvoted." Flint laughed.

I was offered rabbit stew but didn't eat. My appetite remained
as extinct as the kindness Darric had shown when he had led me
by the hand to the Hovel. I had never been unwanted. Lords
and ladies of the Rose Court had always tried to earn my favor.
No one dared insult or threaten me. I had a household waiting
to tend to my every need. Even though I wanted a life away
from the constraints of Alamantia Palace, I was not prepared for
such an immediate and drastic change. I was suddenly infantile,
powerless, a nobody. Adjusting would take time.

The sound of Flint slurping his food brought me out of my
daze. He ate without a spoon, putting the bowl to his mouth and
chugging large gulps that made his exaggerated larynx bob. He
belched loudly when he finished.

After eating, Bromly and Flint worked to create more pelts.
I watched them scrape fat and sinew off several rabbit hides and
toss the fleshy pieces into the fire, though Flint seemed more
interested in picking sprigs of purple lupine growing near the
entrance of the cavern. Sitting next to them in silence generated
a strange form of humiliation. I didn't know how to help or even
perform something as simple as tending a fire.

Eventually the sun dipped low in the sky, preparing to vanish
behind the mountains. The breeze created a haunting howl as it
rushed past the cavern. It sounded misplaced among the beautiful,
flourishing landscape full of greenery and wildflowers.

A grumbled snore broke the silence. Flint slept against the
seating log, his neck arched and his mouth hanging open. His feet
almost touched the coals, and his collected lupines fell from his
hand. Bromly muffled a swear and disappeared into the house.

A devastating sense of despondency took hold of me. I was suffocating and needed air. I strolled out of the cavern before anyone could stop me.

Gritting my teeth against the pain in my ankles, I rested by the riverbank. A single tear dripped down my cheek, and wiping it away caused the cuts on my palm to sting. Dirt caked under my fingernails, and I could smell body odor wafting off my skin.

Pull yourself together, Ayleth.

I sniffled, catching my reflection in the water. The radical change in my appearance stopped me cold. My curls lay over my shoulders in a scattered mess. Scrapes and cuts blemished my jawline. My swollen bottom lip was split down the center. I looked dirty, my clothes stained and ragged. The Divine Princess who had once stared back at me had been replaced by Aya. Aya, who had survived death. Aya, who had listened to the song of a plow horse and tripped over the ripples of water. Aya, who was trying to find herself in a world where she shouldn't exist.

I plunged my hands into the icy water and tore through the image. The stream shuddered, sending waves lapping against the bank and churning white peaks in two directions at once. Ignoring it, I drank until my hands were numb, then rolled up my sleeves to wash away the blood and dirt clinging to my fingers. I splashed my face to clear the tears. It wasn't much of a bath, but the small cleansing helped me feel human.

The cat meowed, calling my attention to a new reflection.

I jolted to my feet. The majestic white stallion watched me from the other side of the river. Untarnished and the color of newly fallen snow, he stood with impeccable grace, a crimped mane that reached past his shoulders floating on the breeze. Up close he was massive, seventeen hands at least, and appeared misplaced among the varying shades of brown and black in his herd, who faded in comparison to his sovereignty. He narrowed his jet-black eyes at me with such intensity that I backed away from the bank.

"*You are quite far from home, little Divine.*"

I locked eyes with the steed, and his thoughts and feelings filled my head. The onslaught of information hit like a battering ram. He knew everything about this valley and its inhabitants. As the leader of the horses, his eyes and ears spanned from the highest mountain to the shortest blade of grass. He could see through me, down to my bones. The etching of the Mandala carved into the side of my skull, hidden beneath muscle and flesh, was not masked to him.

He reflected my own image back to me, and I saw myself standing across the river, disoriented, hurting from the amount of information boring into my brain. The Mandala pulsed under my skin. I fervently pushed the image from my head so the mark wouldn't appear and cupped my hands over my ears, but the noise was internal.

"*What is your purpose here?*"

"My name is Ayleth. I'm the Princess of Alamantia," I whimpered.

The stallion cocked his head. "*I would not have believed a Divine exists that is also a Fae. Miraculous.*" He turned his gaze behind him. My throat collapsed when Darric appeared, gliding his hand along the steed's immense back. Darric laced his fingers into the alabaster strands of his mane and scratched behind his ear, muttering something I couldn't hear.

Threads of amusement seemed to enter the horse's eyes.

"What are you doing out here?" Darric hissed at me.

I quivered with terror. *Run.* I couldn't move.

"Do you have any idea how dangerous it is right now?" he yelled, revealing a frightening stentorian tone to his voice that made my ears throb.

"*You know this mongrel, Fae Princess?*" the horse inquired.

I gave a small nod, afraid to answer verbally.

The stallion's pink mouth pulled into something resembling a smile. He nudged Darric's shoulder with his nose, and my stranger responded with an obdurate glare. In three large steps, Darric crossed the shallow brook and stood so close I could smell the floral scent coming off his skin. I craned my neck back to see his face.

"Trying to leave the valley on your own?" he asked snidely.

"*We shall speak again, Fae Princess.*" The white stallion eased away from the river with the herd trailing behind him.

The cat hissed from beneath my dress and slapped Darric's boot. He furrowed his brows at her, then eyed me suspiciously. "Where are you from?"

I bit my lip and shrugged.

"Fine." He briskly drew his sword. The fine blade rang with a musical chord—a weapon fit for a king. Impossible that he could have acquired it without theft. He moved effortlessly with a weapon in his hand, as if he was built for combat.

My teeth chattered, terrorized nerves taking over my body.

He grew a devilish grin upon witnessing my fear. "You really wear your emotions on your sleeve." He tapped the face of his sword against my shoulder. Satisfied with scaring me senseless, he slid the blade back into the scabbard.

I breathed a sigh of relief. When had I become such a coward? Had the bandits broken me? The days blurred together. It felt so long ago that I had successfully escaped Alamantia—only to be threatened with death in every moment left of what could be a short existence.

Darric Ursygh!

My temper blazed. This was all his doing. I was in this valley because of him. I had tried to abandon my pursuit, but he had insisted I continue following. If not for him, I could be settled in that forest by now, trying to begin a new life.

"You owe me an explanation!" I demanded, finished with his intimidation.

He raised an eyebrow.

"You lied to them." I stomped my foot on the grass.

"Whom?" He crossed his arms over his chest, grinning at my tantrum.

"Bromly and Flint. You helped me here. I remember. You saved my life. You detoxed me. You caught me when I fell. You waited for me at the bottom of the cliff. You even . . ." I held my breath, trying to ignore the burn filling his eyes. ". . . took my hand to keep me going." I felt as if I was recapping a dream he had no way of understanding.

He chuckled nervously. "I'm flattered you think I'm capable of such heroism, but none of that happened."

"Yes, it did."

"You were intoxicated."

"I know what I saw. I know what you did. The forest of wisteria, that's how we got here," I pressed, anxious for him to admit the truth.

"There is no wisteria in these mountains."

"Yes, there is!" I squealed.

"No, there isn't. You were under the effects of a deadly poison. A hallucinogen." Why was he denying this? I may have been poisoned, but I had not completely lost my senses. "Go back to the Hovel. I'm sure someone is waiting for you." He proceeded to follow the herd.

Aggravated, I trotted to keep up with him. "I'm not done talking to you yet."

"Well, I'm done talking to *you*."

"You roam the countryside breaking into prisons, stealing, killing for pelts, tracking horses—"

"Horses are expensive, and I would like one." He skidded to a halt, causing me to grind my shoes into the dirt to keep a distance from him.

"That one?" I pointed at the beautiful herd leader.

"Unique things intrigue me, and he is the fastest."

"You're a thief." Antagonizing my stranger may not have been the wisest decision, but at the moment, I hardly cared.

"Occasionally."

"A bandit—"

"Salted pork for my brother—"

"Who kidnaps women—"

"No, just you."

I gaped, and he laughed, running his eyes over my body in the same lewd manner as Prince Marcus. "Come on," he grumbled. "You need to go back to the Hovel before you die out here."

The sun had left the sky by the time Darric and I arrived at the cavern. I stayed a step behind him, letting the wind roll his rustic scent over me. I never imagined the only thing pleasant about my stranger would be his appearance.

"Good job keeping her here," Darric snarled, kicking the log where Flint was sleeping. Flint's red head hit the ground with a thud.

Bromly gave a hardy laugh from deep inside his belly. "I see you found Darric, Aya."

"Not intentionally," I said flatly.

"You're still alive, so it can't be all bad." He winked.

Flint rubbed a fist into his sleepy eyes and offered me a single sprig of lupine. "I picked this for you," he said sweetly.

An awkward silence fell over the cavern. Bromly focused harder on peeling a potato.

My cheeks seared red. I was used to receiving gifts, but Flint presenting me with a flower in front of his brothers felt painfully embarrassing.

Darric watched from the doorway of the Hovel, leaning against the frame. He crossed his arms over his chest as he tried to stop a laugh. *Ridiculous.* I had never met anyone more purposefully infuriating. Anger added an additional layer to the humiliation. I'd had enough of *Darric Ursygh.*

"If it wouldn't pain you too much, Darric, would you stop staring at me?" I fumed. "Does my face have spots?"

Now he laughed. "No, it's red, actually."

I pressed my lips together and snatched the lupine from Flint's grasp. "Thank you. That's nice of you." I quickly brought my attention back to Darric. "Don't you have a horse to chase or a rabbit to kill?"

He pulled the hood of his cloak over his head to shade his brow, once again becoming the cryptic stranger from the bandit cave. "Keep the fire low," he said to Bromly and left the cavern.

Chapter 11

Darric disappeared for three days, though my new companions insisted he was nearby. A basket of fresh trout appeared outside the front door every morning as proof. Apparently, he never truly left the valley without giving some indication of when he would return, but he never said where he was going.

"He wanders, occasionally to towns and cities. He tends to seek solitude. He's always been that way, even when we were kids," Bromly explained. "He would be home a lot faster if he had a horse, but he's being rather stubborn on that subject."

"Is he gone often?" I asked.

"Not as much as it seems. It gets lonely out here, so even when he's causing a ruckus, it's nice having him home." He rubbed his beard. "He stays long enough to create work to keep us busy. He does his share—hunts and crafts—then heads out."

"He's an ass," Flint jumped in, crinkling his pointed nose in contempt. "I don't miss him much. It was his idea to come up here, yet he gets to travel, an' we're stuck. He'll leave again soon, an' it'll be peaceful 'round here."

With Darric missing, Bromly and Flint familiarized me with life at the Hovel. I learned to collect firewood and where to find kindling. The firepits generally had coals buried just below the surface layer of ash, but Bromly insisted I wade through the entire process. He promised to teach me to tend the garden outside the cavern once I mastered starting a fire.

The wonderful thing about Bromly Keene was his discretion. He taught me what I needed to know to keep Darric pacified about my living at the Hovel and didn't question my history or how little I knew of household chores. By the end of the second day, I could peel and slice vegetables quicker than either of them.

"You're a fast learner," he complimented.

Flint was oblivious to the idea that I was anything other than a lost peasant girl. He didn't care to help with the chores and opted to spend the evenings playing a flute Darric had made for him when they were children. Darric hated it, as noise carried throughout the valley, and often Flint would play just to annoy him. After hearing his music, I didn't blame Darric for disliking it; Flint was a horrible musician.

The evening of my third day awake, the three of us sat by the cavern fire. The sun had not yet fallen behind the mountains, and Flint's fragmented tunes disrupted the spring twilight nestling into the valley. I looked forward to the change in season. Winter lasted a minimum of six months in Brisleia, and summer was always welcome.

"It's a good fire." Flint winked flirtatiously.

Bromly poked the coals with a stick, sending sparks into the air. "I think we can probably leave you alone to tend the flammables, Aya, and not worry that you're going to burn down the Hovel."

A rustle in the brush abruptly halted Flint's playing, and the crickets ceased their early night's song.

"Is something wrong?" My voice unsettled the still forest.

"Shh, shh." Bromly waved his hand, his face hard as he listened intently. An impending sense of doom moved over the Hovel.

The rustling grew louder. Something was rapidly approaching.

Darric exploded from the brush, his drawn sword sending glistening rays from the dying sun in all directions. He rushed towards us, urgency written across his face.

Bromly and Flint sprung to their feet as quickly as Darric bridged the distance to the cavern. Flint's flute twanged as it bounced off the stone; he stumbled for a bow and quiver resting by the Hovel door and nocked an arrow into place. Bromly gripped an axe and took refuge behind his log.

My stranger leaped across the flames and swung his body around me, tucking me to his chest with one strong arm around my waist. His cloak landed over us, hiding me beneath him and blocking my view of the cavern.

He held his sword in front of us like a shield and clutched me in a protective grasp so formidable one would think I was about to fall to my death. His skin felt hot and slick with sweat, and his chest heaved as he tried to catch his breath. Any chance I had of staying calm was shattered by the rhythmic pounding of his heart against my ear. His breath parted my hair as his lips grazed the top of my head. "Don't move," he whispered.

Fear flooded my veins. My eyes darted, trying to see past the mess of wool, metal, and flesh.

"He went that way," said a gruff, gargling voice. My entire body shook at the crunch of footsteps. "Damnable rogue."

I couldn't breathe quickly enough. My lungs were going to collapse.

Flint pulled his arrow back at the ready. Bromly crouched behind his log, a shaking hand clutching his axe.

The figures appeared as vague silhouettes through the brush. Four men. I recognized their clothes and demeanor, their toothless gapes and dirty faces. Bandits. And not just any bandits, but grotesque residents of the cave where Darric had freed me. I inhaled to scream, and his free hand flew over my mouth before a sound could escape.

"There!" one bandit yelled, and the four charged to the cavern with a fierce determination.

Flint let his arrow fly. It pierced the closest attacker in the shoulder. The bandit grasped the wound, his ankles buckling in unnatural directions.

"Get inside!" Darric roared. He shoved me towards the Hovel, sending me skidding across the ground until I slammed into the wall of the house. The cat ran to my side, hissing and spitting furiously at the intruders.

Darric jumped over the fire and caught the injured adversary. His cloak blocked most of the attack from my sight as he drove his sword into the man's chest. The bandit cried out and retched, his eyes bulging as blood filled his mouth and dripped from his lips. *Dead.* Darric withdrew his blade, the miraculous silver coated in shiny crimson, to block the first downwards swing from the second assailant.

Horrified, I lay in a crumpled mess by the fur door. Darric fought with more grace than any swordsman I'd ever seen. Each attack was executed without a stutter. Each left me in awe of the swift movement of his sword and the amazing flex of his lean muscular arms. He flowed from one maneuver to another effortlessly, anticipating each oncoming action from his enemy.

Flint mounted a log to gain leverage and shot another arrow. It grazed Darric's opponent's lower back, but the bandit continued his uncalculated strikes even as blood soaked his dirty clothes.

"Damnit!" Flint groused and snatched another arrow. His aim moved between targets, unable to find a suitable opening that wouldn't injure his brother.

Bromly exploded from his hiding place to plunge his axe deep into the spine of the third bandit. The man arched his back and crashed to the ground with the thick metal blade buried in his body. Planting his foot on the bandit's back, Bromly pulled his weapon free and landed another crushing blow. Blood flooded out of the gaping wound, exposing the white of severed vertebrae. He struck again. The crack and crunch of shattering bones filled my ears, and broken ribs pierced the man's fabric and flesh.

I couldn't hold it in anymore. I screamed, pouring all the air from my lungs into the chaos.

A fourth bandit crept around the outside of the Hovel, trying to remain undetected. He grinned with teeth the color of bark, delighted to see me helpless and cowering alone.

Noticing the sneaking villain, Darric spun around to grab the man's shirt and hurled him away from the Hovel. The bandit tumbled across the cavern, regained his footing, and drew a pathetic rapier from his belt.

Darric grasped the hilt of his sword with both hands and, in one fluid motion, pulled the handle apart. A dazzling spark of white light ran up the center of the blade as it split in half, creating two separate weapons. The sing of metal lingered in the cavern. Such a blade couldn't exist. It bent the laws of nature.

Darric held one sword in each hand, dual wielding against two opponents. His skill evolved into preternatural agility and unprecedented power. He blocked every attack made against him with ease, and the intruders soon exhausted themselves trying to stand against him.

He almost seemed to be toying with them, enjoying the fight, until one brilliant flourish of his left sword stabbed the fourth bandit through the abdomen. The blade reemerged, jutting out of the man's back. A demented smirk encompassed Darric's mouth as he ripped the blade back through the bandit's core, sending a flurry of bloody entrails scattering across the ground and into the fire. The sickeningly sour smell of burned human flesh filled the cavern. Utterly stunned, the bandit dropped his rapier and clasped the chasmic hole, holding the tumbling pieces of his own viscera in his hands. He fell, landing in a puddle of blood and chopped organs.

The final assailant wavered, terrified of the futile fight. With his back bleeding down his legs, he couldn't withstand the constant blows Darric dealt with one sword, then the next. The barrage became too much. He tripped over the seating logs and screamed in horror as he crawled to get away.

Darric snatched a handful of the bandit's greasy black hair to expose his neck. He ran his dripping blade over the man's throat, slitting him open from ear to ear. Trachea and tendons popped apart like strained ropes before the blood flowed. The man retched and jolted. Darric released his grip and let him fall, the bandit's head nearly severed from his shoulders. Red gushed onto the cavern floor in the violent spurts of his fading heartbeat. Then all movement ceased, and the brutality ended.

The forest went deathly silent, and the sun dipped behind the mountains. Darric stood in the last rays of the evening light shining into the cavern—the silhouette of a menacingly dark figure with sparkling swords against a dying day. Blood dripped off his blades and coated his hands. His chest heaved, and the lean muscle in his arms rippled with fading adrenaline. His eyes fell on me, and a form of relief lessened the tension in his shoulders.

I couldn't move, disturbed and stunned by how perfect he appeared when placed in such a horrific scenario. Even in that moment when I should have been terrified of him, I wanted to run to him for safety. Even when I knew I should have fled for my life.

If I were to die in this valley.

If that was my fate.

If Darric was going to kill me . . . eventually.

Dying at the hands of such a man would be an incredible way to end.

Would I even know pain? His sword cut flesh without resistance. The blade was sharp. Darric was efficient. Would I die before I began to bleed? Now that I had seen death at his hands, I felt more at peace with it. Would I be eviscerated? Would I suffocate with a severed throat? Would the steel blue of his beautiful eyes be the last thing I'd ever see?

I didn't realize I wasn't breathing until Darric wiped his swords off on his cloak. He touched the hilts together, and a white glow fused the two pieces back into one blade. My mind dazzled with questions, but I was too petrified to speak, and the strange, aching need to embrace him troubled me.

I remained hunched on the ground, mouth open, my dress askew and my legs still tangled where I'd landed.

"Aya, are you hurt?" Bromly broke my helpless gaze. Splattered blood sprinkled the threads of his beard, and I stared, mesmerized, into the little red specks. He placed a hand on either side of my face to turn my focus away from the gore. The cold stickiness of his palms turned my stomach. "I think she's in shock."

"If she is, you are not helping," Darric said with imperturbable tranquility as he tapped the bodies with his sword to be sure they were dead.

"Is . . ." My voice squeaked, and I gulped. "Is there blood on your hands?"

Bromly released me to examine his hands. A drip escaped his beard and hit the ground. "Oh, I'm so sorry. I didn't realize."

"How could you not realize?" I questioned.

Darric tried to hide a smile.

Flint rummaged through the pockets of our dead intruders, tossing his findings into a pile next to the fire: small knives, coins, biscuits. He took their weapons and lined the decrepit blades against the seating logs.

Blood pooled on the cavern floor around the demolished bodies and chopped entrails. I moved my foot to avoid an oozing river, unable to stomach the carnage. The iron smell was adding a headache on top of my growing nausea. This was worse than a decaying prisoner. This was life bleeding out. The men I depended on for protection were murderers.

Worry flickered across Darric's face as he witnessed my discomfort. "Bromly, go down to the river . . . now."

Bromly tugged at his bloodied shirt. Without saying a word, he left the cavern. Darric gave a nod to Flint and, sheathing his sword, followed his brother .

Flint held out his hand for me. "Let's go inside."

I graciously fed my fingers into his palm, and he helped me onto unsteady feet.

Inside the Hovel, he eased me onto a wooden bench and retrieved a blanket from his room to wrap around my shoulders. The wool smelled strongly of Bromly's charred potatoes—a stench Flint carried because he loved the hot mush covered in a layer of charcoal crunch. They were disgusting.

I clamped my pale, shaking fingers to the blanket. My teeth chattered, and sweat moistened the curls around my temples. The little feline lay at my ankles, purring against my skin to offer her own piece of comfort.

Flint sat next to me with a bucket of fresh water and a frayed rag. He touched my shoulder and rubbed his thumb into the stiff muscle. My whole body ached from Darric's protective hold. I could already feel the bruises forming.

"Do ya want somethin' to drink?" Flint asked. "Ya look really pale."

I shook my head and closed my eyes, taking in a deep breath. My chest rattled as I let the fear flow out of my lungs.

"It's over now." He dipped the rag into the water and wrung it out. "We can relax."

"I don't understand." My voice gargled. The scream I'd let out had reopened old wounds. "What happened out there? Why did you . . ." I couldn't finish.

"We can't let anyone know what we're doin' up here. Sometimes we're attacked by other nomadic groups."

"Does this happen often?" I murmured.

"No." He clumsily wiped the rag along my jaw, washing away the blood Bromly had absentmindedly smeared on my cheeks. "We're wanted men. We didn't want ya to know that. We've been tryin' to ease ya into the truth."

Wanted. The evidence was all around me. In the eyes of Brisleian law, these men were criminals.

"I don't want to be here anymore." I tossed the blanket off my shoulders. "I could handle what you do—the hunting, the pelts, the illegality. But I cannot handle murder. With or without Darric, I'm leaving. I don't belong here."

"No!" He snatched my wrist. "You do. Don't go. Jus' wait. Give us a chance to explain," he begged. "It's not whatcha think."

I clutched the fabric of my dress and allowed Flint to continue cleaning my face. He grew nervous, and his fingers started to tremble.

"What happens now?" I muttered, watching a small flame come to life over the dying coals.

"Darric an' Bromly are takin' care of it. I'll stay here with ya. They'll let us know when they're done." He looked over my features, making sure he had removed all the blood.

"What are they going to do?"

"Dig a grave. Bury 'em. Get themselves cleaned up."

An escaped tear traveled down my cheek. Flint raised the rag to wipe it away but missed and stabbed the rough fabric into my eye.

"Ow!" I threw a hand over my face.

"Ssssorry, sorry. I didn't mean to—"

"I'm fine." Water welled up in my eye. I rubbed my fist into it, trying to soothe the burn, and pushed away from him, but he inched closer.

He faked a smile, displaying every tooth in his mouth, then laughed awkwardly and ran a shy finger along the back of my hand. "I'm really glad you're here. I mean . . . it's nice to have someone new to talk to other than Bromly an' Darric."

I listened, but nothing registered the way it was supposed to. The last few days had been overwhelming and exhausting. I could no longer process my thoughts. Courage failed me and I broke down, letting the tears flow freely.

"Aya." He encased me in his arms. "Shh, don't cry."

Stupid, naive Divine Princess. Inexperienced. Idiotic runaway.

I buried my face in his shoulder. His sharp, bony frame was such a contrast to Darric's. I tugged at his shirt and sobbed into the fabric.

"It was hard for me too the first time I killed someone. It's probably harder to sit by an' helplessly watch it happen. I shoulda made sure ya were in the Hovel to spare ya the memories."

I opened my eyes at his words. The crying turned to hiccups. It had been Darric who had run to protect me, while Flint ran for a weapon. Darric who had thrown me towards the Hovel in hopes of omitting the gore, not Flint. Darric, who claimed to want me as dead as the men outside yet acted like a shield of valor every time my life was in danger.

Something was amiss, and I wasn't entirely sure I wanted to know what plagued *Darric Ursygh.*

Chapter 12

Flint attempted to entertain me by playing his flute. The offbeat music set my teeth on edge, but I tolerated his sweet efforts to make me smile.

Sometime after midnight, the others returned, clean with wet hair and damp clothes. Bromly moved the stew cauldron into the main room and finished cooking, but only Flint ate.

Executions were common in Alamantia City. I had seen death, although I viewed it from afar from the security of my chamber. Never so close. Never smelling the blood or witnessing a man's insides fall out of his belly. This had been no execution; it was a slaughtering.

My mind couldn't stop replaying the gore. If Darric had offered to take me to a town, I would have graciously accepted and begged to leave before daybreak.

Something was different about my stranger upon his return. He was content, relaxed, satisfied. He sat on the ground, leaning against the sanded bench and whittling a piece of wood, which began to take on the shape of a horse.

As Flint requested, I agreed to give the three an opportunity to explain their actions. I needed to understand the cause of a merciless murder before I ran from my only haven.

Bromly wrung his cap between his fingers, waiting for me to ask the first question.

"I thought this valley was remote. Aren't we miles away from towns or villages?" I stumbled over my words.

An instant passed when they all looked at each other, expecting another to speak. Flint crossed the room and sat next to me, so close his skinny leg pressed against my thigh.

"It is inevitable that someone will eventually discover the Hovel, either by accident or design. The valley echoes. There is smoke from the fires. The smell of meat and blood." Darric spoke slow, each word distinct. "The cavern can't conceal everything. It doesn't happen often, but when a passerby strays into this valley, we have no choice but to defend our livelihood. Secrecy is everything, and that is the consequence of this line of work." He paused to slice a curl away from his whittling.

"Your line of work?"

"The King of Brisleia puts restrictions on hunting. It's illegal for all citizens except his nobles. The law has become so rigid that even getting caught with arrows in a wooded area will get you arrested. Blunts only. You can't kill a deer with hunting blunts." It was bizarre to listen to him talk about my family. I pretended to be indifferent. "The complication with that law: it starves people of living necessities."

"It's hard enough to provide for a family without ending up in jail," Bromly interjected.

"Those of low birth have no means of keeping themselves warm, let alone fed," Darric continued. "Materials such as pelts and dried meat have become priceless commodities in Brisleia. Our work means clothing and bedding for those outside the circle of wealth—the difference between surviving the winter and freezing to death. I'm tired of witnessing unnecessary suffering."

I tucked my arms against my belly. I had never heard my father's laws discussed from an outside perspective. I admit my lessons on Brisleian law were sparse, but it always made sense to protect our land and animals. I never thought of how it would affect the public. How many peasants had died of exposure and famine?

"Darric brought us into these mountains to live this way. Though it risks our lives, we all agreed to the consequences." Bromly slid his cap back on his head and folded his hands in his lap.

"Not *all* of us agreed," Flint muttered for only me to hear.

"Every summer we travel to Burge to sell a year's worth of stock," Bromly explained. "It's the best trade city in the country. Once out of our hands, our wares can easily travel to other places in Brisleia."

"If anyone found us and made it back to a town, our location would be compromised, and our way of life would be over," Darric went on. "There are families who depend on us to bring warmth and food just before the winter months. They would lose something precious. Killing intruders is the only way to ensure the cycle continues."

"We are looking out for the greater good," Bromly added. "I've seen citizens save every coin they can spare to buy our wares. We make it affordable. The people of Brisleia need to come first. Sometimes the King fails to realize that. The Divine tend to be concerned with the land's survival instead of its people."

I shook my head, still perplexed. "But you're *killing people*." The cat jumped onto the bench and lay beside me.

"Tonight wasn't about protecting our location." Darric sighed, frustrated. "The group that came here tracked you. I'm not the easiest person to follow."

"That's an understatement," Flint remarked.

"But you"—Darric pointed the end of his knife at me for emphasis—"left quite the path to track. I knew it would only be a matter of time."

"You're saying this is *my* fault?" Of course he would blame me for this, since he never wanted me here.

"I'm saying I think you recognized those men, as they were residents of your *affable* bandit cave—sent to track you, find you, and bring you back to their prison."

I hung my head in disgrace. So, I *was* to blame.

Darric returned to his whittling. "I've been watching them since they tumbled into the valley days ago. This was no accident. They had an agenda."

"That doesn't make sense." Flint blinked, bewildered. "Why would someone be after Aya?"

I looked up to find Darric's eyes full of apprehension. The old hag had been enthusiastic about discovering me astray in the woods. She had celebrated my capture because, like the Onyx Guard, she had known I was a Dreamer when she saw me.

Darric's mouth formed a hard line as he stared at me. "I don't know," he answered, and his glare intensified, warning me to stay silent.

I held my tongue. "I guess if you were going to kill them, at least they had ill intentions. They were murderers themselves."

"They have not been the only ones to find us," said Darric.

"You've killed innocent people too?"

"We can't trust anyone. I've had no choice," he said, taking responsibility as if the decision had been his own.

"We have done what is needed for survival," Bromly added, pulling a portion of the blame towards himself.

"And what about me? Would you have killed me?" I witlessly asked.

Darric hesitated. "Yes."

"But you didn't." I had not understood the grave danger I had been in by following him to the Hovel until it was displayed before me. I had placed too much trust in him. I'd assumed any rescuer would bring no harm. I was wrong. As I trailed after him, a meek and broken creature, he had decided to spare my life if I survived the poisoning, but he never believed I would live. It was a privilege the Hovel brothers had never granted anyone.

Darric half smiled, baring only a few teeth. "No, I didn't. Not yet anyway. I don't always know the reason behind the stupid decisions I make, only that in the moment it was the right thing to do."

"And not killing me was the right thing to do?"

"I haven't decided yet." He slid the knife back into his bracer.

"I won't let him hurt ya," Flint said with unexpected seriousness.

"So, that's it then." I lightly kicked one of the fire logs with the tip of my shoe, causing the coals to crackle. "A noble intent that sometimes requires murder to achieve."

The three looked at each other.

I took deep breaths, and my unease began to lessen. It would be hypocritical to oppose their lifestyle. The Divine royals committed murders all the time, justifying their actions by calling them *executions*. Treason, theft, rape, homicide. There were many reasons my father might sign a death warrant, claiming protection for Brisleian society. I was part of that. The Hovel brothers were merely enforcing a law they had created in order to give back to the people neglected by the royals. It was honorable in its own right.

Darric tossed the finished piece of artwork at me. Surprised, I caught it. He nodded, appeased, and retrieved his cloak and haversack from our room. "I'll be back at dawn." He slipped the hood over his head and closed the front door behind him.

I examined the wood figurine. To my astonishment, it wasn't a horse at all but a dragon, intricately carved with dozens of tiny scales, four legs complete with claws, and a magnificent set of delicate wings jutting from its back.

"Psh, another dragon." Flint plucked the sculpture from my fingers. "Good thing kids have imaginations."

"Kids? Yours?"

Bromly laughed. "No, not ours. We give toys to the children of our patrons. Kids seem to like the mythological stuff." He removed the stew cauldron from the fire and placed it under the workbench.

"That's incredible." *And generous.* Darric had carved the elaborate toy in just over an hour. He was either part genius or seriously disturbed . . . or both. "Darric makes all of these?" I snatched the dragon back from Flint and turned it over several times.

"Forks, spoons, bowls, toys—anything we need really." Bromly plucked a kettle from the bench and filled it with water before placing it in the coals. He dug into his woven baskets and extracted three balls of herbs wrapped in loose linen cloth, which he dropped into the simmering water.

"It's not that impressive." Flint took the toy from me and tossed it onto the workbench.

"I assume you make an ample profit in Burge if you are giving away toys," I observed.

"It's not about the coin. We do it to bring a smile to underprivileged children," Bromly explained. "Most of our earnings are spent before we ever leave town."

"Spent or given to the Pragues." Flint puckered his lips, making kissing sounds towards his brother.

Bromly took off his cap and slapped Flint across the mouth with it. "What I do with my share is my business."

"Share? So, you split profits?"

"Yep." Flint beamed. "Bromly always gives his to Hazel an' her mother."

"They need the money more than I do, and it keeps Hazel out of the tavern." Bromly smoothed his wavy black hair away from his face and shoved his cap back onto his head.

"Bromly don't want other men touchin' his girl." Flint snickered, nudging me with his elbow.

"I wouldn't blame him for that." I inched away, but the sleeping feline locked me in place. "So, you have a girl?"

"Hazel Prague," Flint answered for his brother.

"She lives with her mother in Burge." Bromly sat on the bench across the fire and detached a spoon from his belt to stir the mixture heating over the coals. It filled the Hovel with a lovely clove-and-mint fragrance. "They run a bakery and rooming house and give us a place to stay when we travel."

"Are you going to marry her?" I blurted.

Bromly's round cheeks reddened. "I'd like to, someday. But I have to save enough coin to buy a home and set up house for us. I wouldn't ask her to marry me unless I could provide for her. I save a little of the money I make each year." He glared at Flint. "I don't give it *all* to her."

"At the rate Bromly's savin' coin, he'll marry her in ten years," Flint claimed. "And less coin to go 'round this year since Aya'll get a share."

My throat tightened. "No, I'm not taking anything from you."

"If ya help us, ya get paid. Right, Bromly?"

Bromly went silent, avoiding the question.

"You assume I'll still be living with you or even alive by the time you travel to Burge. I doubt Darric will allow either of those options."

Flint frowned. "Ya will! You're stayin'. Darric'll get over it."

I shot a hard look at Bromly, hoping he would intervene. Instead, he left to retrieve three wooden cups from a basket under the table.

"Why do ya always have to be so silent 'bout everythin'?" Flint scolded.

Bromly returned to his seat and spooned a cup of tea for each of us. "Burge is months away. Best to take this new situation on a day-to-day basis for now. I'm not taking sides in this mess you two created."

Flint crossed his arms over his chest with a *humph*.

"Still, it would be nice to have an extra set of hands to help sew pelts. I suppose there's a point about payment. Aya, it wouldn't be right to use your labor and not give you something in return."

"You have given me enough," I insisted.

He ignored me. "I'll talk to Darric, see how he feels about it."

Great, let's poke the grumpy brother.

"I'll go find him." Flint chugged his steaming tea until his face turned the same color as his hair. Once finished, he took a large gulp of air and squeaked, "That was hotter than I thought it'd be."

Unfazed, Bromly blew steam away from his cup. "Leave Darric alone right now. You know better."

Flint also should have known better than to chug scalding tea, but I was beginning to suspect he was a bit of a buffoon. He gargled and slapped his knee as his face turned ever more crimson. I tucked my lips under my teeth to keep from laughing.

"Where does Darric keep going?" I asked.

"The last few days he's been tracking our short-lived visitors to make sure they didn't discover the Hovel before we were ready." Bromly tipped his teacup to his mouth, testing the heat. "Darric leaves for a while after something like this happens and spends some time alone. None of us enjoy this part of living in the mountains."

"He feels like he needs to serve as guard to us. Keep things safe 'round here," Flint rasped. He cleared his throat and punched his chest to find his normal voice. "Me an' Bromly are here all the time without him. We can take care of ourselves. Insomnia can give ya a bad grasp on reality." He twirled his finger next to his temple.

"Darric is an insomniac?" I questioned, intrigued.

"Worse, he never sleeps, an' when he does, he's violent—"

"Flint!" Bromly interrupted. "Let him decide if he wants her to know any of that."

I had to give these men credit. They had a talent for creating awkward encounters. Despite being *brothers*, they didn't ever seem to belong in the same room together. "Forgive me for saying so, but the three of you look nothing alike for being brothers."

"We aren't brothers by blood," Bromly confessed, tea dripping off his mustache. "My mother had a heart for adopting homeless children. When I was three, she found Flint freezing to death in a gutter in the poor district. We looked for weeks for his family, but no one ever claimed him. So we took him in."

I looked at Flint, and he shrugged. "I don't remember. I was one."

"After my father died, my mother made a meager living baking bread to sell at market. We were barely surviving. Yet, she found ways to keep a roof over us, leaky but still a roof."

Flint laughed. "Hey, tell her 'bout how I used to teethe on flint stone an' that's where my name came from."

Bromly gave me a quizzical look before continuing. "Flint became like a brother to me. He *is* my brother. My mother worked twice as hard to keep us fed, so Flint and I used to beg for coin outside the noble district. But, um . . ." He set down his cup and rubbed his hands together. "She didn't have to go into prostitution until we found Darric."

There was only one city in Brisleia large enough to have districts segregated by class: Alamantia.

"We were pedaling for extra copper the day we met Darric."

Flint narrowed his eyes at the memory.

"Flint was too young when we found him to realize he'd been abandoned. He was innocent and just needing love, but Darric . . ." Bromly let out a long breath. "It was like all the life had been sucked out of him. His eyes were just . . . dead. He was beyond weary and dirty. It took Flint and I hours to convince him to follow us home. But once he did, he slept for days and only woke up to eat. It took him a year to tell us what happened to his family and that he'd traveled all the way from Vegathyad, alone."

I gripped my teacup so tightly that my fingers turned white. "What had happened to him?"

Bromly shook his head. "It's not my place to tell you Darric's history, and I'd rather not talk about it. I'm sorry."

"I understand." The reality that the three of them had lived below me in Alamantia City astounded me. Could I have seen their house from my private garden? Had I ever watched them chasing a town cat down the street or gazing at the palace towers for a glimpse of the Divine? Recently I'd been lost in a massive universe, but this simple revelation made the world feel comfortingly smaller. "How old was Darric when you found him?"

"Uh . . . six." Bromly avoided looking at me by refilling his teacup.

"And he'd come from Vegathyad?" I mused, astonished.

He nodded. "We aren't sure of his exact nationality, but it was nice having another brother. With Darric around to help with chores, our mother could find new means of income."

Flint's hand clenched around his empty cup. "She never would've had to do those things if he hadn't shown up."

"That's not a fair thing to say." I furrowed my brows, shocked he would make such a horrible accusation. "Your mother went to amazing lengths to take care of the three of you."

"She got sick 'cause of it," he said through his teeth.

I turned to Bromly for confirmation, and he nodded. "That's when Darric started traveling. He felt responsible. He swore he would find a way to make money so she wouldn't have to sell herself anymore. We were all against it, so he ran away in the middle of the night while we were asleep."

My anticipation grew. I'd forgotten about my tea and clutched the cold cup.

"He was gone almost a year, but he did come home. Sort of in one piece. And with money, a lot of it."

I let out the breath I'd been holding.

"He wouldn't tell us how he'd acquired so much coin. He said we'd have a hard time with the truth. But mother knew with one look at him. She begged him not to go back. It went on that way for years. Darric became someone we rarely saw, but he always returned. Always with money, but not always without injury. Sometimes he was hurt significantly. Our mother continued to oppose him leaving, but she didn't have to work anymore, so Darric never listened."

"What was he doing?" I leaned forwards, ready for anything. After witnessing Darric kill our intruders so mercilessly, there wasn't much I could imagine that would be worse. But Bromly shook his head, filling me with disappointment. Humbled by his dedication to keeping his brother's secrets, I accepted his silence. "So, Darric has your best interests at heart."

"Indeed." He half smiled but seemed troubled by the old memories.

"Psh." Flint sneered. "Darric didn't consider anyone's interest when he brought us into the mountains to live like criminals."

Bromly's upper lip twitched.

"If you hated the idea so much, then why did you come here?" I asked.

"Mother eventually took a turn for the worse," Bromly provided. "Darric almost missed her. He arrived home the night she passed. He disappeared for a long time after that. We weren't sure he was going to come back at all."

"An' when he did randomly reappear, he took one look at our situation an' decided it was best to bring us up here." Flint fluttered his hand in the air, indicating the Hovel.

Bromly slowly shook his head, silently telling his brother to be mindful.

"I was handlin' it just fine," he spat in return. "I had a plan."

"Flint was not fond of the idea that we would live as nomads, cutting off most of our connection to society and visiting towns only when we needed to sell wares," Bromly added before Flint could say more. "It's not all bad. The time Darric spent on his own taught him a great deal about living off the land and what dangers to avoid."

"It is beautiful here," I admitted. When they weren't killing wayward travelers.

"It's home." Bromly yawned, lifting his arms high above his head. "It's late, and it's been a terrible day. I need rest. We all do."

"I'm not tired one bit!" Flint proclaimed and leaned closer to me so he could snake his arm around my lower back.

"Well, I am." Bromly took to his feet. "Don't stay up much later. We have to finish sewing those hides before the bears wake up."

"I know, I know." Flint waved him off.

Bromly eased the kettle out of the coals with his boot. Giving a slight nod, he slipped behind the center fur door and left me alone with Flint, who suddenly had a devious smile radiating into his emerald eyes.

"You should go to bed too." I set my teacup on the ground beside my foot.

"Oh . . ." His smile faded. "Are ya tired?"

No, I haven't slept since I woke up from being poisoned.

I shook my head. "I'm still pretty shaken."

"I'll stay up with ya. I don't mind. I don't want ya to be afraid. Or if ya want, ya can sleep in my room with me." He winked, his hand cupping my hip.

"No, thank you." The temperature of my blood spiked at his forward invitation. "Go to bed," I hissed, scooting away from him and thus pushing the cat off the bench. She shook her head, stunned by the disappearance of her bed.

Flint's jaw dropped. He couldn't be *that* ignorant. "Oh, but I thought you an' I could . . ." His hand slid over my knee. *Not ignorant.* "If ya wanted . . . I saved a few coppers. We definitely could—"

"Goodnight," I snapped, folding my arms over my chest and crossing my legs so his hand fell off me.

Flint's head drooped, and he rose from his seat. He scuffled to the fur door at the far end of the room, chewing his bottom lip. "I saw that goin' differently in my head. Figured you'd be open to it," he admitted, confused, and closed the fur behind him.

I buried my face in my hands and groaned. I was absolutely disgusted by the amount of men who kept gawking at me as if I was a piece of meat, something to be claimed and possessed. Princes, bandits, nomads—it didn't matter; they were all the same. At least I could count on Bromly to be civil, since he only had eyes for some woman in Burge.

And Darric hated me.

Chapter 13

The Hovel's quiet was broken only by the soft crackle of dying embers. Bromly and Flint slept soundly in their beds, with an occasional snore to remind me of their presence. For the first time, I sat by the fire instead of cowering in Darric's room trying to make the others believe I slept regularly. Eventually, I would need to find something to do.

The palace was always active. The kitchen never closed, and court entertainment often continued until dawn. There were books to read and Elizabetta to act as my companion. Even the things that used to be so deathly boring would be welcomed now that I was faced with a substantial lack of activity. Being at the Hovel had given me a better appreciation for the extravagant life I'd lived before Ambrosia cured my perpetual boredom.

My grandmother had roamed the countryside for weeks before worrying soldiers would look for her. Being *the Spare* had benefits in that regard. Unlike future monarchs, our appearance remained unknown to the public. It was supposed to be a safety precaution, but it didn't stop stories. I'd heard rumors I was known as beautiful—*up for interpretation*—but impertinent and arrogant—*not so unverified*—so my elegance accounted for little.

If Darric made up his mind to kill me, I would have to reveal the Mandala to save my neck. Until then, it was best I pretend to be ignorant of the royals or risk becoming a hostage.

The cat purred on the bench beside me, curled into a tiny sleeping ball of burgundy. "I will have to think of a name for you."

She opened her wide amber eyes as if she'd never been asleep, stretching into a long arch and clawing the wood.

"Why won't you talk to me?"

She cocked her head to the side with an intelligent gaze full of wonder.

"Granted, I've never met another cat, but why should they be so different from horses or birds? What if cats are no different? What if it's just you?"

She meowed and commenced licking her paw, smashing the wet fur into her cheek.

"Are you . . . are you deliberately ignoring me?"

The discourteous feline sat perfectly still, tufts of fur on her face feathered in disarray from where she had abruptly abandoned her cleansing.

"That's it, isn't it? You can talk, and you are choosing not to." How dare she not let me in? What would a feral cat have to hide?

She yawned, plopped onto her belly, and shut her eyes.

I scoffed. *Pest of a feline.* "You can forget me giving you a name."

Her whiskers twitched upwards, as if she laughed at the idea.

The front door swished open, and my heart leaped into my throat. I lost my balance and toppled onto the bear rug, spilling my leftover tea.

Darric stood in the doorway, looking at the sprawled mess of me lying on the ground. He stepped over me and placed his haversack on the workbench to begin untying his cloak. Being alone with him wasn't any better than if a fifth bandit had entered the Hovel.

"You scared me." I lifted myself back onto the bench.

"Good."

Insulting swordsman.

He uncorked a brown glass bottle from his pack and chugged a monstrous gulp. His hands were coated in dried blood and his bracers splattered with red. I shuddered, unnerved that he kept such an impressive physique in constant dishevelment, yet the blood suited him somehow.

After talking to Bromly and Flint, I perceived Darric differently. Violence defined him. Even the vast destructive force of a hurricane can be beautiful. Maybe we weren't so different. I felt like a trapped tornado. It made me wonder if I could kill too.

Thinking about death brought back the images of his blade disemboweling a bandit, and I massaged my temples with my fingers.

Darric casually approached my bench. "You look like you could use a drink." He offered me the decanter. The smell of red wine hit my nose.

"Are you serious." My question came out as a statement. "So, *you're* trying to poison me now?"

He furrowed his brows. "What about me saying I don't condone suffering didn't you understand?"

I accepted the bottle from him and took several long swigs.

"Don't treat it like the water I gave you before." He half grinned and tugged the wine away from my mouth. I swallowed quickly, catching leftover drops on my sleeve. "You're a bit of a lush, aren't you?"

Elizabetta always said the same thing.

I wiped my lips, savoring the flavor. The wine was not fine, cheap and possibly old, but I appreciated the gesture. "Where did you get that?" Spirits were not common among nomadic peasants.

He suddenly became more aware of the blood on his bracers and set down the bottle to wipe his palms on his drab leather pants. It did little to remove the staining. "Don't worry about it. Restless night?" He took a seat on the end of the bench, leaving the cat between us.

I nodded. "Most are these days."

The cat hissed at him, and he coupled a smile with a laugh. "I hate your cat." He took another sip of his wine.

"She is not my cat."

He reoffered the bottle, and I kept my gulping to a minimum. When I handed back the decanter, a faint glimmer of red smeared off onto my hands. I discreetly tried to wipe it on my dress.

"She follows you everywhere," he said, watching my fingers clutch the fabric.

"That doesn't mean I own her. She does what she wants. Apparently, that is following me around."

"And you have no idea why, do you?" he prodded, making me believe he knew something about this burgundy feline that I did not. "She's not that different from you. She follows an enigmatic girl through the woods who pursues even stranger men to their homes."

"Again with this denial," I huffed. "I tried to stop following you in that forest. You would think you'd admit the truth when we're alone together, even if there is something you don't want your brothers to know."

"What forest?" He grinned slyly, but taking heed of my disdain, he sighed and ran a hand through his hair. He looked queerly at his fingers afterwards, forgetting they had been coated in blood.

"I thought you weren't coming back until dawn?"

"It *is* dawn," he informed. "The inside of the Hovel tends to remain dark no matter what time of day it is. I would have thought you had noticed that with your lack of sleep and all."

His observation churned my stomach. "How did you know I haven't been sleeping?"

"I'm here a lot more than those two let on." He recorked his bottle, nodding towards his brothers' bedrooms. "It's just easier to keep to myself."

The thought of Darric lingering just outside the cavern made me fidget with my dress sleeve. "Where were you?"

He shrugged.

"What is there to hide?" I held up my hands, showing him the blood staining my palms. "It's no secret what you're doing out there."

His eyes darkened. "*That's* none of your business."

"Maybe it's not, but do Bromly and Flint know the real number of people who come into this valley that you murder? The amount of innocent lives you take when you are ambling around on your own?"

Tension stiffened his shoulders. "Do you honestly believe I run about killing every man I see?"

"No, there are women and children too," I snidely remarked.

"You are out of line." His voice rang with controlled anger.

I scooted away until I found the end of the bench. "Perhaps I'm not the only one."

His expression changed to amusement as he watched me shy away from him. "All right, fine. It's animal blood. A stag, to be specific. You can go outside and see for yourself. Some animals are easier to hunt at night."

"And the wine?"

"Asking anyway? Call it a gift from a friend. One I was content to share with you until you opened that pretty mouth of yours."

I covered my lips at his words. *He thinks I'm pretty.* My cheeks flushed. I quickly composed my thoughts before they ran me into senseless trouble.

Darric retrieved the half-empty bucket of water Bromly had used for tea. He set it between his legs and dipped his hands into it. The rusty dried blood turned red as he washed.

I rubbed my fingers together; the staining wasn't going anywhere.

When his hands were clean, he connivingly left the bucket beside his feet. If I wanted to wash, I would have to move closer. He shook excess water from his fingers and leaned his forearms on his knees.

Even without the fear of dying, Darric Ursygh made me inconsolably nervous, but I hesitantly crept towards him and eased my hands into the bucket, concentrating to prevent the water from exploding. *Relax.* I rubbed my fingers together and avoided eye contact, since he was staring at me with a devious smirk. "Do you always hunt at night?"

His mood reverted to contempt. He breathed out heavily, as if he would have preferred I'd stayed silent. "No."

I wiped my wet hands on my dress and waited patiently for him to continue.

"It's safer if I stay away from the Hovel at night. It gives my brothers peace to rest." He leaned closer, looking satisfied that his mere presence sent me into a timorous disarray.

"Insomnia." I stared at my feet, poking at a fur tuft on the rug with the tip of my shoe. "Flint told me you have violent tendencies when you sleep."

He scoffed. "And how I'm damaged and he is an innocent bystander? And how Bromly's mother rescued the lot of us from a childhood hell?"

The derisive edge in his voice captivated me. "Actually, I found it remarkable that you care so much about their well-being. I didn't expect it. Everything about you has seemed so . . ."

"Sadistic?"

"I was going to say *impassive*."

He laughed. "You've learned a lot in my absence."

"Not as much as I'd have liked."

"You're interested?" he inquired, still studying the side of my face.

I felt too exposed to him. I desperately needed to back away for my sanity. "I'd be lying if I said you don't intrigue me."

He got up before my head completely fogged and carefully peeked behind Flint's bedroom door. Certain that his brother was still snoring, he dropped the fur back into place. "You're not tired?"

"No."

"Not even a little?"

"Uh-uh."

He clenched his jaw. "Then I think you and I should discuss some things. Come for a walk with me."

My breath hitched. The cat arched her back and hissed, her hair standing on end in obvious detestation.

"Can't we talk here?"

He methodically shook his head and went into his room to retrieve my cloak. He set it on the bench beside me. "What if I promise not to kill you?" He held out a hand to help me up, but I stood without taking it.

He retracted his palm. "Independent or stubborn?"

"Chivalrous gesture, Darric, but I'm not giving you another thing to deny later."

"Fair enough."

The blue glow of fading night spread along the horizon. Spring warmed the valley, and a sheen of morning dew clung to the grass instead of frost. Deer drank from the river in the peaceful silence and only looked up when they heard our footsteps.

The carcass of a freshly killed stag lay next to the Hovel door with its throat sliced.

Darric walked several paces in front of me. I watched the wool of his cloak sway as he moved, and the golden strands of his chaotic hair caught the first yellow rays of the morning sunlight.

The cat trailed by the back of my dress, half hiding under my skirt. She seemed just as disturbed as I was by the fascinating atmosphere of terror Darric created. He made my skin tingle—the thought of his solid arms wrapping around me, burning and tense from running; the roughness of his hand holding my mouth shut. I couldn't forget the feel of his touch when he had led me away from a hallucinated wisteria forest towards the Hovel. His complicated persona tugged at the inner recesses of my sanity, and I wondered if I would ever understand him. Why did he keep protecting me when his attitude was the opposite of his actions?

Following the most withdrawn of the Hovel brothers across the valley reminded me of an execution. I could have been walking to my own death. My only consolation was his promise not to kill me. Maybe I could still turn back.

Darric splashed through the stream, trudging knee deep through the icy water. I continued trailing him across the rushing brook.

When we reached the other side, he stopped abruptly and turned to face me, gazing at my dress with riveted perplexity. I chased his eyes to find dry fabric, except for an inch around the bottom of my skirt. My heart hit my ribs in hard thumps. I couldn't think, and my jaw fell open. I had unconsciously walked over the water, and it had not gone unnoticed by my ever-vigilant stranger.

"Let me make something perfectly clear." He placed his finger on the underside of my chin to lift my head higher, forcing me to look into his stabbing gaze as he towered over me. "There *is* a reason why I haven't killed you yet, and if you are going to lie to me, then I see no incentive to disclose anything further to you. So I'm only going to ask you this once." He removed his finger, leaving me iced in fear. "The night the bandits caught you, were you running from the Onyx Guard?"

My chest tightened with dread, and I doubted I'd ever be able to breathe again. "What?"

"If the Onyx Guard is tracking you, they *will* come here. I can't have that happen."

I hiccupped, gulping in short erratic breaths. "Why would they be tracking me?"

"Don't. Lie." He pointed a stern finger between my eyes, and the cat spat at him.

"And you never thought to ask me this before you decided to bring me to this valley?"

"A mistake I can correct, and *that* is why there is the solution of killing you." He gripped the hilt of his sword. The cat's hair stood on end, and she bared her claws, ready to pounce.

"No!" I flew forwards, laying my hands over his bracer to prevent him from drawing. He instantly ceased all movement, as if my touch shocked him. "Stop, please!" His shoulders relaxed at my desperate plea. "They were not following me. You gave your word not to kill me if I came on this walk with you."

"My word can be shot to hell if I need to protect my interests." He jerked his arm free and took a step back.

Addled by the mention of the Onyx Guard, I simply stared at him, holding my breath. Darric turned and kept walking, the muscles in his back going rigid.

Then everything detonated.

Lightning streaked across my brain, and all the pieces connected.

Years ago, Darric brought his family to these mountains to live in secrecy. He was restless and killed anyone who came near his home. Except me.

My lungs broke free of the ice. I inhaled a colossal breath and gathered every ounce of courage left in me. "You're a Fae!" The words fell like loose rocks on a ledge.

Darric halted so rapidly his boots dug into the ground, making little piles of dirt. His entire body went stiff, and his brows turned down in a scowl. He grabbed my arm and hauled me with him at an expedited pace. I struggled to keep up, stumbling, my ankles rolling over every rock and dip.

He dragged me to the edge of the valley, where the mountain cliffs touched soft grass, and tucked us behind a flowering spirea shrub growing against the rock. I dug in my heels and tore my arm from his grasp, but he snatched my shoulder and spun me around, slamming my back on the stone and pinning me to the granite. My head whirled from the onslaught of strength that rushed through him. I shoved his chest, but I may as well have been pushing on an oak tree. He didn't wobble. He didn't budge. My wrists buckled, sending painful shocks up my arms. I could do as much damage to him as an ant could do to a bear. Where was the cat? Why wasn't she helping me? *Swat at him! Claw at him! Do something!*

"Have you completely lost your fucking mind?" he growled, so close to my face that his breath bounced off my nose.

"You're like me!" I yelled, done being intimidated, especially if he was going to continue to treat me like a rag doll.

"Lower your voice." He tightened his grip. My pulse throbbed in my elbow and down into my sore wrists, and my fingers began to tingle from the lack of blood circulation.

"No!" I said, determined. "You have the symptoms of a Dreamer!"

He slammed his fist on the stone, trying to scare me into submission. Dirt fell from the ledge above us. "Did you draw that abhorrent conclusion from some story you heard from my brothers?"

"Please . . ." My voice shook as my resolve wavered. "I just need to know. I need to know I'm not alone. I need to know there is a chance for my survival."

He loosened his grip and let out a deep breath, his eyes softening. Clenching his hands into fists, he leaned his head against the rock and closed his eyes. "You can't say things like that. It's suicide to say it out loud. You can't trust anyone."

Too petrified to move, I stayed glued to the granite. "I know what it means. I know the consequences." The cat reappeared, brushing against my leg. I jostled her away, perturbed that she had done nothing to stop him from slamming me into the cliff base. "I'm a Fae," I whispered. Hearing myself say it aloud for the first time caused bile to rise in my throat.

"Please, stop saying it." He opened his eyes and looked at me. "I know."

"How? You keep forcing me into silence about the bandit cave, and you're clearly lying to your brothers."

He rubbed his hands over his face. "Because I've been trying to figure out what to do with your ass ever since you woke up in my room," he snapped, momentarily losing control. "You weren't supposed to live . . . We are in a secluded location, but if the Onyx Guard is trailing you, they *will* find this valley."

Defeated, I laid my forehead on the stone. "So, you live hidden to prevent the inevitable. They would imprison you and kill your brothers."

He bristled. "Yes, but not for the reason you think. I'm not a Fae, Aya. I'm a deserter. I tired of the brutality involved in abducting children while their parents watched in horror. I tired of torturing the families protecting them, the murder, and dragging helpless kids to the senators." His mouth quivered in disgust. "If you have a conscience, you can only stand so much before you break."

I swear my heart stopped beating. "You're a . . ." *dark assassin.* I backed away, preparing to flee for my life and run faster than I'd ever dared attempt.

"Was," he corrected, following me like a predator.

"No!" I yelped, leaping out of his reach. I dug my nails into my scalp. "You can't be!" I tripped over the shrub branches and landed hard on the ground. I was going to be sick.

Darric was a *Sight*—a dark assassin of the Onyx Guard, a man born with the talent to identify Dreamers. He would destroy everything. It was done. It was over. I was going to Medial Alexandria.

He knelt in front of me, taking my chin in his hand and cranking my head back so I was forced to look at him. "I knew the instant I saw you what you are. *Insane*, as some call it. But I've never seen a free Fae as old as you are, and poisoned or not, it would have been wrong to leave you to die. Though the more I've thought about it, the more I've realized what a stupid mistake I made bringing you to the Hovel."

"You're going to turn me over to the Senate, aren't you?" I went brittle, and a tear rolled down my cheek.

"No." He let me go, sinking down next to me and tucking himself into the small space behind the brush. "I have no intention of taking you to Medial Alexandria. They would murder me faster than they would imprison you."

I smeared the tear over my face. "Why?"

"Once you are in the Onyx Guard, you're in it for life." He tugged at the white bandage wrapped around his forearm, redistributing the linen over his skin. "It's death to soldiers who abandon their post, and for me *life* was a very long time."

"You deserted?"

"Yes, and desertion is hardly the lifelong allegiance I swore an oath to."

"Idiotic of me to believe you were a Fae." I shuddered. A balmy wind blew through the valley, significantly warmer than any spring breeze, and it tangled hair over my face. The warmth helped coax me out of my numb, terror-stricken cocoon, and I tucked a curl behind my ear. "Bromly and Flint said you travel frequently. I should have suspected you made it to Medial Alexandria."

"I was desperate to find income. If the Senate figures out you can identify the Fae, a *Sight*"—he grimaced at the word—"they will make a coin offer that is difficult to refuse. The money is astronomical. It would be a wealthy living, if they ever let you leave after you swear dedication. Once you swear the oath, they own you, body and mind. I was recruited at twelve. I used to sneak back to the Keenes as often as possible to bring them money."

I clumsily pulled at several blades of grass. "That's young."

"Most of Medial Alexandria's soldiers are adolescents. The younger their recruits, the easier they are to influence—to brainwash into believing what they are doing isn't kidnapping and murder, that the law is on their side. But law isn't always what is right. It's just what is popular or convenient for the time. I've done what I can to protect my brothers from my past. That doesn't mean I enjoy getting my hands dirty. I just have the Onyx Guard to *thank* for my ease in it."

When I was ten, a wellborn merchant who supplied trade goods from Duval to Brisleia lost everything to Medial Alexandria. He sought an audience with the King and begged my father for justice after the Onyx Guard abducted his daughter and killed his wife and son. King Hugo sided with the Senate and had the merchant executed for harboring a Fae.

I fell onto both sides of a rarity in a world where everything I was made of meant a death sentence outside of Alamantia Palace.

I touched my temple and traced my fingers over the place where the Mandala should have graced my skin. A Fae couldn't hide from Darric Ursygh, but there was no possibility I would reveal my Divinity.

Another dry, hot draft ruffled my hair, similar to the heat coming off coals. "It's getting warm. I've always loved spring in Brisleia," I mumbled, moving my hair off my neck to allow my skin to breathe.

He chuckled at the change in subject. "That breeze isn't caused by the season." He glanced up the rock face. "We are at the easternmost part of the valley right now. Can't you hear it?"

In truth, I had been so disturbed by the news that Darric was a former dark assassin of the Onyx Guard that I hadn't looked around me. The temperature in this part of the valley was torrid, and waves of heat warped the air. My chemise stuck to my legs, and a low rumble lingered on the wind. "What is that?"

"The Riving. This valley sits parallel to it." He stretched his legs so his shoes hit the spirea shrub. "I'm . . . addicted, in a way, to being near it. And I'm a little partial to the heat."

"I've never lived anywhere except Brisleia. All I know is the cold."

"I thought somehow you escaped from Medial Alexandria." He gave me a pleasant smile, lessening the shock of his former employment.

"I've never been there," I confessed, cringing internally at my suffocating upbringing. "I've never been anywhere."

"That's a shame. Most of Athera is beautiful." He tilted his head towards me. "I'd prefer not to go back to the Senate headquarters any time in the foreseeable future, but"—he glanced up at the cliffs a second time—"I can show you the Riving."

"You can see it from here?"

"We are practically sitting on it." This time when he extended his hand, I accepted. Let him deny it later. I wasn't intoxicated, no matter how much wine he had offered me.

I followed him up a steep stone pathway that cut through the cliffs. Moss grew on the rocks, making them difficult to grip. Eventually we reached the beginning of a vertical climb, which led one hundred feet above us to an oddly steaming ledge.

I stepped back, intimidated. "I've changed my mind."

Darric laughed, hopping onto the first rocks, and pulled me up beside him. I cautiously gripped the stones. Once I was secure, he released me and climbed higher until I stared at his boots. Again, he reached down and took my hand to help me up.

The climb was slippery and tedious. Darric didn't let me out of his careful grasp for more than a moment, switching between tugging my arms and pushing my lower back. When I looked down, we were high above the trees. The fall would cause serious injury. Even the cat took extra precaution as she sprung from one rock to the next.

Darric excelled at climbing. He looked down repeatedly to gauge distance, and the increasing altitude seemed to exhilarate him.

"You really love heights, don't you?" I strained over another mossy ridge, his free hand supporting my spine.

"More than I should, though I did break both wrists once when I fell out of a pine."

I groaned. "Comforting, Darric."

My arms begged for relief by the time we reached the steaming flat shelf. The cliff gave way to a level space the size of the Hovel, surrounded by boulders with an opening at the far end. The rumble had increased, and the ledge vibrated under my feet. Singed moss lined the rocks, and the horizon glowed a brilliant orange-red.

Darric placed a hand on the small of my back and led me to the edge. "Be careful," he warned.

I peered over the captivating chasm. The igneous wind hit my face and dried my eyes. The Riving was magnificent and enigmatic—beautiful in a horrifying way that paintings and books had failed to capture. The ledge sat directly above it, providing a spectacular view.

The tear in the planet split the crust, revealing a massive bright yellow river of magma flowing in a dazzling display of light with no end. The exposed mantle jutted from left to right as far as I could see. The intense heat burned my skin, and the scorched air was difficult to breathe.

Everyone in Athera knew the story of the Riving—how the planet had bared her inner core to save humanity and deliver the Divine into existence—but none alive knew how to heal it. The Podarians had tried to bridge the gap, only to find no material or structure could withstand its distance and heat.

I leaned far over the shelf to seize every detail, but Darric grabbed my waist and pulled me back. A spiral shockwave jolted from my core and into my throat from the feeling of his calloused hand on my stomach. I spun around to face him, catching myself on his hard chest.

"I said *be careful.* Falling into the Riving would be a sick way to die."

"It would." I exhaled heavily and awkwardly took my hands off him. Despite my fear, nothing stopped my body's natural reaction to my handsome stranger.

I turned back to the ledge and rested my elbows on the stone. Biting my lip, I nervously drummed my fingers on the rock. "Somehow I thought the Riving was a myth. Too impossible to be real."

Darric leaned into the space next to me and surveyed the mantle. "It's supposed to be impossible for people to dream, and yet here you are. The Riving is easy to dismiss as folklore for those who haven't stood at its edge."

Another wave of heat tossed my hair. "You're from Vegathyad, right? Bromly and Flint said you traveled from Podar as a child."

"Actually, I don't know where I'm originally from. My parents died without telling me much about our family history. We were only living in Podar at the time, but I'm not Podarian. Or Brisleian. Or Duvali. I'm . . . without country." He flicked a pebble over the edge, and it disappeared into the chasm.

"Can I ask you something?"

"My opposition has never stopped you before."

I ignored his snide comment. "If you don't dream, then what causes the insomnia? It's just . . . you never seem tired. You're restless. Like me."

"I . . . uh . . ." He stuttered and pressed his thumb into the palm of his hand. "I never said I didn't dream."

"That doesn't make sense. Do Sights dream?" I asked, surprised.

"No, just me." He groaned, giving in to my persistence. "It's more of a curse. Call it a *trade-off* because I didn't stay away from the Riving. I tend to have an odd talent for being in the right place at the right time. It's rather annoying."

"A trade-off for what?"

He swiftly drew his sword. The bloodcurdling sound of the metal raking against the scabbard sent a chill down my spine, and I jumped back, nearly tripping over the cat as the blade sang into existence. He briefly paused, admiring the miraculous sword. I stared in both wonder and terror at the deadly weapon ringing in his strong, deft hand.

Apart from the blades of Medial Alexandria, Divine royalty had access to the most elaborate swords Atheran blacksmiths could design, yet this weapon was entirely different from any Atheran blade I'd ever seen. It lacked gems or crystals, yet light danced off the metal as if it were inlaid with fine stone. The grip was composed of shimmering black granite with spiraling silver threading. It lacked a cross guard, and the small pommel glistened with an indecisive incandescence. Flowing from the hilt were two lines of ethereal lettering carved into the metal. The foreign text continued all the way to the sword's point, divided by a thin sparkling indentation running down the center of the blade.

Darric gripped the hilt with both hands and pulled in opposing directions. The indentation illuminated with a fluid white spark, and the blade split into two separate weapons, each holding one side of the carved text.

Starting with the sword in his left hand, he drove the metal into the rock. It scraped out an unpleasant chord as it cut into the granite. He released the grip, leaving the sword stuck halfway in the stone. Flourishing the blade in his right hand, he repeated the action, embedding the sword in the stone an arm's length away from the first half. When he finished, he leaned onto the ledge with an exhausted expression and rubbed his fingers into his eyes.

My mouth hung open in bewilderment. I was unsure which to react to first: the beauty and brilliancy of Darric's sword bending the laws of nature or the fact that he had not killed me with it.

"Any more questions?" he said curtly.

I slammed my jaw shut. "Yes!"

"Aya!" Interrupting my interrogation, someone called my new name in drawn-out, panic-stricken howls. "Aya!"

Darric peered over the valley and chuckled. "My brother is looking for you."

I joined him at the edge. Flint scurried by the river, darting erratically in one direction after another.

"It's almost noon." Darric looked at the high position of the sun. Between the Brisleian spring and the heat of the Riving, my chemise was soaked under my dress. Darric had droplets of sweat trickling down his temples, and much of his blond hair clung to his forehead. "We need to get you back before my brother overreacts and becomes hysterical."

Flint jogged along the tree line, cupping his hands around his mouth to strengthen his call.

Darric pulled each half of his sword from the granite. When he touched the blades together, the weapon re-fused into one piece.

"Is it standard issue?" I asked, watching him slide the sword back into his scabbard.

"What?" He gave me a quizzical look.

"That sword. The Onyx Guard is full of secrets and superb craftsmanship. Is it something they gave to you? Does it help you find people like me?"

"Uh, no."

"I've never seen anyone as talented as you with a sword." Not even Luken, who was better than any militiaman in Alamantia.

"And you never will." He hopped over the edge of the precipice and descended several feet towards the valley basin.

I sat down and dangled my feet over the side. Unexpectedly, he ran his hand up my leg and grasped my hip to pull me towards him. I fell into his chest and clung to his neck; my feet tingled with no place to land. "Did the Onyx Guard teach you?"

"Some of it." He secured his arm around my back and looked down to find his next footing.

"Who taught you most of it?" I tightened my grip, my nails digging into his shoulders.

"Are you really going to trust me as your sole support to stop you from plummeting to your death?" He raised an eyebrow. "I still have not decided if keeping you alive is judicious."

"I'm starting to believe you might be bluffing."

He laughed and used his free hand to pry my fingers from his skin. I slid off him, scraping my nails across his shoulder as I fell. My stomach punched my throat. I clawed the air, trying to find anything to grab on to.

Without a moment left to spare, he caught my waist and tucked me back to his chest. I tangled my fists into his shirt, nearly ripping through the cotton.

"Don't ever do that again," I gasped out as my lungs attempted to untwist. He smelled intoxicating despite sweating by the Riving.

"Do you want to see it coming, or should I surprise you?" He chuckled, clutching me in a protective embrace.

After scaring me senseless, he used one hand to descend the mountain. It didn't faze him. We reached the ground in half the time it took to climb. Landing on the grass, he eased me out of his arms and headed in the direction of the Hovel.

I rubbed my neck, taking languid steps. I'd survived the excursion, but something plagued me; my future ended in either death by the hands of Darric Ursygh or eventual imprisonment by the Senate. Neither option was appealing.

Ambrosia never would have suspected how dangerous it was for me outside of Alamantia Palace. Defending myself would be necessary when I finally figured out how to escape this valley. Luken had promised to one day teach me to wield a sword, but during my experience with the bandits, I had not even had the mental wherewithal to draw the dagger he had given me.

"Darric." I trotted up behind him. "Teach me how to wield a sword."

"No," he quickly retorted without looking at me.

"No? That's it? You won't even think about it?"

"Absolutely not."

"If I truly am this rarity, then I need to know how to defend myself," I argued.

"No, you don't."

"I'm tired of peeling potatoes!" I stomped my foot like a child.

He stopped walking to face me. "There is no scenario where I could control my temper long enough to teach you anything. Besides, even if I wanted to, you're not ready."

"Not ready?"

"You're erratic and too impulsive. You have no control over anything you say or do. Not to mention you are naive." He continued walking.

If that wasn't an accurate description of my personality, then I didn't know myself at all.

The brush next to us rustled, and Flint burst from the greenery. His feet caught in the branches, and he stumbled, plowing into Darric. The onslaught didn't budge my stranger's balance. He grabbed Flint by the shirt and flung him aside, sending him crashing into a blackberry briar on the opposite end of the grassy path.

Flint sprung to his feet and took hold of Darric's shirt. "Where's Aya? Where is she? What have ya done with her?" he squeaky-screamed into his brother's face.

"Flint?" I said, attracting his attention to where I stood several feet behind Darric.

Flint released his grip with a huff and threw his long arms around me, constricting my chest and plucking me off the ground.

"I was worried sick." He backed away to look at me. His emerald eyes were edged in red with unfallen tears. "Please, don't disappear again." He exhaled a shaky breath and embraced me once more.

I pushed against his chest, trying to pry myself from his bony grip. "I'm fine." I tossed hair away from my face.

"Did he hurt you?" He examined my head for damage.

Darric raised an amused eyebrow. A thin trickle of blood dripped down his bicep from the three deep scratch marks on his shoulder.

"I've been lookin' for ya all mornin'. I was afraid Darric had—" Flint turned to look at his brother and wrinkled his pointed nose. "Why are ya bleedin'?"

Darric glanced at his shoulder, noticing the damage I'd caused, and laughed. My face turned red, and I put my head down to hide a coy smile.

"C'mon, Aya," Flint grumbled under his breath, "let's go home." He slid his fingers down my arm and tried to take my hand, but I skipped out of his grasp to follow Darric back to the Hovel.

Chapter 14

Where were ya? I looked all over the valley." Remnants of alarm still riddled Flint's voice and posture. He walked alongside me the entire way back to the Hovel.

"Darric was showing me the Riving," I replied innocently.

"Ya were with Darric? The whole time?" His response simmered with animosity. "That's dangerous for ya."

We entered the cavern. Bromly sat by the outside fire, spooning stew into his mouth.

"Well, he hasn't killed me yet. He seems to be able to keep his temper when he tries."

Darric smirked in my periphery as he strolled into the Hovel.

"He's a loaded cannon!" Flint squealed. "An' the Riving isn't easy to get to. He coulda pushed ya over the edge. Ya shoulda told me ya were goin'. I woulda gone with ya to make sure ya were safe."

I blinked, astounded by his possessiveness. "We didn't want to wake you."

"I wasn't tired." He blew a puff of hot air. "It coulda ended really bad. Don't do it again, okay? Promise?"

Risking my neck by disappearing into the woods with Darric had been my decision. I didn't run away from a future as the Queen of Podar to have this redhead tell me what to do with my time. "Flint, you do not own me, and after the way you acted last night, be grateful I am even talking to you."

His eyes widened, and his hand flew to his head in distress. "I didn't mean it like that."

"Really? Then what did you mean exactly? Because what *I* understood was an invitation to spend the night with you."

Bromly guffawed with a snort, and he cleared his throat. "Sorry, it's not my business," he mumbled, unable to suppress his entertained expression.

"Aya," Flint grumbled, searching for the right words. "I figured you're from Burge. I assumed Darric brought ya here for—"

"Don't say it!" I interrupted before he could openly declare he thought I was a prostitute.

"It's just, you're really pretty an' . . . it jus' came out."

"If you want a civil relationship with me, you will not insult me so lewdly again."

He gave a dejected nod. When he looked up, his eyes had caught fire. He snarled at the Hovel door and went inside.

"Don't be so hard on him," Bromly advised, setting his bowl on the log. "He has no idea what he's doing. He hasn't been around many decent women."

"How could he accuse me of being a—"

Yelling inside the Hovel silenced me. Then a crash—metal blasting against wood.

Bromly cursed under his breath and pushed to his feet by pressing his hands into his knees.

"What's going on? What are they fighting about?" I asked, worried.

"Um, they get into it sometimes . . . brothers." He stuck a finger under his cap to scratch his head. "Could I ask you to stay here while I sort this out?"

I nodded hastily, not wanting to be caught in the volatile confrontation.

After Bromly went into the Hovel, the unintelligible rage abated.

The cat jumped onto the log and softly meowed. I sat next to her and ran my hand along her back. She purred when my fingers dug into her fur. "I'm not afraid of Flint. He is no more intimidating than a bunny," I confided. "But Darric . . . there is something unnerving about him. I've never known anyone so confident in who they are. It's like he knows his own future."

She grunted in agreement.

"I wonder what made them so angry."

The burgundy feline emitted a low growl.

"I appreciate you trying to communicate with me, but it would be easier if you just spoke."

The fur door flew aside. Darric rushed through the cavern and out into the valley. Flint quickly followed, stopping at the stone entrance. His eyes watered. His fair skin was ablaze. He let out a fitful holler that echoed inside the cavern.

"That's enough!" Bromly's round belly puffed, and his bushy eyebrows cast an intimidating shadow over his walnut eyes.

Flint furiously plopped down next to me. He tucked his shaking arms into his belly and stared ferociously into the fire.

I tilted my head, trying to catch his gaze. "Are you all right?"

His chest quivered. "It's Darric." He spat the name as if it had a foul taste. "He jus' . . . he makes me so damn mad."

I placed a hand on Flint's shoulder and massaged my fingers into the muscle. Irked as I was by his recent assumptions about my past, I still didn't enjoy seeing him in such disarray.

Bromly took a seat across the fire, and the cat surprised me by lying next to him. She pressed the top of her head against his hand and purred.

"I'm sure he didn't mean whatever he said," I offered.

"What would ya know about it?" Flint seethed. I retracted my hand. "Ya don't know what it's like livin' in his shadow. Havin' an' older brother who thinks he can control ya."

"Stop being so contemptuous and dramatic," Bromly said, moving his fingers to the cat's chin.

"And don't be so quick to assume I haven't experienced something similar," I added, sliding away from him. He would never understand the oppression of having a Divine sibling who would be King. I knew well the shadow of an older brother. Luken and Darric weren't different in that aspect.

"You have a brother?" Bromly perked up, his cheeks warming back into their rosy color.

I nodded. "He always tried to protect me. Isn't Darric doing the same for the both of you?"

"An older brother?" He ignored my question by asking his own.

"Yes."

"Just the one?"

I stared at my shoes, avoiding his inquiry. Bromly had noticed my ignorance towards peasant life. I had no intention of allowing him to figure out any more about my past. "It doesn't matter. I'll never see my family again."

"Hmm . . ." He squinted at me and grunted. "It's frustrating that you refuse to tell us a single thing about yourself. What province are you from? What's your surname?"

"I don't have one." Was that unusual? Divine royals are named after the court of their fathers. Born under the Rose Court, *Rose* followed my name, but it wasn't a surname. It simply identified me as Brisleian royalty. As if the Mandala wasn't enough.

He stroked his beard, obviously curious. "The Duke of Burge has four sons. They are promiscuous." I did not need to be schooled on the lifestyle of the Sloan brothers. I knew well their love for women. "I've heard when they produce a child out of wedlock, the duke takes it upon himself to care for the *accident* so it doesn't cause a scandal. They're just rumors, but the Burge manor is awful big."

It was reputed the Duke of Burge, Richard Sloan, and his four sons housed a multitude of young girls borne from years of infidelity and married them to wealthy merchants before they came of age. It was not an uncommon practice among all dukes of Athera, but it was always done furtively.

It was an insult to be thought of as one of too many illegitimate daughters resulting from the Sloan brothers' hedonism, but if it kept my companions' minds away from Alamantia Palace, then so be the misconception. My former life had to be a forgotten memory. Apparently, I dropped out of the sky at eighteen like a falling star.

"Maybe you'll be more likely to talk after we visit the tavern in Burge." Bromly chortled and plucked his empty soup bowl from the log to ladle himself a second helping.

"If Darric doesn't kill her first." Flint scoffed, his tone still belligerent.

"He's not going to hurt me. It's just an empty threat." Though knowing Darric's motive hardly brought comfort.

Flint slammed his fist into his palm. "Damn it, if I could wield a sword, I could stop him."

Bromly raised both eyebrows in skepticism.

"You can't wield a sword?" I asked.

Flint shook his head. "Only a bow, an' a bow is no good against Darric. He won't teach me weaponry. He says I'm too unstable." His lips quivered. "What does he know?"

"He wouldn't teach me either. He said I am erratic and lack control," I confided.

Flint gasped. "Ya asked him to teach ya to wield a sword?"

Bromly's eyes widened, a spoonful of stew paused near his mouth.

"Yes. I've never seen anyone so skilled. I can't stay here forever, and if I can fight, it may prevent me from being kidnapped by bandits again."

"You wasted your breath," said Flint. "Darric won't teach anyone."

"He has commendable reasons for that, Flint," Bromly expressed, putting his full spoon back into the bowl.

"Like I care 'bout his reasons. I'm his frickin' brother."

"Why won't he teach anyone?" I asked.

"He was forced in the past." Bromly placed his bowl on the bench, as if he'd lost his appetite. "He's always been exceptional with weapons, and he's cocky because he knows it, but I'm not sure he's capable of becoming anyone's instructor. His technique is his own, and no one fully trained him."

"You expect me to believe Darric is just preternaturally gifted in violence?" When I said it out loud, it didn't seem that unfathomable.

Flint reached over the fire and stole the remainder of Bromly's meal. He gulped several mouthfuls from the side of the dish before wiping his lips on his sleeve and burping. I slid to the end of the log to avoid the bits of stew flying from his mouth.

"I was lucky to make it this far," I continued. "I won't be able to travel without some general knowledge of combat."

"I'd volunteer to teach you if I knew anything about it, but my skills are centered around cooking and tanning hides," Bromly explained.

I shot him a sidelong glance. He may not have known how to beautifully flourish a sword like Darric, but he had strength he humbly refused to admit. He had gruesomely killed one of the bandits. Though clumsy and lacking skill, he wasn't helpless.

Finished with the stew, Flint scooped a charred potato from the coals. The spud looked dreadful and burned to a crisp. He dug his finger into the flesh and peeled away the skin, revealing the bland mush, and blew at the steam before sinking in his teeth. "I taught myself to use a bow." He let out short puffs of air to cool the burning morsel in his mouth. "I'm not the best shot, an' a bow isn't much good in hand-to-hand combat unless ya whack 'em upside the head with it, but I can teach ya to shoot straight."

"Flint!" Ecstatic, I flung my arms around his bony shoulders and pulled him into my chest, knocking the spud from his grasp. "That would be wonderful!"

He leaned into my hug, and his large hand covered my back. "I'll teach ya, but no more talk of ya leavin'. I like havin' ya here." He smiled widely, displaying bits of mashed food stuck in his teeth. "I'll make a bow for ya right now!"

"We have a lot of work to do," Bromly interjected.

"Right, right, but I have to make Aya a bow first." He licked the last bits of potato off his fingers and stole the axe on his way out of the cavern.

Bromly took a deep breath, his chest and stomach expanding into one bulbous mass. "He's becoming too scatterbrained."

I had not intended for Flint to vanish into the woods in search of material for a suitable bow. My insistence on learning to use a weapon would put them further behind in their work. As penance, I offered my assistance, but Bromly claimed teaching me to work hides would take longer than the time available.

Flint returned in under an hour, dragging the trunk of a skinny, flexible tree into the cavern. He immediately began stripping the bark with an undeniable twinkle in his eyes. As the afternoon turned into evening, the tree changed from a stripped piece of wood to a small bow roughly three and a half feet long. The bow was simple—wide in the grip, tapered at the limbs—and bent beautifully into a crescent after he tied handmade cordage from one end to the other. He finished by nightfall and, as a tribute to his creation, shot an arrow out of the cavern, allowing it to sail away without a target.

Darric emerged from the darkness, his eyes following the projectile until it disappeared. He raised an eyebrow at the new weapon.

"I'm gonna teach Aya to use a bow!" Flint enthused.

Darric looked in my direction, as if he was trying to determine who had suggested the ridiculous idea. "When?" he inquired skeptically. The heavy lids of his eyes were rimmed in red, and the forbidding posture he generally held had weakened into a slight slump. He appeared exceedingly exhausted.

"Tomorrow, after breakfast." Flint smiled as he revealed his plan.

"Good luck with that," Darric demeaned and proceeded into the Hovel.

"Darric?" Bromly called, causing the grumpy brother to pause by the door.

"I'm fine," Darric muttered and went inside.

Bromly and Flint ate the remainder of the stew for supper, and Flint fell asleep playing his flute. He snored in a haphazard position, his legs sprawled messily on the ground and his upper half propped against the log. His neck craned back so far it almost looked broken, and his mouth hung open.

"He looks uncomfortable," I said to Bromly.

"I've often thought the same." He busily rinsed the dinner bowls in a warm bucket of water. "He'll sleep through the night that way. I used to attempt moving him to his room, but he's a heavy sleeper, and several times he nearly rolled into the fire when I disturbed him. I don't fight *that* battle anymore."

I giggled, tugging a rag free from his belt to help dry the wet dishes. Each was identical. Darric had superb craftsmanship. When we had finished, I collected the stack and offered to take them to the workbench.

I cradled the armful of dishes against my belly and stepped inside the Hovel. It was dark save for the occasional flame sparking to life over the glowing orange embers. Next to the dwindling fire, Darric sat leaning against the wooden bench, one leg stretched out and the other bent close to him. His hand was clamped, ever ready, on the hilt of his sword. His chest slowly moved as he slept.

The eye of the storm.

"I thought you never slept," I whispered, tiptoeing to the worktable. Only sheer exhaustion could have forced him to close his eyes.

After our walk, I felt more connected to him. Internally, he was more like me than any person in Athera; images floated in his brain too. I didn't feel so alone anymore.

I set down the bowls so quietly I wouldn't have roused a mouse. Next to the additional cutlery sat the collection of Darric's whittled dragons. Each piece of artwork was carved in immaculate detail, some with scales, some with wings, some with two legs, others with four. Lying on its side amid the standing creatures was the single dragon Flint had stolen from me and tossed away like scrap wood. I plucked it from its fallen position and placed it upright to join the fleet.

When I retracted my hand, my elbow smacked into the stack of freshly washed bowls, sending a cascade of objects skidding across the worktable and tumbling the mess of dishes to the floor. I'd spent hours of despised *etiquette training* perfecting grace and poise, only to clumsily knock over a collection of cutlery when I should have been quiet.

Darric's eyes shot open.

He vaulted to his feet, sword drawn; the echo of a raked scabbard lingered in the air, and the brilliant sparkle of shimmering metal danced off the walls. I caught only a fleeting image of his body accelerating towards me before he slammed me to the ground. The leaf litter crunched under my back, and my bones rattled on impact. It happened so rapidly my head spun as I tried to make sense of up and down.

He hovered over me, his eyes foreign, shaded to a dark gray and searing with fear, confusion, and pain. The stability always present through his body had disappeared, replaced by demented, calculated movements. His muscles tensed, ripped with adrenaline. The edge of his sword found my neck. Cold. Sharp.

This was it!

Darric Ursygh was going to kill me.

I screamed until blood emerged in the back of my throat. The blade sliced into my skin, followed by a paralyzing sting as my flesh started to separate. I closed my eyes, feeling the first trickle of blood seep down the side of my neck.

"Darric! Stop!" Bromly's shriek exploded inside the Hovel. His husky frame plowed into Darric, and they both tumbled to the floor. Darric rolled like dead weight, giving his brother no fight, and his sword slid out of his reach. Bromly pinned his brother to the floor with his knees, took two fistfuls of his shirt, and violently shook him. "Wake up, damnit! Wake up!"

I grasped my wet and sticky throat. The top of my dress was soaked from the steady stream of blood.

Flint's hands came from behind and helped me sit up. He wrapped his skinny arms around my torso and pulled me into his chest. "She's bleedin'!" I could feel his ribcage through his clothes. The fragility of his body and scarecrow-like arms failed to dispel the absolute terror coursing through my veins. "You're gonna be okay, Aya."

I gasped, finally filling my lungs with air.

The darkness in Darric's eyes flickered, then faded into a beautiful shade of steel blue. He shoved his brother off his chest, and Bromly tumbled backwards towards the embers. Darric stared blankly at the ceiling, then rubbed his palms over his face before slowly sitting up and reaching for his sword.

Without taking a moment to rest, Bromly rushed to where Flint cradled me. He wiped sweat from his brow as he tore a rag from his belt and shoved it against my neck. "Keep pressure on it."

Flint slapped his hand over the cloth to hold it in place.

Raking his fingers through his disheveled hair, Darric closed his eyes and let out a long breath that made his body quake. He stabbed his sword into the ground and laid his forehead on the pommel, gripping the hilt with such force his knuckles turned white. A chorus of the most obscene language I'd had ever heard burst from his lips.

"How could ya let her in here with him?" Flint scolded Bromly. "She coulda been killed!"

"I had no idea he was asleep," Bromly retorted. "I asked him earlier. He said he was fine."

"It was too close." Flint's face contorted unpleasantly. "What if we hadn't gotten to her in time?"

Bromly pulled Flint's hand away from my neck so he could assess the damage. "It doesn't look deep. I'm so sorry, Aya. I never would have allowed you in here had I known he was asleep. He hasn't slept inside the Hovel in a very long time."

"He can't control himself. He's going to murder one of us." Flint's angry heart pounded against my back, and the smell of burned potato and sour meat on his breath turned my stomach. He peered around Bromly at Darric. "Why the hell are ya here? You're not supposed to be here when you're like this."

Darric looked up from his sword. "Both of you, get the fuck out," he said in a menacingly deep rumble.

Bromly took to his feet as if his toes had been burned by hot coals. Flint placed his hands under my arms to lift me from the floor.

"Leave her here," Darric instructed, his words low and clipped.

"Not a chance in bloody hell!" Flint shrilled, pulling at my arms.

Darric squeezed the bridge of his nose. The fear coursing through me began to dissipate. His actions had not seemed intentional, and he was clearly reeling with remorse.

"Let's go." Bromly wrapped his hand around Flint's bicep to tug him from the ground.

"No! I'm not leavin' her with him." Flint slapped Bromly's hand. "I'm not goin' anywhere without her. Not tonight. Not ever."

Bromly twisted his fingers into Flint's tunic. "You need to give him a chance to explain."

"GET OUT!" Darric's rage broke the surface with a blast like canon fire. It sent a new wave of panic rushing through my weakened muscle. An eerie quiet fell over the room, pierced only by the crackle of leftover embers.

"Do as he says," I said feebly. No threat of death was going to make me leave the Hovel. Darric had been dreaming, and I wanted his explanation even if it meant facing him alone.

Flint's face morphed into heartache. "You can't be serious?"

"Go," I whispered near his ear.

"I'm not leavin' ya," he murmured.

"Yes. You. Are." Bromly jerked him by the collar and dragged him across the floor. Without the support of Flint's arms, I dropped to the rug, and the rag fell from my neck.

"This is suicide, Aya," Flint blubbered. "Bromly, stop!" He tried rolling to break loose, but Bromly shoved him through the front door. Flint's hysterical wailing became incoherent, and Bromly's calming words were lost among the erratic sobbing.

"He is so stubborn," I muttered, reaching for the rag to place it back at my neck. I tugged at the bright red fabric of my chemise.

Darric released a breath and pulled his sword from the ground. Pointing it towards the ceiling, he rotated the grip and gazed hatefully at the blade. The light reflected off the metal, casting eerie shadows across his features as he ran his thumb over the smear of my blood. He rubbed his fingers together and examined the strange glittering red that came off on his hands.

I shivered. Had I made a mistake by staying alone with him?

Finally, he stood and slid the sword back into his scabbard. My pulse regulated once it disappeared.

Darric took a firm hold of my arms and lifted me onto the fireside bench. Sinking beside me, he pushed my almond curls away from my face and tilted my head to expose the bleeding cut. "The only Fae I've ever been able to protect, and I almost kill her," he mumbled.

"What?" I jerked my head down. "What are you talking about? You wanted to kill me. You said—"

"I know what I said." Irritated, he pulled a handful of my curls to force my head back once more. I stared at the ceiling. "If I am going to kill you, I want to be awake for it." The tips of his fingers grazed the gash. "If I do something that psychotically abhorrent, I want to remember it. I would want your death to haunt me."

"You're not making sense."

He retrieved his haversack and brought it to the worktable, shoving an armful of wooden carvings out of his way to dig into it. When he returned, he held a damp pristine white linen cloth.

I spotted the burgundy cat slowly walking the perimeter of the room, the hair on her back fluffed and her silver claws bared. *Now you decide to come to the rescue?*

"This is going to sting." He ran the cloth over my collarbone to wipe away the blood, each swipe inching closer to the cut until the linen hit the wound. A sharp pain singed my neck. I hissed in a breath and tried to pull away, but Darric kept a hand on the back of my head and pressed the cloth firmly to the torn flesh. Within moments the shocking sting had dulled to a lingering soreness.

"I saw you asleep," I exhaled when the pain faded.

"It's been weeks since I've slept." He took the cloth from my neck and folded it. "I should have seen it coming, but I've been distracted. Still, my inattentiveness doesn't excuse this. I'm not going to ask you to forgive me."

"Distracted by what?"

He gently patted my skin with the fabric. "You look better than I would have expected. Not everyone who wakes me up fares so well."

Frustrated by his deflecting, I snatched the linen from his grasp. "Stop changing the subject and answer me!" I demanded. "Don't apologize. I don't care. My days are obviously numbered in this valley. I just want answers. I don't want to die and never know the truth about you. Don't you understand that you are the first person to make me feel like I'm not alone?"

He stared into my eyes for a long moment. I stiffened as the flash of courage I had managed to summon dissipated. "I know that, Aya. It's reciprocated."

A small smile crossed my lips as he ran his thumb along my jaw.

"What do you dream about?" he asked.

I fumbled with the linen. "That's rather personal."

"I've never been able to ask someone that question." He turned away and rubbed his palms together uncomfortably.

"It's difficult to explain." I lowered my gaze to the wad of fabric. It was no longer pristine but smeared with blotches of bright crimson.

"And?" He leaned towards me, resting his elbows on his knees. His eyes caught mine, and my cheeks flushed. What an inappropriate time to feel coy. My stranger had almost ended my life, and I could still go to pieces under his charm.

"I'm sort of . . . floating . . . or flying."

He half grinned and released a small laugh. "Flying?"

"That's the closest thing that describes it. I'm on a blank slate where I can create anything I want. But I never do. I only know that I can. I've always been so disturbed by it that I force myself to wake up. That's why I decided to stop sleeping. I wanted to avoid the insanity. Of course, I don't seem to need much sleep either."

He took the cloth from me and refolded it back into a square.

"It's strange to say that out loud," I admitted.

"I envy you."

"Why?"

He wiped a trickle of blood from my chest, running the linen from my sternum up to the wound. "I've never had to explain myself to anyone other than my brothers." He took my hand and placed my fingers over the cloth. "Keep pressure on it so the bleeding stops."

I nodded so he would continue.

"My dreams are not pleasant. I'm certainly not flying. I'm preyed upon by my past. I relive things I want to forget. Over and over. Never able to look away. Always seeing the same scenes as vividly as the day they happened. It makes me volatile. I'm going to end up killing someone I care about someday."

"I've never dreamt anything like that."

"You are a Fae. I'm not," he pointed out. "My dreams are the result of a side effect." He eased his sword out of the scabbard and laid it on the floor in front of us. "They began after I acquired this. Ever since, it's been chaos. Reaching for a sword has always been my first reaction, so when the dreams started, it became a lethal combination. Especially when I can't wake up quick enough to stop my actions."

"So, you didn't know what you were doing?"

"Sometimes I do, sometimes I don't."

"And tonight, did you know?"

"Let's just say you would be dead if I had not managed some form of consciousness. I've attacked Bromly and Flint, but they are used to being cautious around me when I start to show signs of exhaustion. Usually I sleep far from the Hovel. That's why I gave you my room. I can't use it anyway. I should have warned you how dangerous I am."

Bromly and Flint were still arguing by the outside fire. I tried to keep my head straight. Time was dwindling; Bromly wouldn't be able to keep Flint out of the Hovel forever.

"If it's the sword causing this, why do you have it?" I asked. "Get rid of it."

"It's not that simple. I've tried to separate myself from it, and things only get worse. I'm bound to it somehow. I must keep the sword in my possession. The responsibility of keeping it out of the wrong hands fell to me. The problem is, I *am* the wrong hands. I wasn't supposed to have it, and it punishes me."

"How did you acquire such a horrific thing?"

He paused, studying the blade. "I'm not ready to tell you that."

My heart sank, and I felt alone again. "You really aren't like me."

"I'm sorry. I know you want answers to your dreams, but I can't give them to you."

"Do Bromly and Flint know about this?"

"Yes, and they know more than I'm willing to reveal to you tonight. I just didn't feel it was in anyone's interest to leave you in the dark now that I've managed to physically harm you."

Flint's whimpering grew noticeably louder. Darric turned his gaze to the door, waiting for it to open, but the fur stayed shut. "I don't need Bromly and Flint knowing you dream. You can imagine the trouble that would cause."

I sighed. "The consensus is still that Dreamers belong in prison, institutionalized by the Senate."

"Precisely." He slid his sword back into the scabbard.

"Great." *More lies to add to my double life.* "And yet you are protecting me because I'm a Fae."

He touched his finger to my bottom lip. "You are eventually going to understand how toxic that word really is. My brothers are right outside the door. This conversation isn't private anymore."

I scowled, pushing his finger from my mouth. "I think it's toxic that you threaten to kill me, yet somewhere behind a dreamlike haze, you were trying to prevent your body from cutting my head off. You aren't an evil person—difficult and deranged, but not evil."

He shrugged. "You say that because you don't know me."

"Why do you deny saving my life? If it hadn't been for you, I would have died in a cave, or in the woods from poison, or at the hands of a corrupt bandit. Nothing you have done has been as heinous as what I've already had to overcome. I thought my life was over the day I ran away from home, but because of you I'm still alive."

He shifted closer, lowering his voice to a murmur. "Where are you from? All of your kind are in Medial Alexandria by the age of ten. I didn't believe there was any place left in Athera out of the reach of the Onyx Guard. I would know. I've been around."

Being so close to him filled my face with heat, and I absentmindedly removed the cloth from my neck. "The Hovel is more exciting."

"Sure, blood and death. Thrilling." He tilted my head to expose my open skin, being considerably gentler this time. "The bleeding stopped." He plucked the linen from my hand and tossed it into the fire. It immediately ignited, adding brief light to the dim room. "Still, I'm not going to keep divulging information without some sort of compensation."

I furrowed my brows. "What sort of compensation? What do you want?"

Darric lasciviously smirked and opened his mouth to answer, but the fur door swished aside. He rapidly slid to the opposite side of the bench.

Flint crossed the Hovel in a few large steps and knelt before me. The whites of his eyes were bloodshot and flooded with unfallen tears. "Are you okay?"

"I'm fine," I replied curtly. My mind burned with curiosity over what Darric had meant by *compensation*. Flint's fingers inched towards the laceration. I swatted his hand. "Don't touch it. It's sore."

Bromly hastily came through the door. "Flint, you're an unbelievable ass. Give him time to explain."

"He's had time," Flint argued. "How much longer can it take for him to explain that he's a psychopath?"

"Flint!" Bromly warned, but Darric raised his hand to stop him.

"Don't worry about it." He joined Bromly by the door. "We're done."

"So . . . she knows?" Bromly pressed.

Darric gripped his brother's shoulder reassuringly. "Enough." He pushed aside the fur and went into the cavern.

"How'd she handle it? How much did you tell her?" Bromly followed, leaving me uncomfortably alone with Flint.

"I'm so mad at him for hurtin' ya. It's unacceptable. He never shoulda come near the Hovel if he was sleepy," Flint grumbled.

"Let it go." I groaned. "I'm alive, and it wasn't his fault."

Disgust warped his face. "You're kiddin', right? He has more control over it than he lets on." He raised his sleeve, showing me the underside of his forearm. His strikingly pale skin was dotted with little tan freckles, and a long pink scar stretched from his wrist to his inner elbow. "He did this to me the last time I woke him up. He had to stitch me shut afterwards." He pointed to the tiny holes on either side of the healed gash. "I'm a bowman. I don't get hurt. I had no scars. I'm not covered in my mistakes like he is."

I sneered, growing tired of Flint's constant disparagement of his brother. What was he trying to achieve by continually complaining about Darric's transgressions?

"Thanks to Darric, I have this reminder that my brother is a—" He stopped midsentence upon seeing my face; my sneer had turned into a scowl. "Okay," he relented and squeezed the meat on my thigh, "I'll let it go."

I softened my expression and shoved his hand off my leg. "Thank you."

Chapter 15

I pulled back on the bowstring. The weight of the draw cut into my fingertips. My muscles ached into a tingling fire across my shoulders and chest and down my back, but I held tight to the grip. I didn't want to seem weak, even when my arms began shaking from the strain.

Flint explained the draw weight on my bow would be around forty pounds. *Forty pounds.* I felt every bit of it. The wood made an odd crackling sound as I stretched the cordage to my cheek. The feathers at the arrow's end tickled my skin.

Darric leaned against the stone arch of the cavern, brandishing a small knife between his fingers. In his other hand he held a chunk of wood he had been transforming into a currently unrecognizable animal shape, but he lost interest in carving the moment the bow was in my possession. His observation made me unsteady; I had not anticipated him lingering around the Hovel to spectate. He was already smirking in a derogatory fashion.

Bromly sat by the fire, sewing together dozens of various-colored rabbit pelts with a large bone needle and thick leather thread to create a beautiful furry patchwork quilt. The work needing to be done had not stopped him from picking a seat close to the edge of the cavern for the best view of the morning's entertainment.

The arrow wobbled. For such a light piece of wood, it created an uncanny amount of pressure on my forefinger. My arms trembled, begging for the release of the bowstring.

Fifty feet in the distance, a skinny pine tree had an apple-sized circle drawn on it with a piece of charcoal. The poor target was difficult to see.

I stared into the black dot, taking in its awkward shape that lumped on one side, and struggled to remember Flint's vague instruction. The position of my feet—apart. Back straight—the immaculate posture of a Divine royal. Both eyes open. I had no idea what I was doing. I had expected more direction before he handed me the bow and blankly told me to "shoot an arrow."

I exhaled a hard breath and tried to force myself to concentrate, but movement distracted me. Darric's half-whittled creature hurtled in my direction. It hit me upside the head and landed with a thud by my feet. Startled, I released my grip, and the bow fell downwards, shooting the arrow into the dirt and sending an explosion of soil into the air.

I narrowed a stern look at my stranger. "Was that necessary?"

He cocked his head to the side with a satisfied expression. "Next time it will be a knife." He spun the blade in his hand for emphasis.

"Ignore him, Aya." Flint retrieved the fallen arrow and handed it back to me. "He does the same thin' to me when I'm tryin' to practice, 'cept he uses rocks."

I tapped the arrowhead on my shoe to knock off loose dirt and restrung the bow. My arms grew sore, and I struggled to make them cooperate. Searching the tree line, I found the pine bearing the black mark.

I inhaled. *Back straight.*

My shoulders shook. *Both eyes open.*

I exhaled. *Feet sturdy.*

Darric's knife spun through the air and sliced the stone head clean off my arrow. The knife landed blade-first in the dirt, his impeccable aim leaving me armed with merely a bow and a feathered stick.

"Darric!" I shrieked, lowering the useless weapon. "What are you trying to accomplish?"

He bent his leg back against the rock. "So, take the shot already. Summer only lasts so long in Brisleia."

Irked, I snatched a new arrow from Flint's quiver. I nocked it against the bowstring, pulled back, and let the projectile fly without care. "Satisfied?" I dropped the bow in a huff just as the twang of splintered wood echoed through the morning valley.

Everyone's attention turned to the marked pine. My arrow pierced the center of Flint's target. I gaped, and Darric let out an enthusiastic laugh.

"Okay?" Puzzled, Flint laid his hand on top of his head. "I don't think ya were lookin' that time. Ya can't always rely on luck . . ." He paused, examining the pine. "We'll keep tryin' . . ."

He brought me a new arrow. I readied myself. After three hard pulls on the bowstring, my arms were too weak to draw back as far as I needed. I quickly found the target and gave in to my body's demand to let the arrow loose. It traveled in a beautiful arch and landed directly on top of my previous shot, continuing through the trunk to leave a gaping hole.

Stunned, I shook my head in disbelief.

Flint rubbed his eyes and wrinkled his tapered nose. "There's no way ya had enough power to do that. I watched ya." He ran to inspect the tree.

"Do it again." Darric concealed his smile by running his tongue over his teeth.

"I most certainly cannot," I said.

His brows lowered, and the smile dimmed. "That sort of doubt is why I will never teach you to wield a sword. That, and your evident lack of actual concentration and control." He slid a second knife out of his leather bracer.

I wanted to wield a sword. Darric's elegant skill entranced me. If I was ever to be the same caliber of lethal assassin, I had to prove I was capable.

I took another arrow, drew my bow, and shot the weapon towards the pine.

"Whoa!" Flint spun around as the arrow whizzed by him. It slid through the hole and disappeared into the forest. "Aya!" I could see the whites of his eyes even from a distance. "That's stupid an' dangerous! Ya coulda hit me! Wait till I'm clear!"

A bizarre confidence filled my chest; it flooded my arms with cool liquid and twisted my brain. For some unknown reason, I was positive I would not hit him, no matter how many arrows I sent gliding in his direction. This weapon yielded to me, even if my muscles loathed me for it.

"Impressive." Darric grinned, crossing his arms over his chest. "Again."

I gulped and reached for Flint's quiver.

An hour later, six arrows had left an additional four holes down the center of the pine.

Flint decided to change tactics. He retrieved a new bit of charcoal from the fire and ran to the forest edge, one hundred feet from the cavern. This time, he made smaller marks on three different trees, each at varying heights and far away from one another.

"It's like he wants me to miss," I observed, watching him scurry between the trees.

"Wouldn't you?" Darric asked. "He offers to teach you to use a bow, and you are better than him. It's not exactly the ego stroke he was hoping for."

"You could have told him you're a talented archeress before you decided to humiliate him." Bromly laughed.

Darric rolled his eyes.

"I've never used a bow in my life!" I insisted. I couldn't start a fire or peel a potato; how could he assume I was an expertly trained archeress?

"Let's rub salt into this wound, shall we?" Darric suggested.

"No," Bromly discouraged, putting an end to his sewing.

"Aya, put on Flint's quiver so you have arrows at the ready, and hit his targets consecutively."

"What good will that do?" My arm was sending shocks of pain into my shoulder. I gripped high on my bicep and massaged my fingers into the muscle. "I don't know if my arm will allow it. Besides, it's too easy. There is no challenge involved," I grudgingly admitted, not wanting to tell him how clearly I could see the targets. They didn't seem one hundred feet away but rather right in front of me. I felt I could reach out and touch them.

"Taking the last three shots perfectly will put an end to this nonsense and get Flint back to work," Darric explained. "Bear season is about to start. He needs to help Bromly with hides instead of avoiding his responsibilities making arrows and new bows. We are behind, and bear kills will overwhelm us if he is distracted by unnecessary archery lessons."

"I can't argue with that logic." Bromly folded his rabbit blanket and neatly added it to a pile of others. "But I wish you'd come up with a less insulting method to get him refocused."

"Aya?" Darric waited for me to acknowledge his plan.

I reached for the bundle of arrows, moved my hair aside, and slung the quiver over my shoulder, tying the fastenings around my chest.

Flint finished marking the pine trunks and jogged towards us. I slipped an arrow from the quiver, strung it into place, aimed at the target farthest to the left, and released. The twang of wood echoed when the arrow stabbed the trunk directly on the black mark. Immediately, I drew a replacement. My weakened muscles trembled, but I let the arrow fly at the last moment before my fingers gave out.

Flint spun to watch the second shot zip past him and replace the middle pine's charcoal circle with a hole. "Aya!" he squealed in alarm. "Stop!"

I nocked the final arrow into place and tugged the bowstring back to my cheek. "Shit!" Flint ducked, covering his head with his forearms as the final shot whistled through the air and made a defiant wooden bang through the last tree.

I dropped the bow and cried out, clutching my shoulder. Sharp spasms ripped into my hand and across my chest.

"That was brilliant!" Bromly shouted and doubled over with laughter.

"You probably should have waited until he was back." Darric chuckled, sliding his knife into his bracer.

"I'm done." I shook my head and winced. "No more archery."

Flint stomped his feet like a child upon reaching the cavern. Sweat dripped from his temples, and he turned a dark scowl on Darric. "I take it that was your dumb idea?"

Darric held up his hands in surrender. Bromly rubbed his fingers into his beard, trying to stop the flow of laughter.

A wave of remorse hit me when I realized I'd been part of a joke meant to torment Flint. "I'm sorry." I grimaced, rolling my shoulder.

"Sorry? You're sorry!" Flint shrieked. "Next time, don't take Darric's fucked-up advice an' ya won't have to be *sorry*. Or better, don't lie to me 'bout your experience so ya can join in on his shitty games an' mock my skill."

Darric uncrossed his arms and laid a hand on the hilt of his sword. Pushing away from the cavern wall, he started to circle like a predator.

"I would never purposefully seek to humiliate you," I told Flint. "I had no idea what I was doing. I would never ask you to teach me if I meant to insult you."

"Really?" He pointed to the hole-riddled pines. "That suggests otherwise. An' ya know what I think? After bein' kidnapped by bandits, ya were disarmed an' needed a bow made. All of this was jus' your way of gettin' somethin' ya wanted so the three of us might take ya seriously."

"Stop it!" I demanded in the same authoritative tone I used to command my ladies. Apparently, anger could bring *Ayleth* out of hibernation.

"I thought ya were smart. I can't believe ya would do anythin' Darric suggested. So from now on, he can teach ya. I'm not wastin' my fuckin' time with someone who disrespects me."

I tore off the leather strap of his quiver. The mess fell to the ground, and I kicked the bundle into Flint's leg. Arrows skidded across the dirt, the shafts snapped, and fletchings flew into the air.

I had to get away from them. I stormed through the cavern and shoved open the fur door of the Hovel.

Tears welled in my eyes as I paced from the bedrooms to the front wall and back again. Of course it had been wrong to brazenly shoot arrows at Flint. I should have waited until he returned, but I had been too enamored by the mind-bending sensation running through my veins—the absolute certainty I wouldn't hit him. How did Darric continue to fog my reasoning to such an extent?

And Flint! How dare he talk to me that way! I might have the appearance of a peasant, but inside I was still Divine royalty. No one should ever speak to me so boldly, or they would risk imprisonment! At a moment's notice I could return to Alamantia Palace, reveal the location of this wretched cavern, and end everything they knew. *I* had power. *I* was vital. What was Flint? Nothing! A no-name nomadic criminal hiding in the Daraban mountains who couldn't wield a sword.

Anger flowed unchecked within me. I wanted to scream, run outside, and flatten Flint's pointed nose to his face. But before I could act on the consuming rage, a burning sensation traveled across my temple, rounded my ear, and flowed down my neck. It stung and pinched, followed by a surge of nausea. I slapped my hand to my face. *The Mandala.* The distinct texture of the mark dazzled beneath my fingers, dauntlessly declaring her presence.

No-no-no-no-no-no.

I panicked. My thoughts crumbled into a thousand pieces.

Stop thinking about being Divine.

I took in a deep breath and let it out.

Again. Breathe deep. Who are you? Aya. Simple, unadorned Aya, who lives in the mountains of Daraban with three rowdy men who saved her from a life she despised.

I became frantic. My attempts to relax turned into hyperventilation.

The front door moved, and I bolted for Darric's room. I had to hide until I recomposed myself. I had to remember how to make the Mandala vanish. What if I couldn't? What if I couldn't force Ayleth back into the recesses of my core?

The cat came into the Hovel and trotted to where I stood.

I had to focus. I thought back to the night Ambrosia helped me change my fate. I closed my eyes, clutching my fingers over the Mandala.

"What do people see when they look at you? The details of who you are to the world are never the same as what you perceive yourself."

I gripped the bed frame, clenching my teeth.

"Somewhere rooted deep inside of you is the person you want to be. She's foreign to you—someone you have never known but desperately want. Who is she? Envision yourself without the Mandala. Who have you become?"

I shoved Ayleth harder, internally screaming at her to leave the Hovel.

"Fight against it. The Mandala wants to be seen. The Divine part of you will not be forgotten easily. It's not enough to envision yourself without our mark. You have to want to be rid of it. You have to know, with certainty, that you are more than the mark that defines you."

I felt delusional—lost in the same senseless up and down I dreaded when I slept. Ayleth was furious to be cast aside. She did not want to be forgotten. She was stronger than I had ever known.

My entire body quaked. When the tremor subsided, I palmed my skin to find that the telltale glowing mark had vanished beneath healed flesh. A cold sweat drenched my hairline, and swirls of sickness churned my stomach.

I wobbled to the bucket by the workbench and sank my arms into the fresh water. It bubbled and overflowed onto the Hovel floor, at the same moment spraying high into the air and hitting me in the face. I splashed the cool water over my skin, droplets dripping from my chin into the agitated bucket. I tossed my wet hair behind me and buried my face in my hands.

I felt destitute and alienated by this new existence. Even if I wanted to go home, there was nothing left for me at the palace. My parents had betrayed me and sold me into marriage. I was scorned, broken, unloved, and erased.

The cat pressed into my thigh.

I broke into a fit of sobs and gripped the bucket for stability, only to cry out when a sharp pain sparked through my shoulder. I leaned back onto the bench until the sniffles turned to hiccups. My little feline companion crawled into my lap.

The fur covering the entrance of the Hovel moved, and Flint's red head appeared in the opening. He hesitated when he saw me on the floor. Darric's bracered arm grabbed the nape of his tunic and shoved him, stumbling, into the room, and the fur swung shut behind him

Flint's shoulders dropped over his chest. A frown had fallen so low on his face it looked as if he might never smile again. In his hands he held a bouquet of pink and yellow peonies, which he transferred nervously from one fist to the other.

I wiped tears from my cheeks and smoothed damp hair away from my face.

He failed to move, apprehension gluing his feet to the rug. "I . . ." He gulped so hard his larynx bobbed, then licked his lips to wet his dry mouth. "I was an idiot. A huge blasted idiot an' . . ." He squeezed the bouquet, nearly wringing the flowers from their stems. "I'm sorry for the thin's I said an' the way I acted." He swayed on his heels and cautiously approached me.

The cat jumped onto the bench in a protective hover. I crossed my arms and tucked my knees into my chest. I wasn't sure I was ready to forgive his insolence.

He lowered the bouquet, waiting for me to accept his apology, but I stayed silent in my defensive ball. He set the flowers on the ground, and the cat hissed.

"I guess I . . ." His eyes watered as I continued to disregard him. "I understand if ya don't want to talk to me." He turned to leave the Hovel in disgrace.

"Flint." I groaned, exhausted.

He spun around at the sound of my voice, and his watery gaze filled with hope.

"I've never picked up a bow in my entire life," I said. "Nor shot an arrow."

He hung his head. "I believe ya. Darric explained it to me."

"Did he?" I rolled my eyes.

"Darric an' Bromly gave me an earful. Darric pays too much attention, so he made me understand."

I scoffed, unfolding my arms, and pushed my legs out. "What did he say exactly?"

"He said your stance was a mess. Ya lack muscle control. Ya didn't hold the bow straight an' ya have no skill. I don't usually see thin's from his point of view, an' his opinion doesn't matter much to me, but he's right."

I wrinkled my nose, perturbed. "You can always count on that spectacular Ursygh charm. Both of you are abhorrent."

"I don't want us to be mad at each other. I shouldn't've blamed ya for takin' his advice. Darric can be convincin'." He took a seat on the wet ground. "I'd give anythin' to be able to shoot like that. When we were kids, I used to beg Darric to take me travelin' with him, but he never would. He said it was too dangerous for me. So I asked him to teach me to fight. Dual wield, like he does. It's a really complex skill, ya know, kinda rare. I learned to use a bow, but he's always held me back. Now he's got us hidin' in the mountains nine months of the year."

"It was wise of him not to take you. You did not have business joining the Onyx Guard any more than he did. I don't care how much money it brought."

Flint went from remorseful to stunned. "He told ya he was in the Onyx Guard?"

I nodded. "He was trying to protect his family. You have to know that."

"From what? Insane toddlers?" He raked his fingers down his cheeks, and fresh anger warped his face. "Since ya haven't figured it out, let me explain it to ya. Darric hides out here 'cause he's a dishonorable cad an' knows it. This *protection* is jus' control over us."

I raised an eyebrow. "I don't believe that."

"Do ya hear yourself? He brought ya here, remember? He changed all the rules we live by an' tried to pass it off as ya trailin' after him like an abandoned dog."

"I followed him." I repeated Darric's story, though I was not a skilled liar. "I tore myself apart to keep up with him. It nearly killed me."

"Is that what ya really think? You've seen him fight. If Darric didn't want someone followin' him, they wouldn't've survived long enough to take one step in his direction. He knew exactly what he was doin' the second ya started trailin' him. He wanted ya to follow him. He wanted ya here, an' I've been wreckin' my brain tryin' to figure out why."

Flint's claim was hard to deny, though I did not accept his assumption of Darric's nefarious purpose. Darric hadn't known what to do with me and came to the only rational solution: take me to the Hovel. He had tried to walk away but couldn't find the callousness within himself to leave me behind. One of us was very wrong about my stranger.

"At first, I thought I knew his reasonin' . . ." Flint continued. "I thought ya were from Burge an' he'd paid ya to entertain us . . ."

I stiffened at the insinuation.

"But when ya didn't wanna get in bed with me . . . It wouldn't be so bad if he'd jus' own up to it. Admit that when he found ya, he threw out every rule. But that's typical behavior. He does what he wants an' takes what he wants, when he wants."

"I don't intend to stay here. This is supposed to be temporary," I reminded him.

"Darric isn't gonna let ya leave."

"You can't hold me hostage!" I balled my hands and smacked the ground, crushing the bouquet.

His gazed flashed to the discarded petals. "Darric will kill ya 'cause ya know our location. That's all he needs."

I ran my fingers through my hair and dug my nails into my scalp. "You three are the most inconsistent, frustrating group of men I have ever met! Darric is not going to hurt me. I trust him. He hasn't brought me any harm." And he didn't intend to.

"Any harm? You're kiddin'. What do ya call the cut on your neck? Why do you keep makin' excuses for him?"

I didn't have an answer. Speechless, I let my hands drop into my lap.

He blew a puff of hot air. "Amazin'. You're as infatuated with Darric Ursygh as those stupid girls in Burge."

"I'm not infatuated with Darric," I said.

"I see the way ya look at him," he insisted. "You're mesmerized until he sees ya, an' then ya look away, cheeks flushed. Ya can almost see the change in your breathin' an' the beat of your heart through your clothes. It makes me sick," he huffed.

I furrowed my brows, trying to pretend I wasn't fully aware of the effect Darric had on me.

"He's obviously given ya some reason to trust him," he said, poking for information.

The private conversations about Medial Alexandria and dreaming were none of Flint's business. "I am done talking about Darric. I know you came in here to apologize, but you are doing a contemptible job. Every time we talk, you either accuse me of being a prostitute or start an animosity-fueled rant against your brother. It's exhausting, and plainly, I'm finished hearing it."

"Fine." He stood and straightened his tunic. He was so skinny sometimes I forgot how tall he was. "Maybe ya could come huntin' with us." He rocked on the balls of his feet, changing the subject in an obvious attempt to let his anger dissipate. "It would give me the chance to behave myself. Three could be fun. Bromly doesn't hunt."

"You mean . . . you, me, and Darric?" I questioned, because it seemed like a disaster waiting to happen.

He nodded uncomfortably. "You're good with a bow, an' I promise I'll do better to not complain 'bout him. You're a new ear, an' I rant a lot." He gripped a fistful of his tunic to dry his sweaty palms.

Was it possible I made him as nervous as Darric made me? I'd never considered it, but he always seemed to be stumbling through his minutes when alone with me.

"You could try ranting about yourself to give me an opportunity to get to know you, instead of your opinions about your brother," I suggested.

"I'd like that." His smile turned genuine. "Anyway, I had to promise Bromly that I'd work on pelts through lunch . . . an' dinner"—he bobbed his head—"an' in between. If the two of 'em have their way, I'll pass out in a pile of scraped deer hides."

"I gather that once you step out of this room, you are at their mercy?"

"Yes."

I giggled, and the light returned to Flint's eyes. "Best not to keep them waiting."

Chapter 16

Almond curls floated in the temperate air. The blank emptiness of space and time surrounded me, punctuated by twinkling sparks of yellow light. A speck of glitter landed in my hand and disappeared into my skin. My veins began to glow, and an emerald stem sprouted in the center of my palm. Roots spread into my fingers and wrist as the plant branched upwards, unfolding two tiny leaves before budding into a pink flower—a rose, though smaller than any I had ever seen. I plucked the bloom from my hand, and the glistening veins faded.

The wind shifted, and a strong breeze ruffled my hair, carrying with it an intoxicating scent. So enticingly familiar— crushed florals mixed with fresh grass. I inhaled, and my heart fluttered. I wanted this fragrance in my lungs. It was safety. The allure of desire. A reassurance that no harm would ever come to me whenever it was near.

Dark green moss grew across the ceiling of Darric's room, nurturing a system of roots that descended from the odd flowers growing on the roof. I rubbed my face into the fur covers, taking in the musky animal scents of the Hovel.

It was May. Spring had brought heat to the valley. I had been living in the mountains for almost a month.

I had grown to love the simple appeal of Darric's bedroom. Now that I knew him better, there were signs of him everywhere. A pile of spare knives waited in the corner beside a variety of sharpening stones; my stranger did not keep dull weapons. The exquisite sword above his nightstand lacked a cross guard, and the hilt was inlaid with iridescent black mother of pearl, a black diamond pommel, and braided obsidian details along the grip that resembled twisting vines. It was a shame such a gorgeous weapon hung in his room unused.

Wooden hooks on the wall housed his spare shirts and two different cloaks, one heavier and lined with dark rabbit fur. Two freshly carved pegs had been added shortly after my arrival, and my own hooded cloak hung from one of them.

The cat sat on the bedside table next to a bucket that hadn't been there when I'd fallen asleep. I rolled over onto a crushed pile of broken petals. "Ugh." I gripped a handful and clumsily threw them at her. "I don't need crumbled flowers." More floral parts fell from my head as I sat up.

The room had gone dark, and the candle I'd lit yesterday was a hard puddle of tallow on the nightstand. I found a clean cloth hanging over the side of the bucket. After all the time I'd gone without bathing, this was by far the best reason to get out of bed since the sugar-covered strawberries at the palace.

I peeked outside the bedroom. The Hovel was empty. Pulling the fur tightly shut, I tugged the lacing on the front of my dress. The cording stuck together and popped as the knots passed through the frayed eyelets. I had been glued into the dress for so long that once the fabric detached from my skin, I breathed a sigh of relief, just as though I'd been released from a corset. I shook the dress out, and a wave of dirt scattered across the rug. I hung the wretched thing on the only available hook and quickly slipped out of my chemise.

My dirty skin looked appalling. The bucket of water must have been an understated hint from the Hovel brothers. Embarrassed, I pushed the idea aside and made a mental note to bathe more frequently.

The water fizzled at my touch and nearly froze my fingers, but it felt amazing to wash off the grime. I wouldn't have cared if it contained snow from the mountaintop. I quickly scrubbed my face, not knowing when one of my male companions might grace me with his presence. Manners and etiquette were something the three practiced sporadically. I wasn't positive any of them would ask if I was decent before barging into the room.

Flint had done a miraculous turnaround after promising to stop slandering Darric. Most mornings he greeted me outside the Hovel with a bouquet of flowers: roses, peonies, daisies, bearded irises, lupines. I suspected the bath water was from him.

It had taken my shoulder a week to heal after the archery fiasco. When the pain subsided, Flint and I spent a lazy afternoon shooting rabbits from the entrance of the cavern. He showed some envy at my ability to use a bow with untrained accuracy but kept his grudge to a minimum. I quickly learned that moving targets were significantly more challenging than stationary trees. Thankfully, the distance prevented me from hearing the frightened voices of the small creatures.

In the days that followed, Flint told me everything about himself. He was seventeen and confident his birthday was in January. He hated the cold despite living his entire life in Brisleia. His mother had abandoned him on the Alamantia City streets as an infant. Years later, he identified her and used to watch her from the roof of their house. Amazingly, he had no interest in reuniting with this estranged woman and felt only animosity towards her for deserting him.

He loved the salted pork Darric brought from the mountains, and bear fillets were the main course he anticipated every spring. Food relentlessly consumed his mind; he had an insatiable appetite. Some days Bromly would cook three meals simply to satisfy Flint's hunger.

He enjoyed dancing and drinking at the tavern in Burge, and with the journey south drawing closer, his enthusiasm seemed to grow daily, especially as it now seemed almost certain I would be joining them.

After thoroughly washing, I dunked my head into the bucket and filtered water through my hair. I wrung out the curls with a giggle. My baths used to be in a marble basin with warm rose water and honey. Elizabetta would leave me soaking until my toes wrinkled, then wrap me in a heated robe and brush my hair. Today my teeth chattered. Washing in a cold bucket introduced me to a new level of poverty.

I threw my chemise back over my head. The thin cotton clung to my wet skin and, once dampened, did little to keep any modesty intact. I took the dress from the wall, fed my arms into the sleeves, and straightened the bodice until I was once again hidden behind the guise of a peasant.

The cat gave a soft meow at my feet.

"How do I look?" I spun around, dripping hair clinging to my back. "I'm cleaner."

Her whiskers twitched upwards in a small feline grin.

I left Darric's room and stepped out into the cavern, shivering when the outside air hit my skin. Bromly was using an iron skillet to cook trout fillets for breakfast.

Over the last week, the cavern had changed drastically to accommodate the start of bear season. Enormous wooden racks had been crafted to strip, tan, and dry bear hides, and the three had also created tripods for smoking meat and collected stacks of apple wood to infuse the best flavor. The cavern was going to be overwhelmed in a matter of days, and I had the feeling I'd be sick of bear stews by the end of the summer.

Bromly greeted me with rosy cheeks and a welcoming smile. "Wet hair can kill you in Brisleia. Sit down before you freeze," he joked.

I took a seat close to the fire and sighed when the waves of heat hit my face. "Thank you for the water." I clumsily ran my fingers through the damp strands of my hair and worked the long mess into a braid.

"Eh, it was Darric's idea. He said you'd been looking rough lately." He filled a cup of tea from the kettle and handed it to me.

I blew on the rising steam. "I thought Flint might have been the one who brought it."

"No, but he offered to wash you."

I hid an abashed grin, taking my first sip.

Flint came bouncing towards me. He jumped onto the log and kissed my cheek. "Good morning, Aya!" He extended a small bundle of candytufts and, seeing my hands clasping a teacup, placed the flowers in my lap.

"Morning," I repeated, rubbing saliva off my face.

Flint's quiver was strapped to his back, stocked to capacity with new arrows. An unimpressive bandit sword hung from a leather belt looped around his waist.

"Was there someone in the valley?" I dreaded the answer as Darric approached, sheathing his own sword.

"Nope, we're huntin' today," Flint declared. "The bears are awake. Darric saw some last night."

Brisleian short-faced bears were massive. I'd read about them in the library at the palace but never seen one alive. Many of their ostentatious pelts covered the floors of my chambers, worked and treated to be fit for royalty with pearls and crystals sewn into the fur. Seeing one in the flesh would be a spectacular event.

"Isn't it dangerous to hunt a bear fresh out of hibernation?" I asked. Two swords and a bow didn't seem like much use against a colossal predatory animal.

"Yeah, but we get the best pelts from 'em, an' they haven't shed their winter coats yet." Flint tore a chunk of hot fish off the skillet and popped it into his mouth. He blew out, trying to cool the morsel burning his tongue.

"Short-faced bears are lucrative at market," Darric added.

"Take me with you," I demanded and stood up, only remembering Flint's candytufts when they hit my shoes.

Darric laughed. I squinted my eyes and shot him a detesting glare.

"Yes! That'd be great!" Flint enthused. "You can use my spare quiver."

"No." Darric stopped chuckling. "We are not experimenting with hunting techniques eight weeks before Burge."

"Hunting short-faced bears is dangerous for someone with no experience," Bromly interjected.

"I've been hunting rabbits with Flint," I contended. Darric and Bromly looked skeptically at each other. "Can you handle the extra challenge of having me along, Darric?"

"No." He shook his head. "Definitely not while I'm armed."

"You're always armed," I said, pointing to the obvious.

"No rationale for you to come along then, is there?"

"C'mon," Flint begged in a whine.

"Look, I've been understanding about her being here, but there is no possibility she is going on this hunt. It's not about danger or an afternoon spent shooting rabbits. She doesn't have any concept of how to hunt bears. We won't kill anything with her scaring everything she comes across."

"I'll teach her to keep quiet durin' trackin'," Flint argued.

"Are you going to teach her the same way you taught her to use a bow?"

Flint's pale skin changed to a heated pink. He snatched an arrow from his quiver and nocked it into his bow.

Darric didn't flinch. "Go ahead, shoot me," he threatened.

"I want her to go. I'll take the blame if she screws up."

"Thank you for the vote of confidence, Flint," I murmured sarcastically.

"Are you sure you want to do this, Aya?" Bromly snickered.

Darric shot him a stern glance that extinguished his grin, then turned back to Flint. "Full responsibility," he warned.

Flint agreed with a doubtful nod.

Darric groaned, running a hand through his hair. "I'm going to regret this."

Flint lowered his bow and, with an ecstatic leap, ran into the Hovel to retrieve his spare quiver. He reemerged much quicker than I expected. Taking away my teacup, he tossed the quiver over my shoulder and pulled the leather straps around my chest. Suddenly, his delighted expression vanished. He froze, his hands lingering over my breasts.

"Flint!" Darric broke his brother's fascinated gaze into my chest. "She is resourceful. She can put the quiver on herself."

I bit my lip, trying not to giggle, and took the straps from his trembling hands.

"Uh . . . Sss . . . sorry," he mumbled.

Bromly laughed, eating fish straight from the skillet. "Entertaining."

"To say the least. Can we go now?" Darric grumbled impatiently and wandered outside the cavern.

I tied the leather straps in a knot, snatched my bow, and followed Darric with Flint at my heels.

"Make sure you hit the correct spot the first time," Bromly called after us. "Hate to see you come back without a face."

We moved across the open meadows and into the forest, where the thick canopy blocked much of the morning sunlight. Spring brought countless blooms to the grass, tripling the number from a month ago. The cat blissfully bounced among the wildflowers and chased tiny creatures with no concern for keeping up with us.

Darric led the way with an uncanny lightness to his feet. He didn't disturb the soil or rustle the brush, his footsteps barely audible above the chirping of birds and crickets. He listened intently for any small sound that might lead us onto the trail of our prey.

The Sights of the Onyx Guard were known as shadows riding through the night. Unavoidable cloaked assassins. Watching him move through the forest, I understood how easily he had walked into a bandit cave full of dozens of armed men and repeatedly lived to tell the tale. He was trained for it, and still lethal.

My movement was unlike Darric's in every way. My dress dragged along the dirt, swishing and tossing leaves beneath the fabric. The wool tangled in a broken root, and I stumbled and fell backwards into Flint. He dropped his bow to catch me, but the momentum knocked him off balance, and we both tumbled to the ground.

"Damn it!" Darric spun around and held out his hand to help me up. "She is noisier than you, Flint." In one swift motion, he yanked me up from the forest floor. "The gown won't do. You make entirely too much noise with it."

I dusted dead leaves off my dress. "Well, I'm not running about in a pair of trousers."

"You won't need *trousers* because you are not coming with us again. The first day of bear season is not the place to start learning to hunt."

"I can tie up the bottom of your dress for ya," Flint offered.

"No." I did not want anyone seeing Luken's dagger. Over the last month, I'd found comfort knowing I had a secret form of protection.

Darric rolled his eyes and continued moving, but I caught the hint of a smile before he turned away. Was everything a joke to him?

We climbed a rock path to a ledge overlooking a small glen near the Riving. Thin birch trees jutted from the stone around our hiding place, and the river branched into a trickling stream that ran along the glen's edge. The surrounding area was full of rocky cliffs riddled with crevices, and a musky scent filtered through the air. Darric took a seat by the ledge and propped himself up on one of the trees.

Flint sat against the rock face and patted the ground beside him. "Now we wait."

I slid next to him and readjusted my dress over my legs. "For how long?" I asked, pulling my braid off my neck to lay it across my chest. The end pooled into an almond spiral in my lap.

"Long, long." Flint had failed to mention that hunting with the two brothers at odds would include sitting in a confined space with them for an unknown period of time. "We'll move in a couple hours if there's no activity here."

"I thought this would be more exciting," I complained, disappointed.

Darric quietly chuckled. "Excitement is the last thing you want when hunting short-faced bears."

"Is there really the potential of going back to the Hovel without a face?" What I'd perceived as a witty comment started to become less amusing.

"Short-faced bears are tough as steel and unyielding. They are aggressive and will pursue a threat until it's dead. Best to kill them before they have a chance to kill you," Darric answered, keeping his eyes on the glen.

"They only got six months to fatten back up an', ya know, make more bears before goin' back to sleep. It makes 'em kinda edgy," Flint whispered.

"And you're hunting them in the first weeks they are awake? When they're hungry and in a fit of bear lust?" I confirmed, astounded.

"Still glad you came along?" Darric provoked.

"It sounds like a death sentence." I wasn't going to give him the satisfaction of proving I should have stayed at the Hovel.

"There is only one way to bring down a short-faced bear," he began. "You have to pierce an arrow through its heart."

"That's why a bowman is handy." Flint pulled an arrow from his quiver.

"There is a location on the side of the chest where widely spread ribs and softer skin meet near the heart. You wait until the animal gives you an opening and aim behind the shoulder. One well-placed arrow will kill the beast instantly. If you miss, the animal will charge," Darric explained, and I gulped. "Short-faced bears don't typically back down from a threat. Good luck if you miss. It will probably be the last thing you ever do."

Foreboding overwhelmed the atmosphere, and my nerves settled like a rock in the pit of my stomach.

Movement in the glen silenced our conversation. Pine trees swayed at the edge of the forest, defiant of the others surrounding them.

Darric balanced on the balls of his feet and peered off the ledge, and Flint crawled to join him. The woods stilled. My heart thumped. A large mass of rich chestnut-brown fur became visible through the foliage, and a face with dark crimson eyes emerged from the greenery.

Darric put a finger to his lips. I held my breath, fearing even the slightest sound would ignite chaos.

The short-faced bear swaggered out of the tree line and towards the stream with heavy steps, limping slightly on his front paw. If I had not been holding my breath, I would have gasped in shock at the sheer size of the animal. Even while he stood on all fours, his head towered six feet from the ground, and his paws were as wide as my shoulders. He lowered his massive head and drank the fresh water as a second smaller bear broke through the forest. *Smaller* was a relative term, because she stood a mere six inches shorter.

"A pair," Darric mouthed to Flint.

"Both?" he murmured back.

Darric shook his head and pointed to the larger potentially injured male by the stream. "He's old," he observed, keeping his voice low. "The female is too young to take."

Flint nodded in agreement.

Their reasoning humbled me—leaving a healthy young female to continue her life and opting to kill an expiring male. Still, I felt sorry for the grand and beautiful bear. It was a shame his epic life would end this way: hacked to bits, eaten, and skinned.

The old bear turned his right side to us, giving special care to his front paw. The correct position. I waited anxiously for Flint to lace his arrow into the bow and take the killing shot. Instead, he handed the bow and a single arrow to Darric.

Darric nocked the arrow into place and, crouching to his knees, pulled back the bowstring. It revealed a source of brotherly scorn; Flint had base skill in archery, but Darric considered himself a better marksman. Always the expert yet keeping the knowledge to himself, he refused to allow anyone to learn from him.

"Wait." I placed my hand on his shoulder. He looked at me, slightly irritated. "I didn't know you could use a bow."

"Of course I can use a bow," he snapped in a careful whisper.

"But I thought Flint—"

"This isn't the time," he interrupted, setting his aim on the bear.

"I can't create the same power Darric does," Flint murmured, crestfallen. "He's never missed."

I furrowed my brows. Were Flint's skinny arms truly ineffective against thick fur, skin, fat, muscle, and sinew? I was not physically stronger than Flint, yet I had more control and strength in archery.

The extraordinary blind confidence rushed through my veins. I slid to the opposite side of Darric and balanced on my toes. Below us, the male bear walked like a majestic piece of living artwork.

I pulled an arrow from my quiver and positioned it across my bow, aiming into the glen. I had to work fast or I would miss the opportunity. The bear's right arm lifted and lowered over the vulnerable location behind the shoulder, the skin moving with the rhythmic beats that pounded life through him. An accurate shot would be about timing—letting the arrow loose at the exact moment when the heart was exposed.

Darric's eyes left the bear and stared at me. He released the tension on his string, and my heart raced. Was he giving me the kill shot? This was terrible. How could he think so little of his brother? I had not thought this through before I'd decided to draw my bow, but I pushed the consequences from my head to concentrate.

The flood of certainty seeped through my muscle. The doubtless guarantee that if I timed my release correctly, I would hit my target. I controlled the arrow's fate. I eased the cordage back to my cheek and let out a slow breath.

"Relax the tension in your right shoulder. Fluid movements increase accuracy. Don't overthink this," Darric uttered softly next to my ear, giving me the courage I needed to achieve this ridiculous act of intrepidity. "It's not questionable. You *will* make the shot."

"What'd ya say?" Flint asked, hearing Darric's whisper. His eyes bulged upon seeing my weapon at the ready.

Following Darric's instruction, I lowered my shoulder, and the muscle tension cooled into a fluid ease. The heart was bared. I let my fingers slip from the bowstring.

"AYA, NO! You'll ruin his shot!" Flint flung his body at me and grabbed the nape of my dress, yanking me to the ground.

I landed hard on his bony fist, which sent a shock of pain through my spine. The bow tore from my grasp, and I watched helplessly as the arrow soared into the blue sky and arched downwards into the glen.

The roar of a bear in absolute agony echoed through the valley.

Darric jolted to his feet. "Oh, shit," he drawled.

I shot up from the ground to survey the damage. The male hobbled to the safety of the forest, a thick stream of dark blood pouring from his right leg, where my arrow had pierced him. He held the injury to his chest and glared at the ledge where the three of us stood awestruck. His crimson eyes stabbed me in the heart with a look of pure malice and sorrow.

Darric's breathing steadily quickened. His eyes darted around the area, analyzing, planning.

The female rose onto her back legs. Her nose twitched, smelling the foreign scent in the air. Her eyes darkened into a terrifying blood red. She lowered her head, and two thousand pounds of brute force barreled towards us.

"Go! Move!" Darric hollered.

Flint immediately turned and fled down the pathway. He stumbled and slid as the rocks came loose under his feet.

The bear tore through the brush. Wind filled her fur, which shook and shimmered over her muscles, making it appear like a solid mass. She crawled up the cliff face, throwing boulders half her size out of the way like small pebbles. The horrific smacking sound her lips made as they pulled back in a snarl shattered the last bits of my courage.

Darric shoved me down the path. I slid chaotically, trying to keep my ankles from buckling as he forced me to maintain speed. We hit the grass just as the bear burst through the trees atop the ledge. Darric slammed into my back, knocking me forwards, and wrapped his arm around my waist to haul me with him.

Above us, the female short-faced bear smelled the rock ledge. She inhaled dirt into her nostrils and expelled it in a puff of dust before swiftly following our path.

Flint raced through the woods, jumping over logs and tripping on overgrown brush. "Where?" he screamed back to Darric.

The bear accelerated down the pathway, her heavy, hot breaths echoing in my ears. The ground shook with each of her bounding leaps. We had to do something. We couldn't outrun her. We were going to die. Mauled to death. Crushed under her weight. Torn to pieces by her claws.

Darric frantically looked for some method of escape. "Flint!" he called, dragging me towards a hole in the cliff face. We dived into a rock crevice with barely enough room for the three of us to stand.

Root systems dangled over us, and loose soil fell from the ceiling. Crawling insects and worms slithered across the floor. A large spider crept down the wall and landed on my shoulder. I inhaled to scream, but Darric threw his hand over my mouth and flicked the arachnid from my arm.

Tears welled in my eyes. I thought nothing could be more terrifying than being captured by bandits, held hostage, and poisoned. Even Darric's sword at my throat couldn't compare to the fury of a short-faced bear trying to tear me to shreds.

My feet sank into the moist soil of our fragile hiding hole. I couldn't grip the wall without pulling back a handful of insect-filled dirt. We tried to keep our ragged panting quiet, denying our lungs the aching need for more air.

The bear paced outside the narrow entry. She huffed into the opening, choking us with a cloud of dirt. Her massive paw reached into the crevice. Swatting with claws as sharp as blades and long as Luken's dagger, she scraped the floor inches from Darric's boot. Frustrated, she shook her head and sent a spray of sand embedded in her fur into the air. She roared into the hole, and the walls vibrated from the rumble exuding from deep within her chest.

I felt faint. If Darric's and Flint's bodies hadn't been smashing me between them, I would have collapsed into a heap to be dragged out and mauled to death. I gripped Darric's shirt and leaned my head into his hand. He responded by tightening his hold around my waist and crushing me to his muscular chest.

I needed the courage to open communication with her. To listen to what she wanted. Talk to her. Reason with her. Beg her to leave us alone.

Then she was gone.

Heavy steps sauntered away from us. Darric removed his hand from my mouth and lowered his head through the opening.

This was insane. We could have been killed. What sort of maniacal thinking had caused Darric to bring his brothers into the mountains to live by hunting short-faced bears? Flint placed his hand on my shoulder, trying to help me relax, but my fitful breaths wouldn't calm. I started hiccupping.

The tumbling of rocks over stone rattled the chamber. Darric backed away from the entrance and looked up. Something moved above us. A pound like a battering ram quaked the walls, and dirt fell in large clumps from the ceiling as the hideout began to cave in. The bear was crushing the ground above to pierce our delicate cage. Another massive bombardment cracked the shell, and beams of sunlight filtered into the crevice, followed by a loud feral growl. With one final blast of her immense frame, the bear's paws smashed through the ceiling and swiped the air.

Darric shoved me through the narrow entry. My dress tangled in my legs, and I fell to the ground. Flint jumped over me and ran for his life. Darric jerked me to my feet. I grabbed the front of my dress and fled. Never had I run so fast. Adrenaline coursed through my body, granting me an otherwise unattainable speed.

The momentary distraction of breaking through the crevice kept the bear occupied long enough for us to gain distance. I heedlessly looked back. She was tossing boulders aside as if they were hollow and burrowing into the roof of our demolished hiding place.

Inevitably, the bear discovered we were missing and leaped from the ledge in a full charge, lips pulled back from her gums, bone-crushing canines the length of my fingers exposed, foam dripping from her mouth and wetting the fur around her caramel face.

We reached the forest edge and broke into the openness of the valley, only to be followed a second later by the thunderous boom of her paws at our heels.

"Flint!" Darric called, pushing me into his brother's arms. "Take her to the Hovel!"

I fell into Flint's chest. He took my hand and kept moving.

Darric came to an abrupt halt and turned to face our assailant.

"NO!" I screamed and dug my heels into the dirt.

"Aya, he can take care of himself," Flint shouted, fighting against me.

I fell to my knees so he would have to drag me through the grass to continue.

Darric drew back on Flint's bowstring with the one arrow left in his possession. The arrow flew at a blinding speed with more power than I had ever created and stabbed the bear in the shoulder joint. The arrow sank into the animal, leaving only the fletching sticking out of her fur. She stumbled and somersaulted, having lost control of her front limb.

Darric dropped the bow and drew his sword as the bear shook her head and righted herself. She reared onto her back legs, towering over him at double his height, and screamed a roar so loud her lips quivered and my ears popped.

Flint kept tugging at my arm, trying to pull me off the ground.

Darric remained unnervingly calm, as though he had no care whether he lived or died. Either he was selflessly sacrificing himself or he truly believed he could kill a charging short-faced-bear with a sword. Either outcome defined true insanity, brawn mixed with sheer stupidity. He held his sword low, the shining blade almost touching the grass, and waited for the bear to lunge.

I couldn't allow this to happen. I couldn't stand by and watch Darric be ripped to pieces. I tore my hand from Flint's grasp and sprinted senselessly to Darric. Flint screamed my name at the same moment the bear broke her gaze and charged, running into her wound, ignoring the pain. She roared, and my eardrums rattled.

I searched for a way to read her. I had to speak to her. I had to tell her to stop. To leave. To spare Darric's life.

"Stop!" I yelled, and our minds fused. The information poured into my brain so forcefully I thought I had taken an axe to the skull. It knocked me to my knees. Her cries were loud to the ear but blisteringly insufferable inside my head. Unmatched anger consumed her. The pain in her shoulder felt unendurable, yet she fought on in a battle to the death. She knew we were here to kill her. Worse, she recognized Darric. She had seen him hunting throughout the valley and was determined to end him.

My thoughts became befuddled, incoherent. Nothing I could say would calm her rage or reason with her. She was too irate to see us as anything other than an enemy.

Biting back tears, I gripped my bow and pulled an arrow from my quiver. *Don't overthink it. Don't overthink that she won't hear your pleas and doesn't realize you're a Fae. Don't overthink the decision to help Darric end her life.*

I yanked back on the bowstring. *Where do I aim?* What made the most sense? My nerves failed me, and remorse replaced my adrenaline-fueled courage at the woeful sight before me.

The bear's colossal paw crashed towards Darric. His quick reflexes spun him out of the way, and her momentum sent her slamming face-first into his blade. The sword sliced open her muzzle. Blood poured from the wound and trailed off her nose, mixing into the foam dripping from her mouth. Red stained her fur, and her arm hung limply at her side. My heart ached as the majestic creature faltered.

Incredibly, she was no match for Darric's agility. He moved around her injured frame with grace and ease, predicting every threat she made against him. Agitated, the bear threw all her weight forwards to barrel into him. Darric skidded across the ground on his knees to avoid her.

I was clutching my bow, unable to loose the arrow, when a brilliant shimmer of burgundy leaped from the forest and bounded towards the bear. The cat propelled herself through the air and landed on the bear's neck. With silver talons fully exposed, she dug deep into the animal's pelt and bit into her skin. Over and over, she ferociously clawed and chomped into the beast.

The bear fell onto all fours and shook her body, trying to rid herself of the feline. When ruffling her fur did nothing to deter the pest, she used her good arm to swat behind her head, but the cat remained, jaws clenched on a mouthful of flesh.

Darric used the distraction as an opportunity. He slid forwards on his knees, positioning himself under two thousand pounds of enraged bear, narrowly avoiding the deadly daggered paws that pounded into the ground beside him. He lay back, lost under the mass of fur, and raised his sword. Grasping the hilt with both hands, he drove the blade into the animal's chest, burying the weapon so deep the metal vanished within her.

The beast instantly ceased moving, and the chaos in the valley quieted. Her gaze fell to Darric, who panted on his back between her front arms. He gripped his sword and twisted. A loud crunch flooded the silence as the blade cut through rib and breastbone. The first drops of blood streamed onto Darric's shirt. He released the hilt and rolled out from under her just as she collapsed into a lifeless heap on the ground.

Stunned, I dropped my bow.

Darric jogged to where I sat frozen on the grass. He knelt in front of me and placed bloodied hands on my shoulders. "Are you all right?" Beads of sweat trickled down his temples, and wisps of blond hair stuck to his wet forehead.

I nodded, tears blurring my vision.

"You're not hurt?" he confirmed, brows furrowed. His thumbs caressed the fabric of my dress.

"I'm okay." Something inside of me cracked. "Darric, you could have been killed." I placed my hands on his chest and fell into him. His heart raced as he breathed a heavy sigh of relief.

"I'm a bit insulted by your lack of faith in my abilities," he said, and the slightest smile on his lips eased my panic.

The cat pranced merrily by my thigh. She had blood coating her fur and flesh stuck in her claws. "You crazy feline." I ran my hand down her back and scratched between her ears.

"That was one hell of a distraction," Darric praised, then suddenly jerked away from me upon seeing Flint running towards us.

"Wow." Flint placed his hands on his knees to catch his breath. "Never done it like that before, huh?" He snickered.

A new wave of anger stiffened Darric's shoulders. He returned to the bear carcass and yanked his sword free. Electrified, he rushed Flint, blade ready, and wrapped his hand tightly around his brother's neck. "You fucking idiot!" he growled. "How could you stop her? She had a clear shot!"

Flint coughed and stammered. He clawed at Darric's bracer, trying to pull the grip from his neck as his face turned bright red. Failing, he collapsed to his knees. "I was tryin' to help," he gargled.

"Do you really think so little of my judgment? Do you really think I wasn't paying enough fucking attention to know exactly what she was doing?" Darric snarled.

"Fuck," Flint squeaked as Darric squeezed harder. His cheeks changed from red to purple. "If she missed, the bear woulda charged!" He gasped uselessly for air.

"She did miss! And the bear did charge!" Darric hollered. "Because of you! Someone could have been killed. Do you want more of that shit on your conscience?"

Flint tugged at his brother's fingers, frantically trying to pry them loose. "I can't breathe," he pleaded.

"Darric." He paused at the sound of my voice. "Let him go." My stranger's strength had always made me feel meek and insignificant, but seeing him incapacitate his brother with a single hand opened a new level of dread somewhere between unbridled terror and respect for his lethal nature. "He was only trying to help. You said it yourself, I shouldn't have been hunting with you. He was attempting to stop a disaster."

Annoyed, Darric released his brother. "He did a fine fucking job."

Flint disintegrated onto the ground and grasped his neck. He inhaled a loud gulp, coughed, and spat thick drool.

I ran my finger over the side of Flint's neck. He would be left to wear the humiliating bruise of Darric's hand. "Are you okay?" I whispered to him.

He nodded wearily. "I'd have a lot more to say if I didn't promise ya I wouldn't complain 'bout him anymore." He cleared his throat as his red-rimmed eyes stared ruefully into the grass.

I reached under his quiver to rub my hand over his back. "I wouldn't blame you this time if you did." I narrowed my eyes at Darric, watching him wipe his sword clean on the bear's fur.

"Denigrate me all you want, Flint," Darric said. "You and I both know why you're doing it." Sheathing his sword, he snatched a strange arrow from Flint's quiver. The fletching was abnormally large, and instead of a stone head, a woven ball of tinder wrapped in white cloth was attached to the shaft. He held out his hand expectantly. Flint reached into his pants pocket and pulled out a piece of flint stone, which he gave to Darric without looking up from the ground.

Darric put his thumb and forefinger into his mouth and whistled. The ear-piercing shrill made my head throb. He pulled a knife from his bracer and struck the blade against the flint, lighting the woven ball with a shower of sparks. He nocked the flaming arrow against Flint's bow, leaned back, and shot it vertically into the sky.

Puzzled, I gazed at Flint, who still refused to make eye contact with me.

"It's to signal Bromly," he said in a crackling voice.

The arrow sailed above the treetops and fizzled out at its highest altitude before diving back to the ground, leaving a trail of smoke floating in the sky. The leftover burned stick landed by Darric's feet.

A deep, foreboding bear cry captured the forest. It bellowed and echoed in a painful chorus that chilled my blood.

"Fucking hell." Darric groaned and glared at Flint.

"What is that?" I hated to ask.

"That would be the injured male," he replied acidly.

"He's in pain," I mused, listening to the heartbreaking cries.

"Your arrow went clear through his leg. He'll be down somewhere in the woods. It's going to be a slow death."

A tear rolled down my cheek, and I quickly wiped it away. I had to stay strong. What was I expecting? Hunting meant killing animals. I knew people in the poorer villages would benefit from fur and meat, but sitting next to the fresh remains of a beautiful young female short-faced bear, I couldn't see it from their perspective. I had looked inside her; I knew her thoughts as she raged. She was a beast, yes, but she wasn't that different from us. She still thought and felt, feared and angered, perhaps even loved in her own way. I grew sick to my stomach with remorse, and the taste of vomit rose in my throat. "How long is it going to last?"

"If it stops, he's dead. Short-faced bears don't have any natural predators. We'll find him tomorrow at first light and put him out of his misery." Darric tossed the bow on the ground, disgusted by the situation.

An hour later, Bromly's plump figure appeared on the horizon. A coiled rope was slung over his shoulder, and several large knives had replaced the spoons that normally hung from his belt. He carried an axe in one hand and a shovel in the other. I didn't need to ask to know what he had been signaled for, nor did I want anything to do with the process.

His gleaming eyes dulled when he looked upon our sullen faces. He approached the bear and frowned. "A female?"

Darric nodded. "Don't start."

"But a female," he scolded.

"I'm aware. I gave her every chance to turn away. She was determined," Darric defended.

Bromly tugged at the arrow jutting out of the bear's shoulder. It didn't budge. His attention turned to her chest, where a gaping hole oozed congealing blood, then his eyes dropped to the purple finger marks on Flint's neck. The sound of the injured male rumbled through the valley.

He hesitated. "What happened?"

Darric crossed his arms over his chest. "We experimented with hunting techniques on the first day of bear season."

Chapter 17

I sat in a patch of wildflowers facing away from the kill, my legs pulled into my chest and my chin resting on my knees. The noon sun offered no shade from the already exhausting day. Living deep in the mountains of Daraban was turning out to be more formidable than I'd ever imagined. Even sleep offered no escape from the mental drain.

I plucked a purple bloom and twirled it between my fingertips. The cat batted the moving flower and bit the petals. She was dauntless and amazing. Weeks ago, she had attacked bandits in the woods. Today, she assisted Darric in bringing down a short-faced-bear at close range. Six pounds of indomitable brawn. Yet I cowered away from the brothers as they dressed their kill.

Bromly was summoned for a specific purpose. He could skin and gut a rabbit in under a minute; behind me, he dismantled a one-ton bear. Not watching allowed my imagination to run rampant every time I heard the crunch of bone or the weighty thump of some hefty body part hitting the ground. I couldn't watch her be cut to pieces.

Eventually, Darric noticed my distress and instructed Flint to take me back to the Hovel.

Flint trudged the entire walk, kicking a small stone, and didn't say a word. I felt sorry for him. His neck looked unbearably sore. Still, I wondered how he could have been so oblivious on that ledge.

When we reached the cavern, he disappeared inside the Hovel and returned with his flute. "I can't stay here with ya. I gotta go back an' help. But if ya need us, ya can blow loudly into this. We'll hear it." He handed me the wooden instrument.

I nodded thankfully.

"An' Darric told me to tell ya not to wander."

"I don't plan on going anywhere," I murmured, turning the flute over in my hand.

He tried to force a smile but failed. "Don't be angry with me. Okay?"

Before I could say another word, he left the cavern.

I couldn't be angry with Flint. Darric had scorned him enough, and none of this would have happened if I had simply observed instead of trying to prove myself.

I unlaced the quiver off my back and sank next to the fire. My legs ached from sprinting for my life. Crossing my arms over the log, I buried my face into the sleeves of my dress. The soothing crackle of the embers helped me shed all the tears backed up behind my eyes.

In the distance, the injured male continued his strange painful bellows. I tried to drown him out by covering my ears, but to no avail—his cries pierced the barrier.

The cat jumped onto the log and kneaded her paws into the back of my head. "I can't keep doing this," I mumbled to her. "I can't keep breaking down like a child every time something goes awry." I rubbed my nose over my sleeve. "How did Grandmother ever think I was strong enough for this?"

Ambrosia would expect me back at the palace by now. Perhaps she had realized returning was never my intention. Luken's homecoming would have brought devastating news about my engagement to Prince Marcus—its irrevocability.

My days at the Hovel were numbered. I would travel to Burge with the brothers and stay behind. Follow the road to another town. Find another life. With my skills in archery, I could defend myself. I longed to show Luken my ability with a bow. I imagined he would exude a mix of horror and pride.

Deep within me, a suppressed desire to remain at the Hovel grew stronger. I'd grown attached to the valley's unparalleled beauty, and despite their flaws, I adored my companions—even Darric, who seemed less agitated by my presence these days.

A single set of footsteps entered the cavern, and I smashed my face deeper into the huddle of my arms. Something heavy thudded to the ground: the first of the bear parts to be delivered to the Hovel.

I waited patiently for the footsteps to leave, but a somber, brooding demeanor lingered in front of my log. Flint must have volunteered to check on me. I felt more comforted by his presence than ever before, safe somehow.

He crouched down and smoothed a loose strand of hair into my braid, his calloused fingers grazing my neck. *Flint doesn't have calloused hands.* The smell of crushed petals and grass permeated my nose. I didn't want him to see me crying. I curled farther into myself, and the flute was plucked from my grasp. *Please, no more flowers.*

"Go away, Flint," I sniffled.

He scoffed and gave a small chuckle. "Look at me," Darric said, sounding mildly insulted.

My eyes shot open. I sprung up to find steel blue staring back at me. "Oh, I wasn't expecting you." I quickly smeared tears from my cheeks.

"Clearly." He balanced the flute at the far end of the log. For the first time, the cat had not hissed at him when he approached me. That was unsettling.

I stared at him, dumbfounded. The increased heart rate and frozen lungs his presence always elicited had not clogged my brain when I thought he was Flint. I felt consoled and relaxed, loving his heady floral scent.

"Listen, about today," he began, "I want you to know, you didn't do anything wrong. Nothing that happened was your fault."

"I didn't envision it being so violent," I confessed.

He nodded wearily. "Normally it's a much cleaner kill, but I can't imagine it was any worse than a bandit attack. So why the tears?"

"It's you and Flint. You didn't have to hurt him the way you did. I'm beginning to wonder how you've lived together for so long and not killed each other."

His pleasant mouth formed a coy smile. "We've come close. Bromly is a proficient mediator. But you're right. I shouldn't have gone after my brother like that. Taking down a bear with a sword is never supposed to happen. We could have died. I lost my temper, and I've apologized to him. However, Flint does tend to hold a grudge, especially towards me."

Another chorus of howls came from the forest as the old male continued vocalizing. "You say it's not my fault, yet none of this would have happened if it hadn't been for me." My eyes welled up. I groaned, frustrated with myself, and rubbed my palms into my face.

"Aya." He leaned forwards and cupped the back of my head. "Stop blaming yourself. I did not have to lower my bow and allow you the kill shot." He glanced out of the cavern, searching the horizon, then turned back to me. "You have a centered strength about you, the kind that can't be broken. It's extremely rare to find someone so willing to expose themselves to vulnerability. Bravery doesn't always manifest in the form of wielding a weapon, and often the internal form is stronger. Don't hide it or be ashamed of it. Your ability to not fear your emotions, to wear them openly, is one of your greatest assets. Very few people are capable of that sort of transcendence."

Darric's touch was distracting, secure and warm. Unconsciously, I turned my head so his hand encompassed my cheek and his thumb traced my bottom lip. "There are a tremendous number of people who would disagree with you," I managed to say.

"Then it's convenient I don't care if I'm being disagreeable." His eyes blazed into me, and his fingertips thumped with the heavy beats of his heart as they grazed the healed cut on my neck he had inflicted with his sword. Not a person alive had ever praised the things about me that I feared, not even Luken. My emotions were shunned as a Divine Princess. Too headstrong. Too free-spirited.

"I have to go back and help Bromly and Flint," he said, standing, but seemed to be telling himself more than me.

Before leaving, he slid a blade from his bracer and knelt by a humongous portion of raw bear with the back leg still attached. He cut a bite-sized morsel and held it in his open palm. The cat meowed and jumped from her perch to pluck the delicacy from his hand, then allowed him to scratch between her ears. My jaw fell open. *You traitor, he hates you!*

"Beautiful pelt or not, I can't skin an animal who helped me win a fight against a bear." He wiped his hands on his leather pants and slid the knife back into his bracer.

Darric acted different when alone with me. The tension in his shoulders lessened, and an ease came over him. He hadn't threatened to kill me in weeks, and unlike Flint, who had fled from the bear in a manner that suggested he didn't care who died as long as it wasn't himself, Darric had never left my side.

"Darric"—I shifted onto the log—"when did you realize I was a Fae? Is it an automatic thing for people like you? You said you knew it when you saw me and couldn't let me die alone. So was it when you were breaking me out of the prison cell, or when you handed me the water and told me where to find the road?"

"Neither." He shifted uncomfortably at the question. "It was on top of the mountains, when we stopped by the willow tree."

I wrinkled my nose, confused by his answer. "But I thought . . ." By the time we had climbed into the Daraban mountains, I'd been following him for hours. He had prevented a hazardous fall and allowed me to stay at his heels. It didn't make sense.

"He brought ya here, remember? He changed all the rules we live by an' tried to pass it off as ya trailin' after him like an abandoned dog. You've seen him fight. If Darric didn't want someone followin' him, they wouldn't've survived long enough to take one step in his direction. He knew exactly what he was doin' the second ya started trailin' him. He wanted ya to follow him. He wanted ya here, an' I've been wreckin' my brain tryin' to figure out why."

"You thought I let you follow me because you're a Fae." He crossed his arms over his chest, reading me before I could fully respond.

I nodded. "Nothing you do makes sense. You are a walking contradiction."

He groaned, running his hand down his face. "Damn this stupid promise, Flint," he grumbled to himself and left the cavern.

"Darric?" I called after him, but he didn't turn around, and he didn't look back.

As the afternoon wore on, the brothers came and went individually with different pieces of the bear. They divided her body into sections and cut the pelt into separate furs. The massive parts seemed incredibly heavy, but as I'd learned over the last month, none of the Hovel brothers were fragile.

Bromly dropped a section next to the drying racks. The entire front of his tan tunic was sopping with blood, globs of fat, and caramel-colored fur tufts. "I was wondering"—he took a knife from his belt and cut away a large chunk—"if you could start a stew? Normally we don't eat on the days we have a bear kill. This animal must be processed on the first day or it spoils, so I can't break to cook. But with you here—"

"Yes!" I stood enthusiastically, tripped on my dress, and almost fell into the fire.

He laughed, handing me a huge fillet of bear. "Spectacular. I'll leave you to handle it then. Flint is getting hungry."

I found Bromly's cauldron under the workbench. Unsure what to do with the giant slab of maroon meat, I temporarily stored the slippery chunk inside the pot so I could drag the iron cooking vessel to the outside fire.

Once it was over the coals, I filled the cauldron with water and hacked the fillet into a series of deformed bite-sized bits. Adding potatoes and carrots seemed like an *innovative* idea, so I plopped a few into the pot.

I kept busy, watching heat bubbles rise and burst across the cauldron rim, wondering where Bromly hid all his spoons. Eventually I found them tucked safely inside a basket hanging over the workbench

Flint arrived carrying a rolled pelt tied together with rope. The bears lovely head bounced over the top of his shoulder. He dropped the heap of fur on the cavern floor with a *splat* and disappeared again.

As early evening descended over the mountains, the three appeared walking side by side through the valley. Bromly and Darric each carried the last portions of bear slung over their backs, and Flint trotted beside them with a bounce in his step, leftover rope hanging on his shoulder while he clutched the axe in one hand and the shovel in the other. They were laughing. Flint gave a joyful howl and wiped a tear from the corner of his eye with his wrist. The day's quarrel seemed momentarily mended, either by my absence or Bromly's mediation.

My heart shriveled and fell into my stomach. Of course, I wanted the altercation between them to be over, but not once had I seen them so content with each other. I was always with them, a constant reminder of a broken rule. This camaraderie coming towards me was a glimpse into the life they had shared before I arrived and caused a rift.

As they drew closer, I could make out the gaiety of witty banter, vague inside jokes containing lewd comments and profanity. I tried to block them out. No matter how much I wanted to fit into their lives—learning to cook or using a bow—I would never be part of what they had as a family. They were raised together. They shared a history. But if I didn't belong here with them, then I didn't belong anywhere.

The thought broke my heart. It was odd to feel so forgotten.

The three quieted before coming into the cavern, but their smiles couldn't be extinguished so easily. Bromly continued to sporadically chortle as they delivered the remaining traces of bear to the pile.

"I'm so hungry I could eat the entire kill." Flint ran to my side and inhaled a lungful of steam. "Smells great!" He grabbed my waist, picked me off the ground, and spun us around, exhibiting a genuine, gleeful smile.

"You might want to try it before getting too excited," I warned.

He set me down when Bromly called his name. They began opening the pelts and hanging them on the drying racks.

I patiently stirred my simple soup until they joined me by the fire. I fetched bowls and ladled four servings, surprised when Darric accepted one, since I never saw him eat. Darric took a single bite, gave a guarded smirk, and placed the uneaten bowl on the log beside him.

My cooking tasted bland compared to Bromly's, but that didn't stop Flint from holding his bowl to his mouth and ravenously gulping. He wiped his lips on his sleeve and belched. "I knew it would be amazing!" he enthused, helping himself to a second bowl.

Darric watched Flint with a disgusted scowl and left the fireside. He stood at the opening of the cavern, listening to the bellows that permeated the valley like a thick fog.

"Are you going tonight or tomorrow?" Bromly asked without turning away from his dinner.

"Tomorrow," he replied. "Two bears in one day is too large a burden. If I make the kill tonight, he'll rot before we can process him. It'll be a waste."

"So he's going to suffer for the night?" I blurted, crushed with grief. No one answered.

The stew cauldron was nearing empty when Bromly patted his round belly and declared they best get back to work. Flint moved the cauldron off the fire and replaced it with a wooden tripod and applewood logs. When smoke began to billow towards the ceiling in large clouds, he stripped meat from bone and laced it over the tripod. Bromly took a paring knife and tediously scraped fat and grizzle from the pelts. Darric left us for the evening.

Night encased the valley. The full moon rose into the sky, and midnight came before Bromly and Flint finished scraping the hides. Witnessing the amount of time involved in tanning made me understand the concern with being overwhelmed during bear season.

"I'm calling it a night." Bromly dropped his knife in a bucket of water and washed his hands. "My fingers are cramping."

"I can't feel mine," Flint added, massaging his knuckles and releasing an overstretched yawn. He held out his hand to help me up, but his arms were covered in greasy bits of fat and sinew.

I raised an eyebrow. "I'll go to bed so the two of you can wash."

"Goodnight, Aya." Bromly laughed as Flint examined his tunic and trousers.

The inside fire had gone out, making the Hovel eerily dark and quiet. Only a faint glow of orange embers burned under the ash, and a thin string of smoke rose to the ceiling. I retrieved a log from the corner to relight the flames.

"How's your neck?" Without the crackle of the fire, Bromly's muffled voice just outside could easily be heard. I froze. *It isn't polite to eavesdrop.*

"Sore," Flint grumbled. "Aya stopped him. He wouldn't've let go till I passed out."

"You had it coming—" Bromly's reply was drowned by splashing water.

"Yeah, maybe," Flint agreed, then scoffed. "I'm givin' it all I got an' he's walkin' backwards an' laughin' at me."

Again, their conversation became unintelligible. I gently released the fire log and tiptoed to the fur door, putting my head against the pelt.

"He's not helpin' either," Flint said acidly.

"Did you expect him to?" Bromly asked.

"I expected him to keep his distance."

"If Darric keeps any more distance, he'll move out of the Hovel."

I wrung the fabric of my dress in my hands.

"You're always tryin' not to get involved," Flint accused. "I've never seen him look at anyone like he does her. I know you've noticed it. All of this is a cover-up or a lie, an' it's gonna sting me in the ass. I jus' know it."

"Aya is pretty and Darric is human. He gave you his word," Bromly defended.

"Darric's word is 'bout as useless as Aya's cookin'."

Cringing, I covered my mouth.

"Aya doesn't know how to cook," Bromly reminded his brother. "She does try, and that's all we can ask. It's her effort that counts."

"She don't know how to do much of anythin' 'cept humiliate me with her archery skills," said Flint.

I'd heard enough. *Serves you right for eavesdropping.* I left the fire unattended and hid inside Darric's room with the cat.

Bromly and Flint eventually came into the Hovel and settled in their rooms.

Sitting on the edge of Darric's bed, I buried my face in my hands as the continuing bear howls vibrated the walls. *What an appalling day.* No matter how much I tried to be of use, I continued to drastically fail. I knew the meal was far from delicious, but Flint didn't need to lie about it. It left me wondering what else he fibbed about. Darric perhaps?

Tomorrow, they would put an end to the male's suffering. Bromly would have to dress another kill. I'd ruined the hunt. I'd almost cost Darric his life. I truly didn't know how to do *much of anything. Useless.*

The short-faced bear's cries penetrated me to the core, a constant reminder of everything I had done wrong. I couldn't stand it. I wouldn't stand it.

If I had stayed at the palace, I would have been alive but living in a state of death. If I died in the mountains, at least I would have lived. Time to make more reckless decisions. Damn my Divine existence. What was the purpose of being Divine if not to help Athera? We were not meant to be locked in a palace, given riches, and worshipped. We were created to serve the life around us. *That* was the true purpose of the Divine, and I was going to shoulder that responsibility, even if none of the other royals ever did.

I threw my cloak around my shoulders and yanked the fur off Darric's bed. Using Luken's dagger, I sliced through the cotton sheets and ripped away a long strip of the fabric. *I'll apologize for destroying his bedding later*, if he ever noticed. Once I'd wrapped the cotton into a bundle, I searched the workbench for any vessel to carry water. Buried in the flatware was a leather pouch like the one Darric had given me outside the bandit cave. I filled it from the bucket and set out into the cavern.

Smoke clouded the exit, billowing up over the drying pieces of bear meat. The valley glowed a brilliant shade of blue as the full moon lit the landscape, and the night's chilling breeze swept through the trees, moving the branches in blurry black masses. I swallowed hard and took a deep breath.

"Darric said I am *transcendent*."

The cat brushed my leg and gave a hushed meow.

"Okay, let's go."

Chapter 18

The cavern disappeared into the distance, becoming a black hollow within the trees. The fading firelight served as the only hint of its location. If it went out, I would never find it again.

If I came back alive at all.

The cat followed my heels as we reached the forest at the far end of the valley. The echoes of agonized cries amplified, and my head spun. It sounded like a dozen bears singing around me. I shut my eyes, trying to pinpoint the origin.

"Strolling through the woods after dark, Fae Princess?"

A tingling jolt zipped through my legs, and I dropped my wrapped strip of cotton. I knew that voice. I turned to find the white stallion peering through the trees. He tossed his long mane away from his eyes, and the alabaster strands glistened under the blue rays of moonlight piercing the forest canopy.

"Or perhaps you seek the boy? He is some ways from here, and you are heading in the wrong direction." His voice was deep and

old, slow and full of memory, containing a beauty that mirrored his regal appearance.

"I'm . . ." Stammering, I plucked the cotton roll from the ground. "I'm not looking for Darric." The bellows captured the night. I listened intently.

"*I see.*" The stallion took a step forwards once the echoes faded. "*You must tread carefully, Fae Princess. The bears are agitated tonight with their old adversary back on the prowl.*"

"One is injured," I explained.

He nodded. "*There will be blood on the horizon if any approach him.*"

"Have you seen him?" I asked hastily.

"*I am keeping my herd at a guarded distance. The bears will kill our offspring. Detestable carnivores. We will retreat to the secret parts of the valley until winter nears and the predators disappear into the crevices of the mountains.*"

"Do you know where he is?"

"*Indeed.*"

"Will you take me to him?"

"*Do you wish for death?*" Concern registered across his brilliant features. "*If so, I cannot assist you. I will not contribute to the worldly loss of a Divine, nor a Fae.*"

"I'm not trying to die. I want to help him. Darric and his brothers plan to find him at dawn. I've caused enough pain. I never should have joined their hunt today, and I am desperate to fix what I have done."

"*Remorse is a human emotion, as is regret. I cannot empathize.*" The steed continued to close the distance between us until I could see my reflection in his black eyes. "*You are a strange anomaly, Ayleth, and though I would seek to keep a Divine human safe from harm, I cannot deter a Fae from fulfilling her wishes. A distressing decision on my part. Do you understand?*"

I nodded. "Will you help me?"

"*I shall take you to him. The Fae in you outwills the Divine. However, I shall not stay once we reach him. Your fate will be your own.*" He walked past me and into the forest.

I trailed behind him until the underbrush transitioned into a grassy forest sprouting an expanse of endless pine and aspen trees. A soupy gray fog hung under the canopy, chilling the day's leftover warmth. I didn't like this part of the valley and sped up so I could walk alongside the steed. "Do you have a name?"

"*Atlas,*" he answered proudly.

"Do all horses have names?" I asked, hoping conversation would keep my mind off the creaking trees and spectral witching-hour sounds of the forest. Darric was alone in this environment every night, yet he feared nothing.

"*Do all humans have names?*" I detected the faintest hint of sarcasm. "*All animals have a title they call themselves in one tongue or another. Most would not be discernable to your ears.*"

"I've only met one animal that I couldn't communicate with."

Atlas's eyes darted to the cat half hiding beneath my cloak. "*Hearing something does not mean you can understand it. You have heard us all your life, have you not? Have you always understood what is being said?*"

"It wasn't until recently I learned I could speak with animals. Where I come from, I'm considered something of a lunatic. The only reason I'm alive is because of Darric."

"*A vexing action that is causing him much torment, I assure you.*"

Confused, I furrowed my brows. "How . . . ?"

"*Forgive me, I am not sharing an open connection with you.*" He lowered his head, and some of his hair fell into his eyes. "*I have no intention of betraying the emotions of Darric Ursygh.*"

"The other animals, I could feel what they felt, but not you," I observed.

"*I am not allowing you to penetrate so deeply into my consciousness.*"

"Because of Darric?" I confirmed.

He nodded. "*His secrets are not mine to reveal. He is . . . something of a friend. I have known him longer than any human, since he first arrived in this valley several years ago. He was a boy then, yet he lacked the innocence I would have expected from a child. He has always been exceedingly heavy with burden.*"

"How much do you know about him?" I inquired, curious.

"*More than he realizes. I can hear when he speaks. His thoughts. His heart. Though he is not a Fae, he is the only human I could understand until you. His companions are mute to me, as are the other humans I have rarely encountered. I have tried to communicate with him in the past, but he cannot hear me. He exhibits several qualities of the Fae yet lacks the blood. It is quite perplexing.*"

"What qualities?" Mesmerized by his knowledge, I began to forget the reason I was in the woods alone at night.

"*Fortitude. Dexterity. Precognition. Untamed communication— though he seems oblivious to that peculiar power.*"

"Precognition?" I breathed, astonished. "I don't have any of those abilities." No wonder Darric was an expert assassin. He was endowed with inhuman proficiencies.

"*Not currently. You are odd as a Fae. I know little about it, only what Athera whispers on the wind. The men dressed in black cloaks who ride black horses through the night have prevented a Fae from ever obtaining omnipotence. If they continue their quest, none ever will.*"

I came to a grinding halt. "Omnipotence? You're joking."

Atlas stopped walking to look at me. "*What is joking?*"

"It means to not be serious." The trees waved and creaked in the breeze. "Or to trifle." My teeth chattered in the eerie chill, and I shuddered.

"*To lie?*" he questioned, insulted. "*What purpose do you suppose I would have for detailing to you a deception?*"

I shrugged, releasing a shaky exhale.

"*Human's truly are a curious species, full of emotion that drives their decisions. And you, Fae Princess, are among the most enigmatic.*"

A bone-quaking grumble vibrated my feet, snapping me out of my daze. In front of us loomed a cave carved jagged into the rock. Stalactites and stalagmites lined the opening like the sharp, bloodthirsty teeth of a monstrous mouth.

Atlas nodded at the foreboding entrance. "*He is in there.*"

My blood ran cold, and my knees began to quiver.

"*He can still run but will not maintain lengthy speed. There may be the chance you can outrun him. Use discretion. Do not startle him, and keep your mind open.*"

I nodded to acknowledge Atlas's advice and inhaled until my chest hurt.

"*Good luck to you, Ayleth the Divine Fae Princess. May you see the dawn.*"

"Thank you," I mouthed.

I tipped my head to enter the cave. A variety of rocks and pointed mineral deposits covered the floor, and I had to sway from side to side to avoid strange crystalline growths on the low ceiling. It smelled vaguely like the Hovel, if the Hovel had been overrun by living short-faced bears. The overwhelming stench made my eyes water. The moonlight illuminated the opening, but after stepping mere feet inside, I became lost in a crepuscular world where my heart threatened to tear a hole through my chest.

The rear of the cave appeared fathomless. How deep would I have to go before I found him? I glanced at the entrance. Atlas was gone.

My eyes failed to adjust to the darkness. Something moved in the caliginous shadows with a blatant huffing breath, and the entire right wall shifted. A fur boulder turned to face me, and I stared straight into the glow of two bloodcurdling eyes.

I threw my hand over my mouth to stop a scream. The creature peered at me and lowered his massive head to breathe in a long whiff of the front of my dress. The fabric stuck to his nose. He blew out, and the force of his breath made the wool cling to my skin. Everything about him was stronger, bulkier, heavier than his mate.

A terrified tear fell down my cheek as I started to hyperventilate.

"*I should. Kill. You. Now.*"

My blood congealed. His voice rumbled in my brain, incredibly menacing and arcane. I had never heard its equal. Truly inhuman.

I worked to unblock my mind. One swipe of his colossal paw and my life would end. He needed to understand I meant no harm. "I came to help you." I hiccupped and drew in several short breaths. "I can remove the arrow from your leg."

"*If you come any closer, I will rip you to shreds.*" He expelled each breath with an audible rumble. I could see the outline of his teeth as he spoke, the darkness of the cave making his canines shine black.

"I knew the risk involved when I decided to find you," I said warily.

"*You deserve death.*" He growled. The painful pulsing of his arm started in my own as the first of his open thoughts filled my head. He was nervous but didn't want to display weakness. He feared I had a hidden weapon waiting to finish him. How could this monster be afraid of a tiny woman?

An image of Darric standing on the ledge looking down over the glen, me crouched beside him, flashed into my brain. "*You were with him.*"

"Yes." I shut my eyes, ashamed, and forced myself not to block him out despite his voice causing insanity.

"*A Fae should have known better.*" Suffering washed over his face. He hobbled back with his injured arm tucked against his chest, the indigo fletching still nestled into his fur.

"Yes," I mouthed in agreement.

The bear peered into my eyes. His steamy, malodorous breath puffed against my cheeks. "*It is not in my interest to destroy a Fae. You would have died this morning if it were. Yet, you wander here lacking foresight. So I ask you: what do you offer to keep me from taking your life?*"

"My name is Ayleth. I am the Divine Princess of Brisleia." My teeth chattered between words.

"*And a Fae,*" he confirmed, amazed.

I nodded as the tears trickled down my neck and into the top of my dress.

"*Impressive combination of talents,*" he said on a growl.

His face was inches from my nose. The brown and crimson swirls of his irises gleamed with hatred, and the sour smell of his pelt penetrated my lungs and twisted my stomach into a nauseated knot. "I can remove the arrow, clean the wound, dress it. It will help you heal."

"*Not good enough!*" He roared and slammed his good paw into the ground, shaking drops of water from the ceiling. "*I see the mark burning beneath your skin, Divine Fae. Your eminence has much to offer.*"

"What do you want from me?" I whispered, petrified of his answer.

"*You are the only one close to the source. The purpose of the Fae is being annihilated by the black-cloaked assassins. Learn your power. Wield it. Become it. There is someone who can assist you in this matter, and you know well the tyrant of which I speak.*"

I shook my head, dismayed. "I can't do that. Darric doesn't listen to me. He won't help me do anything."

The bear ruffled his snout in displeasure. "*You are his mate, are you not?*"

I gaped, continually shaking my head.

"*Ignorant human beings. Make him. It is his penance for this atrocity. To kill a young female of my kind is degeneracy at its greatest.*" He tilted his head, analyzing my fear.

"Darric knows it is degeneracy. We tried to get away from her. He never wanted to kill her." My hands went clammy, and I clutched the wrapped cotton bundle. I couldn't possibly be as cold as I felt. "We were trying to kill you. He said you were old and limping. I got in the way. It is my arrow in your arm."

An acrimonious roar tore through the bear's throat. He lunged, barreling into me and knocking me to the ground. My back crunched onto the rocky floor. He stood over me with bared teeth. Drool seeped from his lips and pooled on my dress. Daggerlike claws scraped into the ground on either side of my body, leaving jagged cuts in the stone. The cat hissed and arched her back but did not attack.

Screaming was useless. I stared up at him. Ready to die. Knowing in his eyes I deserved death.

"*You are afraid.*" His voice lowered to something like a whisper but hissed when it bounced inside my skull.

"I'm terrified." My mouth went dry. I clutched the bundle to my chest and waited.

"*Your courage is admirable.*" He grunted, slinking off me, and sheltered farther in the cave. "*Last warmth, I was injured by a competitor and lost the right to breed.*" His raging drastically lessened, replaced by a mournful grumble. "*As it happens, your Darric Ursygh eliminated that adversary. The arrogant sword-wielding bowman is correct. I am in the finality of my life.*"

My spine creaked, and I cautiously maneuvered into a sitting position. "I don't know how to convince Darric to teach me anything, but I give you my word I will do what I can."

"*It goes against my instinct to allow you near.*" He stepped over me, carefully placing his paws so as not to crush me, and laid his massive belly on the floor in the light of the full moon. A painful, discordant groan rumbled from deep within his chest as he extended his leg into the nightly glow. "*You have two minutes,*" he warned.

The wooden shaft of my stray arrow had vanished beneath his elbow, leaving the head visible on one side and the purple fletching on the other. I gulped, tentatively pushing the fur aside to examine the wound. Though warm and dirty, the pelt was identical to the rugs inside the Hovel. "This is going to be painful."

The bear grumbled and laid his head on the stone. "*You are wasting precious time talking.*"

I set the cotton and water aside to pull Luken's dagger free from its scabbard. The bear snarled at the blade, revealing half a canine. I smoothed fur away from the arrowhead to locate a small section of exposed wood and began to saw. Within two strokes, the rocky head fell to the ground with a muted clank. I sheathed the dagger and lightly tugged the exposed fletching. It didn't budge. "You should take a deep breath," I advised.

"*My patience runs thin, Fae.*"

My hands shook as I firmly clasped the feathered end. I took to my feet and yanked the arrow from his arm in one smooth motion.

The bear launched from the stone, filling the cave with an ear-shattering roar.

Rage fueled him. He tried to rear onto his hind legs but hit his head on the ceiling. Frustrated, he threw his paw at a nearby mineral deposit. It exploded, sending rocks flying towards me. I ducked and covered my head. Frightened tears flooded my eyes until the sounds of breaking stone faded.

Why did I come here alone? Darric was not so unreasonable. I should have waited until dawn. I could have pleaded with him to help this bear. Instead, I would die in this cave and never see him again. A disturbing need consumed me. I wished more than anything to have Darric here, protecting me, sheltering me.

The beast ceased his tantrum with a snort and ground his teeth. "Apologies *I believe is the term humans use.*" He returned to lying on his belly. "*You attempted to notify me of physical distress, and I ignored your warning."* Fresh blood poured from his arm, soaking into his fur and pooling on the cave floor. *"You may continue."*

I was trembling so uncontrollably I doubted I could open the water container.

"Is courage failing you?" He offered me his injury. *"Perhaps the phrase 'there is a reason why I haven't killed you yet' would ease your trepidation."* The words mimicked Darric's threats, even his diction and delivery. An image of my cloaked, hooded stranger flashed through my brain.

I eased onto my knees and pulled the cork from the leather pouch. "How do you know about that?"

"As I have let you into my head, so you have allowed me into yours. Your resolve keeps me from harming you. Your potential. If you are ever going to become what is needed of you, I cannot end your life. 'I'd want your death to haunt me."

Pushing aside a thick layer of fur, I poured water into the gaping carmine hole.

"I would encourage you not to put your life in danger in the future. A Fae has been born Divine. The unification may prove useful. Don't squander it."

The cat meowed, drawing both of our attentions. She stood just outside the cave. Her shimmering pelt appeared almost metallic in the moonlight.

"You have interesting friends," the bear mused, looking at her. *"Still, I must caution you against Darric Ursygh."*

Having exhausted the water, I reached for the cotton fabric and carefully wrapped his leg. Thankfully, I'd brought enough to fit around his immense front limb. "Darric has repeatedly saved my life. He is protecting me because I am a Fae."

The cat gave a low growl; she sounded like a mouse when compared to the bear.

"Yet, tonight you disregard his sacrifice and put your life in jeopardy." He shifted his head to meet my gaze. His eyes appeared

more chestnut, bordering on friendly. *"Do not be foolish and believe he has anything to gain from your Divinity."*

"I never told him I was Divine," I admitted mournfully. "The three of them, Darric and his brothers, they don't even know my real name."

"There is sorrow in your voice." He shook his head, displeased.

My heart fell. I tied off the bandage and tucked the fabric into itself.

The bear stood, shaking his pelt so it sprayed dirt. *"Resist your sentiment for Ursygh, Fae, though I fear it is too late. Your head is muddled with thoughts of him. I see invasions of the swordsman in your brain, consuming you like a plague. Obsession is dangerous to the human mind."*

I stumbled to my feet, trying to stop my knees from buckling.

The bear shifted his weight onto his haunches. He raised his paw and swatted at me. I faltered backwards to avoid him, but his agile claw caught my hand, ripping the flesh of my palm.

I gave a short cry of astonishment. A pink-and-white fleshy gash stretched from my wrist to my fingers and had yet to begin to bleed. I balled my hand into a fist and crumpled it to my belly.

"Something to remember me by." He growled slyly with a hint of amusement. *"As I have something to remember you."*

Blood commenced pouring from the wound. It dripped through my fingers and stained the front of my dress.

The bear wiggled his nose. *"Fae blood has an exquisite smell, and I am still starving from winter. Does it taste as distinctive?"* Any notion of friendliness vanished from his eyes. *"Get . . . Out . . ."*

My stomach launched into my throat, and my heart rate reached an unprecedented speed. I lunged for the cave exit, tearing past the boulder of moving fur, and fled into the moonlit fog. Behind me, a blaring roar shredded the quiet forest. My legs burned; the muscles in my thighs and calves ripped from being pushed to the extreme twice in one day.

The barren woods turned to brush. I raced through it, narrowly avoiding branches and roots. I had to keep moving. My ears strained for the familiar pounding of heavy paws pursuing me.

I held my torn hand against my dress. It bled and throbbed with each racing beat of my heart.

I didn't know the contours of the valley and fled blindly, hoping I would somehow stumble upon the main clearing by the cavern. In my periphery, the cat dashed as a burgundy blur in and out of the brush.

By a stroke of luck, the river stretching away from the lake cut across my path. I raced up the rocky bank towards the shining body of water, needing the cool liquid to help numb the pain. Ignoring all reason or caution, I scurried awkwardly across the lake and dropped to my knees at the center, plunging my hand beneath the glassy surface.

The lake convulsed and exploded, sending sprays into the sky that rained down to soak me. Specks of blue sparkles hung in the air and crested each wave.

The wound fed a steady stream of blood into the frothy churn, and my cries of agony broke through the crash of the waterfall against the cliffs. I cursed through the pain. This affliction was more than anything I had ever experienced. Divine life had not prepared me for such an injury; I didn't know how to work through the anguish.

What am I supposed to do to fix this?

I glanced at the cat for answers. She sat by the water's edge, swishing her tail in an annoyed fashion. Her brows pointed towards her nose, creating an anxious mask over her amber eyes as she looked at something past me. I turned to see the object of her concern, and an entirely new wave of alarm rushed through my body.

Darric stood by the stony bank on the opposite side of the lake. His inquisitive gaze turned into a cryptic smile when I noticed him.

I panicked, and the water went out from under me, sending me plummeting below the surface. The icy lake choked the breath from my lungs. Working with one hand, I couldn't right myself and searched for something to grab on to. My chest screamed for air. At last, one of my frantic swipes found the rocky ledge of the bank. I dug my nails into the stone, driving sharp granite into my sliced hand and sending lightning stabs of pain up my arm. I cried out and swallowed a mouthful of water.

Darric reached down the embankment and grasped my wrist. I surfaced and took an enormous breath, immediately followed by uncontrollable coughs and gags as I hacked up a lungful of water. He dragged me onto dry land and ripped at the knot holding my sopping cloak to my back. Tossing the garment aside, he removed his own from his shoulders and wrapped me in the dry wool.

His heady scent entered my lungs through spurts of gasped air. I knelt into the shelter of his chest until I stopped choking. Surprisingly, his arms circled my back and pulled me closer, allowing his warmth to penetrate my core.

With the commotion of my gagging at an end, the nightly chirp of crickets refilled the void between the stillness of the forest and the waterfall. The beauty of the valley returned. I released a tremendous sigh of relief. I was alive. I had walked into the den of the beast and lived. My hand was not important when compared to the outcome.

I rubbed my nose over Darric's chest; his soft cotton shirt created a pleasant contrast over his hard muscle. The worry of never seeing him again dissipated. How implausible it seemed that I should feel this at peace in his arms. He exhumed strength from somewhere deep within me, the fogged brain he created a mere prerequisite to how he assuaged my fears.

"I saw a kid from Varanus do that once." He stifled a chuckle, his lips brushing my hairline. "I've been waiting for you to do something aberrant. I knew dreaming wasn't all there was to you."

"So, I'm more valuable to you now that you know what I'm worth?" My teeth chattered with such intensity I almost bit my tongue.

He laughed. "That's a little nonsensical, don't you think?" He shifted onto the balls of his feet and wove his fingers into mine to pry us from the ground. I graciously accepted one of his hands but avoided taking the other. His amused expression changed to worry as he gazed at the unmissable trail of blood falling down my dress.

He tugged at my wrist. I tried to resist, but physically I could not prevent him from taking what he wanted. The moon moved from behind the clouds, and rays of white light illuminated the lurid gash dividing my flesh. It ached, and my fingers pulsed.

"What the hell did you do?" he asked reproachfully.

"You won't like the answer," I warned.

He released my damaged hand, tightening his fingers around the other. He hadn't held on to me like that since the day he brought me to the Hovel; the same calloused grip from years of wielding a sword pulled at my delicate skin. I tried not to overthink his actions.

"We need to get this treated," he said. "Come with me."

He plucked my wet cloak from the ground. I huddled into the side of his chest, mashing our joined hands between us, terrified he would let me go and disappear. The bear could be watching from the woods, waiting to find me alone. I scanned the tree line. No mass of forbidding chestnut fur loomed in the forest, but black eyes framed by a shining alabaster mane intently watched us. Darric nodded in Atlas's direction, and the stallion faded into the trees with the slightest smirk across his muzzle. *You snitch!*

"It's quiet," Darric noted. "Much quieter than it was an hour ago."

"It is." I didn't know how to tell him why the echoes of an injured bear no longer congested the valley. How could I explain what I'd done, how I'd survived? Dreaming, water's peculiar reaction to me, communication with animals. *No, one preternatural abnormality at a time.*

"Though cussing and defying the laws of nature does have a tendency to draw attention," he added with a pointed grin.

I took a shaky breath. "I was afraid you weren't going to acknowledge the reason I'm soaking wet."

"I had planned to circle back around to it after I appeased my curiosity on several other subjects."

"I'd rather circle back around to it now," I huffed.

He shrugged passively. "You're not the first Fae I've seen."

"Your dismissal is rather unnerving."

"What's unnerving is the reason you came out here alone. Has everything that has happened over the last month not been enough to make you understand the risk?"

He knows. Of course he knows. I lowered my head, ashamed. "I know you claim that nothing was my fault, but you're wrong. Everything that has happened is because of me. The bandits. The bear. You and Flint. All me."

"How narcissistic of you." He sighed. "Don't concern yourself with anything going on between my brother and me. Our dynamic changes hourly. Better you ignore it than get involved."

"You said I didn't fear vulnerability, so I took matters into my own hands."

His eyes darkened. "*That's* what you got out of what I said? That it was acceptable to risk your life because you're blindly audacious?" He stopped walking and pulled my shoulder, turning me to face him. I avoided his eyes and stared into the fragile threading of his shirt. The V-shaped neckline plunged to his breastbone, where the edge of a scar defaced his tanned skin. "Remind me to never pay you another compliment."

"I couldn't stand those bellowing echoes another minute. I don't want anyone or anything to suffer because of me."

He released my shoulder and kept walking. "Is he alive or dead?"

"Alive."

He raked his hand through his hair and took a deep breath. "What possessed you to do something so stupid?"

Flustered, I pried my fingers loose from his grip. "I can't explain it, but it was the right thing to do."

"Then you want to explain to me how you're alive?"

"I don't want to tell you anything. You were in the Onyx Guard. I'm sure you can figure it out. Do you have any idea how difficult it is to be around you? To tiptoe through your contradictions? To have you look at me knowing exactly what I am and never understand how much I fear that?" I scraped my nails against my scalp. "Maybe . . . I'm not going to keep divulging information without some sort of compensation."

He gave an amused grin when I repeated his words. "What sort of compensation? What do you want?" He repeated my response verbatim. "I'm not used to having my own words used against me," he said, touching the pout in my bottom lip.

The cavern came into view. I would have certainly missed it without him, as the fire had reduced to a clump of embers.

Darric slid the tripod off the coals and added wood to the fire to relight the flames. "Sit down," he instructed and went inside the Hovel.

The heat tingled my toes as my boots warmed. I wrapped his cloak tighter around my shoulders, briefly holding the woolly fabric to my nose and breathing in. I had yet to figure out why his smell made me lightheaded or why I wanted to continue to put myself in such a ridiculous state.

The injured bear had peered into my head and seen the constant flood of my stranger. Was I truly obsessed with him? If my reaction to his smell was any indication, then the answer was a startling *yes*.

Finding Darric captivating, a man who had spent most of our early acquaintance threatening to slice me in two, was no better than having an attraction to Prince Marcus. The Podarian heir was strikingly handsome; only an idiot would think otherwise. Graceful and poised, powerful and regal—I knew the supposed description of physical attractiveness. Darric looked nothing like Marcus, though their physiques were hauntingly similar, as though war had sculpted both their bodies.

Darric looked rough around the edges, unpolished. Not one blond hair on his head was the same length. And his eyes— inscrutable and enough to make me dizzy.

Despite not being a Fae, there was much I could learn from him, if I ever managed to stop the fog every time he came close to me. My brain was confusing curiosity for desire. *Desiring Darric?* I smiled and laughed at myself. What a preposterous idea.

The Hovel door opened. Darric stood in the doorway, his heavy cloak laid over his arm and his gray haversack slung over his shoulder. *Ridiculous. Inconceivable.*

After setting the pack by my feet, he pulled his cloak from my shoulders and exchanged it for the one lined with rabbit fur. It was double the warmth and as soft as my robes at the palace. "Do you want me to wake up Flint?" he asked.

I wrinkled my nose, exasperated. "Why would I want you to do that?"

"Comfort?" he answered with a shrug.

I raised one eyebrow. Flint would only cause an altercation by accusing Darric of lacerating my hand.

He smiled. "Bromly?"

I shook my head.

"Then may I suggest you stay silent during this process so as not to wake them."

He removed two bottles from his haversack: first the brown decanter of red wine, then another made of clouded dark green glass. He set folded white linen on his knee and uncorked the wine. "Bottoms up."

I bashfully took the decanter and drank a conservative mouthful. It tasted terrible, worse than it had the first time. I grimaced, and he pushed the bottle back towards my lips. "You'll need it."

Conceding, I gulped several times before noticing his fingers positioned on the underside of the bottle to prevent me from stopping. I pushed away his hand, and wine dribbled down my chin. "Stop!" I scolded, wiping my face.

He frowned and urged the decanter towards me a third time, but I shied away from it.

"You are going to regret not drinking more of this," he said. "I'm sorry I don't have anything stronger."

"My day might have been hell, but I don't need to be drunk."

He gave a defeated nod. "Suit yourself. Being stubborn doesn't always pay off though." He corked the decanter and set it next to his foot. Reaching for the clouded green bottle with one hand, he offered me his open palm with the other. "Give me your hand."

Wearily, I extended my injury. He snatched my wrist and tightened his grip so I couldn't pull away, then uncorked the new decanter with his teeth and spat the stopper onto the ground. "Hmm . . ." He looked over the atrocious tear. "I should have brought you some leather."

"Why would I need leather?"

"To bite down on. Too late now," he said.

Everything dawned on me at once. Trying not to awaken his brothers. The grip he had on my wrist. The wine. The linen. The new green bottle. Terror shot through me. What was in this decanter? I tried to break free of his grasp, but he didn't allow me to budge.

"Wait—wait—wait. This is going to hurt, isn't it?" I asked frantically.

"Yes." In tandem with his reply, he poured a large splash onto my hand.

The crystal-clear liquid felt like molten metal. Intense, fiery pain blazed up my arm as it washed away blood pooled in the fleshy gash. I wailed in agony, going weak at the shoulder, and tears welled in my eyes.

"I'm sorry," he added and released my wrist.

I drew my hand into the protection of my lap and doubled over, tucking my head down as the tears broke the barrier.

Darric placed the evil bottle on the ground and brought his arm around my back to pull me to his chest. I buried my head in his shoulder and let the tears flow onto his shirt.

"I know it hurts like hell," he whispered beside my ear. His lips brushed my skin, sending an enticing tickle down my side. He gently rubbed the arch of my spine until the radiating pain began to subside. "You can't scream like that again. You'll wake my brothers. Unless you want them around now?"

Quivering, I shook my head and smashed my sniffling nose against him. "You should have warned me."

"I did warn you."

"I wouldn't consider *yes* a warning. Nor shoving alcohol down my throat without providing a reason."

"If I had given you any more warning, you wouldn't have allowed me to do it." He angled his head, trying to find my eyes. I fought the temptation to look at him, unsure my body could handle another rush of adrenaline. I didn't want him to see me with a red nose, glazed in tears. "Aya," he murmured, running his fingers through my almond tresses to pull the strands away from my face. His calloused fingers grazed the back of my neck. "We are going to count backwards from six."

"Six?" I blinked numerous times to refocus and met his gaze. Even as close as we were in our tiny private circle, the intoxicating blue of his irises became lost in the dim light.

I found it increasingly difficult to concentrate. I pushed away from his chest, needing to reduce the fog. My heart regulated, thanking me for the increased distance.

He exchanged the bottles for a wooden spool of thick black thread with a silver needle tucked into it. I puzzled at the odd items; black threading was costly and silver no less expensive. He threaded the needle and waited patiently for me to reextend my hand.

"Why is that necessary? Can't we wrap it?" I argued in alarm.

"It's necessary if you plan to use your hand again."

Disheartened, I offered my hand, wishing I'd drunk more wine to counteract the pain.

He reached under the cloak to wrap his arm around my waist and slid me close to him. "Hold on to me if you need to. You won't hurt me."

I gripped his back and buried my face in his shoulder to avoid watching.

"Backwards from six, all right?" His voice steadied in concentration.

I nodded weakly.

A sharp pinch zinged through the sensitive wound. It paled in comparison to the fire liquid, but at least I'd only had to endure *that* once. I smashed my mouth into his shirt, swallowing a cry that turned into a pathetic, muffled squeak.

"Six," he said softly and drove the needle through a second time. "Five."

My arms began to shake, radiating the vibration into my fingertips. The thread pulled my skin relentlessly, tugging at the wound and closing the gash. I dug my nails into Darric's back and twisted a handful of fabric as the needle pushed through again.

"Four. You're halfway," he continued.

I held my breath, unable to subdue my violent trembling.

Once more, the needle traveled through my flesh. "Three." He tugged gently on the string, tightening the center stitch. My skin felt tight, as if I should close my hand or risk tearing open the stitching.

I drowned his next count with the scream I muted into his shoulder, gripping hard on his back. My nails sliced into his skin, but he didn't react. Instead he drove the needle through my flesh the final time and pulled the thread taut. The pain lessened when the cold air could no longer torture the open muscle. I exhaled, and my entire body shuddered.

He tied off the threading and lowered his head to bite through the remaining string. "It's really advantageous that we didn't have to do this to your neck. I would have lost as much blood as you. Your nails are a formidable weapon. That's twice you've dug those things into me."

"I'm sorry," I mumbled.

He slid the needle back into the spool and tossed the thread into his pack.

Physically and mentally drained, I held tightly to his shoulder. I wasn't ready for him to push me away. If his past transgressions had not still dominated my thoughts, I might have considered falling asleep in his arms.

"You don't need to be sorry." He ran a finger down my cheek and hooked it under my chin. Lifting my eyes to his, he searched my exhausted expression as his hand massaged my spine. My lungs forgot how to take in air. "If you ever come to understand what a baneful thing I've done by allowing you at the Hovel, you won't feel sorry for anything." He traced his thumb over my chin. "I might have to tell you sooner than I planned, if only to get you to stop looking at me like this."

A surge of nervous spasms nullified my fatigue.

He brought his thumb to my bottom lip, catching his callous on my skin. "Aya . . . breathe."

I snapped away from him and let the trapped air out of my lungs.

He turned over my palm. A spiral-like stitch fastened the wound shut with six strokes of black thread. "I need to wrap this." He reached for the linen and gingerly bound the fabric around my hand. "I want you to promise me something. Don't go into the woods alone anymore. Animals and bandits are not the only dangers. I'm out there too, and if you walk up on me while I'm asleep . . ." He grimaced, tucking in the end of the fabric to complete my bandage. "I'm as much of a threat as everything else. I can't always be there to rescue you."

I tightened his cloak around my shoulders. "I don't need you to rescue me. I can stand my own ground."

"The way you did in the bandit cave?" He stood, displaying a mocking grin, and leaned down next to my ear. "And with the bear?"

I shoved him—with the wrong hand. My wrist buckled against his hard chest, and renewed pain seared across the stitched muscle. I grasped my hand and winced. "I've never known anyone who could go from being so charming to so offensively abhorrent in the same sentence."

Darric laughed as if he enjoyed when the twists of his personality caused me anguish. "Pleasure to have met you too, my lady."

"I have yet to decide if I feel the same way." The sting of anger erased any lingering traces of fog.

"That's a good thing. You should take it easy tonight. You're going to need your off hand." He wrapped his damp cloak around his shoulders, then took my hand without asking and helped me up. "Dry out your clothes. You can use one of my shirts in the meantime. Try to get some rest. I have a business proposition for you in the morning." He lifted his hood over his head, becoming someone terrifyingly familiar: the stranger who, despite his reservations, had beckoned me to follow him.

"You're going into the woods, aren't you?"

He plucked his haversack from the ground. "I don't have a room."

I bit my lip apprehensively. "What kind of business proposition?"

"You might find that patience can be something of a virtue."

"So can respect, integrity, and temperance," I replied spitefully.

He smirked and turned to leave. "Goodnight, Aya."

"Wait." Regardless of his brutish change, I still owed him gratitude. "Thank you."

"No need. I couldn't let you fester."

"Even so."

"You'll pay me back, you'll see."

"Compensation?" I rolled my eyes.

"We'll talk about that tomorrow." He set his hand on my waist, waiting until he had my eyes to speak. I could just detect the outline of his face darkened by the hood. "I know over the last month I've been . . ." He gave a wicked smile. ". . . I really can't make you understand why right now. But I don't regret saving your life nor bringing you to the Hovel, even though I should. Aya, you are the most unique thing I have ever come across. I don't want anything to hurt you, and I'm going to make it so nothing ever does."

My throat stiffened. Without waiting for me to respond, he took several steps backwards and left the cavern.

The cat rubbed into my leg. Had she been here the entire time?

I watched him fade into the darkness, my stranger's figure becoming indistinct as he disappeared into the night. The short-faced bear was right. My head was toxified with Darric Ursygh, and it was absolutely unacceptable.

Chapter 19

A business proposition.

Darric's voice repeated the words inside my head.

How did he expect me to rest? He knew I didn't sleep. He knew I would wait in his room, naked and antsy, for the rest of the night.

I fell back onto his pillow, causing the mattress to poof when I landed, and twisted the fur blankets around my lower body. I had nothing on below the waist. Darric had four shirts to choose from: two lacking sleeves and two bearing them. Hiding in his room, scantily clad, was going to be immodest enough, especially with Bromly and Flint sleeping in the adjacent rooms. I opted for sleeves.

I wrung out my clothes, hung them on the extra wooden hooks, and threw Darric's shirt over my head. The adequate cotton material covered all the important areas, though the neckline almost touched my navel and the arms drooped over my hands. The thin fabric left little to the imagination.

I opened the laces of my shoes to help the leather dry and left Luken's dagger on the nightstand, then hopped into bed for warmth.

The cat addled my nerves, anxiously pacing the room and swishing her tail in restless jerks.

How long was it until daylight? Inside the Hovel, it would be impossible to know the time.

My injured hand throbbed. Whenever I moved my fingers or made a fist, a painful burn triggered lightning strikes up my arm. No more hunts for me. Divine Fae or not, the old injured male would kill me if I ever joined them again. He had sliced my palm as a punishment, a reminder of how I had permanently altered him. It would leave a scar, but thanks to Darric's expeditious attention, I would still have a working hand.

I drifted in and out of thoughts until the fur door cracked open, allowing a thin sliver of orange light into the room. I snatched the covers to my chest, and the shirt fell off my shoulder at the abrupt movement.

"Get dressed and meet me outside," Darric gently instructed and closed the fur.

I leaped out of bed and snatched my chemise. The dry fabric held a remnant chill, but I quickly dressed, threw on my shoes and tightened Luken's dagger around my ankle, grabbed my cloak, and raced through the Hovel and into the cavern.

Darric waited next to the fire, arms crossed over his chest, his figure silhouetted against the morning sun and the hood of his cloak pulled down to shade his eyes. He slipped the hood back and looked at me with a sedate expression. "Do you still want to learn to wield a sword?"

"Yes!" I exclaimed, covering my mouth in disbelief.

"Shh." He put his hand up to quiet me. "Don't wake anyone up."

I bit into my lip.

"Come with me." He headed for the exit, and I followed him into daylight.

Darric walked beside me, leaving the cat between us. In time, we reached the waterfall and passed into the tree line, where he took a sharp left and continued through the woods. A mysterious feeling of familiarity pervaded my mind. I couldn't recall ever coming to this edge of the valley, yet it felt as though I'd been here before.

The cliffs grew closer, and I began to fear we would be climbing. Darric may have found enjoyment in scaling the side of mountains, but the amusement was lost on me.

He walked up to the rock, turned right, and vanished behind the stone. I gaped. The cliff rock wasn't flat but layered. Two separate ledges created a pathway between the crag, impossible to detect until standing next to it. Following, I turned into the stone, and my legs went weak at the sight before me.

Millions of wisteria blooms grew in a canopy under the trees. The petals fell readily to the ground, littering the supple grass with floral sprinkles of color. Thin and delicate trees intertwined their branches, creating woven masterpieces of natural beauty. The immeasurable number of pink and purple blooms blocked most of the sunlight, leaving limited rays of yellow crystalline beams to illuminate the forest.

It's real. The wisteria forest was real. It had not been an intoxicated delusion after all.

The cat swiftly scaled a tree and perched on a high branch. She contentedly watched petals drift to the ground, mesmerized by the flicker of color.

"You've brought me here before . . ." I breathed, stunned.

Darric set his haversack by the base of a tree. "You happened to be in tow the last time I was on my way back to the Hovel.

I'd call it an accident, but . . ." He scoffed, shaking his head, and chuckled to himself. The cliff we had descended a month ago towered to my left, covered with a complicated system of roots.

"You told me this place wasn't real. You had me believing I hallucinated it," I tried to scold him, but the striking beauty of the forest kept my anger muted.

"And it worked." He grinned cheekily. "This forest is the most remote part of the valley and the farthest point away from the Hovel. I've never seen anyone enter from this direction, because the above cliffs are too steep. You too almost fell to your death. It was incredible you followed me down here without injuring yourself. I've never seen anyone so compelled to stay with me, no matter how difficult the terrain became."

"It wasn't easy," I stated.

"Nor did I try to make it such." He paused, nervously taking his cloak from his shoulders. He laid it over the tree behind him and leaned against the bark. "No one will ever see us here or know where we are. Not even Bromly and Flint know about this place."

My jaw dropped into an inaudible gasp. "*That's* why you didn't want me to remember it?"

"I've kept this location to myself. I've always tended to seek isolation and . . . I like it here. The privacy gives me a chance to lower my guard. When I'm not at the Hovel, I'm usually here."

"It's beautiful." I turned in a circle, gazing into the treetops. Petals landed on my face, tickling my cheeks and sticking to my curls. "I couldn't fully appreciate it last time."

"You were in a poison-induced haze." He watched my amazement, then uncomfortably shifted his lean. "I have a proposition for you. I am willing to teach you to wield a sword."

"You've changed your mind?" I blinked rapidly at this new development.

"I believe you are capable of learning. I wouldn't waste my time otherwise. Though it's going to be difficult for you. And for me. So I hope you are prepared for that. I've never willingly taught anyone to wield a sword. Flint has asked for lessons in the past, but the way I learned . . ." He drifted into thought but quickly resurfaced. "I use techniques I'd rather not reveal to them, but everything I have in my arsenal will be at your disposal. And here"—he waved his hand to indicate the surrounding forest—"is where I'll teach you."

"We'll be alone?" I questioned, my stomach twisting into an uncertain knot.

"Against my better judgment, yes. But it's necessary. Flint has never forgiven me for refusing to instruct him. He's not going to take this well. It will be hard enough on him without having to watch."

"Are they allowed to know you are teaching me?"

"Yes, but I will decide when and how we tell them. And they will never know where we are. I'm protective over this spot. I won't be able to get away from them completely if they know all my hiding places."

"All? You have more?"

He deflected the question with a condescending smile.

I folded my arms over my chest. "What about being able to get away from me?"

"I'm less concerned about you." He casually rested his forearms on the branch above his head. The sunlight scattered glimmering rays across his intense stare.

Elated as I was that Darric had finally agreed to instruct me, I still wasn't confident I could handle spending that much time alone with him and not combust. Trying to manage a fogged brain and a pounding heart every day was a daunting proposition.

"In the beginning, we'll train in the early morning while my brothers are asleep and there is work to be done at the Hovel. It will keep them occupied. In the past, they have respected my need for solitude, but I doubt they will be so accommodating if I have you with me. Eventually, we'll practice at night. Everything about combat is different in the dark."

"Why the secrecy?"

"I'm used to moving in the shadows. It's a trait I developed in the Onyx Guard, and I've never been able to sever myself from it. It's something you will learn. Stealth will become critical in your future. Many of my teaching methods are bound to be somewhat unorthodox. Swords are as much a mental game as a physical one. You are not going to learn just how to wield a sword. I'm going to teach you to fight like *I* do."

The longer I stood in the desultory sunlight and floral disarray, with Darric's unapologetic stare holding me, the more I became wary of his motives. "There's a catch."

He nodded. "In point of fact, I'll teach you everything I know about weaponry and swords, and you will act freely as yourself around me. No more hiding any ability you have. Everything out in the open. That is the intention of instructing you in a secret location. A Fae trained under my direction . . . well, it could be inconceivable the amount of damage you could inflict."

"You're curious," I observed and rolled my eyes. "Compensation."

"Both ways." He tossed a petal out of his hair by flicking his head back. "If I knew what you were capable of, I could work it to my advantage when instructing you. I'm not going to pretend I know more about the Fae than I do—members of the Onyx Guard are not allowed into the inner sanctum of Medial Alexandria—but I am well aware that dreaming isn't the only idiosyncratic quality of the Fae. In Varanus, we took a boy who could control water. He could unhinge it. Manipulate it. Bend it to his will. In Aogar, there was a girl who communicated with a colony of rats, and another in a rural village outside of Zullas who displayed an artistry with weaponry. These talents are the true purpose behind the Senate sending the Onyx Guard to hunt the Fae. Each and every one has been taken to Medial Alexandria to be killed, experimented on, or brutalized. All. Except you." He pointed a finger at me. "If you knew how to defend yourself, if you knew the skills I know, the Onyx Guard would never be able to touch you."

The more Darric spoke of the Senate and the Onyx Guard, the less likely it seemed they would care I was Divine. I was at their mercy outside of Alamantia Palace. He knew I needed protection and, for some reason, wanted to ensure I had it. It should have been an easy decision: trade exposing my abilities for defensive instruction. Yet, I was panicking. I rested my forehead against the closest tree trunk and held my stomach.

Darric massaged his fingers into my shoulder. His warm hand ran under my hair and covered the back of my neck. "One of the first things I'm going to teach you is control. You fall into hysteria much too easily." He put his hand on my waist and turned me to face him. "Why are you afraid?"

The tremors amplified, and my thoughts blurred. I pushed on his chest, trying to put distance between us. "Darric," I pleaded, releasing the sweet smell of blossoms from my lungs and unintentionally inhaling his heady scent. *It's the wisteria, permeated into his skin somehow.* I shoved harder. He released me and I backed away and sank into the grass.

"Hmm, you do realize to train you properly, I can't always maintain my distance."

Everything that makes you a Fae, Ayleth. Agree to it, under one condition . . .

"I want to add a clause," I blurted through short spurts of air.

He folded his arms over his chest. "I'm listening."

"You won't ask me anything about my life prior to the day we met. I will show you everything I can do, but my former existence will be at my own discretion to reveal and do so under my own terms."

He scanned me, then scoffed, disliking my counteroffer. "Agreed," he said after mulling it over. Taking my hand, he pulled me from the ground. "Bear in mind that your additional clause entitles me to my own."

Afraid to ask, I stared at my feet, watching the breeze blow petals across the grass. "What do you want?"

"One request of my choosing to be defined in the moment, however I deem appropriate, and to be carried out immediately by you, no matter the context or task," he answered quickly and without apprehension. "Let's call it an *ambiguity*."

"That's ridiculous!" I shrieked, and the cat gave an angry howl from her perch.

"If I'm supposed to ignore any question I have about your past *and* teach you to wield a sword, then I'm going to have a condition of my own." He eyed the displeased feline. The tension in his muscles increased, and he rolled his shoulders.

"The terms of my condition were defined. You're trying to add vague, exploitative stipulations," I argued.

"If you want an obscure past, then I want an ambiguity. Otherwise, we can go back to my original proposition—weapons training in exchange for exposing your Fae abilities to me, both of which benefit you exceedingly more than me."

I balled my fists contemptuously. "This is extortion."

"I prefer to think of it as strategizing for the future."

Of all things to possibly want. Backed into a corner, I would live in terror wondering when he would call upon his self-defined *ambiguity*, but I couldn't have him interrogating me about my past.

"Do we have a deal, my little cave Fae?" he proposed.

I furrowed my brows, setting my hands to rest on my hips. "Yes, we have a deal, my arrogant antagonist."

"Presumptuous, Aya." He unfolded his arms and drew his sword. "Not that I disagree with you." He began circling me like a hawk. "Now that the contract is out of the way, allow me to explain several . . . oh, let's call them rules." He walked slowly and with purpose, using his sword as an exaggerated emphasis to his words. "Revealing anything to my brothers about this forest or what takes place within it is strictly forbidden. I will train you in control, focus and concentration, balance, attention to detail, physical conditioning, speed and agility, defense and offense." He stopped and faced me. "I am the instructor and you are the student. There will be consequences for disrespect. For questioning me. For disobeying me. You will accept that I will not shed mercy upon you, because neither will any opponent you ever encounter. Chivalry and benevolence are beautiful sentiments but account for nothing in combat. Ruthlessness is the only true way to ensure you are standing when the fight is over. Your lessons will reflect these concepts, and you will endure anything and everything I decide is constructive to your training. Thus, a day's lesson is over when I say it is and not a moment sooner. If you ever walk out of training due to anger, misplaced emotion, or exhaustion, your lessons will come to an abrupt and immediate end. In return, you will show me every Fae ability you possess. I will not interrogate you about your past, and you will consent to my ambiguity when I call upon it."

The shadow of an assassin emerged through his menacing words, and my core iced. I remembered him coated in bandit blood—how he terrified me by the way he had skillfully ended their existence. Staring down the first day of real weapons training, I grappled for composure. I felt hollow. Intimidated. Daunted by the task.

When I failed to answer, he flourished his sword and released the grip. The blade stuck in the ground, and he rapidly crossed the distance between us. "Aya, breathe." He grasped both sides of my face.

I inhaled with a sharp high-pitched gasp.

"Stop doing that," he scolded. "Take deeper, steadier breaths. Don't pant so much and don't hold your breath. You were turning blue."

I gulped air and exhaled.

"Slower." His hands slid down my arms and gripped my waist. "Take your time, hold the breath, then let everything out. Force the anxiety from your chest. You must fight your subconscious mind. If you can't win that battle, you'll be hopeless in a real one. Stop letting your emotions control your reactions."

I closed my eyes, feeling his thumbs graze my ribs. Each steady breath cleared the fog.

"We really are going to have to start with the basics if I have to teach you breathing techniques." He hooked his finger under my chin. For the first time, my heart didn't break into a frenzy when he studied me. Satisfied, he retrieved his sword and took a seat against one of the many twisted wisteria trees. "You wear your emotions like a second skin."

I sank into the grass. What had happened to the iron Princess always in such perfect balance and control? She could strike fear into her ladies with a single glance. Now she cowered like a kitchen mouse in the cupboard. When Aya replaced my reality, all my royal training disappeared. I'd lost all sense of restraint or discipline to a clumsy peasant. "It's strange that you've seen my affectivity so exposed. There was a time, not so long ago, when most thought I was made of stone."

"That's exponentially hard to believe." He adjusted his back against the bark.

"Dispassion is embedded in the person I used to be. It was something of a requirement."

He cocked his head to the side. "Our agreement has me silenced on this subject. Define it for me. Am I allowed to ask questions, or am I supposed to sit here and feign aphasia?"

A tiny laugh escaped my lips. "I suppose you can ask, but no interrogating, and I want the luxury of refusing to answer without repercussion."

"I can live with that." He dropped the hilt of his sword, letting the blade fall to the grass as though he didn't care about the weapon.

"Considering I have to live in dread of your ambiguity, it's hardly a sacrifice."

He suppressed a conspicuous grin. "It's more problematic than you realize. Addressing the past while learning to wield a sword has benefits. Facing who you really are is difficult for most people, and tapping into one's driving force fuels power. Becoming more deeply aware of your own sentiments and predilections will help you control them. You're making me circumvent that. I'll have to come up with a more *creative method* to get you to employ this *dispassion*, though I can't say I'm looking forward to it. Your exposed affectivity is one of my favorite aspects about you. Training you correctly will cause you to lose much of that asset."

My cheeks flushed. "I'm surprised you find anything about me appealing. I thought I was a nuisance."

"You are absolutely a nuisance, but that doesn't suppress the things I do find engaging about you."

"Water and dreaming?"

"Among other traits."

"I doubt I'll ever master the same level of control you have." I tucked in my feet, taking care to keep Luken's dagger hidden beneath my skirt.

"It's just practice," he confessed. "Flint likes to spread the idea that I'm a lit cannon, and maybe that's true. I've been judged on my actions, but not even my brothers understand the options I've had. Keeping my emotions contained doesn't mean I don't feel. I've just learned to manipulate them, because I wasn't given a choice. For instance"—he leaned forwards and shuffled his hand through the back of his hair to remove stuck petals—"when battling an enemy, you must take emotion out of the situation. Anger is likely to cause you to make a fatal error or lose your footing, kill gratuitously, or take unnecessary risk to injure an adversary. Sorrow will cause you to fight weakly and ineffectively, leading to suicide. Quelling emotion until the fight is won is critical. Remaining detached is a weapon. It does immense psychological damage to an enemy. Your opponent assumes you don't care if you live or die as long as he is destroyed in the end. If they are afraid, you gain the upper hand. Fear is lethal."

"That's psychological warfare," I discerned, recalling how he had stood, cold and immovable, against a two-thousand-pound short-faced bear.

"The basic aspects. It's not something you can master unless you dominate your own sentiment." He chuckled. "I'm not expecting you to become a bloodcurdling psychopath overnight."

"I suspect it was easy for you to employ such maniacal behavior," I said snidely.

"Of the two of us, I am not the one who is legally considered insane, and remember what I said about disrespecting your instructor, Aya."

I bit my tongue, timidly lowering my gaze.

"We need to head back before my brothers wake up. It's become blatantly obvious Flint doesn't like you disappearing." He stood, shoving his sword back into the scabbard.

I took the hand he offered and dusted blooms off my dress. "He's oddly possessive."

"Well, he really didn't want me to kill you." Darric plucked several petals from the top of my head. "We'll come back at first light tomorrow. We are going to examine that water anomaly of yours in further detail."

I bounced with excitement. "And stay until Flint starts screaming my name across the valley."

During the walk back to the Hovel, I paid special attention to the landscape, trying to record the trees and the placement of rocks. I wanted to remember the forest's location.

In revealing his most secret hiding place, Darric had shown me a side of himself I'd never imagined existed, a gentleness he kept reserved. Something about sharing in his mystery fascinated me, and the growing number of similarities between us became an intriguing concept.

The cat trotted under my cloak as I paced several feet behind him, using his breathing techniques to stay calm. The clouded view I had of my stranger became lucid, and parts of him emerged that had gone unforeseen. His entire body always seemed relaxed, except for his shoulders. Often, he rolled one or the other, as if he carried every burden he had ever encountered in the tension of his upper back. The lean muscle of his triangular torso, vaguely outlined under his shirt, and the slack in his sword belt hanging low around his hips adjusted into a clearer image. Despite his knowledge and long history, he could not have been much older than me.

The details of his contemptible past were written in the telltale scars defacing his striking biceps. Flint said he was covered in his transgressions—the marks of an assassin with insane audacity. But despite the visible mistakes, he was wildly and bewilderingly handsome.

My cheeks lit fire.

Combustion was likely.

I trailed away, forcing myself to stop lustfully imagining him in a way that would allow me to see *all* his scarring—an amorphous image anyway, since my life had been kept chaste under the King's repressive guard.

Darric turned around and gave me a quizzical glare. I touched my cheek, hoping the heat had dissipated. Never in my life had I thought of a man so lewdly, and of all people in Athera to invade my head without a stitch of clothing, Darric Ursygh. What the hell was happening to me?

We reached the cavern minutes before Bromly emerged, sleepy-eyed, from the Hovel. He greeted us with a lazy yawn and commenced pulling smoked pieces of bear meat off the tripod to place in a woven basket.

By the afternoon, Flint still had not come out of his room.

Bromly created a bowl of foul-smelling gray slurry, which he smeared on the bear skins while whistling a merry tune. Wanting to avoid the stench, I offered to rouse Flint.

Inside the Hovel, the last fur door remained closed. "Flint?"

"Aya?" he replied immediately.

I eased the pelt away from the doorframe. Flint sat on the edge of his bed, fully dressed and fiddling with his flute. Unlike Darric's room, Flint's had clutter everywhere. Articles of clothing were draped over the bed and nightstand and littered the floor. Two woven baskets hanging from the wall overflowed with a variety of random items: unsharpened knives, cups, dried flowers, spoiling vegetables, and old bowls full of moldy food. The sheets and furs on his bed were twisted into knots, and some of the stuffing was falling out of his mattress. In the corner, a pile of bandit swords collected dust beside his quiver and bow.

"Are you all right?" I asked, taking in the depressing condition of his room.

"I'm great." He smiled wide. "Better now that you're here."

"Does your room always look like this?" I eyed the empty clothing pegs on the wall.

"Uh . . . yeah." He scratched the side of his nose. "It's my space. I do what I want with it."

I backed out of the door to escape the pungent odor. "Lovely."

He joined me outside his room, and the fur swung closed behind him. "What time is it?"

"Afternoon. Darric and Bromly are expecting you to be working."

His upper lip quivered. "They sent ya to fetch me, huh?"

"No, I volunteered." My eyes drifted to the unsightly bruise circling his pale neck.

"Really?" A flirtatious twinkle entered his eyes. He attempted to clasp my mangled hand, but I jerked away. "What happened to your hand?" He seethed when he saw the white bandage, his skin turning a flaming red. "Did Darric do this to you?"

"Flint, calm down," I said, annoyed. "Darric didn't do anything. I had a small accident, and he treated it for me."

"Psh, like I believe that shit."

"Believe what you want. It's the truth." I crossed my arms over my chest.

His angry coloration lingered as he quickly changed the subject. "At least it's nice to see your sweet face wakin' me up instead of Bromly's ugly mug." He swallowed nervously, and his larynx bobbed. "Your eyes look so pretty on your face."

He wavered on the balls of his feet, licked his lips, and dipped his head. Alarm rushed through me when his morning breath surged through his teeth. I pushed against his chest and twisted out of the way as his lips grazed the side of my mouth.

"What are you doing?" I shrieked, flattening my back against the wall.

"I thought ya were . . . I thought ya wanted me to," he stammered.

I slammed my fist into the doorframe. "Flint! I didn't come in here to *entertain* you!"

"I meant . . . I didn't . . . I just . . . ." He held up his hands, his fingers trembling in midair.

"What? What then?" I raged.

He covered his reddened face with his hands.

I shoved off the wall and ran from the Hovel. How many times did I have to explain that I was not for the taking?

I stormed past Darric and Bromly, ignoring their confused expressions, and left the cavern.

The sun beamed down on the open valley. I lay in the grass just outside the cavern entrance and stared at the clouds. The fresh spring breeze from the mountains filled my lungs, eradicating the rancid potato breath clinging to the side of my mouth. I wiped a trace of Flint's saliva from my cheek and listened to the lull of water rushing over the rocky riverbed.

Flint scurried out of the Hovel. His brothers eyed him suspiciously. "Women." He shrugged with a laugh.

I sent one malicious glare in their direction and turned my attention back to the blue sky. Flint's indecency would not get the better of me.

I spent the afternoon outside the cavern with the cat pressed against my side, staring at the puffs of white clouds as they changed shape. Everything else disappeared when I looked into the same sky that encompassed all Brisleia.

My entire life I'd craved freedom. The engagement to Prince Marcus should have provided the solution. My reasoning for opposing the marriage was becoming less clear. Perhaps this had never been about our union or relocating to Podar but my desire to run from the life of a Divine royal.

When Luken and I were younger, we would lie in the grass and stare at the blue dome above us. I wanted to turn into a bird and touch the sky. He always brought veracity. He was grounded, attached to the land the same way a tree weaves roots into the soil.

By the time Prince Marcus paraded into the Rose Court, years had passed since my brother and I wandered the palace gardens. Responsibility at Parliament and court ruled our lives. The days spent imagining our future changed from childish fantasy to reality.

"If you could have anything, anything your heart desired, what would it be?"

Luken was older than me by four years and a model of Divinity.

In the past, our parents had tried to create more heirs. It was beneficial for the Divine to produce many descendants—King O'dern and Queen Nadeani of Duval had six children—but our mother was unable to carry future pregnancies. Each expectation ended in disappointment and risked the queen's life. Luken and I were the last of the Brisleian bloodline. *The Heir and the Spare.*

He lay beside me, our ears touching. The warm summer breeze pleasantly tickled our skin.

It was July the year I turned fourteen. The dreams were consuming me; I had not slept in weeks and desperately wanted to tell my brother, but I couldn't find the courage.

In those days, Luken wasn't being conditioned by the King to rule Brisleia. His duties were not extensive. He spent his time lazily wandering the palace, flirting with maidens, hunting, and enjoying endless hours in the bliss of childhood. It wouldn't last. He would turn eighteen that summer and come of age.

"We have everything." I groaned. "I don't want more jewels or dresses."

"I meant in a nonmaterialistic sense," he revised.

"I don't want to be Divine," I whispered.

I felt his head turn towards me; his nose brushed my cheek. "That's not something I can change for you."

"Being King doesn't mean you have to fix everything. I know there are things that, no matter what you do, you can't change. But that won't stop me from wanting it. You asked, so I answered."

He tugged a lock of my hair and tossed the curl over my face. "If I can't provide happiness to my own sister, then what kind of callous King would that make me?"

"A normal one." I smoothed back the misplaced curl.

"I don't understand. Why would you want to wish away your Divinity? It's such a grand honor to be Divine. Everyone relies on us. Needs us. Our lives matter more than anyone else's in Athera. We're special. You're special. We have the liberty of never needing to guess our purpose for living." He pointed into the sky, directing my attention. "Look at that cloud, pristine white and soft. It's there because the Brisleian Divine are alive."

"Don't you ever feel like we are in a prison?" I squeezed a handful of grass in both reality and my memories. *"A beautiful prison where our shackles are disguised as fine amenities? The Divine lose their humanity in exchange for service to the people, and we have*

no choice in the matter. Forbidden to transcend our circumstances. Why can't I see it like everyone else? Why can't I understand the honor behind it and just be happy with my fate?"

Luken paused for a long moment before answering. *"I can't imagine my life any other way. I was born to this privilege, without regret. I have always been sure of one thing: I am Divine, and someday I will watch over Brisleia as the Divine King. It is my identity. That certainty keeps me strong when I feel scared about the future. I was meant for this, as were you. The honor lies in our ability to know our own sacrifice to Athera and be willing to give ourselves for the benefit of the planet."*

I tore my handful of grass. *"It makes me selfish, doesn't it?"*

"I want to say no."

I sighed. *"But you can't."*

He lightly shook his head. *"Turning your back on the Divine and leaving the fate of millions up to chance, that would be selfish. You wanting to be like everyone else is an unusual trait for a Princess, but you deserve happiness, and I can't blame you for it. In fact, I love you for the way you see the world. You make me think of my own Divinity in ways I never would have if you hadn't been my sister. It's a part of you I'm always going to cherish."*

"You're the only one. I know I'm alone in my thinking." I paused, seeing Elizabetta walking up the stone path. She tried to give us space to talk privately but had difficulty maintaining her distance. *"Haven't you ever thought about what it would be like to not live in the palace, to be somebody else completely?"*

"No," he answered quickly, *"and for the sake of myself, I can't. The idea of not being Divine, of waking up one day and finding the Mandala missing, terrifies me. I'm not sure I would survive if I was a nobody. I don't want to be a nothing. I want to lead. I want to help. I want to leave my name in history, to be a better King than my forefathers. Gentle but firm. Kind and fair. Generous."*

"Maybe the only reason you think that way is because you were born to it. Because you don't know anything else. It's ingrained.

Shouldn't you want to be those things without needing to be Divine?
Can't ordinary people provide as much as royalty?"

"Yes, of course. But Divinity allows me to become everything
I aim to be. As royalty I have always known which direction to
go." Luken sat up, twisting onto the balls of his feet, and plucked a
flower from beside my head. I closed my eyes, feeling his fingers brush
my temple as he laced the stem behind my ear. Momentarily, the
memories invaded reality. I could feel the change in pressure from
his feet pressing into the grass. I breathed in, and my lungs filled
with the smell of crushed wisteria petals. Where were the roses of
Alamantia Palace?

"I'll never rule a country. What can I possibly bring to the Divine
circle? I feel stranded. Extra. Without purpose. The Spare. I'll never
be as important as you. I want to wake up and not see the Mandala
staring back at me in the mirror. I want to know what it feels like
to be ignored and forgotten." The horrifying truth of my dreaming
lingered over my uncertain future. *"Luken, if one day I turn out to be*
. . . different . . . will you still care for me?" I murmured.

"You're my sister. Even when I am King, nothing will ever
change that. Our bond as siblings surpasses all others. I swear, when I
am King, you will have everything you've ever wanted. I will always
be there for you, no matter who or what you decide to become." He
touched the top of my head and ruffled my hair. I felt a callous. *"Are*
you all right? You've been acting strange lately."

"Bromly wants to know if you are hungry."

"What?" My eyes shot open. Darric leaned over me in the
same manner Luken had that day in the gardens, his face darkened
by the setting sun. The smell of wisteria blooms coming off his
skin had overpowered the reverie about my brother. "I'm not
hungry," I said, trying to disentangle my memories from reality.

"You can't stay out here much longer. The sun is going down.
I don't want you vulnerable." He twirled a small white flower
between his fingertips, and a second fell from behind my ear.

"The Hovel is thirty feet away from me," I argued, annoyed by his demands.

"I don't care if it's thirty or three," he sternly replied, dropping the bloom so it landed on my forehead.

I glared at him bitterly. "Do grounds for punishment count at the Hovel or only when we are training in the forest?"

He raised an amused eyebrow. "If that's your tactic, don't fault me for being passive aggressive."

I flicked the flower off my face. "If you weren't such a brazen ass, I might believe you were being protective."

"Chaperoning your kind was never on my immediate agenda until recently."

I sat up. "Amazing that you can be quite charming when you want to be."

"Brazen ass and all." He chuckled.

Chapter 20

The glow from the Riving mixed into the first traces of sunrise, giving the eastern sky an unusual complexion. An hour before daybreak, Darric and I headed back to the wisteria forest.

"Why are we taking Flint's bow?" I asked as we rounded the hidden crag. When Darric outlined the categories in which he would be instructing me, archery had not been among them. Yet, clasped in his hand was Flint's bow, with the quiver dangling from his wrist.

"Flint pissed me off yesterday," he said.

"Me too."

He waited for an explanation, but I remained silent. The thought of Flint's lips coming towards me in a clumsy gesture of affection was mortifying. I had done nothing to merit such appetency from him. Assuming he no longer believed I was a prostitute, why would he think I would want him to kiss me? How could he have concocted such an appalling idea?

I glanced at Darric, who seemed to be thinking of something rather pleasant, as his mouth was slightly upturned.

We continued through the floral woods until the sound of rushing water filled the forest. A towering cliff face appeared in front of us, and a narrow waterfall tumbled from a protruding ledge through the blooming canopy, crashing into a small crystalline pond.

"Wow." I gaped at the spectacular location.

Darric let the bow and quiver fall to the ground and removed his cloak. "Ready to get wet?" He gave a bawdy, self-satisfied smirk.

I narrowed my eyes, preparing a cutting remark, but quickly remembered we were officially in a training session; his clear rules about disrespect would demand disciplinary action. I snapped my jaw shut, and my cheeks flushed. He leaned against a nearby tree, widening the smug grin decorating his handsome face.

I turned my back to him and sat in the petal-covered grass to unlace my boots, secretly keeping Luken's dagger in place, then braided my hair and knotted it high atop my head. "I've never done this in front of anyone," I said, touching the chilly water with my toes. The cat gave a reassuring meow from a high perch within the trees.

"Technically, you have. I bore witness to your entire lake fiasco." He shrugged. "There is nothing to be apprehensive about."

"Nothing to be apprehensive about?" I scoffed, stepping onto the pond. "You're an ex-assassin of the Onyx Guard. Why should I be apprehensive about that?"

"*Ex* being the pivotal word in that statement."

Conceding, I walked across the pond, using my arms to maintain stability as the hem of my dress took on water. When I reached the center, I turned to face him. His head tilted inquisitively to the side, and his intense gaze had become inscrutable.

"You could say something," I squeaked.

He pushed off the tree trunk to approach the bank. "Can you do anything else aside from stand on it? When you ran onto the lake, something happened when your hands broke the surface."

I nodded. "Water tends to explode when I become overzealous, the way it would if you threw a rock into it."

"You need to discover your limitations and push through them. The Fae we kidnapped in Varanus attacked the regiment with well water."

"I don't know how to make it happen," I admitted. "It occurs when I'm upset or scared."

Darric held up a finger. Snatching Flint's bow, he hastily nocked an arrow, aimed at my chest, and released. The stone head rotated as it sped in my direction. I shrieked and covered my head, ducking over the pond.

The cat's howl of panic vanished behind the sound of crashing water. An explosion pulsed under my feet, and the vibrating pond knocked me off balance. I tore my hands free to catch myself as a circular wall of water surrounded me, creating a protective cocoon that floated in the air. The morning sunlight caught the motionless wave, exposing suspended blue sparkles that scattered across my skin and the surface of the water. Encased in the wall, the halted arrow slowly continued to rotate, unable to reach its target.

Stunned, Darric dropped Flint's bow.

I carefully stood and examined my creation. The water parted as I reached into the wall for the spinning arrow. The instant the weapon was in my hand, the defenses fell, crashing into the pond all at once and sending waves lapping up my legs. The blue sparkles dusting the floral trees steadily dimmed until they disappeared.

"You could have killed me," I murmured, unable to muster an appropriate reaction.

"Somehow, I find that unlikely," he mused, awestruck.

I tossed the arrow onto the bank

"Aya, the water is reacting to you. When I sent that arrow, you panicked and wanted protection. The water gave it to you. Tell it what you want."

I dropped to my knees. Leftover ripples washed over my thighs, sending a chill up my spine. I peered into the churning pond. It wasn't deep, and tiny confused fish swam among the murky weeds.

"This is where you need to employ focus and concentration." He sank onto the balls of his feet to meet my eyes. "The day Flint attempted to teach you to use a bow, I threw two objects at you. Do you know why?"

I gave him an aggravated glare and shifted uncomfortably. The cold, gelatinous sensation of the water under my legs still bewildered me.

"Try to answer without being spiteful. I understand I tried to shoot you, but I have validity," he expressed.

The urge to berate him became increasingly difficult, but I shoved back the anger and took a breath. "You threw a block of wood and then a knife." I groaned.

He grinned at the memory. "When fighting an adversary, concentration and focus are not about using all your energy to aim at one target. They are about opening your mind to everything around you." He set his elbows on his knees and clasped his hands together. "If I am concentrating on only one opponent or focusing all my energy on a single target, I'm going to miss the attacker coming from behind. Or hit an obstacle I didn't see. You were determined to make the perfect shot and ignored the fact that I stood behind you, well-armed, and could kill you at any moment. I broke your concentration to force you to pay more attention to your surroundings. You must see everything at once. Death is always going to come from the place you were not looking. Under no circumstances should a dragon sculpture have caused you to lower your bow. Note the activity, take the available shot, then rearm to face the next opponent."

"You're saying I should have hit the tree and then attacked you?" I confirmed skeptically.

He laughed. "*That* would have been impressive."

"And highly satisfying." I tapped my finger across the water, sending ripples towards the bank.

"Then work through your irritation and give yourself gratification. What's stopping you? Have I not given you ample reason to have animosity towards me?" He pulled a hunting knife from his boot.

I stuck my finger into the water and twirled it. The liquid formed a thin whirling vortex that spiraled to the murky bottom of the pond. Fish darted out of its way and hid among the sunken logs.

"I can provide more hostility if you need additional motivation." He brandished the blade.

Rise. The pillar of swirling water instantly shot skywards, wobbling over the pond's surface and sending me tumbling back onto my elbows. The spout smashed into the tree canopy and scattered hundreds of blooms and twinkles through the air.

I righted myself and held up my hands, closed my eyes, and imagined what I wanted. The cyclone moved across the churning surface, tearing through the beautiful flowers in its wake. I pushed it to the bank where Darric waited, motionless, blade ready. When the whirling vortex reached him, I abruptly lowered my arms. The water stopped spinning and fell, sending a crashing wave to the shore and soaking him in the process.

Foamy crests lapped over the grass, and trapped water rained from the branches. Darric's wet hair stuck to his forehead. His white shirt clung to his skin, contouring over his svelte muscular frame and allowing me to glimpse the history of scars covering his chest.

My face burned at the alluring sight, and I averted my eyes. *Stunningly handsome. Be quiet, Ayleth.*

He chuckled and pinched the front of his shirt, pulling the fabric away from his skin as he ran his other hand through his wet hair. "Now, that's more like it."

As the morning hours passed, Darric and I discovered the simple premise behind my water control. I could do anything I desired by imagining what I wanted; the water always complied. The act generated a soothing feeling mixed with a chilling freshness that skittered through my veins.

I raised thousands of droplets skywards so they rained down upon us. I cupped water into my hands to create dewlike globes, which I gratifyingly threw at him. Focus and concentration were crucial for complex actions, such as summoning multiple vortexes or transforming floating globes into shapes. The larger the quantity of water I controlled, the heavier the burden on my body and mind. We found my limit when he suggested I lift the entire pond into the air. Yet, shoving waves or strong jets onto the bank was relatively effortless. I laughed each time I sent another bombardment in his direction. He endured the drenched morning with enthusiasm and seemed fascinated by my preternatural ability.

The strangest aspect was the miraculous blue sparkles left behind after each feat of water control. They stuck to my hands and decorated every wet surface. "What is this stuff?" I finally asked.

He brushed the glittering specks off his arms. "The Senate calls it dust. It's a trace left behind from Fae power."

I fell onto the middle of the pond, thoroughly saturated, with wrinkled toes and a muddled brain. My muscles turned to jelly as

I crawled to the bank. "I'm exhausted," I said, transitioning back onto dry land.

Darric lay in the grass, and I plopped onto the ground beside him. He moved a long strand of dripping hair away from my face, and an electrified pang tightened my chest. "Phenomenal."

I hid a shy smile. "Nothing you haven't seen before."

"No, I've never seen anything like you." He gave a small laugh. "At least not while I was conscious."

I pulled my hair free of its knot, and the heavy tresses toppled down my back. "What about the kid you took in Varanus?"

"There is a substantial difference between a scared ten-year-old boy and a beautiful woman." He ran his fingers through my loose curls. "Especially when she's soaking wet."

"You think I'm beautiful?" I asked softly, knowing any answer would frighten me.

"It doesn't matter what I think," he grumbled, tucking his hand behind his head.

Confounded by his answer, I rested my head on the underside of his rigid arm. There was nothing yielding about him, and his bicep somehow managed to further stiffen. He lay beside me, immobile, my shoulder pressing into his ribs as we watched the tree canopy move with the breeze. Traces of cloudless blue sky were visible through the foliage, and the flickering sunlight filtered through the branches.

My weary mind settled. The tension in his arm lessened.

I craned my head back to look at him, and he swallowed hard. "Why doesn't it matter?"

"I've already broken enough rules by allowing you to stay at the Hovel and training you to fight," he said. "I'm trying to refrain from also becoming a traitor."

I wrinkled my nose. "A traitor? Like a betrayal?"

He unexpectedly sat up, and my head fell the short distance to the ground.

Unrelenting, I sat up next to him. "Does this have to do with Flint wanting to learn to wield a sword?"

"No." He set his wrists on his knees. "But I'm never going to teach him weaponry. I've thought about helping Bromly in the past, but out of respect for Flint, I've abstained."

"Why? You are already giving lessons to one. What's two?" I asked, leaning over his shoulder.

"I can't tell you without defaming him. I know he's been outspoken in his opinions of me, but I can't do the same to him."

The little feline jumped from her tree perch and pranced over to where we sat on the grass. "I could stand a little defamation of Flint." I tucked my knees under my chin. "He tried to kiss me yesterday."

Darric laughed and fell back onto the grass. "And did you enjoy it?" He acted amused, yet one of his fists was clenched.

"I said tried, not succeeded," I quipped with a frown.

"You didn't want to tell me that, did you?" He stopped his chuckling but did nothing to hide his delight.

"No, especially since you find it so comical." His contagious charm made my face redden, and I couldn't stop my lips from pulling into a smile. "It was a rather mortifying experience."

Darric rolled his tongue over his teeth. "And that may be the reason I took his bow."

"You stole his bow because he tried to kiss me?"

"Possibly." His fingers trickled up the contours of my spine, and I let out a gasp that didn't go unnoticed. "Or because he has a habit of foul mannerisms, and though my tolerance for his inurbane behavior is high, I am human."

Hoping to stop the tingling he was creating, I fell onto my back. He propped himself onto his elbow and hovered over me, cradling my head in his palm so his calloused fingers gently gripped my scalp. My fingers twined into a handful of grass. Wisps of damp blond hair still clung to his forehead, and I shut my eyes against the steel-blue irises drilling a hole in my heart. Feeling him was enough to cause the dizzying circles of fog.

"Flint has made no secret of thinking you are a prostitute I brought back from Burge."

My eyes flashed open. "I know exactly what Flint thinks of me, thank you, Darric," I said, miffed.

"Don't blame him for it. He hasn't been exposed to many other types of women."

"Have you . . ." I ripped up the blades of grass. ". . . brought *those* types of women to the Hovel before?"

"No." His face scrunched up. "I would not do something that nonsensical. I've never allowed anyone to stay in the valley, until you."

The last sweet traces of his breath hit my nose. My stomach did a backflip, slamming my heart into my rib cage. The intoxication he caused petrified me, and worse, he didn't seem to hate me at all in the moment. He almost seemed to . . .

My mouth went dry. I clenched my fist and shoved it against Darric's chest, only to be met with stonelike resistance that left my arms weak. As if sensing my desperation, the cat leaped forwards and pounced on him. He released his grip and jerked away from me.

The cat placed her paw on his shoulder. She gazed into his eyes and hissed, baring her teeth in a menacing warning.

"Damn cat." He drove her off him by pressing his palm into her forehead. She shook herself free and backed away, silver claws exposed and spine arched. Darric ran a hand over his face, mussing his wet hair. "Did you know your cat is a Sage?" he asked in frustration.

The burgundy feline let out a fitful screech. The fur on her back fluffed, and her brows pointed downwards.

I shook my head free of the clouds. "A what?"

"A Sage," he repeated more slowly. The cat jumped behind the base of a tree bordering the rock face. "A Shepherd. A protector of Athera. They are attracted to the Fae. I wasn't sure at first if she was indeed a Sage—they are difficult to detect—but it's becoming more obvious by the day."

My brain finally emerged from its haze. "What are you saying? She's not a cat?"

"No, not really. No one knows the true appearance of a Sage. They use whatever guise suits them for the purpose at hand. This one has taken on the form of a cat. The Onyx Guard keeps watch for them. Where there is a Sage, there is usually a Fae. And she never leaves your side."

"Do all Fae have them?"

"No, there are not many left. Over the centuries, the Onyx Guard has killed most of them. She is only the third I've seen. The Fae seem to have a better chance at evading Sights when a Sage is protecting them. The Senate found that Sages can suppress Fae power to a certain extent, making it harder for the Onyx Guard to find them."

I stared into the feline's amber eyes when she peeked around the tree trunk. *That's why you don't talk to me. You're not a cat at all.* She looked at me wonderingly, then tucked her head back into her hiding place. "But you still saw me . . ."

"I'm really talented." He smiled.

"I had no idea such a thing existed."

"I figured as much. When did she find you? When you were young?"

"No," I stammered, "in the woods the day before I met you. She practically attacked me."

"You're positive you've never seen her before?" he pressed.

"Yes." I didn't think it likely that Sages wandered the grounds of Alamantia Palace. Why had I never read a single thing about them in any of the books Sir Jonathan Helms brought me? Was there no written account of their existence? Perhaps, like many things, the Senate had erased them from history.

"How the hell have you managed to avoid not only the Onyx Guard, the Senate, and Medial Alexandria but any Sage that happened to be passing through?"

Because I'm the Divine Princess of Alamantia.

Darric huffed. "I said it when we were traveling to the Hovel and I'll say it again. It's disturbing how clueless you are. The answer, I'm certain, is hidden in that past of yours I'm not allowed to mention."

I gnawed on my bottom lip. "If it means anything, I'm starting to feel horrid about not telling you where I'm from."

Satisfaction twitched at the side of his mouth. "I like that."

"I'm not going to break. I just want you to know that I understand the absurdity of what I've asked."

"As your instructor, I hope you don't break. It's best to keep an adversary guessing." He extended a leg towards the pond, bending the other close to him. I wished some of his natural ease would wear off on me. His control was perfection—every action a calculated plan. "But, as myself, I can't say I feel the same way."

"Am I an enemy to you?" I asked fearfully, especially after glimpsing a Darric who seemed to want more from me than knowledge of Fae power.

"In a way," he confessed.

"Is that why you haven't told me about the other abilities you have that are symptomatic?" I pried, hoping he would admit everything Atlas had told me.

"Just what is it you think I can do, Aya?" A hint of condescension flashed into his eyes.

I fumbled with my skirt. "Precognition."

He laughed, making me feel foolish. "That's fairly perceptive."

I pressed my mouth into a firm line. "There is more to *you* than dreaming too."

"Your constant curiosity is making me want to figure out a way around our contractual agreement."

"You have an ambiguity!" I scolded. "Which, might I add, cannot be used to force me to reveal aspects of my past. That's a contract violation."

"Absolutely." He nodded in agreement. "It doesn't mean I'm not going to start coming up with an alternate plan."

I lost the battle against his magnetism. Remaining frustrated with his enchanting laughter swirling around my ears was simply too difficult. "I was just wondering if I have it too."

"I don't have precognition. It's more of a clairvoyance—an immediate sense. Fractions of a second for me to realize what's coming. That's why my reactions are . . . a bit faster."

"I don't have that."

"Yes, you do," he informed me, as if it should be obvious. "I wouldn't be able to teach you to fight as I do if you didn't possess every combative quality I have."

I shook my head, befuddled. How could I have more hidden abilities?

"How can you know that about me?"

"Call it precognition," he teased.

"Ugh." Aggravated, I shoved my hands in my hair and tossed the wet strands off my neck. "Enough with this cryptic Ursygh behavior."

"I am not the one who should be accused of being cryptic. I've answered everything you've asked, save the subject of my younger brother. A courtesy you are not going to bestow on me."

"I have one more question," I blurted.

He rolled his eyes. "Sure, why stop now?"

"When did you start dreaming?"

"After Bromly's mother died, when I left the Onyx Guard and this sword came into my possession." He slowly drew the blade from its scabbard and pointed it skywards. "Something about this weapon gives me a few of the qualities of a Fae." He ran his finger along the center indentation. "I've tried to separate myself from it, especially after the dreams turned horrific. As it turns out, I'm bonded to the blade, and even if I endure the consequences of leaving it behind, I'm still affected. The damn thing punishes me for abandoning it." He let the sword fall through his hands as if he despised its existence. It raced towards the forest floor and buried itself deep into the soil, halfway to the hilt. "Wielding it has honed my skills." He reached for Flint's bow and pulled an arrow from the quiver. "But I didn't discover I could do this until we started hunting in the mountains."

He rolled to his knees and faced the twisted arrangement of trees, then strung the arrow and pulled back on the bowstring. Letting out a slow, controlled breath that turned his shoulders fluid, he released the tension.

The arrow shot away from us with such speed that waves of disrupted air visibly moved out of its path. It hit one of the trunks with an explosive crash of splintering wood, cutting straight through the bark and flesh with unprecedented force. Weakened by the gaping hole, the entire tree snapped and fell to the ground, sending a cloud of multicolored blooms into the air.

Darric cocked his head and smiled at the destruction. "I'd be lying if I said I didn't enjoy the weapon enhancement it gives to me." He touched the underside of my chin to push my mouth closed. "I could do without the horrific dreams, however."

"And I gather no one taught you how to use a bow?"

"Did anyone teach you?" he replied, knowing the answer.

"How did you handle it—when you realized that as far as everyone in Athera is concerned, you're insane? Weren't you afraid of the Senate?"

With a glance through the trees, Darric checked the position of the sun and stood. He tugged our cloaks from the branches and wrapped his around his wet shoulders. "We need to head back."

"You're not going to answer the question?"

"You've asked enough questions today."

Bitterly, I snatched my cloak from his grip.

He chuckled. "You're entertaining when you're angry with me."

"I have no right to be." I clumsily searched for the strings to tie my cloak. He stopped my fumbling by feeding his hands into mine and pulling me from the ground.

"You do." He cupped my cheek and leaned close to my ear. "We aren't coming back here tomorrow."

Chapter 21

Darric used everything in his arsenal to infuriate me over the next week. He was hostile, condescending, and insulting. He shoved me out of his way and routinely threw knives at me with incredible precision. The chill of metal would graze my skin before slamming into its target. He always left me intact. No blood, no injury, but enough torment to make a harrowing shiver run down my spine.

Unable to scold him per our contract, I wondered what punishment could be worse than the heart-shattering terror of never knowing when a razor-sharp projectile would fly towards me.

After three days, the fear constricting my chest began to diminish. I watched carefully for any attack he might execute. A knife. An insult. I expected him to appear around every corner, ready to barrage me.

In addition to the knives, his voice became a weapon. He fueled the fitful rage burning inside my core by whispering streams of vulgar and degrading language by my ear. I had to call upon every ounce of control I possessed to bite my tongue and keep from slamming my fist into his jaw.

As Darric worked to invade my senses, Flint expelled every bit of anger I concealed. He rebuked his brother for his cruelty and tried to convince him to stop slowly killing me. He assured me I would learn to tolerate Darric's erratic moods.

The first day of training in the wisteria forest had led to a moment where I found myself questioning if Darric truly hated me as much as I originally thought. Now the gentle, tingling touches he had given me felt like an illusion. Had it really happened the way I remembered? Had he truly lingered above me, searching for a glimmer of something more lasting than our contract? I tried to rid myself of the memory, but not even his recent asinine behavior or the spiteful cadence of his attractive voice rattling through colorful expletives could erase the mind-numbing feeling of his hands cradling me.

Two more days passed in which he didn't speak to me as anything except an antagonist. Had he changed his mind about training me?

At night, Bromly and Flint slept while my fickle instructor disappeared into the darkness. Alone with my Sage in the safety of the Hovel, I was free from bombardment. I practiced my talents using a leftover bucket of dreggy water.

I held a tainted brown globe in my hand, watching tiny specks of debris drift inside. The blue sparkles glittering over the circumference were an odd contrast to the dirty water.

My nerves felt tightly coiled and unable to unwind due to a perpetual awareness. The crackle of the fire normally dominated the inside of the Hovel, but tonight strange ghostly echoes haunted my peace. The wind howled by the cavern. I could differentiate between the gentle snaps of the applewood wafting billows of smoke around the drying bear strips and the crackles of the oak logs breaking down at my feet. I could hear the subtle changes in

Bromly's and Flint's breathing patterns as they drifted in and out of deeper sleep. It made me weary to listen to it all.

When the quiet footfalls of leather soles on stone pierced the silence, it dawned on me. I could hear his slow, definitive movement through the insulated walls. Leave it to Darric to think of the most unusual, maddening method conceivable to force me to start paying attention to my surroundings. This had all been deliberate.

Control. Focus. Concentration.

I dropped the globe into the bucket, then snatched my cloak and a teacup. As I pulled the fur aside, the clairvoyance flooded my brain. The introduction felt like someone driving a needle into the center of my forehead. I jolted to the left, smashing my small body against the doorframe, and watched Darric's knife fly past my head and slam into the wall.

I gripped my stomach, waiting for the anxiety to pass.

Darric stood by the cavern fire, the hood of his cloak pulled down over his brow. "Finally," he said, letting out a long breath.

"Unorthodox practices indeed." I kept my displeasure muted.

"It took less time than I thought. Bromly was right, you are a fast learner."

I mouthed, "*Fae.*" Beneath the shadow of his hood, a smile upturned his lips. "Are you going to stop being such a cad now?" I asked.

"That depends on how much you've retained this week." He sauntered forwards, keeping a cautious eye on me.

Nervously, I pulled my cloak tighter around my shoulders. "There is something I want to show you."

He glanced at the teacup before easing his fingers along the sides of my neck and collecting my mess of curls to tuck inside the nape of my cloak. "You are focusing on your surroundings well enough to start hiding what you are." He raised my hood and tugged it down over my brows so it covered much of my face. Satisfied, he leaned in close to me, his mouth hovering just above mine. "Shading your eyes is vital to your survival. That's how people like me identify you." He hooked a finger under my chin and raised my gaze. His eyes locked on mine and he paused, seemingly watching my irises as his pupils dilated ever so slightly. "It only takes a glimpse, the faintest sliver of eye contact, to know what you are."

"What can you see in my eyes?" I asked almost inaudibly.

"They glimmer," he murmured and slipped his thumb across my chin. "I can see traces of your dust, even when you aren't using your Fae power. That's why the Senate calls us *Sights*. Most of us join the Onyx Guard, but nomads exist—an old woman using a cave of bandits as a guise, for example." He twisted his hand into mine, interlocking our fingers. "Ready?"

Without waiting for a response, he led us from the cavern, and we disappeared into the night.

We traveled at a slow run—the same speed we had maintained when I followed him to the valley, only this time it was different. With the clairvoyance activated, I easily kept up with him. I could avoid branches, roots, rocks, and unforeseen obstacles. I understood how effortlessly he traveled without disturbing his path or making a sound.

We moved through the shadows, our footsteps furtive. The hood obscured much of my vision, yet I didn't need to see everything anymore to perceive my surroundings. I could hear the movement of deer in the brush, the distant trickle of the streams, and the scurrying of tiny beetles through the leaf litter. The wind tickled my skin like tiny electric sparks, and even the touch of Darric's callouses were more defined compared to the smooth spots on his palm. Nothing was numb. I was alive, my frail senses exposed like an open wound. Sharper, clearer, crisp. I absorbed the feelings without reservation.

We rounded the crag as the first pale yellow light appeared through the trees, and I dug my heels into the grass to stop our jog. Perplexed, Darric turned to face me, and I flung my arms around his neck, beckoning his unyielding frame into my arms. I jerked the hood off his head and buried my face in the curve of his throat, breathing him in, allowing the dizzying sensation to overwhelm me. The new control I had over my body crashed into the nervous onslaught of what his presence normally did to me. Enthralled and gratified by everything he had done, I didn't fear the frantic beating of my heart.

His strong arms wrapped around my back, crushing me to his chest. His mouth grazed my cheek, and his hot breath tumbling over my neck sent prickles down my side.

"Thank you," I breathed, my lips brushing his heated skin. "Thank you for all of this."

He slid my hood away from my face. "How long did it take you to realize I've been training you, not being an insufferable ass?"

"Too long," I admitted.

He moved his hands to my hips, putting some space between us. "You controlled your emotions exceptionally well this week." A charming half smile emerged. "Until just now."

"You're still an insufferable ass," I taunted, feeling myself light up as I teased him.

"That's undeniable, but occasionally I know what I'm doing." He smirked, a little overly pleased with himself.

"I want to repay you."

"I haven't given you anything you weren't already capable of."

"You're wrong," I insisted. "Since the moment you found me, you've done unfathomable things for me. By the end of this training, I'm going to owe you more than I have to give."

"Maybe *that's* when I'll use my ambiguity." His enticing chuckle reddened my cheeks. He watched the rosiness spread over my skin with evident enjoyment until he regained his lost composure and pried my fingers from his neck. "What did you want to show me?"

I lowered my chin, suddenly abashed by how I had thrown myself onto him. "Um . . ." *Concentrate.* "At night, there isn't much to do at the Hovel besides listen to Bromly and Flint snore." I wrapped his hand around the cup. "The water Bromly leaves in the buckets is disgusting, so I've been practicing." I curled my finger over the edge and closed my eyes. The refreshing sensation started deep within my chest and swirled as it branched out into my arms. A sweet taste lingered in the back of my throat and tickled my tongue.

I opened my eyes to be sure it was working; water slowly filled the teacup, and shimmering blue dust gathered around the wooden rim. I retracted my finger to stop the flow. "Apparently, not only can I control water, but I can conjure it."

Darric skeptically examined the teacup's contents as the glimmering dimmed, then turned the cup over and poured the water onto the ground.

"You could have tasted it!" I stomped my foot. "It's a lot sweeter than river water."

He raised an eyebrow. "It's weird."

"Weirder than me throwing tornadoes of it at you? After everything you've seen me do, this is where you're going to draw the line?"

He rolled a leftover droplet between his fingers, testing the feel. "This is begging me to ask questions that are more sexually explicit than I'm willing to express right now."

"Darric Ursygh!" I glowered, snatching the cup from his hand. "I'm not leaking!" The embarrassment reflared. "The water comes out of thin air."

He laughed and tugged at the string of my cloak, catching the wool when it fell from my shoulders. "I could get used to you turning such a lascivious shade of pink around me."

I dropped the cup and covered my face. The cat meowed at my feet, and I peeked at her through my fingers.

"Getting back to the reason we are here . . ." He draped our cloaks over a tree branch and drew his sword. After surveying the area to find the largest tree, he drove his blade into a thick trunk, slicing through the width. The falling timber crashed into the branches of a smaller tree twenty feet away and stuck, creating a wooden beam suspended four feet off the ground. "All right." He hopped onto the trunk and sheathed his sword. "Come up here."

The log wobbled as I struggled to climb it and my feet dangled in the air. Darric grabbed my hand and jerked me up beside him. I crouched and dug my nails into the bark, unable to stand on my suddenly flimsy legs.

With little effort, he strolled to the opposite end as easily as walking across solid ground.

I repositioned and straightened my back.

Shifting his weight, he purposefully caused the log to turn.

I waved my arms, but my feet went out from under me. Darric sprinted across the wood and caught me in the crook of his arm, and I clung to his shirt until I corrected my footing.

"Keep your feet apart, offset." He looked at my shoes, causing a lock of hair to fall into his eyes, and he blew a puff of air to move the blond tress from his forehead.

Once I was stable, he released me and strolled backwards, curling a finger towards himself to beckon me forwards as his eyes stayed locked on mine. Enchanted, I watched his elegantly lazy footwork and followed across the log.

When I reached the midpoint, he jumped to the ground, making the beam bounce. The abrupt change quaked through my legs. I knelt and wrapped my hands tightly around the trunk.

"Stand up," he ordered.

Fighting the tingles in my knees, I pushed up again. He walked next to me as I continued down the thinning beam.

Finally, I gripped the floral branches that had once been the treetop.

My brazen instructor nodded. "Turn around and do it again."

I walked the length for an hour, eventually finding a rhythm to solve my instability. Growing more confident, I increased the length of my strides and moved faster. Just as I began to feel comfortable, Darric abruptly shoved his weight against the trunk. The tree twisted. My balance vanished. I toppled over, and the ground rushed towards me at an astonishing rate, sending my stomach lurching into my lungs and forcing the taste of bile up my throat.

Darric caught me inches before I smashed into the forest floor. My body shook as I tried to untie the nauseated wreck in my core.

"Concentrate on your footing." He pushed me back onto the beam. "Maneuver with the spring of your surface. Don't work against it. Allow it to move through you."

I regained my equilibrium and took one step. Again, he violently shoved the log. The trunk spun, and my feet flew out from under me once more. My back landed on the bark, arching my spine with a crunch, and I rolled to the side, clutching my stomach as I fell.

Darric scooped my limp frame into his arms and eased me onto my feet. My head bobbed like a doll, and he put his hands on either side of my face to steady it.

"Are you all right?" he asked, trying to meet my disoriented gaze as my eyes rolled in my head.

I nodded, stifling a small cry, and palmed my back in search of the forming bruise. "Your brutal tendencies are going to get me killed."

"Not today." He grinned slyly and massaged his fingers into the thumping ache in my spine. "When you walk across water, you careen, transferring your balance to maintain stability. This is the same concept, but you are letting the fear of falling control you."

"I could crack open my skull doing this." The soreness in my back waned with the soothing motion of his hand.

"I'm right here. I'm not going to let you break your neck," he reassured me.

I put my hands on his chest and gently pushed him. He complied with my silent request for distance and lifted me onto the beam. I clung to the bark like a vise as he hopped up next to me.

Wrapping his hands around my wrist, he pried me off the trunk and pulled my back into his chest. "Feet offset," he reiterated, nudging my calf with his boot.

His fingers trailed over my stomach, and my increased heart rate sent throbs through my belly. The soft breath from his smile moved the hair behind my ear. *Ridiculous, Ayleth, pull yourself together.*

"Hmm, my lessons on self-control haven't yet stopped you from wearing your emotions on your sleeve."

I clutched his bracer and spun out of his hold. He countered by weaving our fingers together and lifting my arm above my head. Gently, he rotated his grasp, forcing me to spin as if performing the slow steps of a dance. Lost in his gaze, my balance remained perfectly intact.

He chuckled and twisted his leg around my knees, deliberately taking my footing. I fell into the crook of his arm, and he arched my back with a mischievous smirk. "You falter when you overthink." He eased me back onto my feet and hopped off the tree.

My head spun. I opened and closed my fists several times to lose the feeling of his skin pressing into my palm.

"Move across again. Quicker this time." The toying lilt in his voice disappeared as he paced before the tree.

I gulped with a nod and set into a light run. I should have expected it; he slammed into the fallen trunk with the force of a battering ram, shifting the entire beam. It vanished from beneath my feet and I fell completely off the timber and into his waiting arms. He immediately shoved me back onto the bark. "Again."

I slammed my fists against the wood. "Let me get my bearings before you rotate the damn thing."

He snatched my wrist and constricted my fingers. I winced, trying to pull away. "Don't question me. You want to be trained? You do it my way." Annoyance vibrated his shoulders, and he raked a hand through his tousled hair. "And don't swear. As much as it entices me, it's unbecoming."

"Then don't touch me like that, you ass!" I shoved his chest, which made me lose my balance and nearly topple off the log.

He jerked me off the beam and pinned me against the trunk. "You're testing my patience," he snarled, the blue in his irises graying. "This morning, you wrap your arms around me and allow those exquisite lips of yours dangerously close to my neck. Even with my proficiency in control, you did not make it easy for me to keep my head straight. We are here for one purpose: to ensure you escape an encounter with the Onyx Guard. I am not your friend. I am your instructor." He punched the bark beside my shoulder. "This tree represents any surface you might move across during a fight. Perfecting balance will make it impossible for an opponent to knock you off your feet, and that's extremely important if you want to survive. To be able to accomplish complex maneuvers, you need to understand your surroundings even when blind to them. Backwards. Forwards. Sideways. So, fall off as many times as you want. You are stuck on this beam until you can flip while blindfolded."

My face fell. "You could have said that without unleashing your savage temper."

He tightened his hand into a fist. "Consider this your first warning, Aya."

I nodded meekly and put my hand on his shoulder to hoist myself onto the log. He clasped my waist to assist me and gave a weary sigh. "I'm sorry."

My gaze fell to my feet to avoid looking at him. I ignored the tiny rip in my heart and walked backwards, raising my eyes to the beauty of the overhead blooms. The blossoms helped distract from the relentless overthinking of my foot placement. If I couldn't hold my balance across a simple fallen timber, then I certainly couldn't handle anything else Darric would throw at me, especially when I seemed to misinterpret his gestures so drastically.

The rolling log snapped me out of my daze. I wobbled but kept my balance as the shuddering in my nerves faded.

By midmorning I had improved significantly, but it came with a price. Contracted into training to exhaustion, my legs were screaming, my hips were sore, and my ankles felt broken. I looked at Darric in desperation. He gave a satisfied nod and fed his hands up my thighs, firmly gripped my waist, and gently lowered me onto the grass. I trembled as my body became accustomed to the stable surface.

He left me resting against the tree and retrieved a strip of white linen from his haversack. I groaned—more training to this morning's session.

"Take a detailed look at your surroundings, not just visually but sensuously too."

I did not follow his instruction.

He turned me to face the bark. Before I could protest, he slipped the linen over my eyes and tied the cloth behind my head. "Let's see how well you've been paying attention. Describe the forest to me."

Drained and aching, I knew my location, but everything else was empty. Nothing coalesced. "I'm tired," I despaired.

"I know," he soothed, pulling my back into his chest. "After this, we are done for the day. I promise."

I tried to visualize the wisteria and the stone, the trees and the grass, the placement of the fallen timber and the waterfall cascading into the small pond, but only one thing came into focus: my stranger. His hair brushed the side of my face. His hard chest moved against the contours of my spine as he breathed. Dominating me and impossible to ignore. "I can't get you out of my head," I murmured.

He forcefully spun me around and tore the blindfold from my eyes. I sucked in a sharp breath, trying to quell the unease welling up in my throat.

He stared at me with concern, jaw clenched. "We're done for today."

Unnerved, I wrapped my arms around myself. *What the hell just happened?* My gaze drifted into the wisteria blooms where the cat had lazily positioned herself over a branch, an obnoxious grin upturning her whiskers.

Darric leaned against a tree and slid down to the grass. He rubbed his hands over his face. "I've been thinking about our contract."

I massaged my fingers into my biceps and bit my lip. "Ready to use your ambiguity?"

He shook his head and motioned to the ground beside him. I joined him against the trunk, his shoulder lightly brushing mine.

"I've been mulling over something you said. The contract doesn't stop me from asking you questions. It just allows you the luxury of not having to answer them."

Tumbling off the balance beam all morning had made my stomach uneasy, and sitting this close to him didn't help my dizzy head. "The purpose was to persuade you to avoid questioning me."

"After your interrogation last week, I would think you'd give me the opportunity to ask a few things." He reached for his haversack. The glass bottles clinked together as he removed a leather pouch and the decanter of red wine.

"Regardless of anything I've asked you, it's a contract violation. That was the deal. You leave my past alone. I give you an ambiguity. No trying to break through our agreement."

"I'm not breaking through it." He unlaced the pouch and retrieved a small handful of the salted pork. "I'm . . . testing the edges."

He held out his hand offering me the pork. I pushed his balled fist, refusing the dried bits. "If I can't berate you during training for fear of some bizarre punishment you've concocted, and if you're eventually going to throw a ridiculous unknown at me, then no, you aren't allowed an interrogation."

"But your end of the contract states you don't have to answer, so I should be able to ask any question I want."

"You read people too well. No thank you."

He pried open my hand and transferred the salted pork into my palm. "I want to know where you came from."

"It doesn't matter where I'm from—"

"It does to me," he said over me.

"—because I'm going to do anything in my power to never go back there—"

"Why?" he asked before the last word left my mouth.

I dumped the pork into my lap and dusted the salt off my hand. "It was a dead end."

He uncorked the decanter and took a long drink; the limited amount of alcohol sloshed in the bottom. "Aya, it means that somewhere in Brisleia there is a place beyond the reach of the Onyx Guard. Don't you understand? No free Fae has ever reached adulthood. You were obviously safe there. You shouldn't have left."

"You don't know the circumstances. It was complicated."

"Uncomplicate it."

"No."

He groaned. "You astound me."

I poked a piece of dried meat clinging to a loose woolen fiber on my dress.

"You're not eating," he observed.

"Neither are you." I flicked a larger chunk in his direction.

"I eat as often as you do," he said passively.

"That means never. I don't have an appetite. It has been dwindling ever since I started dreaming."

"Apparently, that's something else we have in common." He extended the decanter to me.

"Are you experimenting with food aversion now?" I grasped the bottle's neck and brought it to my mouth.

"There is something about you I can't figure out. A missing element. My intuition is notoriously accurate, but with you, it's like I'm walking around in a volcano blindfolded. You are completely exasperating and dangerous, yet entirely addictive."

I handed back the decanter. "I'm trying to forget my past. I left because I want to be someone else. Someone more like myself."

"You ran away?"

"In a fashion."

"Escaped?"

"That too."

"Was the decision prompted because you're a Fae?"

"Maybe a little. I didn't start dreaming until I turned thirteen, and I didn't know there were other qualities involved. I kept the secret to myself. I didn't want to be insane. I wanted to fade into obscurity, but I'm starting to realize that is an unlikely possibility. So now, I suppose I'm just looking for answers until the Onyx Guard captures me." I lowered my head, since he refused to part his gaze.

He shoved the cork back into his wine and tossed the bottle onto the ground. "If I have anything to do with it, that will never happen."

I scoffed. "And when I finally tell someone I'm a Fae, of all people, I picked you. A former Medial soldier."

"You couldn't hide it from me even if you wanted to."

"And knowing that, you still haven't made any of this easy—threatening to kill me and hating me. And now you—"

I fell silent when he wove our hands together, rubbing his thumb over my knuckles. "I do hate you, but not for the reasons you might think."

I was so distracted by the caressing of his hand that I missed the burgundy feline with furrowed brows climb down the tree and fall at his feet.

"I tried to refrain from making you realize your potential," he continued. "You may have eventually discovered it on your own, like you did with archery, but Bromly and Flint would have become too involved. I have to protect my brothers. I'm not sure what they are going to do to me when they find out I've hidden a Fae at the Hovel. Bromly will be livid. So, to avoid the risk of you *conjuring water* around our campfire, I had to intervene." He once again fixed his eyes on mine. "But it is nice to talk to someone who understands what I've been experiencing the last few years."

"When you told me you could dream, I felt a little less alone," I said. "It was like finding a piece of myself. Even when I think back on how scared I was of you at first and everything I went through to get here, I know it was worth it. I would never have found answers back home, and my future was turning grimmer by the hour. The constant ridicule and control was never going to allow me the freedom I craved." My voice slowly died as I rambled. I leaned closer to him, so I could no longer see the entirety of his face. My nerves and my new sense of contentment around him battled to the death.

"Whose?" His silver voice pulled me back to the surface.

"Um . . ." I tried to loosen his grip, but he refused to let go. "My parents."

He sat up straighter and shifted uncomfortably. "You've never mentioned your parents before."

I shrugged. "They are extremely set in their ways." Luken would be furious with me by now. If everything went according to my plans, I would never have the chance to apologize for abandoning him. *Terrible sister.*

"Are they the reason you left? Ridicule and control, as in abuse?"

"No, nothing like that," I hurriedly corrected. *Be cautious how you word this, Ayleth.* "My father is . . . was forcing me to get married to . . . someone."

His expression lightened into an amused smile, and he rolled his tongue over his teeth.

"What?" Annoyed by his disregard for the grievous situation, I jerked my hand from his.

"Nothing." He laughed.

"You think it's funny?" I shrilled.

"That's just not what I thought you were going to say."

"And just what did you think I was going to say?" I folded my arms over my chest, waiting for his explanation.

"Not that," he said derisively, and I glared at him. "All right, I'm sorry." He pursed his lips, a smile tugging defiantly at the corners. "So, you obviously didn't like this arrangement."

"No! I didn't." I balled my hands into tiny fists. "If I was the person they wanted me to be, then he would have been perfect. He was attractive and articulate. All the things I should have wanted in a husband. Everyone seemed to believe it was a brilliant match. My brother understood my perspective. He knew I wanted something else."

He pulled my hand back into his. "A different guy?" he asked, finding my eyes, and his pupils dilated when he watched the Fae glimmering come to life in my irises.

His curiosity brought an abashed smile to my lips. "No, there was no one else."

A single purple wisteria bloom fell onto our interlocked fingers. "You have a fiancé." He let out a long breath and ran a hand through his hair. "That may break Flint's heart."

"I *do not* have a fiancé," I declared sternly.

"Flint likes you. A lot." His voice held a new caution I wasn't used to hearing.

"Enough to be upset by my betrothal?" I challenged. "Flint isn't exactly the future I had in mind."

"You don't seem to want the future your parents planned for you either."

I shuddered. "I spent so long ignoring the years as they passed that I didn't realize how numbered my days had become. I panicked. The engagement was unexpected after so much monotony, and yet I should have seen it coming. I'm eighteen. I was bound to end up married soon. If not him, it would have been someone else."

"Ah, parental expectation and the passage into adulthood." He casually bent his leg and rested his wrist on his knee. "I'm eighteen, and I'm not married."

My disbelief was impossible to hide. "How are you only eighteen?" I glanced over his entire body. Suddenly the traces of a boy exactly my age emerged, and he looked the part. Why had I never truly beheld how young he was beneath the appearance of a seasoned assassin?

"Why? Do I look older?" he teased.

I shook my head, haunted by the reality of his worldly experience when naive wasn't substantial enough to describe my sheltered existence. "You're eighteen?" I repeated, trying to convince myself.

"Well, I think I am." He laid his head against the bark.

"Don't you know your birth date?" I asked, edging closer to him.

"Not exactly. I was so young when my parents died I can't be sure of the exact day or even the month of my birth."

I tightened my grip around his fingers. "That's horrible."

"Not really." He shrugged, his eyes flicking to our hands. "What's a birthday? A means of tracking time? I never knew how much time I had left, so what was the point in tracking how much I'd gained?"

"And eighteen is your best guess?"

"It's simple math. I remember my birthday occurred sometime after the first snow in winter. So when I wandered across the border after my parents died, I started watching for the snowfall each year. Twelve snows since coming to Brisleia makes me eighteen."

"Infallible logic." I decided to shamelessly test the strength of my settling nerves and examine this startling information in detail: Darric Ursygh, the hooded stranger who had rescued me from a bandit cave and terrorized me senseless, the former soldier of Medial Alexandria's elite regiment, an assassin—age eighteen.

He smirked wickedly. The unfathomably beautiful blue in his eyes swirled into recesses of leaden gray. I looked down before the fog could take the edges of my vision. "How long were you alone until you met Bromly and Flint?" I asked with a blush.

"Months." He chuckled, watching me hide my face. "It was an incredible stroke of luck I found the Keenes. Staying in one place has always been difficult for me. I left Vegathyad, one foot in front of the other, and I've never really stopped wandering since. Being in the Onyx Guard allowed for constant movement. I saw many places, from the most remote tribal villages in Hydrodawn to cities carved out of lava flows in Balakaya. If it weren't for your being at the Hovel, I'd be gone. I usually only stay long enough to keep my brothers busy with pelts." He pushed the bottom of my chin to raise my gaze. "Flint keeps asking me when I'm leaving."

"Are you planning to leave anytime soon?" I asked ingenuously.

He shook his head. "No."

The instant his thumb grazed my smiling bottom lip, an unfamiliar fiery current shot through me. The elation I felt from his staying at the Hovel spilled across my entire body.

Abruptly, the cat-formed Sage gave an irate growl that disturbed the silence of the forest. We turned simultaneously to see her swishing her tail through the grass, tossing petals into the air.

Darric slinked away from me just as she bared her claws and swiped his boot. "All right. All right." Surrendering, he narrowed his eyes at her. "I hate that fucking cat."

Chapter 22

The days turned into weeks. The time when the Hovel brothers would pack their wares and travel to Burge approached at an astonishing rate. The date was set; we would leave the first week of July. That left six weeks for Darric and me to continue training in the forest.

The three were at odds regarding what to do with me when the time came. Everything from abandoning me in the woods to taking me back to the bandit cave, escorting me to Burge, or simply leaving me in the valley had been suggested around the nightly fireside suppers.

Darric expelled the most despicable plans for my disposal, though I suspected he voiced them only to maintain a facade. Flint wanted me to go everywhere and anywhere they went until the end of eternity, and Bromly was indifferent, as long as the outcome didn't involve killing me.

After three weeks of combat training, I had not touched a single weapon. The lessons were divided into two sessions:

balancing on the beam until my legs gave out, then being blindfolded and forced to recall my surroundings. This did not always take place inside the wisteria forest. Darric dragged me to many locations throughout the valley and tested my memory after giving me a brief moment to observe the area. The aggravating task became easier with practice.

At the end of the third week, he broke the routine to relax against a tree base and watch me struggle to lift the entire wisteria forest pond out of its basin. My mental strength had increased, and though I was unable to raise the water completely, I could lift it significantly higher before my concentration waned. That was the day I finally convinced him my conjuring came out of thin air rather than some bizarre form of leakage from my skin. I created crystalline droplets that rained under the tree canopy, complete with the associated blue dusting of sparkles. Darric contentedly lay in the grass watching the sunlight filter through the drizzle and didn't ask me to stop until we were both thoroughly saturated.

The following day started the most stressful and intense week of the entire training process.

That morning my instructor paced between two lovely twisted trees. Reservation warped his movements, as if he didn't want to proceed with this exercise. "Today is going to be rough."

I shifted my weight from one foot to the other, my arms tightly crossed over my chest. "I'm ready."

He stopped in front of the closest tree and took a huge breath. Slowly releasing the air, he unbuckled his leather belt and pulled it from his hips. My eyes bulged. Never had he removed his scabbard. Sliding the sword from the sheath, he drove the blade deep into the roots, where it stuck, hard and immobile.

Perplexed, I lowered my arms.

Reaching into the top of his boot, he detached one of his hunting knives and stabbed it into the trunk, then did the same with the other forbidding blade tucked in the opposite shoe. From a pocket always hidden beneath the hang of his sword, he removed a unique dagger with a twisted tri-edged blade and carelessly let it slip from his fingers. Lastly, he slid the knives from his bracers—three from each wrist—and methodically stabbed each one through the bark. I found myself silently counting. Ten weapons in total.

"This part of your training will require both of us to be completely disarmed. I don't want any accidents."

I stared, stunned at seeing him unarmed. It filled me with a surge of dread. He couldn't kill me with a sword now, but his physical strength could produce an entirely different and horrifying type of blunt injury I had never considered— something I suspected would be a lot more painful.

"Now, Aya, I would be mistaken to assume you don't have a weapon hidden in that dress." He held up a finger. "Excuse me, let me rephrase that. A weapon made of metal."

Luken's dagger. My stomach clenched, and a familiar knot tightened my throat; there would be no more hiding the comforting blade.

He crossed his arms over his chest. "I'm waiting, my lady." His eyes darted to my ankle. *He already knows about the dagger.* Someone had removed my shoes and reapplied the weapon for safekeeping while nursing me back to health. Of course, Darric. How stupid of me to think otherwise.

I huffed and knelt to the ground, moved my skirt, and revealed the knife caked with a layer of dirt. Luken's gift was firmly attached inside the scabbard, as if it would never be used.

"That's what I thought," he said as I untied the fastening and pulled the dagger from its dusty black sheath. "Fine blade for a girl who claims to have no connection to Medial Alexandria."

I rubbed my dirty hands on my dress as I approached the weapon-filled tree.

"I used to have one just like it." He reeled with skepticism.

"I didn't steal it."

"I didn't say you did. Such a thing would be practically impossible. Do you think I stole my sword?"

I stared at the mystical hilt ensconced in the tree roots. "Did you?"

"I earned it."

I rolled my eyes. "Well, for all intents and purposes, let's say I earned this too." Mirroring his actions, I attempted to stab the blade into the trunk. The dagger went a mere inch into the bark and stopped.

His chuckling flooded anger into my blood. I shot him a harsh glare and examined the variety of weapons stored in the wood, each one buried to the grip. He leaned his shoulder against the tree in enjoyment and waited with a condescending grin. I stabbed into the trunk a second time, but my effort was even worse, and the blade bounced off the bark.

He slid his hand over my wrist, plucked Luken's dagger from my grasp, and shoved the metal deep into the trunk. "Don't ever let anyone take your weapon." He pointed a scolding finger at me.

I scowled. "You took it from me!"

"You let me."

"I thought you were trying to be helpful."

"You can't trust that's everyone's intention." He left me by the tree. "We'll discuss why you're carrying a dagger designed for the *Hell Squad* of the Onyx Guard later. Today we start physical conditioning: grappling and unarmed combat."

I gaped, wanting to shrink back to the Hovel.

"First, if you find yourself grappling, you have already made a few tactical errors. Your goal becomes to incapacitate your opponent long enough to draw your sword or create distance. These defensive maneuvers will also apply in scenarios where deadly force is unnecessary. Let what I teach you today serve as a warning. Women don't commonly fight. You are unique in that aspect. Men who fight have egos. The more you defeat, the more hostile they will turn. You need to be prepared for the consequences men tend to be capable of when trying to dominate a woman they see as a threat."

I tilted my head, trying to understand what he was hinting at.

Seeing my confusion, he elaborated. "In other words, as a woman, being killed is not the worst outcome you face *if* you allow a man to gain physical power over you. Enemies you encounter are going to see you as a conquest in more ways than just combat."

I bit into my lip. "Sexually."

He nodded, letting his warning traipse through my head. He took my hand and balled it into a fist, pulling my thumb free of the grip, then pointed to the middle knuckle. "This is your impact point. Anywhere else will break your hand. Keep your wrist straight. Don't allow it to buckle." He mimicked the positioning. "Dominant leg back. Hands up. Chin down."

I corrected myself accordingly.

Next, he pointed to various locations on his face: the eye socket, the jawline, the underside of the nose. "These are facial targets. Never hit the cranium. It's rock."

After providing minimal information, he instructed me to throw a punch directly into his chest. I resisted until he started laughing. "You can hit me as hard as you want. You won't hurt me." His arrogant, patronizing tone was the motivation I needed.

Hitting Darric was like beating into fleshy stone, but it felt undeniably amazing to slam my fists into him. The anger I kept buried came to the surface and escaped through each punch.

I hated him for mocking my weaknesses. I hated myself for loving the lustful way he looked at me. I hated Flint for believing I was a harlot. The accursed thoughts evolved into memories of the palace. My parents' betrayal. Being sold into marriage. Prince Marcus. Dreams. Fae.

He snatched my wrists mid-swing. "Stop-stop-stop."

I panted, on the verge of tears.

"You're getting angry. Don't let emotion impel your force." He released me, setting a hand on my shoulder. "Dare I ask what you were thinking?"

I shook my head, pulling myself together, and huffed out the last piece of ire circling my brain.

"Try again."

Further instruction introduced additional parts of the body that could be used for incapacitation: the knee, the elbow, the forearm. Locations of impact: the stomach, instep, throat, and groin—the last being particularly vulnerable in men. I didn't need him to explain why.

Sparring was common among the knights of Brisleia. Luken enjoyed the occasional brawl. But it didn't take me long to realize Darric was a dirty fighter. He fought without respect. No chivalry. No limits. No rules. "In a scenario where grappling has become a life-or-death situation, you do anything it takes to live." Scratch. Bite. Pull hair. Gouge eyes. "Look for weapons of opportunity. Never fight fair." Sticks. Rocks. Dirt. "In the end you are in charge of your own moral character. You bring the outcome."

I bristled. "You've won fights being this callous?"

He refused to answer.

The days Darric taught me grappling techniques bled seamlessly into one another. Overloaded with information and exertion, I couldn't differentiate one day or even one moment from the next.

"I want you to attempt to incapacitate me using any of the methods I've shown you, but this time I'll be fighting back," he challenged sometime midweek.

I nodded hastily, gulped, and lunged for him. He caught my fist and twisted my arm backwards. I had to spin to keep my elbow from dislocating, and my back slammed into his chest. Darric held my wrist in an uncomfortable arch against my spine. His nose grazed the side of my neck, breathing in the smell of my hair. The feathery touch sent a heated wave down my legs and weakened my knees, making me momentarily forget the ache in my arm.

He let me go and took several steps back, then curled a finger towards himself, beckoning me to reengage.

This time when I threw my fist at his face, he let it make contact. Instant pain shot up my fingers and throbbed through my wrist. I clasped my hand and was immediately tackled to the ground. He pushed me into the grass, pinning my arms above my head, and his knees straddled my hips.

"Never let your guard down. No one is going to wait for you to bandage your hand," he chided. "Your small size is useful when evading attacks, but the second you are in *this* position, it's over."

I struggled beneath him, thrashing my torso and trying to slide out the way he had shown me.

He leaned forwards, applying more of his weight to my chest, and the fight instantly ended. I couldn't breathe. "Once you've got your opponent on the ground, keep them there and do not turn your back. Smash their kneecap, crush their larynx, or make sure his stones are too obliterated to ever *love* another woman."

I couldn't help but giggle at the reddening spot under his eye, and he slithered off me. "Take it seriously, Aya."

"You're so strong," I panted. "It's like you are solid muscle."

"The Senate puts the Onyx Guard through extensive physical training," he explained, unfazed.

I stared into the purple blooms, catching my breath, and several petals fell onto my head. "I'm ready to go again."

There was too much instruction to process. How did he expect me to remember every move, every placement of my foot? Clinching. Sprawling. Submission holds. Balance throws. Turnovers and reversals. Escapes.

He repeatedly pinned me into submission as I heaved and gasped labored breaths, trying in vain to gain any advantage. The smell of his skin had long since rubbed off on my clothing. Petals stuck deeply in my curls. Grass stains defaced Ambrosia's dress. Each time he touched me, our skin stuck together from the heat of our bodies entangled in a wrestling brawl I couldn't win.

He claimed I was improving, but it felt like spectacular failure. Each time I stabbed my elbow into his stomach, I met stony resistance. Each time I threw a punch, he slammed me into the ground, and the strength of his hands left the same fingerprint bruises over my legs that appeared across Flint's neck.

Having him so close to me day after day created maddening interference for my clairvoyance. He yelled at me to concentrate, to put inhibitions aside, to focus on the fight. But the fight was an unrelenting battle against my reason. He affected me in ways I couldn't control. I would senselessly allow him to gain leverage just to feel his body pressing against mine.

In the end, the tumbling act of grappling would prove an unsurpassable obstacle for both of us.

Darric's arms encased me like a vise. His heart pounded into my back—slow, heavy, threatening knocks that caused my chest to cave over my stomach. The instruction regarding how to escape this particular submission hold was forgotten, and my body went weak as I neared the ground in a losing fight.

"Aya, focus!" he scolded in a harsh rasp.

His rough hands dug into my sides. My knees carved holes in the dirt with his svelte frame curved around my back. My insides were starting to twist over themselves in ways that made me doubt they would continue functioning properly.

"Darric," I pleaded, desperate for release. I couldn't get out of this. If he held me any longer, my chest would collapse, but he refused to relent. "Get off me!" I fumed, throwing my head back to hit his face with my skull and missing. Instead, his hard shoulder absorbed the collision. My eyes rolled, and I groaned from the bewildering pain.

He finally loosened his hold to knot his fingers deep in the strands of my hair. "You okay?" He massaged the sore point of impact. The exposed skin of my throat caught the onslaught of his heated breath.

I let out an unintentional moan that transformed my fight into submission. "Yes."

He chuckled low, grazing his lips down my neck. A rush of electricity shot through my spine when his mouth made contact. It felt as if a flaming coal had been pressed into my skin.

My body spasmed as he trailed slow open-mouthed kisses along my throat, punctuated by his warm exhales. The intense heat between us was quickly growing to a fever. His grasp slackened and he set me free.

Instead of listening to the scolding in my brain, I wrapped my arm around the back of his head and laced my fingers into the feathered locks of his hair. Inspiring to know at least one part of him was so soft. I shut my eyes, dizzy and unsure I was still experiencing reality, and allowed the forbidden ecstasy of Darric's mouth to warp my senses. His hand trailed up my body and coursed over my breasts, toying with the lacing on the front of my dress as he gripped hard handfuls of my chest.

A deep growl came from the back of his throat as he pressed me against his front, grinding his own reaction to touching me into my lower back.

I turned to face him, and our lips brushed in a tortuous sting that caused an unfamiliar warm tingle to spiral between my legs. I leaned in to eliminate the last piece of distance between us and give in to my blatant lack of control, but he suddenly lunged away from me. I dropped to the ground with barely enough time to catch myself.

"FUCK!" He expelled a fitful roar, digging his nails into his scalp. "Damn it, Aya. You're not concentrating on anything!" The boom of his frantic, stentorian voice scared me. "I can't train you properly if you refuse to remember the first thing about physical combat when a man comes close to you. Are you truly going to allow your defenses to fall if someone tries to kiss you?"

"What?" Confounded, I tried to stand, but my legs had yet to recover.

"I don't care what lascivious thoughts are going through your head. If someone is trying to kill you, yielding to an attraction isn't going to keep you alive." His chest vibrated when his shoulders reached a new level of tension.

"That was training? Are you kidding me?" I shrieked, slamming my fists into the ground. It couldn't be possible. What kind of monster could fake emotion like that? The ardency in his breath. The massaging of his lips on my skin. It had felt real. Was I that naive? "How dare you!" I reached an unpleasant octave. "You're supposed to be instructing me, not seducing me!"

"Intriguing to find out what happens to you, Aya, when you're aroused by the person who is attempting to kill you." He ripped his hair as he tore his hands from his head. "As it turns out, you aren't that difficult to seduce."

I screeched and stumbled to my feet, only to stomp like a child throwing a tantrum. "I would never be attracted to someone who is trying to kill me."

"Oh no?" He took a menacing step in my direction. "Then explain what's going on with you and me."

My legs recommenced their quivering. "You are so insane! What are you talking about?"

"Do you think I don't know about the lustful effect I have on you?" His shoulders bunched, as if the words had been extremely difficult for him to say.

My jaw fell. All my efforts to hide the way my body betrayed me around him had not gone unnoticed, but whether Darric was acting on something he personally felt or training me, neither was acceptable. I covered my mouth, trying to control the rising inferno of rage and humiliation.

"This is your second warning," he threatened in a blander tone.

My blood turned molten. "Go to hell, Darric!"

I had to get away from him. I had to get out of this forest. I headed for the exit, my feet stumbling over piles of fallen petals, but once I reached the layered crag, I stopped dead.

I couldn't leave.

If I left, it was over.

My training would come to an *abrupt and immediate end.*

No abandoning a lesson due to emotion or exhaustion.

Contracted to endure anything and everything *Darric Ursygh* decided was conducive to my training.

I took a step back from the crag and screamed, forcing the anger and frustration from my chest. After the violent howl faded, I gulped in a sharp breath and tried to extinguish the urge to march back to Darric and punch him.

As much as I wanted to berate him for kissing my neck, I couldn't. Not because I feared punishment or losing my training but because I was furious at myself for loving it. I hadn't stopped him. I hadn't fought back. I had pressed into him and dug my fingers into his hair to pull him closer. I had turned my head expecting to feel his lips cover mine, and in that moment, I had wanted nothing else.

"*We'll be alone?*" I had asked.

"*Against my better judgment, yes.*" His statement made more sense now.

My legs gave out, and I crumbled to the forest floor. Tears flooded my eyes. I tilted my head back to prevent them from falling, but they spilled over and dripped down my temples.

I heard the crunching of footsteps, then Darric let out a heavy sigh. "I thought you were about to walk out of here." His knees raked against my spine as he knelt down behind me.

I curled into a tiny ball. "Me too."

"Thank you for not leaving," he whispered. The trembling in his body transferred into my back.

My watery eyes darted around the colorful blooms. "I can't leave. We made an agreement. If I walk out, it breaks the contract."

"You care that much about learning to fight that you would allow me to subjugate you? There's something profoundly disturbing about that."

"You told me I had to endure anything you decided was constructive. You said your methods were unorthodox. I accept that." I buried my head in my knees, muffling my voice. "I'm sorry. I've never been touched like that before."

A crestfallen growl rumbled in his throat. "And you still shouldn't have been. I don't want you to think sexual gratification is part of your training." He paused for a moment, the rustling of wind through the branches and the distant chirp of birds seemed amplified by his silence. "You asked me . . . and I never answered you. Actually, I avoided answering you." He pulled my hair away from my face so the locks tumbled down my back, then leaned next to my ear. My shoulders shivered when his breath hit my skin. "Aya, you are the most beautiful woman I've ever seen. You push the limits of my self-control to the very edge of breaking. And, to add insult to injury, you have this captivating and tenacious little personality that is making me damn near insane."

I swallowed hard. The lump in my throat didn't move.

"What just happened should not have occurred. I caved. I was not expecting your reaction. I thought you'd be angry—fight harder. And instead of apologizing for my actions, I twisted it and tried to blame you."

Finding my courage, I turned to face him. He was so close I was sitting between his legs. "But you weren't wrong about what you said. The lustful effect you have on me." I leaned back to see him in his entirety.

"I know." His eyes fell. "I was hoping you'd realize it's the same for me. Being in this forest alone with you has been challenging, to say the least."

Speechless, my lips parted. How could Darric feel anything towards me except the hatred he openly displayed?

"I am your instructor. I had a weak moment. It won't happen again. If I don't swear this to you, I'm not sure that us coming out here together will be able to continue."

My heart missed a beat as I listened to him vow never to touch me again. The thought cut deeper than I expected. "If I asked you to end today's lessons, would you allow it?"

"You want to go back to the Hovel?" he confirmed.

I nodded, brushing tears from my temples.

He hesitated, revealing the enormity of his want to force me back into compromising positions under him. Finally conceding, he held out his hand to help me from the ground. "We're done for today."

I revisited the strange events in my mind the entire walk back to the Hovel. Analyzing every word Darric had said. Reliving every disorienting touch. Imagining what his lips might have felt like against my mouth.

"Aya?" He finally spoke in the last seconds before we reached the cavern. "Where and how did you obtain a Medial *Hell Squad* dagger?"

I agonized for a moment, wishing for the first time he knew I was Divine. "I can't tell you."

He scoffed bitterly. "Of course not."

The fire was blazing as the cavern came into view, the bear meat tripod replaced with a steaming cauldron.

Darric tensed when he spotted Bromly moving around the fire. "Shit," he drawled.

"Where have you two been?" Bromly pried, eyeing the reddish bruise along Darric's cheekbone. "What happened to you?"

"Is Flint awake?" Darric deflected.

"Lucky for you, no." Bromly forced a wavering smile. "Good afternoon, Aya." He scratched his beard, observing the conspicuous tension between us, and cleared his throat. "Both bear pelts are drying and most of the meat has been smoked. Flint and I are ready for another kill. We should be able to process one more before Burge. Just nab a male this time."

"It's still early. There should be a few by the river." Darric left to rouse his younger brother.

"Aya." Bromly tapped his cheekbone, pushing into the chubby skin under his eye. "I don't know what happened or how you did it, but thanks. He's deserved it lately."

Flint stumbled through the front door, catching his leg in the pelt and barely managing to maintain his footing. "I'm half-asleep," he hollered. "I haven't stretched."

Irritated, Darric shoved the fur aside, Flint's bow in hand. He tossed the weapon at his brother, hitting him in the chest.

"You foul jackass." Flint rubbed his fists into his eyes to remove the crusted sleep in the corners.

Darric pulled the hood of his cloak over his head and left the cavern.

Flint snatched his bow with a mumbled half yawn, then frowned at my comfortable seat by the fire. "Aya, you're comin' too, right?"

"Flint!" Darric called impatiently.

I raked the tip of my shoe against the stone floor. "I'm going to stay behind." I did not want to witness another kill of that magnitude, and I had a permanent reminder of the first chaotic experience marring my hand. "Bromly could use some help around the Hovel. You two go without me."

"Bromly'll be fine," Flint griped.

"It wasn't a pleasant experience, and I—"

"A fiasco," Darric interrupted. "It's not happening again. She is staying here from now on."

"No, we need her." Flint took my wrist, intent on pulling me to my feet.

I held my ground and stayed seated. "Please don't make this a problem."

Flint sneered at Darric and dropped my hand.

"This is my decision," I added, but Flint's pale skin had already gained the fiery color he turned when angry.

"It's not right." He plucked his quiver from the side of the house and trudged outside.

"So eager to get her killed," Darric provoked, and the sounds of an ensuing argument faded into the distance.

"Are they going to be all right on their own?"

"Black eyes are usually the worst of it." Bromly snickered, handing me a potato and carving knife. "So, spending some *quality* time with Darric this morning?"

I avoided looking at him and shaved a long brown curl away from the spud. "Darric isn't as callous as Flint makes him out to be."

He grinned in the same derisive manner I'd often seen on Darric. "I know that. And yet you decided to give him what looks like a damn good right hook."

"That was because of . . . something else." I rotated the knife in my hand. "An extenuating circumstance."

"It's okay by me." He laughed. "It's about time someone decked him. I'm just surprised he let you do it."

"It's a little like hitting a stone wall."

"Don't I know it." He tugged at the hanging bear pelts, and the skins dimpled in his hand, having dried into supple blankets. "You've been spending a lot of time with him."

I abruptly stopped peeling my potato. "I don't know what you mean." *You are a terrible liar.*

His forehead wrinkled. "I'm not getting involved with any of it, but don't think things go unnoticed around here by everyone."

I nodded, refocusing on the spud. Thankfully, he dropped the subject.

Within an hour, the quiet afternoon was interrupted by a long, deafening whistle, followed by a flaming arrow rising high above the tree line. It left a trail of gray smoke in the cloudless blue sky.

"Time to go." Bromly had already loaded his belt with a variety of hunting knives. He tossed a coil of rope over his shoulder and grabbed the shovel. "Are you going to be all right by yourself? You can come with me."

I gathered my hair and tied the mess of curls into a braid. "No, I'll finish the stew for you."

"I'm starting to like having you around." He chortled and turned his husky frame towards the smoke signal.

The cat plopped onto the log and stretched. *Where have you been?* She cocked her head with a snide whiskered grin.

"What?" I said defensively and rubbed my neck where I could still feel Darric's mouth. "I know you saw everything that happened this morning."

As the afternoon progressed, a steady delivery of new bear pieces came to the cavern until I was greeted by the familiar sight of all three Hovel brothers walking across the horizon.

Flint let the shovel hit the floor and inhaled the smell of stew. "Aya, your cooking always smells amazing."

Still irked that he had lied about my earlier attempts, I frowned and shoved a steaming bowl into his hands. I provided Bromly with his supper next, then offered a bowl to Darric, who declined, and Flint plucked his portion from my grasp.

"How did the hunt go?" I asked.

"Great," Flint said with his mouth full. Tan liquid dribbled down his chin. "As always, Darric was a perfect shot." Jealousy edged his tone.

"No distractions," Darric quipped and stole one of Bromly's cloths from the stack. He ripped the fabric in two, creating a long strip.

Flint slurped from the side of his bowl, and Bromly elbowed him in the ribcage, trying to give him a spoon. It was the last thing I saw before Darric lowered the fabric over my eyes and tied a hard knot on the back of my head.

"Are you serious?" I shrieked.

"Describe it to me," he instructed.

This was going to be his way of telling his brothers about my training? Blatantly shoving the lessons in their faces? "I already know how the cavern looks," I said in annoyed disbelief.

"Even the most memorable places can become foreign when you are blinded to them. If you know the Hovel so well, this shouldn't be difficult."

The cavern went silent for an eternity, then someone's spoon clanked hard against their bowl. "You're teachin' her to fight?" Flint screeched, his voice echoing off the stone. His bowl smashed onto the floor, and the fire sizzled where the stew splattered into the coals.

I tore the blindfold from my head. Darric stood beside me, a statue of strength ready for the onslaught.

"For years I've begged ya to teach me to fight! Years!" The whites of Flint's eyes quickly became bloodshot, and he stomped on the crushed remnants of his bowl. "Ya won't teach anyone, yet ya teach her? Some girl ya find in the woods?"

Bromly set his half-full bowl down beside him, apparently having lost his appetite.

"Some girl?" Darric questioned. "This doesn't have anything to do with you."

"Like hell it don't!" Flint's hysteria grew with every word. "I'm your brother! But I'm always gonna be useless to ya. Your promises are fuckin' worthless. Why do I ever trust ya?"

"Instructing Aya in combat does not break the promise I made to you," Darric stated earnestly.

"That's bullshit!" Flint kicked the nearest seating log, but Bromly's weight kept it from moving, and he stumbled backwards.

"You've broken every rule you've forced us to live by. Ya bring a stranger to the Hovel, threaten disgustin' things, an' now you'll betray me."

"For reasons beyond your comprehension, she needs to know how to defend herself. That should elate you. She lives protected, and I'm one step closer to leaving."

"Fine! She can learn, but not taught by ya."

"Who then?" Darric retorted. "You? We know how that turned out."

"Ya swore to me," Flint hissed.

"She's gifted in weaponry. She has the potential to be as deadly as I am. Would you dare hold her back for your own depraved interests?"

"You're a damn liar!" Flint balled his hands into fists as water welled in his eyes. "What's she givin' ya in exchange for lessons with a sword? How often is she liftin' her skirt for ya?"

I flew from my seat, ready to land my newly learned right hook on Flint's jaw, but Darric snatched my arm and forced me behind him. I dug my nails into his shoulder, trying to quell the rage.

"Flint, it would be wise of you to never utter anything like that again," Darric warned. "If she doesn't break every damn tooth in your mouth, I will."

"Darric wouldn't be doing this if he didn't have a good reason, Flint." Bromly's calm voice seemed misplaced among his brothers' yelling.

"You!" The heat in Flint's face pulsed like the veins in his neck. "Ya knew, didn't ya?"

"I . . . I saw them, just once . . . this morning," Bromly stuttered.

"Ya didn't tell me?" Flint closed in, about to let his fury overflow onto the wrong brother. "You're always tryin' to play *dumb*."

"I didn't know," Bromly mumbled.

"Don't blame him for your unbalanced sense of reality," Darric ridiculed.

Flint dragged his nails down his cheeks, leaving pink streaks on his face. "This is fuckin' unbelievable." He jumped over the seating log and kicked the empty water bucket. The canister flew high into the air before tumbling down to smack his head. The impact further infuriated him, and he ran from the cavern.

A wicked grin spread across Darric's face. "That could have gone better."

My jaw dropped. I shoved his arm, completely astonished by his lack of remorse. "You didn't have to tell them like this!"

I stormed into the Hovel, the cat following at my heels.

Chapter 23

Flint refused to speak to any of us for a week. Bromly tried to reason with him by reiterating that he had no idea Darric was instructing me, but it didn't make any difference.

Though the secrecy premise had been Darric's decision, I still felt responsible. We had unintentionally put Bromly in the middle; it pained him to see Flint so inconsolable.

By the end of the week, the raging tantrum had lessened. Bromly's persistence paid off, and Flint began acknowledging him.

Witnessing Flint hold a grudge was everything Darric had described. After begging for years to learn a skill his brother willingly taught to a strange little woman with no history, he had a right to be angry. But as the days of ignoring our presence at the Hovel continued, I began to find Flint's attitude childish. In the end, Darric had to take his brother's place in processing the new bear kill while Flint sulked in his room.

Between Bromly's pleading, Flint's silence, and Darric's indifference, something remained unsaid among the three. A grimace. A glare. Words written across their faces but not voiced. A plight I couldn't figure out. Darric teaching me to fight was not the only cause of Flint's tantrum. However, the additional element stayed hidden, and none of them were going to say exactly what it was out loud, at least not to me.

Despite the oppressive emotions choking the cavern, Darric and I continued leaving for the wisteria forest every morning well before dawn, when he was certain we wouldn't be followed. He insisted it was imperative his brothers not find out I was training in combat *and* a Fae in the same week.

The guilt of learning something Flint longed to obtain weighed heavily on me. No, he did not possess our strange anomalies, but he could learn the basics. Why couldn't Darric teach him something to pacify the situation?

"Stop thinking about it." Darric pulled apart the tightly wrapped knot of my arms across my chest. He reached into a crevice created by a system of three intertwined tree trunks and removed two long sanded sticks, the same length and width as a sword, complete with smooth grips. "This is a waster," he explained, flipping one stick so he held the imaginary blade and extending the handle to me. "It will be the first weapon you'll learn to use. We don't start with anything sharp. You would lose a limb. Or die."

I took a firm hold of the polished grip, and he released the weapon. The weight surprised me. My wrist buckled, and the end smashed into the grass. "It's heavy," I exclaimed.

"It's ironwood," he stated, as if it was obvious. "What would be the purpose of having you train with something that wasn't the same weight and length as a sword?"

"Valid argument." I readjusted and lifted the waster. It fought my wrists, straining the joints.

"You'll get used to the weight. Eventually, you won't notice it." He circled me as I familiarized myself with the feel of a training sword.

I rolled my eyes at the odd "weapon." Though I trusted his methods, this seemed ridiculous. Did he truly perceive my skill as so underdeveloped that I couldn't be trusted with an actual weapon? "At least there isn't much you can do to me with a stick," I quipped.

He gave a devious chuckle. "Don't make the mistake of thinking that because this weapon has no blade, it cannot bring you harm." He passed behind me, and a firm blow from his waster slammed into the backs of my knees. I tumbled towards the ground, shocked, as my own waster fell from my grasp and rolled across the grass.

Darric caught my hand, stopping me from hitting the dirt at full force, and eased me onto my back. He grazed his waster over my forehead and made a light tap with the edge. The hard wood knocked murderously against my skull.

"This is a heavy wood. In the right hands, it can be as deadly as a sword. With enough force it can crush a skull, break a bone, or simply bludgeon to death. It *is* a weapon." He took my hand and jerked me from the ground. "And it's the only one you're touching until I decide otherwise."

Defeated, I plucked my "useless" waster from the grass, holding it limply at my side.

"Time for review." He recommenced his predatory circling. I watched intently, only losing him for a split second when he passed directly behind me. "You've learned concentration. Focus. Balance. Some haphazard grappling skills." He disappeared and slammed the waster against the backs of my thighs. I buckled and fell, but this time he wrapped his arm around my waist to prevent me from hitting the ground. "And you are still not paying attention to your surroundings." I pushed his chest, trying to wriggle out of his arms. He ignored my struggle and tightened his hold. "You keep making it this easy and I won't need a sword to sweep you off your feet." The gruff, rich tone of his voice left my knees weak.

"You are not as charming as you think you are, Mr. Ursygh."

"I don't recall ever claiming to be. Is that lustful effect getting to you again?" He raised a devilish eyebrow.

"Ugh, let me go." I rolled out of his arms and scooped my waster back into my hand. Without thinking, I swung for his head.

He ducked and countered by smashing his waster into mine. The force of his impact tore the wooden sword from my grasp, sending unpleasant vibrations up my arm.

He laughed. "It would be advantageous for you to keep the weapon in your hand."

Jackass. I snatched the waster and took a calming breath, attempting to lock my emotions back in their pit. He came at me before I could swing. By some insane reflex, I avoided his attack, and the wood grazed my hair as it sped past my head.

Surprised, I stumbled backwards, and a surge of fury broke free of its cage. "That would have killed me!" I hissed.

Bam! My legs went out from under me, and my stomach hit my throat. He was at my side in an instant, cradling me in his arms. "You are not trying, and you are not concentrating. Be aware and alert. That is what makes you accurate." He set me back on my feet.

I swung. He blocked. I was too slow. His movement increased. I felt him brush alongside me and grab a tight handful of my hair. He pulled my head back, forcing me to meet his penetrative eyes. "You're tense, and you are staying in one place too long. Agility and fluidity are key. You are small and nimble. Use it. I've taught you to see when blinded. You can anticipate your opponent's actions. Why are you not employing your clairvoyance?"

I narrowed my eyes at him. "Maybe I've decided I don't want to see it coming," I retorted.

He clenched his jaw, suppressing an amorous grin, and released my hair with a gentle tug to the curls.

I tried to catch him lingering behind me, but he maintained a perfect illusion in my blind spots, only occasionally flashing into my periphery. I grew dizzy from rotating.

Another yank to my hair. This one hurt.

Finally, a full glimpse of him. I swung and hit nothing. He gripped my shoulder and spun me completely around so I faced the opposite direction. What the hell was the point of this?

Legs gone again. Righted once more.

"Use what you have learned."

Darric aimed to relentlessly knock my knees out from under me. This time I observed a definitive change in his muscle tension as he prepared to strike, his arm held to the side ready to catch me. I turned at the last possible moment to avoid the attack, but he swiftly changed tactics and planted his foot on the train of my dress. I landed on the ground with a thud.

"Aya, that was terrible."

I rubbed my hands over my face.

"This dress is a hindrance." He pulled at the woolen fabric. "I'll have Bromly sew you a pair of—"

"I'll learn to move in it," I interrupted. "I'm not wearing pants."

"If you intend to ever fight like a man, you will."

"I don't intend to fight like a man. I intend to fight like a *woman* who can *kill* a man."

A satisfied smile crossed his face. "Fair enough." He helped me to my feet. "My brother is going to resent you when he realizes you've become a skilled assassin while wearing a hideous frock."

"It's an heirloom," I informed him, "and your brother wouldn't resent the idea so much if you had half a heart to teach him."

"I'm never going to teach Flint combat." He plucked my waster from the grass and tossed it in my direction. I caught the fake blade without issue.

"It isn't right. You've made him feel worthless. He's eager and enthusiastic. He envies you."

"Envy . . ." He scoffed.

I controlled my anger exceptionally well. It transitioned into something lighter, almost aerial. The breeze rushed through the forest and ruffled my hair. "Why not him? Why only me? He's your brother, and I can't possibly be more important than that bond."

"This is not a subject we are discussing right now," he said, looking around at the sudden change in the wind.

That was it! I'd had enough! I gripped the edge of my waster and threw it at him.

He moved nimbly away from the wooden sword and stared at me, stunned. His lip curled into an unpleasant shape, and his shoulders tensed. Every ounce of friendliness vanished from his eyes, and an impending sense of doom slithered up my spine.

He slammed his waster to the ground and sped towards me. I jumped, the blood draining from my face. *Run. Run now.* But my feet stayed firmly attached to the grass, as if I were part of the landscape. The cat hissed, disembodied, from some unknown location.

Darric towered over my frozen form, running a hand along my waist and slowly up my back. My heart spasmed as a wicked grin parted his lips. "Three," he growled.

He violently twisted his fingers into the nape of my dress and hauled me to the nearest tree. My ankles bent and I stumbled, trying to grind my heels into the dirt to stop him. He pulled a coil of rope from his hiding place.

"No," I yelled, contorting my body in an attempt to slip out of his grip.

He caught my wrist. "I told you there would be consequences. I've been lenient. Now I'm punishing you."

Punishment? He was going to punish me?

He dragged me to the ground, pinning me to the grass with one knee, and leaned his weight on my torso. Uselessly, I bucked and wiggled beneath him and hammered my fists into his leg; nothing slowed him. He snatched my flailing arm and tied the rope so tightly around my wrist that blood throbbed in my fingertips. I threw a punch, narrowly missing his jaw. My puny fist landed on his bracer, and the knives stored in the leather caught my attention. I tore one free and sliced into the space between us.

"Fuck," he drawled, avoiding the blade, and caught my hand. "Vicious little cuss when you're angry, aren't you?" He pried the small knife from my grip and flung it, then continued binding my wrists together.

With my hands bound, rage bellowed from deep inside of me. I screamed and let the insults fly, calling him every foul name I could remember from a lifetime. Adding to the indignity, he began to chuckle at my erratic swearing.

He pinned my bound arms above my head. I had never felt so exposed, as if my chest were bare and he could see everything. He wrapped his hands around my wrists and studied the increased pulse in my neck.

Lying under him, the same senseless mania that had snared my rational thinking during grappling training began to overtake me.

My heart fluttered.

I wanted to feel his lips on me.

His body over me.

I wanted him to engulf me.

I thrashed, inhaling a sharp breath, and pushed the lustful thoughts out of my head. *Stop thinking such repugnant things about this ill-bred sadist while he has you pinned into submission!*

Darric's chuckling turned into depraved laughter as his mouth descended to my chest and his lips torturously dragged over the arch of my breast. "Emotions on your sleeve," he sing-songed and flew off me.

He pulled hard on the rope, jerking me from the ground, and threw it over a branch above my head to heave my body into the air. I dangled limply with my toes barely scratching the grass. My arms screamed at the joints as I swayed with the breeze. Darric tied off the rope and cut the excess.

Next, he knelt to my ankle and unlatched Luken's dagger. I kicked him and squirmed, trying to prevent the theft of my only piece of security, but he won and tossed the blade far off to the side. Using the remaining rope, he bound my ankles.

Pleased with his handiwork, he observed me hanging with satisfaction. I suspected he would have lit a cigar if he had one. "Get out of it," he said through a dark and psychotic expression. "Use anything you know. Take all the time you need. Neither of us sleep anyway." He settled by the base of a tree across the forest and leaned against the bark, ready to spectate the torment he had created.

Of all the impertinent.

Unorthodox.

Barbaric.

Ridiculous methods.

I craned my neck back and had to squint against the sunlight. I couldn't look up for long. The pressure in my chest wouldn't properly allow air to fill my lungs. My fingers had taken on a cyanotic hue as they brushed the bark. My shoulders ached, and my wrists felt as though they might snap under the strain. I needed to separate from the pain and work through the problem. I had to relieve some of the burden.

The forest grew quiet, letting me hear the creak of the rope as the wind swayed my body. I gripped the trace of extra line and pulled myself up so the pressure in my chest decreased. My stomach muscles scolded me for the action, and I groaned as my energy rapidly depleted.

I shot a quick glance at Darric. He smirked sardonically, resting his wrist on a bent knee and grinding his nails against the inside of his fist. *When I get out of this, I'm going to stab Luken's dagger into your throat.* The breeze moved flecks of blond hair across his forehead. Why did he have to be so stunningly handsome when I hated him? *Arrogant dual-wielding swordsman.*

Despite his warning about succumbing to emotions, I let the rage take a firm hold on my senses. Between us, fallen petals whirled in a light vortex with faint white glimmers at its edge. The wind's speed increased until the blooms flew out of the little tornado in a miniature explosion of glittering color.

I gaped, then quickly slammed my mouth shut, my brows knitting together to shade my eyes.

A new breeze flooded the forest. This time, I mentally grabbed the strings of flowing air. They came to life with iridescent sparkles and twisted towards my trunk, smashing into the space below me. Agony shot through my arms as the gusts propelled me into the air and over the top of the branch. I tossed my legs to catch the bough, and my stomach collided into it with a hard thud. The frenzied sway of the branches slowly stilled, leaving only fading white sparkles and an array of new foliage tumbling to the grass.

"Wind," I exhaled, awed by the newly discovered talent. "Wind!" I squealed ecstatically.

Darric leaped to his feet.

I tugged at the bindings, forcing the rope knot to the top of my perch. Raising my ankles to my hands, I loosened the ties and wriggled my legs free. My insolent instructor paced below, running an anxious hand through his hair. My ankle restraints fell at his feet, and I flashed a derisive smile at him.

I sawed my bound wrists back and forth against the bark, trying to cut through the rope, but the harsh cord rubbed burns into my skin. I needed something sharp or . . .

Air is abstract. It's light. Fickle. A changeable energy that doesn't luxuriate in staying in place.

Instead of waiting for the breeze, I envisioned it. I let the aerial ability vacate my core. It felt like someone cracked open my ribcage and ripped my lungs from my chest. I cried out. A powerful gale hit my branch, splintering the limb down the middle and shredding through my bindings. The force of the blast reverberated through the tree, violently tearing the trunk in two. The entire mess of broken wood, leaves, petals, sparkles, and myself fell to the forest floor.

Darric slid to his knees in just enough time to catch me before I slammed into the ground. Two loud thumps crashed on either side of us, sending a flurry of petals into the air, and morning sunlight spilled through a new hole in the tree canopy.

I blinked rapidly, staring into his astounded face. "I can control and conjure wind." My chest heaved between words. "I venture you didn't take *that* into consideration when you decided to tie me up. Have I rendered you speechless yet?"

His mouth twitched into a halfhearted grin, and he eased me out of his arms. "You've rendered me a lot of things." He twisted onto the balls of his feet and rubbed his palms together, losing his amazed expression. "Flint is a cynic, Aya," he stated dryly. "There is a perverse side to him that only needs to be nudged in the right direction to turn iniquitous. Teaching him to wield any sort of weapon would be like setting oil on fire."

I wrinkled my nose, having never heard him say anything so disparaging about his brother. "He knows how to use a bow," I said defensively, still catching my breath.

"He's not very good."

I raised an eyebrow. "Flint seems harmless. A bit dimwitted and ignorant, but nothing more nefarious than a bunny rabbit."

"If handled wrong, a rabbit can still bite. Flint lacks control. He doesn't know how to hold himself together in a crisis or how to move forward and recover. There are too many deep-seated vexations addling him, and fear rules his mind. He will end up getting himself killed. I don't want the disaster of what he would become on my conscience."

"You are under the impression he would become some sort of mass murderer?" I realized I didn't know every detail about their history, but it didn't seem likely Flint would hurt anyone on purpose.

"Letting fear control your every action, without using it constructively, has insidious consequences. He is terrified of being abandoned and forgotten. His memory is extensive, and his grudges are deep. I brought Flint into these mountains to protect him when he didn't deserve mercy. I feel no guilt for refusing to instruct him in combat."

"Flint said you didn't give him a choice about leaving Alamantia."

"That's accurate. Though considering his unrelenting want to travel with me, his teaching himself to use the bow that would become his downfall, one would have thought he would be elated by the opportunity. Flint didn't want to leave Alamantia because he didn't think what he did was wrong. He still doesn't. He lacks the ability to empathize and refuses to take responsibility for his actions. The apologies you have received from him have been a new, somewhat forced, occurrence."

I rolled onto my side and pushed into a seated position. My arms tingled. My shoulders drooped, and every part of me ached. "What did Flint do?"

Darric shook his head, hesitating. He left me sitting by the broken tree in a pile of wisteria blooms and retrieved the bracer blade I'd stolen. He brandished the weapon before sliding it back into place. "When the three of us lived in Alamantia with Mrs. Keene, Flint always claimed to know his mother. He had no tangible proof other than her tall, thin frame and red hair. He would watch her from the roof of our house with pure hatred. When I decided to leave to find work, he begged to go with me, but I couldn't risk his life. I had no idea if I would be successful or even return. I convinced myself I would find a way to bring a steady income to the Keene's or die trying. I owed it to them for giving me a home.

"When I returned, I was in the Onyx Guard. Knowing the dark assassins the Senate makes of Sights, Flint began asking me to instruct him in combat. But I couldn't stop thinking of the way he always looked when he saw the woman he thought was his mother. The resentment in his eyes. The enmity. I feared what he might do to her if he knew how to wield a sword. When I refused, he began crafting arrows and taught himself to use a bow." He groaned, sweeping a hand down his face as if seared by a painful memory. "I swore if I ever left the Onyx Guard, I would relocate the family. Anywhere other than Alamantia."

"And that's why you brought everyone here?" I confirmed.

He plucked Luken's dagger from the grass and edged his thumb over the Medial crest. "We all had a form of psychotic breakdown after Mrs. Keene died. Bromly fell into depression. He stopped eating and slept for days at a time. The hatred Flint had towards his mother finally metastasized into something physical, and he attacked the woman he believed to be her. We had to flee into the mountains before the city guards could trace the crime to Flint."

I threw my hands over my mouth and spoke through my fingers. "Was she all right?"

His stare pleaded with me not to be naive.

My heart shattered. "Flint killed her . . . didn't he?"

Darric knelt in the grass and took my ankle to reapply Luken's dagger. "He blames me. He claims if I had just let him travel with me, then he wouldn't have had to watch her every day and remember that she abandoned him." He sat back and groaned. "Maybe he's right. Maybe I should have taken him with me. Maybe if I had brought him along, I wouldn't have fallen into the hands of the Onyx Guard and that woman would still be alive."

I mulled over the demolished remains of the wisteria tree. "The three of you . . . There's so much death . . . It's heartbreaking."

He smoothed a loose curl away from my face and tucked the strand behind my ear. "We are criminals, and we ran from our crimes. We've all committed our share of murder. Flint succumbed to his emotions. Bromly fights by my side, killing any intruder that threatens us without question. And I . . . Let's just say the Onyx Guard is not the only sordid part of my history."

I shook in denial. "You've never seemed like criminals to me."

"For some reason, you see the best in all of us. Despite our flaws." He took my hand and laced his fingers in mine. "I love how you find beauty in everything."

I raised a finger and gave it a little twirl, controlling the wind to make blooms fall onto us. "It's human to be flawed. We can't change our pasts. The only thing that truly matters is what we do with the future. I believe a person should be judged only by the inner workings of their heart. Good people make mistakes as often as evil ones appear as perfection."

"See?" He peered into my eyes, watching the Fae glimmer travel over my irises. "Beautiful."

Chapter 24

My lessons changed drastically in the two weeks following my punishment. After introducing the wooden wasters, Darric opened the doors to combat. Despite my using clairvoyance, he was still faster and stronger. A sword was in the near future, but before my intimidating instructor would allow it, he wanted to be certain I bordered perfection in all the aspects he had taught me thus far.

I developed an eidetic memory and learned to navigate the landscape and block attacks while blindfolded. To explain the extent of this ability, he blinded himself one morning. After recalling the entire landscape in more exquisite detail than I could ever have imagined, he allowed me to assault him in any way I saw fit. He instantly incapacitated me.

"You trust your eyes too much," he said. "Vision should be an additive, not a requirement. Rely on your other senses."

I adjusted accordingly out of necessity. My lesson the following day involved both of us sightless in a full brawl with the wasters.

I often forgot about the danger involved with the ironwood swords. In the end, every part of me bore round bruises from being too slow to avoid Darric's attacks. Each time I was hit, he reminded me that not only was he curbing his force to prevent mangling me, but if it had been a sword, I'd be dead. "If you must take a hit, an injury to the arm or leg will offer a better chance of survival, though any impairment of magnitude can prove fatal."

I lost track of how many times he killed me.

Balance was still a tribulation. I had grown to hate the trunk beam, especially now that Darric was throwing knives at me. Once I accomplished the insane flipping he adamantly insisted I learn, he added the blindfold. Listening became the only way to avoid his blades. The metal made a distinct song slicing through the air, growing louder as the knife drew closer. The predicament: he didn't want me to avoid his projectiles—he wanted me to catch them. Attempting to snare his daggers without losing a finger was terrifying. In addition to the sing of metal, I had to pick up on the trace whomping sound of rotation to grab the handle instead of the blade. Luckily, I kept all my fingers.

Between the bruises and full-body soreness, something was changing; I looked different. The skin on my face had darkened from spending many hours outside. My arms and shoulders were toned. The waster had become weightless. I felt lighter on my feet. I could move with agility and more fluidity, bending in ways I never thought possible.

The hours spent away from the Hovel steadily increased. We left before dawn and often would not return until sunset. Darric had carefully chosen the moment to tell his brothers about instructing me, waiting for the time when our training sessions would extend until the evening and prevent us from returning to the Hovel for most of the day.

Each night, he dropped me off at the cavern and occasionally joined us for supper before disappearing into the caliginous valley.

While Flint and Bromly slept, I practiced my balance and footwork on the seating logs and worked on flourishes with a stick. I felt ridiculous, but I was determined to perfect my skill.

I talked to the cat for company, though she never replied. As the long nights wore on, I inevitably would scan the blackened tree line for some sign of my stranger. I could have made it to the wisteria forest alone, but I'd promised him I would stay at the cavern. It was aggravating that he kept leaving me behind, and I was not sure how much longer I could tolerate the monotony.

The evening I decided the perpetual nightly boredom would come to an end, he was teaching me about rhythm.

"Swinging a weapon isn't a haphazard action," he instructed. "There is a rhythm to attacks, blocks, and parries. Finding the flow of a battle is critical for success. Once you discover it, you can control it. Knowing how long it will take you to make each move is essential. Each action must be carefully calculated against your opponent. Use their weaknesses. Everyone has a weakness. Your goal is to find it and use it to exploit your adversary."

I sidestepped Darric's swing, and his waster grazed my lower back. It was hard to imagine him with a weakness.

"A sword just flayed your back open," he reprimanded. "You are going to die when we begin using swords if you don't start moving more efficiently."

"Do you have a weakness?" I purposefully stepped out of our practice battle.

"Everyone does." He snatched my arm and touched my ribcage with the edge of his waster. "What did I tell you about protecting your body? You're dead again." He groaned, frustrated.

I rolled my eyes, recalling the many days of verbal abuse I'd endured under Darric's instruction. Days when he repeated himself multiple times and I still made the same errors. "What's my weakness? What have you been using against me?"

"Do you mean now or in the past?" He laughed.

I wrinkled my nose, waiting for an answer.

"All right," he finally said, "you fight with your emotions. You don't trust your senses. You have Fae power yet never use it when you fight. You lack focus and can be easily distracted. The lustful attraction you have towards—"

"Okay, okay, that's enough," I interrupted. "I wasn't expecting a snide list."

"There's more." He gave me a smug grin.

"So, what's yours?"

He scratched the back of his head, ruffling his hair. "There is no reason to tell you. You never want an enemy to know where your skills are lacking."

I stubbornly crossed my arms over my chest, awkwardly holding my waster to the side.

He chuckled at my obstinate stance. "I have two. The first: daggers. When an opponent fights with a dagger in their off hand, I rarely escape without injury. I tend to focus too much on their sword and miss the dagger, as it becomes easy to conceal. Bracers are an exceptional solution to that problem." He held up his shielded wrists.

"Will you teach me to dual wield?" I gazed at the dark brown leather covering his forearms. The three knives he kept tucked into each bracer were almost undetectable.

"I intend to teach you to fight as I do. Yes, you will learn to dual wield."

Excitement surged through me. "Then when the time comes, I want to use my dagger as my off hand."

Smirking, he lightly shook his head. "Absolutely." He scanned the horizon, checking the position of the sun. Orange and pink hues pierced the blooming tree canopy.

"What's the second?" I pried.

"You'll figure it out someday. It's time to go."

I gnawed at my bottom lip. "I don't want to go back to the Hovel." I hated to admit how much I enjoyed Darric's company. I didn't see him as my instructor anymore. Perhaps I never did. He was a friend who had rescued me from the depths of hell to show me how to continue in this new existence. The first person in my entire life who knew me as I knew myself. I loved that small miracle.

"It's not really optional." He plucked the waster from my grip and placed the two wooden swords inside his hiding tree.

"Yes, it is," I argued. "Every night, you leave me at the cavern and disappear. What are you doing all night anyway?" He hadn't brought a new stag kill to the Hovel in weeks.

He shrugged, pulling his cloak around his shoulders.

"Let me stay with you," I pleaded.

"I can't." He lifted his hood over his head.

"Why not? Sure, the woods are dangerous at night, but as long as I'm with you, nothing will happen to me."

He tugged my cloak out of the branches. "You are *disturbingly* confident of your safety with me."

"I am," I asserted, then rolled my eyes. "We can keep training."

"No training. You are not ready for night fighting." His gaze drifted into the tree canopy. "Though the concept of allowing you to stay with me is tempting, we have to go back, for Flint's sake."

"What does Flint have to do with it?"

"If we stay out all night without showing our faces at the Hovel, it's going to look a bit . . ." He smiled, running his tongue over his teeth.

I laughed, throwing my hands over my mouth.

He chuckled at my reaction and handed me my cloak. "Are you prepared to further infuriate my brother?"

I tied the wool around my shoulders. "Flint is not stuck enduring hours of boredom after you leave."

He ran his finger down the side of my cheek. "Just tonight."

"We'll see about that. I'll roam the valley alone if that's what it takes to convince you."

He pulled my hood over my head and tugged it down to shade my eyes. "Stubborn Fae."

"Insolent instructor."

Night took the valley as we left the forest and headed in the direction of the Hovel. I stopped walking when the cavern came into view, protesting my return.

"Doubting my word?" Darric asked, noting my sudden stop.

"You said yourself your word can be shot to hell if you need to protect your interest."

He slid his hand down my arm and wove our fingers together. "True, but that's wildly unlikely when it comes to you." He retreated into the tree line, and we crept into the brush by the entrance of the cavern.

"You eavesdrop!" I accused, shoving his shoulder.

He shushed me with a wicked smile. "I can't protect my brothers a mile away from the Hovel. Most nights I'm a lot closer to the cavern than I let them believe."

A metallic clang made me jump, and a bucket rolled out of the cavern. "Where the fuck are they?" Flint snarled.

"You might not like everything you hear," Darric murmured into my ear. I tucked myself under the shelter of his arm.

"She's fine, Flint," Bromly grumbled. "She's safe with him."

"A little too safe." Flint spat on the ground and kicked dirt over the sticky glob. "Why has he changed? Why does he suddenly wanna keep her alive?"

"That's what you wanted, wasn't it? Darric accepting her and allowing her to come with us to Burge? It all worked out for you." Bromly chortled. "Obviously, he's found a use for her. From what he says, she's gifted with weapons. Maybe he thinks she'll be a good defense during the trip south this year."

"He's gonna betray me," Flint growled.

"I'm surprised he agreed to your insane demands, especially since he seemed so . . ." Bromly paused and grunted. "You need to make peace with the outcome, even if it isn't what you want," he warned.

"What did you agree to?" I whispered under Darric's chin. He let out a long breath and didn't answer.

"I'm not acceptin' that," Flint snapped.

Bromly shook his head. "You're not helping yourself. Lying to her. Bashing Darric to make him out as an evil cad. Aya is too smart for that."

"Yeah, she sees right through it." Flint plopped onto the seating log and stared aimlessly into the fire. "He was suppose'ta leave. He always leaves. But he chose to stay."

"You need to stop thinking ill of him, because it makes you think ill of her. Jealousy is no way to win someone's affections." Bromly handed Flint a paring knife, encouraging him to go back to work.

Flint thumbed the wooden handle. "Alone in the woods with her after dark, I bet he's winnin' every affection she's got under that dress."

Enraged, I leaped to my feet. Darric urgently grabbed my waist and jerked me to the ground. He lay on top of me and covered my mouth with his hand, forcing me to stay still. The rustle we created in the brush silenced Bromly and Flint's conversation, and they both eyed the woods.

"If you don't want me to leave you here, then be quiet," Darric scolded in a whisper.

"How dare he?" I mumbled furiously against his fingers and dug my nails into his hand to pull it from my mouth.

"I figured you'd be used to Flint sexualizing you by now."

I pressed my palm to my forehead. "How long do you listen to this?

"Sometimes hours. I especially love it when you talk to your cat." His mellifluous voice rang through a sly half smile.

Embarrassed, I wiggled beneath him, trying to free myself.

Delighting in my struggle, he lowered his mouth to my neck. "Heard enough?"

His lips brushed my ear, and I leaned into him ever so slightly, hoping to feel more of his mouth against my skin. "I don't need any more reasons to dislike Flint," I breathed.

Satisfied, he rolled away and wrapped his hand around mine to lead us from the cavern.

Darric kept me close as we strolled through the woods to an unknown location. I pressed my body into him, and it seemed to lessen the tension in his shoulders. "Why does Flint keep talking about you betraying him?"

He groaned and kept his eyes locked on the wooded path. "I made him a promise, one I knew I was never going to be able to keep. It was a mistake, and it isn't likely he will forgive me if I renege. The complication is, it's no longer a matter of *if* but *when*."

"Darric!" Angered by his confession, my heart broke for Flint. "Why would you do such a thing?"

"When I made the pact with him, I wasn't thinking straight. My judgment was . . ." He scanned my face before looking away. ". . . clouded. I was concerned with more pressing matters. I didn't realize something that minuscule would become so significant."

"What did you promise him?"

He shook his head, clenching his jaw.

I dug my heels into the ground, grinding us to a halt, and spun in front of him. "I don't understand you two. Blood or not, you're family."

He cupped my cheek and traced his thumb along the side of my mouth. "You ran from your family, did you not?"

I pushed away his fingers. "That's not the same thing."

"Right." He reintertwined our hands and continued walking. "The heinous fiancé. Worlds of difference," he said scathingly, and the silence that followed was deafening.

The azure glow of the moon illuminated the flowers scattered across the valley. Various shades of purple and cobalt, nestled in a carpet of black strands, covered the ground.

"Where are we going?" I asked, ending the quiet between us.

He shrugged. "You asked what I do at night. I wander."

"Doesn't that get lonely?"

He didn't answer.

My gaze shifted upwards when the last clouds dissipated to reveal the stars. My jaw fell; the sky had changed. Millions of stars glittered across the charcoal slate, twinkling over mysterious milky bands of amaranth and indigo.

Darric followed my bewildered gaze.

"It didn't look like that before," I said in awe, my feet slowing.

"It's the solstice. Summer is here. It's more apparent this far from the cities."

I stopped to absorb as much of the sky as possible.

A pleasant smile spread over Darric's face. "I know where we can go tonight, but it'll involve some climbing."

I rejected the idea at first, my nose wrinkling. "Only if you promise not to let me fall to my death."

He squeezed my hand and pulled me deeper into the woods. "Only if *you* promise not to dig those damn nails into me again."

Darric led the way to the layered crag. He tucked me to his chest and wrapped my arms around his neck. "This will be easier if you hold on to me." He took a firm hold of the rock and lifted us up the cliff face, placing his hands in near invisible ledges I never would have found on my own.

We passed the tree canopy and ascended high into the mountains, leaving the darkened colors of wisteria stretched far below us. The cat comfortably perched on the lower levels of rock and closed her amber eyes, allowing Darric to take me away from her.

He held on to my lower back to ease me onto a flat mossy stone platform. Soft, spongy lichen squished under my fingers, and the scent of nearby flowers drifted on the air. He tugged us to the center of the ledge and spread his cloak over the moss before lying down upon it and patting the fabric beside him. I crawled onto the wool and leaned back, losing myself in the awe-inspiring dome of solstice sky. With no mountains or trees to obstruct the view, I became mesmerized by the beauty.

Darric tucked his arm behind his head. "This is the best view anywhere in the valley."

"Incredible," I muttered, focusing on a cluster of stars twinkling more vividly than the others. "Do you do this every night?"

"Not every night. Usually only when I need a place to think without disruption."

"Darric Ursygh's meditation precipice," I mused. "I think you've been up here a lot recently."

"*Recently* complications have been more present in my life," he admitted.

A fidgety exhale left my chest. I had the feeling this ledge was another of the hiding places he concealed from his brothers.

"It looks like Fae dust," I observed, gazing into the endless cosmos.

"I never thought of it that way." The side of his mouth twitched into a reluctant smile. "In Vegathyad, you can't see the sky. The country is cloaked by the volcanic clouds, so most Podarians have never seen the stars. I remember crossing the border the first night I set foot in Brisleia. The haze vanished in an instant. It was . . . overwhelming, and the first time I experienced the drastic seamed change from one country to another. It made me feel a little . . . less dead."

I stayed quiet a moment, formulating a response. "You really don't know your nationality? Where you're from or your birthday?"

He shook his head. "I know I wasn't born in Vegathyad, though my family lived there for a time. I guess I could be Podarian. I know I'm not Brisleian, and obviously my lack of an accent eliminates Duval."

"Do you want to know?" I asked, astounded by his indifference.

"Of course," he confessed. "But even when the Onyx Guard took me all over the world hunting the Fae, I never found another family with the name Ursygh. My parents said if anything ever happened to them, it would be critical I seek a man named Roweley. He seemed to be some sort of elusive relative who opposed us traveling, but I never found him either. It was defeating, though my parents probably didn't expect to die when I was too young to understand their instructions.

"There are many gaps in my memory from those days. The images are dim, seen through innocent eyes. I was too young to realize any of it was important. My birthday. My nationality. All mysteries I've never been able to solve."

My heart ached. I inched closer and pressed my body into his side to lay my head on his shoulder. He inhaled a sharp breath.

"Do you miss them?"

"They are difficult to remember." His eyes darted from the sky to my small frame curled beside him. "Do you miss your family?"

I placed my palm on his chest. His heartbeat knocked in fast jerks against my fingertips. "I miss my brother more than anything." I buried my face in his shoulder and rubbed my nose over his shirt. The intoxicating smell coming off his clothes made my head spin. "He was my best friend, and he is never going to forgive me for running away."

The tension coursing through Darric's body lessened until he felt pliable.

"Sometimes you remind me of him, but he never threatened to kill me or took joy in pretending to."

He released a throaty chuckle, then pulled his arm from under his head and wrapped it around my back. "I don't want to kill you. I never did. I wish I had been able to. It would have made everything so much simpler."

I smiled, looking up at his face. "You're not used to physical comfort, are you?"

"No." I barely heard his answer. "But I could get used to it." He tucked me tighter into his side, and the underside of his chin brushed my hair.

"Darric?" I held the words on my tongue, unsure if I should pose the question.

He twisted his fingers into my dress and pulled me further into his embrace. "It's okay. You can ask."

"What happened . . . to them?"

"They were killed by Caldera soldiers. I remember I was sitting on the floor in the hallway of our manor, listening to my mother sing a lullaby to my sister, the night they broke down the front door. We had a small collection of guards who serviced us, and my father was a talented swordsman, but it didn't matter. They ambushed us while our guard was down. My mother was hysterical, and I witnessed most of my father's death. I saw his hands and feet bound. The struggle. The gutting they performed to pacify him. Podarians have an uncanny ability to be savage."

I swallow thickly, ashamed I'd made him relive the memory, and fumbled with a handful of his shirt.

"The corruption taking place in Podar back then was inconceivable," he continued. "It wasn't enough to take my father's life. They had come for my entire family. My mother used the distraction of our failing guards fighting off the soldiers to flee with my sister and me, but the soldiers set fire to the manor and chased us down. She tried to run with both of us, but it was too much for her, and I couldn't keep up. So she shoved me into a thorn bush for safety. The soldiers caught her and killed her in cold blood in the middle of the night. And then they killed my sister." He looked down at me and squeezed my frozen side. "Are you okay?"

I shuddered. "I want to say I'm sorry, but it's not enough."

"It was a long time ago, but it's still vivid. Nothing about that night fades. I doubt it ever will." He sighed. "I dream of it often."

I looked up from his shirt. The stars were reflected across his eyes. No matter how much comfort I offered, nothing was going to heal a wound this deep. "You had a sister?"

"She was an infant when she died. I don't remember much about her. I have vague memories of an older brother as well, but he disappears around the time my sister was born."

"And you were six?"

He nodded. "The soldiers searched for me and concluded I'd died in the fire. When they left to inspect the wreckage, I ran to my mother. She was still alive, but barely. That's when she told me to find Roweley and that my future was with him, but she died before telling me where to go—or anything else for that matter. So I started walking, one foot in front of the other, until the sky opened and I saw the stars for the first time. It was easier to survive in Brisleia. I slept in trees and barns, living off what I found in the woods. Thieving isn't difficult when you are small and nimble."

My chest tightened as I realized the true depth of my naivety. "I always wanted to wander. To have the liberty of going anywhere I wanted, any moment I willed it. All this time, I've craved your freedom and the careless ease you possess, yet I had no idea it stemmed from something so execrable."

"Detachment became a part of me because I didn't want to rely on anything. I've tried to prevent growing attached to anyone, since most people I've cared about have been ripped from me. "

"What about Bromly and Flint? Aren't they your family?"

"The Keenes gave me a home. I promised Bromly's mother I wouldn't leave her sons to fend for themselves. But soon, Bromly will marry Hazel Prague, and they will start a life together. He is an absolute fool for this girl, and they are going to have a quiver full of kids. Once a year they help us sell wears, so naturally I give them a percentage of our revenue. Bromly will be happy. It will be a fine life for him and a perfect location for him to settle. But once he stays in Burge permanently, I'm not sure where that will leave me."

"You aren't going to continue living at the Hovel?" A tiny hole bored into my heart at the thought—I didn't want the valley to become a memory.

"I don't want to profit by hunting mountain game forever, though it is tempting to stay here."

"Would you consider moving to Burge? You are not short on talent. There must be plenty of opportunities for work in town."

"There are, and perhaps I could. But having a history in the Onyx Guard makes it difficult to stay in one place. I've got the same target on my back as the Fae."

"And Flint?"

"Flint is going to stay wherever Bromly resides. He'll do well with roots."

Tears welled in the corners of my eyes. "I feel like the most selfish person in existence. I've taken so much for granted. I never truly knew everything I had."

"Don't be so despondent, Aya. It won't change anything that's transpired. Personally, I wouldn't want to be married off to someone I despised either. Come to think of it, if my parents were alive and things were the way they should have been, I probably would have fallen into an arranged marriage myself. So, in that regard, we aren't different. I'd have run too."

I sniffed. "Leaving my home was a spontaneous decision, not solely based upon marriage. I abruptly found myself in a world so unfamiliar that everything I knew was turned upside down. I had spent my entire life looking out over the mountains imagining how different my life would be if I left. I could see the world. Be someone else. But that was naive. The reality is so different."

"Seeing the world changes you," Darric said softly. "Experiencing different perspectives starts to alter the way you think. It breaks the foundation of ideals you've accepted. Sometimes not knowing is better. I can't extirpate the corruption I've seen. Or the suffering I've caused. The lives I've taken. I have memories of pure evil and malevolence burned into my brain. Those images will never disappear or fade. I will carry my past with me forever, silently letting it rip me apart for the rest of my life, however long that may be."

I drifted under the spell of his horrifying words. Darric had braved more suffering in one lifetime than any person should ever witness. He had a right to be bitter, yet somehow, beneath his callous attributes, a remaining faith in kindness endured.

"How do you even know how to form a smile?" My voice cracked as I swallowed tears.

"Well, you've helped." He readjusted his back against the woolen fabric, and his thumb grazed my ribs, sending a spark down my leg. "Training a Fae is more enjoyable than kidnapping them," he added with a smirk.

I released a heavy, disbelieving breath. How could he find humor in any of this? "Why aren't you still in the Onyx Guard? You said you swore an oath of lifetime servitude."

"I did, but when Bromly's mother died, I lost my sanity for a while. She had taken me in when I had nothing, and after she died, I had nothing all over again. She was the final event that broke me. I didn't return to Medial Alexandria with my brigades.

I abandoned my horse, stripped off the uniform, and burned it. Nothing could force me to continue the spiral of death I'd created when I joined the Onyx Guard. I was filled to capacity with blood and carnage and sought to bring it to an end." He rubbed his hand over his face. "But leaving it behind completely is impossible. No matter how hard I try to forget, the scar is permanent. No matter where I go or who I become, I'll always have the Onyx Guard etched into my skin."

Darric shifted onto his side and pried my grip away from his shirt. He took my hand and massaged his thumb into the new reddened callouses forming at the base of my fingers.

"The Onyx Guard makes it seem like a choice to join their ranks, but it's not optional," he said. "The Senate relies on Sights to find the Fae, so they make sure their soldiers understand the contract is irrevocable."

Still holding me in his embrace, he untied the white linen bandage he kept wrapped around his arm and let the fabric fall from his skin. It landed on my chest, revealing a healed burn on the inside of his forearm under the curve of his elbow. The unmistakable crest of Medial Alexandria was seared into his flesh—the same circular geometric pattern of the four Mandalas merging together that decorated the hilt of Luken's dagger.

I shuddered when I saw it.

"A burn lingers, aches, and pulses with each beat of the heart," he began. "Your skin screams for relief that doesn't come for weeks. That's why the senators brand their soldiers. To remind them of their commitment to the Onyx Guard. To make the memory painful and the allegiance permanent.

"In addition, the location of a Medial brand means everything in reputation and pay. A mark on the back will label you a coward. It means you ran from the senators during your branding oath. Not everyone is so keen to give their entire life to forced servitude. Few soldiers who are marked on the back survive through their first months, if they make it past basic training at all. The chest or stomach means the senators had to restrain you. It signifies you couldn't control yourself enough to endure the pain, but at least you aren't classified a coward. I knew a lunatic who willingly took the branding to his face. He was the highest paid soldier in the entire regiment, save the Alpha."

I wrapped my fingers around his forearm and brushed my thumb over the scar. The slightly raised flesh felt soft and smooth and was a distinctly different color from the rest of his skin. "And this?"

"Offered willingly. Pain endured without reaction. High pay and"—he gave a fiery smirk—"something of a reputation for audacity."

"Darric . . ." I groaned, covering the emblem. I didn't want to see it anymore. I had tried to convince myself his history in the Onyx Guard was a lie, but staring into the Medial brand forever burned into his skin pulled his dark history out of abstraction. He truly had kidnapped young Fae, murdered their families, and dragged children to the senators.

I found the fallen strip of linen and redressed the brand, concealing a piece of him that vitally needed to stay hidden. "You have more scars, don't you?" I gripped his arm, touching the traces of his past carved into the lean muscle.

He nodded, his fingers trickling across my stomach.

"A lot?"

He nodded a second time. "There are consequences to wielding a sword. I hope you never find that out for yourself."

I tried to push away, but he was reluctant to release me from the comforting embrace. I sat up, forcing him to drop his arms. I couldn't hold back the sobbing another moment. Tears streamed down my cheeks. I hiccupped, and my chest bounced with each sniffle.

He eased up behind me and gently pulled my hair back from my face. "Why are you crying?"

"I can't relate. I don't know how to fathom any part of what you've been through," I whimpered, hiding my face, but he absolutely refused to distance himself.

He lifted my chin so I had to meet his eyes and worked his fingers into the curls stuck to my neck.

"It's June." I gulped back a sob. "We're leaving for Burge in a month. The Hovel, living here with the three of you, is the only other home I've ever known. " I could see my reflection in his irises, the beautiful steel blue tinting the mirror image of me breaking.

"You're coming with us."

"I know." I wiped away a tear. "So I can start a new life. It's just, I'm terrified to continue on my own after we reach Burge. I don't want to fade into Medial Alexandria or face the Onyx Guard alone. Able to defend myself or not, I don't think I can do it on my own. I don't want any of this to come to an end and—"

"No," he forcefully interrupted.

"No?"

"I couldn't live with myself if I abandoned you in Burge. You'll have a home with us anywhere we go. No matter what happens."

"Why?" Confusion fueled another wave of silent tears. "I thought this training was so I could leave this valley. Aren't you worried about me traveling with you? Staying with you? I'll bring nothing but chaos."

He chuckled, grazing his lips over my ear. "Aya, you already bring nothing but chaos. Eventually, I have to face the truth. I brought you here, and I can't make you pay for something that's entirely my doing."

"But I thought—" I hiccupped. "I thought I just kept up with you unusually well and followed you against your will."

He pressed his forehead to mine. "We both know that isn't true."

Relief crashed through my core at hearing him finally admit it. My heart swelled, and the rush of air leaving my lungs shook my ribcage. I wrapped my arms around him and fused myself to his hard chest, tucking my nose into the curve of his neck and purposefully flooding my throat with his heady scent.

"I promise I will never let Medial Alexandria or the Onyx Guard hurt you," he murmured against my hair, kneading the strands between his fingers. "I'm not mediocre with a sword. I can handle them. I can't handle losing you. I'll give my life before they touch you. I'll die protecting you. I swear it."

"Why would you do that?" I sniffled, pulling back to see his face.

"Because you give me strength, Aya. A reason to be inspired— to believe there are still mysteries yet to be discovered. You let me know that Medial Alexandria and the Divine royals don't have everything figured out. That beneath the genocide of the Fae and oppression from the Senate and the Kings, there is still beauty and grace left in the world."

I kissed his neck, allowing my lips to linger on his skin. He released a long, blissful groan—as if he was about to come unhinged—and his fingers dug into my back. I laid a second kiss on his chin, and my heart seized when my mind caught up with my sudden confidence. Freezing, I rested my forehead on his shoulder to await consequences.

He shook his head, eyes alight with amusement. "I'll never be able to leave you at the Hovel at night again."

Chapter 25

Inever had a reason for wanting a moment to linger. I never experienced anything so monumental I wanted to preserve it as a treasured memory. Then I met Darric Ursygh.

Until the day of my eighteenth birthday, I moved through life as if it were disposable, blindly waiting through my childhood until a future with Prince Marcus Ember of Podar stretched before me like instant mortality. But with Darric time was nonexistent—irrelevant yet never enough.

Even through every insane method of his weapons training. Even when his normally collected mood turned asinine. I would keep those instants locked safely inside my heart to remember a time when I had not recognized what was slowly happening to me around the frantic beating in my chest. I wouldn't have replaced anything or traded a single memory.

Eternity is always the same. A minute doesn't alter its length because of fear or rapture, though it tends to feel otherwise. You cannot stop the flow of the universe, but you can luxuriate in the beauty it provides for the allotted moments you're given.

Wrapped in Darric's arms, his breath coming in slow swells against my skin, I wanted nothing more than for the clock to stop ticking. For the steady march of time to freeze and put us inside our own private world. Let him continue brushing his lips over the shell of my ear. But the starry sky will always fade, and the sun will rise over the mountains. He released the intoxicating hold he had on me, and a new ache settled in my core.

After that night, I knew one thing was absolutely certain: I couldn't ignore the truth of my feelings for Darric Ursygh forever.

When we returned to the Hovel, Bromly was asleep by the outdoor fire with an apple wood log clutched in his lap. Flint was sprawled on top of his bed with the door open. The two had stayed up all night to finish processing the new bear.

"We don't leave for Burge for three weeks. Why the rush?" I asked quietly as Darric moved the tripod off the smoking embers.

"There's one more project we have to finish before we can leave. I'll be helping them with this one, so we won't be able to train as much in the afternoons." He plucked the dried meat off the tripod, dropping the bits into a half-full basket.

After carefully sliding the apple wood from Bromly's grip, I untied my cloak and laid it over him, tucking the ends around his bulbous belly. He pleasantly smacked his lips and snuggled under the makeshift blanket.

I joined Darric at the tripod. "What's the last project?"

"The transportation vessel to Burge. It's been rotting for the last year and needs repair."

"Vessel?" I wrinkled my nose. "A boat?"

"Did you think we were going to walk to Burge with several hundred pounds of illegal cargo?" he teased.

We worked silently through the morning, carving the last of the meat and leaving it to dry over the apple wood. Bromly awakened in early afternoon and suspiciously eyed my cloak. He yawned, rubbing his eyes, then gave Darric a scorching glare.

"Aya, you should get some rest," Darric suggested, returning Bromly's scowl. "We won't be training again until tomorrow morning."

I started to protest until the cat rubbed my leg and looked up at me with a nod.

Reluctantly, I went to our room with the tiny feline. The instant I fell into bed and tugged the covers around myself, I could no longer keep my eyes open. The cat curled into a warm ball of burgundy against my body. I yawned, accepting the musky scent of the Hovel deep into my lungs, and drifted to the dream world.

I stood on water, yet I was completely dry, even my feet. The water beaded and slipped off my skin. Soupy gray fog hung in the air; I couldn't see more than a few feet in front of me. A gust of wind viciously whipped my hair around my face and sent waves rushing over my ankles.

I started to feel my way across the silvery pond, but a wall of fire burst from the water and cut off my path. Startled, I spun around, only to be confronted with a second fiery barrier erupting from the churning waves. I was trapped.

The agitated surface beneath me began to violently shake. I dropped to my knees just as stone breached the waves and lifted me high into the air. The dripping rock rose above the swirling tornado of wind and flames, and I looked down from my perch at the chaos below. The fog suddenly split, forced apart by golden beams of brilliant light from above. It grew brighter and brighter, blinding me until I had to shut my eyes.

———————•⟨⟩•———————

I burst up from the pillows, clutching a hand to my chest, and rubbed my eyes. They burned as if I'd stared directly into the sun. Concerned, I looked over the side of the bed. No water. No flames. No wind. No stone.

I lay back into the mattress, and my head crushed a pile of delicate vines growing cerulean flowers. I rubbed the tiny perennials between my fingers; a faint dusting of green glitter dimmed inside the stems.

The cat poked her head out from the torn cotton blanket. "You aren't bringing these flowers, are you?"

She cocked her head to the side, her whiskers twitching upwards.

I dropped the handful of flowers to scratch the underside of her chin. She closed her eyes, tilting her head so I could reach the fluffy tufts on the side of her face. "Atlas said a Fae has never reached omnipotence because of Medial Alexandria. The bear said he wouldn't kill me so I could be everything Athera needs of me." I groaned and rolled over, smashing my face in the pillow. The cat stood on my back and kneaded her paws into my shoulder.

Muted voices clashed in the distance. Three young men in a heated argument. "They're fighting again," I mumbled into the pillow. They must have been outside the cavern, Darric ensuring a private conversation.

When I finally gathered the courage to open the front door, the three irate brothers instantaneously ceased their squabbling. The six disconcerted eyes that stared at me were worse than any number of gawking lords. I took a cautious step back into the Hovel.

"Don't worry," Darric said to Flint, his tone coated in acid. "She didn't hear anything." He left his brothers and squeezed past me to disappear inside his room.

I scanned the horizon, strangely disoriented. The evening sky was not cast in its normal orange-and-violet beauty. Everything was indigo, and the sun was shining in the wrong place.

Darric came back with his hood covering his brow and handed me my cloak. "We're leaving."

"What? Now?"

"It's dawn," he asserted.

"Dawn?" Confused, I studied the sky a second time.

"You were tired." His acrid tone warned me not to question him.

I tied my cloak and trailed after him. How had I managed to sleep so long? And what fracas had occurred between the brothers during my absence?

Bromly gathered tools and piled them next to the seating logs: a basket of nails, his axe, knives, and every bit of spare rope that existed in the cavern. Flint sat on the grass, seething, his head tucked between his legs. Darric snatched my bicep as we passed him, unwilling to let me stop.

When we reached the layered crag, I tore my arm from his grip. "What the hell is going on?"

"We're training," he replied acerbically.

"Before I step one foot into that forest, I want to know why everyone at the Hovel looks like they're about to kill each other."

"You don't need to be concerned with—"

"Don't tell me I don't need to be concerned with it! You told me the Hovel is my home. If I'm going to live with the three of you permanently, then I want to be treated as part of the family. I want to know what's going on."

"Aya, please don't ask about it."

I stubbornly crossed my arms over my chest.

"You're right." He groaned, raking a hand through his hair. "You're our sister and you should know."

Sister? My heart ripped between beats.

"But I can't have you thinking ill of me. Not yet. It's critical that you and I are civil with each other, because you need the defensive skills I can teach you. If you keep asking about me and Flint, I will tell you—unfortunately, I'm finding it incredibly difficult to say no to you—and you'll hate me for the answer I'll give. I have every intention of betraying him, and I don't want you knowing the irrationality I promised. Not until you're fully trained in combat." His shoulders tensed, and he ground his teeth as if pain was settling deep within his body. "After that, you can hate me. I'd prefer it. That's the way it's supposed to be."

The growing feelings I had for Darric shriveled into a pit in my stomach. I held myself together as something fatal wrapped around my chest like a snake constricting its prey.

Ayleth, you are capable of such idiocy. Absurd to think that any feelings you had towards him would be reciprocated.

Darric had admitted an attraction to me; *No better than every man at the Rose Court.* He thought I was beautiful; *So did Prince Marcus.* It made no difference what Darric thought. He was being true to our contract until the end, nothing more. Then life at the Hovel would continue as normal, with the addition of their *sister*.

I forced the sting of my thoughts into the background, ignoring the crushing pressure in my chest. "Let's get this over with," I grumbled, walking past him and into the forest.

Darric laid his cloak over the tree where he kept his training items. The rays of light coming through the canopy broke into yellow and orange flickers that sparkled against his svelte frame.

The magnitude of his violent capability and the callous person he had become due to his history slammed into me. How could I have thought he would care for me as anything more than a friend? Or *sister*. The platonic word made bile rise into my throat.

Viewing my dejected expression, Darric rubbed his hands over his face. I noticed he was wearing two leather belts, both hanging loosely around his hips. The sword that had so long hung above his bed now lay beside the brilliant black hilt of his own blade.

My lips parted when he unlatched the extra belt and flipped the extraordinary sword into his palms. The darkness of the Hovel had not done the weapon justice. The shimmering black mother-of-pearl hilt bounced light into the trees, and every detail of the carved obsidian vines on the grip shone in vivid clarity. In the morning sun, the black diamond pommel morphed into otherworldly rainbow hues.

The scabbard had also changed. Its tawny brown leather, smooth and flawless, now displayed an intricate swirled pattern down its length—like some form of ethereal writing, but not in a language I had ever seen written.

In all my life, I had never beheld a more beautiful weapon.

"Ready for an upgrade?" Darric asked.

I went entirely inarticulate. I'd known he would eventually introduce me to swords. I'd known someday I would have a blade in my hand instead of an ironwood waster. Yet I hadn't considered where he might obtain a suitable sword for me.

"This was my sword. I learned everything I know with it." He unsheathed the blade and spun the grip in his hand. The metal glistened and danced in the light. "Despite its abhorrent history, it has served me well. It's seen more bloodshed than I care to remember, but considering where it came from, I can't imagine you wielding anything less." He revealed an impression inlaid on the blade just below the hilt: the crest of Medial Alexandria. "You already wear a dagger from a specific grouping of weapons called the *Alpha's stock*. Now you'll wield the sword issued to a Sight of the Onyx Guard."

He slapped the sword back into the scabbard and untied the string of my cloak with one pull, letting it fall to the ground. Placing a hand on my waist, he eased me towards him to slide the belt around my hips. The heavy sword pressed against my thigh.

"This sword has taken me many places, and I've become who I am as a result." His fingers lingered over the belt buckle, lightly tickling my belly. "It's yours now. It suits you."

I ran my fingers over the diamond pommel. "It's beautiful."

"Ironic that something that resplendent has produced so much carnage." He lifted my hand above my head, rotating me into a spin as he eyed every inch of my armed body.

I stepped away. This was too much. The sword was too beautiful and its history too graphic. I couldn't allow him to part with it. "I can't accept this."

"You'll have to if you intend to continue learning to fight," he insisted. "You are going to need a sword capable of standing against mine. One that won't fracture under the force I create. " He tucked a curl behind my ear. "Besides, you'll be doing me a favor by taking it. I don't need two swords that haunt me."

Relenting, I nodded.

"Aya." He put his hand on the back of my head and refused to continue until he had captured my eyes. "More than any weapon you've trained with thus far—the wasters, the throwing blades— what we are about to start today, training in this manner, can kill you. You must apply everything you have learned. You have the advantage. You are a Fae. Use it." He put his other hand on my cheek, forcing my utmost attention. "And there is one critical rule you must abide by on pain of death: under no circumstance do you ever grip the hilt of my sword. Do you understand me? Under. Absolutely. No. Circumstance."

I let out a fidgety breath. "Okay, I won't."

"Are you ready?"

"Yes."

Darric backed away, worry etched across his face. His chest shook with each slow exhale. He pulled his blade free of the scabbard and waited.

I fumbled with the grip of my new weapon, unsure of the exact placement of my fingers.

A light breeze whistled through the wisteria and feathered wisps of blond hair across Darric's forehead. The soft trickle of the waterfall emptying into the forest pond echoed off the rocks. I was aware of these details, yet the world fell silent, leaving only the silvery metallic song of my blade raking against the scabbard to linger in my ears.

The moment I pulled the sword free, my hearing came back with a vengeance. Sounds were amplified. My muscles warmed and pulsed. The feeling was extraordinary. Nothing had ever felt so natural, as though I'd been crafted specifically to wield a sword.

Darric moved too fast for my eyes, but I could hear everything. The sing of metal cutting the air sounded unlike anything in existence. Unmistakable. A light whistling that held a winsome delicacy in the same way blood can be beautiful.

It felt as if it took me forever to respond. Time slowed until I could physically see the flow of it resonate through the battle. I lifted my sword above my head and blocked the fall of his blade. His sword landed hard onto mine. The forceful clash sounded like glasses breaking and vibrated up my arm, sending tremors through my shoulders and down the full length of my spine. I didn't realize I screamed until the shriek echoed off the cliffs. I raked my blade against his, using his own crushing strength against him, and spun out of his blow.

"That was good," he breathed steadily.

I degraded his compliment by wrinkling my nose. He was the enemy. Someone wielding a weapon intent on destroying me. The stinging rip on my heart fueled a surge of strength through all my new muscle.

I unleashed an attack, and he met my sword. Each new block and counterblow of lustrous alloy materialized faster than I had time to process. He laid me to shame. Suddenly, I was forced into one defensive move after another. His nimble strides quickened. The blows of his sword became heavier. My vision flashed with sparks and swings of blurred metal.

I lost my rhythm, and his blade came within a hairsbreadth of my head. He snatched my arm and tripped me. I plunged into his chest, finding the sharp edge of his sword at my throat.

"You're going to have to do better than that," he growled in a heavy pant against my neck, sending a shiver down my spine. "You're dead."

I shut my eyes, attempting to block out his entrancing voice that brought ice to the warmest summer day.

"Stay controlled while making defensive moves," he said as I shook free, careful not to rake my throat on his sword. "Fluid, relaxed swings make the sword heavier and inflict the maximum amount of damage. When you feel as though you are on the losing end, keep up your defenses and patiently wait for an opening. The moment you tense, your enemy gains leverage. Mastering damaging attacks while blocking defensively is key, and doing both at once is what separates the living from the dead."

I rotated the grip to try my first flourish with an actual sword, and my feet went out from under me when Darric's shin slammed into the backs of my knees. He caught me before I hit the grass and raised an eyebrow. "Aware and alert makes for accuracy," he reiterated.

"Ugh, I hate it when you do that." I dropped my sword to push against his chest.

"Then stop allowing me to do it." He steadied me as I regained my footing.

Truly fighting against Darric was exhausting. Avoiding his constant barrage brought a new level of torment to my aching muscles. Unlike with the wasters, the danger felt real. The rush of wind whipped past me with each of Darric's blisteringly fast swings, as if I'd be cut cleanly in half if I didn't instantaneously get out of the way. I learned to move at speeds I didn't know I could achieve. My ankles felt broken from the footwork. The repeated rolling of my shoulders, elbows, and wrists caused my joints to feel loose and cry for relief.

"You're getting faster," he complimented, giving me a moment to rest. I watched his boots pace in front of me while I panted on all fours into the grass blades. He had knocked my sword from my grip, and it lay several feet from me, shining in the noon sunlight. "I'll increase my rate of attack tomorrow. In a week, we'll start dual wielding."

I huffed out a groan and pushed back onto my heels. The thought of fighting him while he had two swords sent my head into a spin. "I can't. There is no chance I can survive if you're dual wielding."

"Stop doubting yourself. You'll be amazing."

"I'll never beat you." I stabilized my breathing, cupped my hand to fill it with water, and drank greedily from my palm.

He furrowed his brows as if it was the oddest thing he had ever seen me do. "I'll always be the only man who can knock your knees out from under you." He retrieved my sword and stabbed it into the ground in front of me. "This is a permanent part of you now. It never leaves your side."

I climbed to my feet and tucked my sword back into its scabbard.

"We're done. Bromly and Flint need my help this afternoon."

"Fine." I dusted petals off my dress. "Just try not to kill each other."

Bromly sat against the stone arch of the cavern weaving new rope, silently counting the knots he created. He was soaking wet, as if he had taken a swim in the lake.

"Where's Flint?" Darric inquired.

"Avoiding work," Bromly answered between mouthed numbers.

Darric collected a pile of the new rope resting next to his brother and slung it over his shoulder. He leaned close to my ear. "Where we are going is technically outside the valley." I was beginning to believe he purposefully brushed his lips against my skin when he whispered to me. "You have the skills. You'll be able to defend yourself while we're gone should anything happen."

I was being left behind? Alone?

"You're safer inside the cavern than outside the valley," he said. "You think you aren't skilled because you've only fought me. I wouldn't leave you if I wasn't confident you could gut someone. We'll be back before nightfall."

I leaned on the rock arch and watched the two disappear into the tree line. Apparently, it didn't matter if I wanted to go; the decision was made without my input. The cat rubbed my leg, shifting the weight of my new sword. She playfully flipped onto her back and batted the tip of the scabbard.

The breeze moved the wildflowers, and Flint's distinctive orange hair appeared by the river. He scooped several handfuls of water to his mouth, and like Bromly, he was soaking wet. After wiping his lips with his wrist, he plucked a stone from the bank and threw it across the river.

The cat gave a stern meow, protesting my decision to leave as I stepped out of the cavern.

"I'm not going far, and it's only the nefarious bunny rabbit."

She held to her argument by sitting on my feet. I giggled, stepping over her.

Flint spun around when I reached him, and a wide smile spread across his cheeks. "Hello, beautiful." He searched behind me to find only the cat. "Where's your guardian?"

"Guard—Darric?" I laughed at the notion. "He's where you are supposed to be: repairing the Burge traveling vessel."

Flint shook water off his hands. "I'll go back eventually."

"They could probably use your help now," I prodded.

He shrugged, leering at me, and his smile suddenly faded, replaced by an astonished gape that contorted into a grimace of hatred. "Is that . . . ?" He balled his hands into fists. "Is that Darric's Medial sword?"

I glanced to my side. Light shot into my eyes from sunshine catching the hilt, and I covered the pommel to stop the reflection. "Yes. It's actually not . . . um . . ." I bit my tongue, seeing the red veins bulge in the whites of his eyes. "This sword isn't his anymore."

"He gave it to you?" Flint shrieked.

"He's trying to have me fully trained before we leave for Burge."

Flabbergasted, he dug his nails into his cheeks. "Don't ya know where he got that thin'? What he's done with it?"

I tapped my foot on the grass. "I know its history. And Darric's. It doesn't bother me."

He fumed silently, throwing another stone from the bank.

"I've never apologized to you about all of this," I said. "I know you desperately wanted Darric to teach you. I'm sorry he's been instructing me and excluding you. I think about it. A lot."

"Tryin' to make yourself feel better?" He crouched, bobbing on his heels. "I can't believe he taught ya. It's so unlike him."

"Well, he doesn't make learning easy." Growing uncomfortable, I crossed my arms over my chest. "The past weeks have been challenging."

"I wouldn't know," he snapped.

I nodded, accepting my defeat, and turned to retreat to the cavern.

"Ya spend all your time with him. He's consumin' ya. Ya can see that, can't ya?" Flint stood directly behind me. His height never failed to come as a surprise.

I gazed up at him as a drip of water fell off the tip of his nose. "It's complicated."

His wet hands grasped my shoulders. "Aya, I've done everythin' I know, an' ya just aren't gettin' it. Do ya want more than flowers? I don't know what else to—" He paused, and the redness in his eyes lessened. "Please, jus' give me a chance."

"For what?" I asked innocently.

Distressed, he rocked on his heels and lowered his head. His wet lips urgently came towards mine.

My hands flew to his chest, and I pushed him back, arching my head to the side to escape his mouth. My resistance didn't deter him. He placed a huge spiderlike hand on the back of my neck, attempting to force me to his lips.

"Flint! Stop!" I cried and drew my sword from the scabbard. The blade cut the space between us, and I leaped backwards to avoid slicing him in two.

The metal trembled in my grip. The tip of my sword hovered a fraction away from his larynx.

Flint's arms hung suspended in the air, his fingers curled as if they still gripped me. Shock and disbelief wreaked havoc over his face. "You're fuckin' Darric, aren't ya?"

I regretted ever having sympathy for him. In fact, I regretted every interaction with him since the day we met.

I slammed my sword back into the scabbard to prevent myself from committing my first murder. "Are you delusional?"

"No one spends that much time alone with anyone in the woods until all hours of the night an' not end up givin' 'em a green gown."

His words cut into my heart's open wound, taunting the senseless, unreciprocated desire I had for my instructor. *You should have listened to the cat.* "Darric was right. You are a cynic."

"That betrayin' bastard! He said that about me?" Flint snarled. "Don't ya get it? Darric don't do anythin' for anyone without gettin' somethin' in return. So, what is it? What are ya givin' to him if it's not your little honeypot?"

"How can you think this way about him? He cares. He's protected you. Provided for you."

"Darric's not my blood. He holds me back," he gritted through his teeth. "I would be jus' as great a fighter. Probably better, an' he knows it."

A tear rolled down my cheek. "I'm going back to the Hovel."

"Why? 'Cause Darric tells ya to keep your ass there?"

"Please, go help your brothers."

He snatched my arm. "Ya aren't goin' anywhere!"

Flooded with anger, I balled my fist and slammed it into his jaw. He stumbled backwards, palming his mouth.

"Don't ever touch me like that!" I roared, storming into his personal space. He fell onto the grass. "If you ever try to kiss me again without my consent, my sword won't stop shy of your throat!"

"Aya!" The aggressive jolt of Darric's voice relaxed my chest. I never thought hearing the stentorian version would bring serenity. My hands fell out of their fists when his soothing touch caressed my lower back.

Bromly helped a wavering and dazed Flint to his feet.

"That damn bitch has a right hook like'a cannon," Flint mused, stunned.

Flint's insolence riled me once more. Darric banded his arms around my waist to stop me from continuing my assault. Like his brothers, he was dripping wet, and the water quickly soaked into my clothes. I tugged at his bracers, trying to break free, but he held me like a vise.

"Calm down," Darric said, so softly only I could hear him.

"Your brother is a pervert!" I snarled.

"You're surprised?" he whispered and lessened his grip.

I pushed out of his arms and trudged back to the Hovel with the cat at my heels.

Chapter 26

It was a beautiful punch." Darric laughed at the memory. "Regardless, as much as we've worked on control, you should have restrained yourself more efficiently. Though I wish I'd been there to see you pull a Medial sword on Flint's throat."

"He deserved it."

A week had passed before I'd been willing to discuss what happened with Flint.

We strolled to the wisteria forest as the sun fell behind the mountains. The exertion of my lessons had become so exhausting I appreciated tonight's languid pace.

"I'm not attempting to justify what he did," Darric said, "but I am trying to understand how the act of someone leaning in for a kiss would impel you to assault them."

I gave him a sideways glare. "Do you want to kiss Flint?"

He raised an eyebrow. "Not particularly."

"He was trying to prevent me from resisting, and my reaction will be the same if he ever forces unwanted affection on me again."

His eyes grayed with the fading of his smile. "Is that so?" A growl rose from his chest. "Now I'm thankful you punched him before I could. I wouldn't have let him remain conscious."

"Please don't steal his bow again," I teased, giggling at the protective reaction. "The two of you don't need more reasons to be combative with each other. Promise me you won't wreak any sort of vengeance. I handled it, and that's what you trained me for, right?"

He ground his teeth. Despite it fueling another wave of animosity between the brothers, I loved seeing my instructor so perturbed that someone had attempted to kiss me.

Tonight the lessons in the dark began. The aphotic sessions were the final instructions in basics. Darric explained that further development of my skills could only be acquired through actual combat experience. To keep my wits sharp, he promised to attack me on a regular basis. I was less enthusiastic about that prospect.

With my heart aching, my training nearing completion, and the journey south in two weeks, I began to wonder what would happen once we all returned to the Hovel. Learning to wield a sword had become part of my life. I couldn't imagine living without it. I was a heinous cook; the time the three had spent outside the valley repairing the Burge vessel had proven it. And I refused to hunt.

After our visit to Burge, Darric would start traveling again and regularly leave me at the Hovel with his brothers. I would join in their concern every time we watched him fade into the distance, uncertain if we would see him again. I would miss him terribly.

I shoved the horrid thought out of my mind. I did not want to think of a life at the Hovel that didn't include him.

The wisteria forest appeared entirely different at night. Without the sunlight piercing the canopy, the colorless blooms became a black mass moving like ominous clouds with the wind. The falling petals reminded me of fluttering beetles rather than beautiful flowers. Even the lovely twisted trees bent into eerie, shadowed abnormalities. I memorized the scenery, growing apprehensive. In a matter of moments, I would be fighting a dual-wielding Darric Ursygh.

Dual wielding. What an incredible discovery. I was as ambidextrous as Darric. With Luken's dagger secured in my left hand, I became lethal. The skill came naturally, as though I had been doing it the entire six weeks. Knowing I held one of my instructor's weaknesses in my off hand gave me an unbridled confidence that he warned would lead to trouble.

Darric was truly deadly once his sword split in two. Over the last months, I had begun to see him differently, but the first time I fought him with both his blades violently swinging around me, the memory of the man who had killed four intruders outside the Hovel barreled back into existence. My handsome stranger melted away, and the seasoned assassin, formally a member of the Onyx Guard, besieged me. I surrendered to him in utter terror. Cowering flat on the ground, I'd questioned every decision that brought me here.

"Aya, you can be afraid. There is nothing wrong with it. Let your fear inspire fight, not defeat. Use it to find your own form of bravery," he had soothed as I trembled.

Now the ominous blackness took over every surface inside the forest. Relying on senses other than sight would be critical.

Darric wore his dark cloak, making it impossible to see his face or even the figure of a man. He began our session by traversing around me as a furiously fast black penumbra. Knowing it was him calmed the terror that knocked at my skull, but to anyone else, the shadowed circling act he accomplished would be horrifying.

Growing up, I'd heard tales of the Onyx Guard wearing black uniforms and black cloaks crafted from a material so dark it absorbed almost all light, reducing the structures of their bodies to mere silhouettes. They rode black horses and traveled through the world during the deepest hours of night. Darric had lost none of the skills associated with Medial Alexandria's highly trained regiment.

At one point, he disappeared entirely. My hand trembled around the hilt of my sword as I listened for any sign of him. Detecting the only unnatural sound tainting the night—metal cutting the air—I spun to find the flash of his sword as he dropped from a tree branch. I blocked him and jumped backwards, making a defensive swing. He avoided it, gripped his hilt, and pulled. The tenebrous forest illuminated from the shimmering white glow that traveled up the center of his blade as the metal split. I was momentarily blinded until the light vanished and darkness recaptured the woods.

I shook my head, trying to find anything through the black. I caught the slightest hint of movement and, with no time left to spare, lifted my blades, smashing against his swords. Disoriented, I blinked furiously, attempting to focus through the blotches clogging my sight and concentrate on listening.

The whistling slice of metal came from the left. I swung but found nothing.

Darric snatched my wrist and twisted my arm, pinning it to my back. The force knocked my sword from my grasp, and his blade met my throat.

"Damn it!" I struggled.

He tightened his iron grip, and my knees quivered. "Trying to use your eyes always gets the better of you." The cold edge of his sword pressed harder against my skin. A low chuckle rumbled in his throat as he slid tresses of my hair off my shoulder, and I felt his wicked grin drag along my neck. "Blinding you was no accident. You should have shut your eyes to prevent it."

"You enjoy this too much." I tilted my head back to take the pressure of his blade off my throat, but he followed the movement, touching the sword back to my skin.

"You make it exceedingly entertaining. I have quite the effect on you." He let out a long, heavy breath that tumbled down the back of my dress. "I aim to use it to my advantage since you've decided to wield a dagger in your off hand. I'm going to make you pay for that decision."

I twisted my arm back in the right direction and ducked under his sword. If he intended to gloat when he killed me, I could at least not fall to pieces every time he touched me. Ignoring his magnetism was challenging, even when I sincerely disliked him.

He abruptly dropped his swords and caught my waist, spinning me into his chest. His hand traveled up my spine, pressing us together, and he smiled tenderly as I molded to the contours of his body. "I love it when I can feel your heart drilling a hole through you," he teased.

I reached a hand around the back of his neck and tugged the hood off his head. "You wanted me to hate you, and yet you make it impossible."

He pried Luken's dagger from my hand and tossed it out of reach, then wove his fingers into my hair. "I've recently learned I have to disarm you to do this." His nose touched mine, and my heart fluttered from the heat of his mouth fanning over my lips.

Before he could act, a noise that shouldn't have been in the forest captured our attention. Darric's perfect smile vanished as his eyes flashed to the wisteria trees, and he carefully moved me behind him.

I jerked my head to see the source of terror that had ruined the moment I craved and gasped at the mass of dark fur circling us, an obvious limp to its front paw. The bear's eyes flashed between cautious brown and deadly crimson, and when he snarled, the immense canines that had threatened to take my life weeks ago shone wet and black.

I burrowed into Darric's side so I wouldn't collapse in shock.

The bear's huffing breaths scattered black petals across the grass. Blocking our exit, he met my eyes, and the communication stabbed into my brain. I grimaced and dug my nails into my scalp, trying to bury the agony.

"*If you would be so kind, Divine Fae, tell your mate to sheathe his weapon.*" The menacingly arcane voice permeated my bones.

Darric held his sword at the ready, the two halves mysteriously re-fused and back in his hand.

"Darric," I whispered frantically, "put away your sword."

Refusing, he gripped tighter on the hilt.

"You have to trust me," I pleaded, rubbing his arm to reassure him. After a moment, his shoulders vibrated in defeat, and he slid his sword back into the scabbard, quickly scanning the area to locate the placement of my fallen weapons.

"*He's angry with you for that request.*" My head throbbed with each syllable the bear uttered. "*Curious. He is savagely protective of you and sincerely believes you are mistaken in your trust.*"

"Am I mistaken?" The last time I met this majestic beast, I'd wanted nothing more than Darric at my side. Now I wanted him as far away as possible. If anything happened to him because of this creature, I would never forgive myself.

Confused, Darric's head spun towards me.

The short-faced bear's ears twitched as he inquisitively examined my instructor. "*His brain has always intrigued me. Full of human emotion I have no interest in understanding. A twisted mess of sadistic and masochistic traits lying under superb Fae qualities, which he uses despite the pernicious consequences.*"

I shuddered. Darric pressed his arm to my back to shelter my small frame against his chest. An increased presence of protection flooded the connection I shared with the bear as he read Darric's thoughts and transferred them to me. My insolent instructor would die for me. Live for me. Protect me until the very last shattered beat of his turbulent heart. From the first instant he had laid eyes on me cowering in a bandit cave, it had never been any other way.

I furrowed my brows, wholly bewildered, and stared into the side of Darric's distressed face. I searched the swirls of his complicated mind, desperate to pry deeper, but hit a moral wall. It was wrong to invade his heart without his knowledge or permission. Despite him telling me of his dedication to keeping me safe, feeling the powerful impulses of emotion flowing through him that evoked such a promise was more than I could handle.

"If I may ask you . . ." I concentrated to block Darric's thoughts and focus on the bear alone. "Please stop transferring him to me. It's wrong."

"Aya, what's going on?" Darric clenched his fists.

"*As you wish, Divine Fae.*" The bear grumbled, and the overwhelming flood ebbed.

Relieved, I inhaled to capacity to clear my head. "I swear I'll explain, Darric."

"*You have healed well.*" The bear eyed my hand digging into my protector's shirt. The gash had long since transformed into a pink scar across my palm.

"As have you." I bowed my head respectfully. "I gave you my word that I would try, not that I would succeed."

"*I hold no ill will towards you. I did not seek you out to bring harm to you, nor your mate. I have heard the songs of the birds and the tick of the beetles. They speak of your growing power. It seems the sword-wielding hunter has proven to be an asset to your abilities. I encourage you to continue to evolve. As it happens, the last of my kin this assailant eliminated opened the opportunity for me to obtain a female. I have your diligence in tending to my injury to thank for this matter.*"

The terror riddling my body parted enough to allow a cautioned smile to cross my lips. "I am dedicated to completing my training."

Satisfied, the bear gave a nod. "*There is a complication you should be made aware of, as it may interfere with your progress. Since you have prevented me from allowing you to perceive his mind, I will bestow it upon you.*" The bear moved towards us. Darric took a step back, pulling me with him.

"It's okay," I soothed, tightening my arms around him. "He's not going to hurt us."

"You can't possibly know that," Darric said.

"*Ayleth, the same consuming plague that exists within you, the sickness that muddles your thoughts and fogs your brain, also resides in him. He thinks of you often and with equal mania. There is a mutual obsession present. The term for such human stupidity is foreign to me.*"

My heart did a backflip. I closed my eyes and spoke the next words inside my head. "*That's why you keep calling him my mate, isn't it?*"

"*Indeed, Divine Fae. For that is precisely what he is.*"

My smiled widened, and heat rushed into my cheeks.

The bear shook his head in disapproval. "*Take caution. You do not comprehend how enigmatic you are. It would be a shame for you to become dormant after falling from such affectivity. As it is, I shall join Darric Ursygh in your protection. As long as I am alive and you are a resident of this valley, you will not have my kind to fear.*"

I slammed an astonished hand over my mouth. Darric responded by jerking me back into his chest and laying a firm grip on the hilt of his sword.

"Don't!" I reiterated, clutching his wrist. "I *am* talking to him. This is the bear I hit with the arrow."

"*That's* how you survived the night you went to him?" he verified, aghast.

"Yes," I admitted. "There's a lot I need to tell you."

"*Do not inform him of your Divinity,*" the bear interrupted.

"Why?" I snapped.

"*Because you cannot exist in his world as a Divine, Princess. The two parts of who you are cannot be combined. They are fire and water. Flying and falling. Living and dead. Be mindful, as the*

Divine blood will not succumb easily. You will have to make a choice, Ayleth, for Darric has already made his."

My lips parted, ready to bombard the bear with one thousand questions, but he turned towards the exit.

"*You may be as you were before my intrusion.*"

Darric and I held each other like statues, watching the immense beast saunter through the crag. Despite his limp, he vanished nimbly into the darkness.

The instant he faded from sight, Darric jerked out of my embrace. "You can talk to animals?" he fumed.

I stumbled backwards, tripped over my sword, and landed on the ground. "I know I owe you an explanation."

"Contract violations, Aya! No ability held back!" He paced, rubbing his hands over his scorned face.

"I never intended to hide it." My bottom lip quivered. "A part of me was afraid you would stop my lessons if you knew too much too soon."

He ceased his pacing, and the dark made it difficult to read his expression. "You truly believe that? Knowing how infatuated I am with you?" He bitterly shook his head, untying his cloak to slip the wool around my shoulders. I only noticed my shivering when the heat of two cloaks warmed my skin.

"Infatuated?" I repeated, stunned.

"You don't swear to give your life for someone you deem mediocre," he mused thickly.

I tightened myself into a ball. "I'm sorry I hid it."

He eased onto the ground beside me. "So you aren't just talking to your cat for entertainment?"

"The cat . . . Sage, whatever she is, is annoying." *Where is she?* I scanned the trees and located an eerie pair of amber eyes peering through the black foliage. "I don't know why I bother speaking to her. She doesn't talk back at all."

He followed my gaze to the same exotic eyes that never truly left my side.

"Untamed communication, the ability to talk to animals, scares me more than any Fae power," I expressed. "To hear them, I have to expose myself completely. Open my brain to anything they are willing to transfer to me. Their thoughts aren't human, and it's not exclusively verbal information. The transmissions include their emotions, sometimes pain, even their readings of other animals. Most of the time it's so difficult to decipher a clear path through everything they expel that it gives me a headache."

The guilt of my contract violation led me to hold nothing back. I told him everything. Leaving out the details of Alamantia, I confessed I stole a horse, only to lose the beast when I scared him senseless upon discovering I could understand him.

Darric listened silently to my story of the bear hunt gone awry—how I'd tried to open my heart to the female he had killed, but I couldn't deter the attack. He ran a hand through his hair and let out a weighted breath. "Can you hear them all the time?"

"No, only when I'm close. Most animals won't talk to me. They keep their distance and aren't capable of complex communication, but I can still sense their feelings. Speaking with animals who possess an intelligent mind comes with a price. It leaves me sore. There is something forbidden about it, like talking to them bends the laws of nature, so I suffer internally for it. There is only one consistency I have found—they all know I'm a Fae. The bear chose to spare my life because of it."

"I never would have left you alone at the Hovel had I known he was a threat. Despite all my caution, your life was still in danger."

I rubbed my thumb into the gruesome scar on my palm. The skin was puckered and pink, complete with six raised dots where Darric had sewn the flesh back together. "It was something to remember him by. He wanted me to understand my actions. That I had been reckless, and a Fae should have known better. I pulled the arrow from his leg and dressed the wound, then he gave me this."

Darric eyed the scar before shrouding my hand with his.

"A short-faced bear's heart is violent," I said, "but he meant it with a noble intention. He is indifferent to most animals in the valley and seems pleased when you dispose of a rival male, but it killed him to see a female die."

Darric groaned, tossing my hand into my lap. "I knew you'd gone after him, but hearing you admit it feels sickening."

I tucked my legs into my chest and wrapped my arms around my knees. "There's something else you should know."

His shoulders stiffened.

"Untamed communication is one of your mimic Fae abilities, though it's profoundly one sided. The animals can hear you. You let them into your head all the time. Atlas told me he tried to talk to you in the past, but you never answered. He peers inside your head and has a deep working knowledge of your heart. I didn't want to believe what he told me about you . . . until tonight, when the bear . . ." My voice trailed away.

He took a long moment to respond. I waited patiently as he absorbed the information. "Atlas is the bear?"

"Oh, no. Atlas is a horse. A white one. He told me he was a friend of yours—"

"You've talked to that white stallion?" Darric interrupted, agitated, and shifted onto his knees.

I nodded apprehensively.

He covered his face, muffling a worried string of profanity.

I clasped his wrist, trying to uncover him. "He refused to share an open connection with me. He said your secrets were not his to tell."

Darric shrugged me away and got to his feet. "But you did share this open connection with the bear."

"Yes," I confessed.

"I'm not an idiot, Aya. I can follow a conversation. Even a one-sided one. 'Stop transferring him to me. It's wrong.' What did that mean? What was he telling you about me?" he asked, guarded.

I gulped. "I don't want to tell you."

"Don't make me use the ambiguity," he demanded.

I narrowed my eyes. "If you're going to threaten me with that stupid part of our contract, then why shouldn't I make you use it?"

"Not for this," he pleaded.

I tightened my hands into tiny fists. "Darric, you were clinging to me like a vise. I could barely discern anything through your overwhelming cloud of protection. It's blinding. As controlled as you are on the outside, every emotion you project has enough strength to move mountains. An open connection means any feelings you expelled were directly transferred to him, so he flooded me with your mind. I asked him to stop out of respect. As much as I wanted it, I couldn't dig through your brain."

"Protection? That's it?" He dropped to his knees and gripped my leg, desperate for more information. "Nothing else?"

"For the rest, I will make you use the ambiguity," I said, reaching my limit.

Irate, he shoved off me.

I grappled with the breaking of my heart. "It doesn't matter. He's a bear. He doesn't understand human emotion."

Darric's entire face hardened. "If it was an open connection and you felt everything flowing through me, why would you not trust it? You've been with me every day for weeks. How could you doubt anything you felt from me?"

My stomach lurched as I realized Darric was painfully aware of everything he had been thinking in the bear's presence. "Because if it's true, then I need to hear it from you." I dropped his cloak and tightened my own. I was leaving this forest whether he decided to continue instructing me or not.

With the wisteria forest behind me, the world seemed lighter, and the landscape welcomed the sun. Darric followed. I knew the distinct sound of his footsteps.

Flint sat alone by the cavern fire. He smiled weakly and plucked a massive collection of morning glory off the log, needing both hands to keep the large bundle together. He cast a dismissing glare at his brother.

Darric nodded at him. "I'll leave you two alone," he said and went into the Hovel.

Flint wasted no time explaining himself. "These flowers only bloom in the mornin'. I wanted to make sure ya got some an'—"

Ignoring his words, I crossed the seating area and threw my arms around his neck. "I never should have hit you. I'd blame it on being around Darric all the time, but really, I did lose my temper. I'm embarrassed by the way I acted. Forgive me."

He dropped the flowers and tugged me into his chest. He felt lanky in my arms—bones covered by sparse muscle and clothes smelling of animal hides and Bromly's cooking.

I pushed away, shyly tucking loose curls behind my ears. "I'm sorry, that was inappropriate. I had a rough night."

"It wasn't inappropriate," he said, excited. "It was wonderful."

"My head isn't in the right place."

"Well, it should be in the wrong place more often." He smiled wide, squeezing my shoulders. "I wanted to say I was sorry too. I shouldn't've accused ya of bein' involved with Darric."

I shook my head. "No, you're right. I know how it looks." I made a fist and lightly pounded it against his chest.

He winced from the playful impact. "You're stronger than ya seem."

I returned a smile. His emerald eyes practically glowed. "Darric has taught me well. Wait until you see me fight. The next time we're attacked by bandits, I plan to show all of you how an assassination is supposed to look."

He laughed nervously, taking me more seriously than I expected. "Aside from the flowers, I wanted to ask ya somethin' 'bout your newly found skills. I was wonderin' if you'll teach me to fight? Since Darric won't."

I took my hands from his chest and folded my arms over my belly. "I can't."

His face fell. "Why not?"

"It's nothing personal. I don't know how to teach. I don't even know how *I* learned. I wouldn't know where to begin."

Disappointed, he sank onto the log.

"In two months, I've somehow managed to learn skills that took Darric a lifetime to master. I'm not exactly normal, and I know I'd end up getting you seriously hurt. Or killed."

"I thought I might've finally found someone willin' to teach me a sword."

"My own training is hardly complete. I'm in no position to take on a student," I explained.

He shook morning glory blooms from his hairy foot and plucked a blossom from its stem, carelessly tossing it to the side.

I sat down in front of him and gathered several flowers into my hands. "They're beautiful. It must have taken you a while to gather this many."

"I didn't think ya were gonna accept my sorry. I thought I'd hav'ta grovel."

I twirled a morning glory between my fingers, watching the petals spin into a violet blur. "What reason would I have not to accept?" I pushed the bloom towards his pointed nose. He breathed in, and his nostrils sucked in the petals. "Especially when presented with such a lovely gift."

Chapter 27

I t was noon. No shadows. The July heat bore down on me, preventing Ambrosia's dress from remaining comfortable. Maybe I could obtain some fabric in Burge to make myself a summer dress. It would be sewn poorly; I wished I had spent more time perfecting my needlework. Divine and Atheran history, musical studies, and dancing seemed so worthless now.

"Stop daydreaming." Darric lowered the blindfold over my eyes and tied it tightly behind my head. "Count backwards from twenty. When you remove the blindfold, I am no longer your teacher—I am your enemy. Do not draw your sword until you are ready to engage. Use any and all techniques you have learned to become the victor. This is a real battle. There are no rules."

Air brushed my neck as he moved away, and the woods fell silent.

Darric was gone.

I breathed in deeply and gathered my thoughts. He was a dangerous foe and promised a daunting fight, but as we had discovered over the last week, I was a formidable adversary. Something he knew had been inside me all along.

Breathe. Twenty.

The purpose of the exercise: a hidden assailant, coming from an unknown direction. He would be watching. Waiting to ambush. *Be prepared to counterattack.* Expecting impending doom did not make it any less nerve-racking.

Control. Seventeen.

My final week of training had consisted of fighting Darric in sword-to-sword combat. At first, it was arduous to put all my lessons into practice at once. My mind exploded with information, and I died within seconds. I had to watch him in action. Observe his technique. Marvel at the way he moved with a sword.

Concentration and focus. Fifteen.

The more Darric and I engaged, the more I advanced. Each fight I incorporated additional knowledge into my execution. Each time I lived a little longer.

Attention to detail. Twelve.

And every time, he defeated me.

Balance. Ten.

When I finally started to employ all my abilities at once, paying special attention to the ones he lacked, I still could not gain leverage over him. To force me to control my anger, he ridiculed me—viciously taunting that no matter how great a fighter I became, no matter how much I practiced, I would never win against him. As long as we lived, he would forever be the only swordsman alive I would never defeat. I despised him for it.

Physical conditioning. Eight.

We were leaving for Burge in two days. The many furs and baskets of dried meat in the Hovel had disappeared. Wooden boxes of cutlery and intricately carved toy dragons had vanished. The remaining vegetables in the garden were picked, and Bromly's small cauldron went with them.

Speed and agility. Six.

Candles. Tea bags. Blankets. Pillows. Gone. The extra sets of clothes the three hung in their rooms were packed into personal haversacks. Bromly made me one of my own out of the torn bed sheet he found in Darric's room. I thanked him, though I had no possessions with which to fill it.

Defense. Three.

The first week of July had brought both the emptiness of the cavern and a striking doom to my mind. Something about leaving for Burge was so final I struggled to stomach it. For the Hovel brothers, traveling was just another part of life. Something they did every year. A chance for Bromly to visit Hazel. An opportunity to socialize and sell their wares. For me, it was worrisome. Burge was a major trade town, and though the Sloan family did not actively partake in court life, I still risked being recognized. Stupidly, that was a risk I was willing to take to stay with Darric, Bromly, and Flint.

Offense. Two.

Darric had promised I would always have a home at the Hovel. That if I chose it, I could remain as their *sister* wherever time took them, for the rest of my life. They were my family now. My brothers. Yet, I couldn't dismiss the feeling that if I left for Burge, I would never see the Hovel again.

One.

I tore the blindfold off my head and spun, taking in the blossoming trees and the surrounding forest. No sign of Darric. I knew he was here. Watching. Waiting. The serene woods became eerily silent. Beautiful before the squall.

My palms began to sweat. I steadied my breathing, trying to loosen the anxiety of an imminent attack, and listened for anything to reveal his location. Footsteps. The rustle of leaves not moved by the wind.

I was a sitting duck. The anticipation was torture. I turned circles in an attempt to see all my blind spots at once. The knot of nerves in my stomach tightened, and I ran my fingers over the pearly hilt of my sword. *No. Don't draw. Not yet. Those are the rules. Not until you engage—there are no rules.* My core ached when I pulled my hand away from the grip.

I backed into the tree line. The fluttering petals made my eyes dart in erratic directions. If he didn't appear soon, I would have to search the woods. The thick brush made it hazardous to move, and defending myself would become more perilous.

A twig snapped.

A sound so faint it would have gone unnoticed had I not been a Fae.

My heart sped. His breath hit my curls. *Behind you!*

I wrested my sword from its scabbard and swung the blade. The clash of metal vibrated up my arm as I crashed into Darric's brilliant weapon.

The first series of maneuvers he performed shamed my own speed. I took several steps backwards to avoid being hit, caught in a swell of unrelenting terror. Too difficult to believe it wasn't life or death. Too impossible to accept that his razor-sharp sword wouldn't slice me in two if given the opportunity.

I had the strength. I had mastered agility. I was efficient. The style of my ability mimicked my instructor, yet he surpassed me. Always stronger. Always more agile.

I would be vanquished just like every other fight.

There are no rules.

To ever come close to defeating the full strength of Darric Ursygh, I needed to be more cunning, to take advantage of the skills he lacked. Using his dagger weakness wasn't enough to overtake him.

In the last seconds before he had a hold on me, I slid under his blade and ran. I had to get away from him. I had to create distance.

"Aya!" he sternly called as I plunged into the forest. I gained speed, jumping over brush and dipping under low branches.

He chuckled darkly at the new game, and the pounding of his footsteps echoed behind me.

This wouldn't last. He would inevitably catch me. And when he did, I would be finished.

The wind moved through the trees, blowing strands of hair across my face, and rustled the leaves and petals above.

Wind.

I flung my sword arm to the side, creating a violent gust that erupted from my clenched fingers. Crystalline white sparkles slammed into the trunk of a passing tree. The wood exploded from the impact, sending the timber crashing to the ground. Darric narrowly missed the fall and jumped over the trunk to continue his pursuit.

I forced a second gale to the left. Wood splintered and burst as another tree fractured and fell.

"Shit!" Darric's sharp hiss cut through the chaos, and he increased his speed.

Unwilling to surrender, I sent gust after gust to either side of me, spinning the air so the trees fell in haphazard directions to prevent my assailant from discerning where the branches would fall. He skillfully swerved and dodged the pandemonium, but the effort needed to evade my devastation slowed his chase. I laughed in disbelief and shook glittering white dust from my hair. *It's working!*

Credulously believing I controlled the rhythm of our battle, I reduced my pace.

The tree to my left cracked at the base and toppled. Darric scaled the trunk, shifting his weight to control its descent, then jumped to the ground, sliding across the dirt as the tree landed and blocked my path. He taunted me with a smirk and flicked a lock of hair away from his forehead.

I gaped, stunned, and composed myself just as his sword slammed into mine. Avoiding his next swing, I tore Luken's dagger free. He countered by twisting away from the small blade and breaking his sword in two.

I matched his spectacular dual wielding, and we broke through the mess of shredded trees. He backed me into the open valley. The sun was blinding after the shade of the forest.

The rush of water plummeting into the lake gave me a flicker of hope. I allowed him to back me closer to the bank until my shoes hit the mud. I hopped onto the water and ran to the center. Out of his reach, I breathed deeply to alleviate the uneasy feeling compressing my chest.

His smile widened, and he shook his head, as if I was the naivest person he had ever met. He fused his swords and dived into the water.

My stomach jumped into my throat. I searched beneath me. The blue twinkles littering the crest of each churning wave disguised his location. Without warning, his hand snaked around my ankle and jerked me under the surface.

Surprised, I accidentally inhaled and filled my lungs with water. I kicked for the surface, but he held me down by the arm, trying to shake the sword free of my grip. *Control. Concentrate. I need air. My chest is going to explode.* I raised Luken's dagger to stab his throat, but he caught my wrist and fought against the push of my attack. My heart pounded, using up my last bits of stored oxygen. I kicked into his stomach with all the strength I had to spare. The forceful blow made him release me, and I swam for the bank.

With my hands full of weapons and my dress sopping wet, I dragged myself onto the grass. I stumbled and coughed, trying to inhale new air into the spaces brimming with water.

Darric snatched the train of my skirt and jerked me back to the ground. Instinctively, I released my sword to catch my fall, and the blade skidded out of my reach. Still clutching Luken's dagger, I tried in vain to slide out of his grip, but he pitilessly shoved me back into the grass and pinned my last form of defense above my head.

Using my free hand, I crashed a hardened fist into his jaw and cried out from the painful impact. He took advantage of my distraction and swung his knee over my hips, immobilizing me and fastening my body to the ground. My head slammed onto the dirt, and his sword met my throat.

Darric held the blade to my skin for a long moment for emphasis.

I'd lost.

Again.

I stared at his silhouette, darkened by the sun, and watched droplets of water leave his disheveled hair. His arms quivered with adrenaline, and his chest heaved. My emotions appalled me when they used his handsome face to morph my hatred into lust.

He rolled away and lay beside me. "Damn, your skill is getting faultless," he said breathlessly. "The falling trees—" he paused, struggling to maintain his breathing "—that was absolutely brilliant."

"You still won," I huffed, ripping up a handful of grass and crushing the blades in my hand.

"That action alone would have killed anyone chasing you. It would be suicide to attempt to kill you. You're lethal."

I blushed at his praise. "I don't feel lethal. I thought you would reprimand me for running."

"No rules, remember?" He propped himself onto his elbow. "How's your hand?"

"Sore." I opened and closed my throbbing fist several times. "Hitting you isn't like hitting Flint. You're harder."

"I'll take *that* as a compliment." He laughed.

I laughed with him, exhausted. Combat made me ache both mentally and physically. I took deep breaths, feeling as though I couldn't get enough fresh air.

Darric trailed a finger across my stomach and up my chest. His callouses brushed my skin as he moved the leather lacing on the front of my dress off the arch of my breast and watched my chest heave with each breath. My heart almost broke a rib as I studied his wandering gaze.

"I'm leaving tonight." His eyes moved away from my breasts. "I need to sleep, since I won't be getting another opportunity until we arrive in Burge. Once we are on the river, we'll be stuck on a boat together for weeks. It's dangerous if I nod off."

"You would probably hate yourself if you sliced Flint in half." I giggled.

"Flint is the least of my worries. I'm only telling you this because I want you to know where I'll be. I've always feared you would go against my request and wander the forest alone. I won't live with myself if I kill you." He peered intently into my eyes, watching the Fae glimmer come to life within them. "Do you remember the ledge we climbed the night I told you about my family?"

I nodded. "Shame, that is exactly where I was planning to spend my evening," I teased, pushing a lock of blond hair away from his forehead.

He caught my hand and interwove our fingers. "I haven't been looking forward to the trip south this year. If it weren't for Bromly needing to visit Hazel, I would have canceled it altogether."

"Why?"

"Let's just say I've enjoyed the weeks we've spent alone in the forest. Even if I have been trying to kill you for most of it."

Chapter 28

Summer moved over Brisleia with a revivifying nurture. The landscape celebrated the warmth, and the animals brought new young out of hiding. Bees and butterflies tasted the abundant wildflowers, and the snow caps receded to their highest points on the mountains. The beauty and brilliancy of the valley never failed to amaze me.

By early afternoon, I missed Darric significantly. He had been gone a full day. My stomach panged, feeling the premonition of the future: I would spend endless hours watching from the cavern for his figure to appear on the horizon. My heart would ache with memories of the wisteria forest until time faded the days I'd spent as his student. Then I might have the chance to be a simple *sister* for the Hovel brothers.

I waited against the rock arch, trying to calm my nerves. Bromly had taken notice of my distress and softly hummed to himself. A sizzle from the coals broke my watchful attention as he poured a full bucket of water over the smoldering fire. The flames hissed a dying breath, and he shoved his boot into the black mess of smoking mud and soot, scattering the leftover embers.

Today was the day I'd been dreading.

He set the bucket in an organized spot next to the Hovel and joined me by the rock arch. "When Darric gets back, we'll be leaving. He wanted to go at noon, but it's past one. Hopefully, he awakens soon. It's odd. He doesn't normally sleep this long." He took off his tan cap and fanned out the heat, then smoothed his black hair before resettling the small hat on his head. "Are you all packed?"

I nodded meekly. My empty haversack lay on Darric's bed next to his own, which had grown fuller as the bedroom hooks went barren.

Bromly set his hand on my shoulder, and his chubby fingers massaged the muscle. "He's fine," he reassured me.

Flint bounced out of the Hovel and skipped across the smoking remnants of the fire, ripping a large piece of dried bear meat with his teeth. "Fire's out inside. Darric back yet?"

"No." Bromly removed his hand from me. "Might as well get comfortable."

"We could jus' leave him here this year," Flint said through chews.

"I know where he is," I murmured absently.

Bromly gaped, a combination of shock and dismay etched into his doughy brown eyes.

"Whoa." Flint stuck a finger into his ear to dig at an itch. "He's never told either of us where he goes to sleep." He flicked a ball of wax off his finger and bit another chunk off his bear meat.

I shrugged, pressing my back against the rock. "I can find out if he's still asleep."

"That's a dangerous idea," Bromly warned, settling on the seating log.

"It is for the two of you, but not necessarily anymore for me." I repositioned the sword at my side.

Bromly gazed at the weapon belonging to Darric's abhorrent history. "Be careful, Aya. You know how deadly he can be."

"I'll grab my bow an' come with ya. It'll be safer that way." Flint zipped into the Hovel, choking on the last bit of his bear meat.

Annoyed, I stomped my foot in protest.

"Be nice, Aya. He wants to help in the protection of our *sister*." Bromly scratched his beard, snickering at the term I hated.

"Sister." I scoffed, rolling my eyes. The cat meowed at my feet. *No, Flint is not coming with me.*

I dashed away from the cavern at full speed, a long bellow of Bromly's laughter echoing behind me. Staying mindful in case Flint pursued me, I scurried through the valley.

Still a distance from the crag, Darric's blond hair appeared in my periphery. Rested and serene, he leaned on a birch tree facing a rocky overhang above the riverbank. Thin trees encompassed the ledge, and water washed at the mud around their exposed root systems.

Lost in a still meditation, he watched the waterfall descend into the basin. His chest rose and fell with each new exchange of mountain air. The ripples of his lean muscle shifted beneath his white shirt as he breathed. Even from a distance, the scars defacing his arms stood out against his tanned skin. A warm summer breeze scattered strands of hair over his forehead and swayed the branches, sending beams of sunlight flickering across his handsome features.

He was indeed the most attractive man I'd ever seen. Impressive, rough, and grim—nothing like the feeble, well-dressed men at court. Jagged around the edges, yet built with such a pure heart I found it difficult to remember the deadly assassin lurking inside of him. How effectively peace had eluded him in the wake of his haunting past.

We had never been different; we both struggled with a history we wanted to forget. Yet, my royal upbringing would never compare to his anguish.

I had made peace with the oddity of our attraction. I knew somewhere deep in the recesses of my core what I felt for him, but I would never allow those feelings to surface. Especially since he considered himself my adoptive brother.

Darric would know the time of day and that the others waited for him. I rocked on my heels, rethinking the decision to disturb him, but the irresistible draw he had on me tugged at my feet.

I gripped the hilt of my sword and pulled it from the scabbard, the delicate ring of metal on leather nearly inaudible between the songs of valley birds and the rush of the waterfall. Cautiously, I slid the blade under his chin, relishing the moment of catching him off guard.

He eased away from the tree, his own sword drawn and a smirk twitching at the side of his mouth. The sharp point of his blade touched my belly. "You are not as quiet as you think you are," he informed me with a chuckle.

"How do you do that?" I asked, both awed and defeated.

"I pay attention." He flourished his blade. "Though the effort you make to catch me off guard is amusing. Do you really want to know what I'm like with my defenses down that desperately?"

Irritated by his provocative behavior, I summoned all my force to crash my sword into him. He blocked the attack with ease and laughed at my futile attempt to fight him. He countered with a blow so heavy my arm flew backwards, and I grasped my stinging shoulder.

Immediately, he caught my wrist, raised my sword, and stabbed the blade deeply into the branch above my head, leaving me clinging to a weapon buried to the hilt within the wood. I pulled at the grip with both hands, trying to free it, and hung off the ground. Nothing. I gazed upwards, trying to decipher how he had managed to jab my blade into immobility.

When the spell of amazement broke, I tore Luken's dagger from my ankle and swatted at him. Dodging the blade, he recaptured my wrist. I let out a shriek as he twisted my off hand and plunged the dagger into the trunk.

He took a step back, eyeing his craftsmanship, and vivaciously slid his sword back into his scabbard. "There are still a few things I could teach you."

"Ridiculous," I muttered, tugging at Luken's dagger.

He rested his forearms on the branch above us and hovered over my dismay. "I assume the coalition sent you, since it's well past noon."

"No." I pushed displaced hair away from my face. "I volunteered."

He pointed a stern finger at me. "You aren't supposed to be out here."

"And *you* are supposed to be asleep." I stubbornly crossed my arms over my chest and leaned my back on the tree.

"I did sleep." His steel-blue eyes penetrated mine, causing me to lose control over my heart. I shifted uncomfortably against the bark. "I need to talk to you about something, and I have to say it before we leave for Burge."

I swallowed hard, hoping my legs wouldn't turn to jelly.

"Aya." He let go of the branch to put his hands on my hips. "What am I to you?"

My heart hammered at the inside of my ribs. I put my hands on his chest for distance, trying to prevent him from noticing the unhinging of my sanity. He pushed them away and gathered me into his arms, pinning my tiny frame to the trunk. A gratified smile grew on his lips when he felt my erratic heartbeats drumming against his chest.

"Why does your heart pound like that when I come close to you? Do I make you *that* nervous?"

Trapped, I gripped his shoulders to support my wobbling. "Yes."

I needed the Darric who fought me to return. I needed the man who used to hate me. I needed him to send me tumbling away, his sword drawn, ready and willing to slice my throat. Instead, he was pulling to the surface a part of me I desperately needed to forget existed.

"You once said I reminded you of your brother. Is that how you see me? Am I a brother to you?" he asked gravely, as if *yes* was the last sound he wanted to hear.

"No," I admitted.

He pressed his forehead to mine. "A friend? Or simply an instructor?" he continued softly.

"Neither." Throbs of blood morphed my tongue, so I struggled to speak.

He shut his eyes and huffed out a breath. "I wish I didn't make you so nervous when I touch you. I can feel it every time I try— that your heart is going to explode if I don't keep my distance. I've been hoping it's a reaction to training, but it's something else, isn't it?" He dug his fingers into my back, tightening his hold on me.

My body shook from head to toe. "No one has ever touched me the way you do."

"I don't want you to be nervous with me." He slid his cheek down the side of my face. "I'm sorry it has taken me this long to tell you, but for someone who wears their emotions so openly, you've done well hiding any amorous feelings you might have for me." The heat of his sweet breath filled my throat. I arched my back and sharply inhaled as he laid a soft kiss on my neck. "Aya, I've tried to keep away from you. I can't do it anymore. Trying not to love you is tearing me apart, and there isn't much of me that's left whole. You said you needed to hear it from me. I want more than what we currently are. If that's what you want."

The entire valley fell into the background at his words.

I went to pieces in his arms, soft and pliable. He trailed his lips up my neck and kissed my jaw before lifting his head to meet my eyes.

"Please, turn me down," he whispered, going still, waiting for me to make the decision that would change everything.

"No." I ran my hands across his shoulders and fed my fingers into the feathery strands of his hair. "You are never going to be a brother to me. You never were. I don't want you to stay away from me."

His entire body shivered against mine. "Stubborn Fae," he growled, gliding a hand up my spine and twisting his fingers into my curls. He pulled my head back, cradling me.

"Insolent instructor," I whispered as his breath fell over me, and he pressed his lips to mine.

My entire body caught fire. Flames blazed along my weakened legs, through the muscle and into my toes. It burned even the almond tresses tangled in his hand. His lips parted as he kissed me, moving in an electrified dance with mine.

Enraptured. Maniacal. I couldn't absorb enough of him into me.

A groan of bliss and relief rumbled in the back of his throat. I clawed at his scalp, forcing him to press his lips harder. Responding to my desperation, he opened his mouth and slipped his tongue over mine. I lost the ability to stand. Thankfully, I had a tree to lean against.

The urge we had to kill each other dissipated, and with one kiss, I knew everything he had wanted to say to me from the beginning. Light shone on his internal war, *the vexing action.* He had tried to prevent us from ever feeling this way for each other.

All this time I'd been training to fight, I'd been becoming a part of him. An extension of my other half. Everything made sense. Every moment of my existence had purpose. I was meant to touch him. Created to stand by his side no matter who or what we became. Everything I had ever felt towards him, all the anger and frustration, had been a way to cope with the reality we had both recognized the moment we met. An uncontrollable force stronger than gravity.

I couldn't stop it anymore. I couldn't ignore the astounding realization of how deeply and irreversibly I had fallen in love with Darric Ursygh. My hooded stranger. My insolent instructor. And I wanted it anywhere, anytime, here, now, everywhere all at once.

I knew I heard it. The sound echoed in my head at first but quickly materialized in the outside world.

Darric ripped himself away from me.

By the time I opened my eyes, he was leaning against a tree far out of my reach, his shoulders violently trembling. He eased down the trunk and buried his forehead in his hands. "I'm so sorry, Aya. I should have done that somewhere else, at a more appropriate time."

I gripped the bark for support. My strength was gone, and I hated to see him so dismayed at such an unfriendly distance.

The cause of his distress hit my ears—Flint calling my name grew louder. I nearly collapsed from disappointment. My lips burned. The places Darric had touched were dying coals where fire had blazed. I wanted him back in my arms.

"Hey, ya left without me, silly." Flint ran up to us, his orange hair lopsided from the breeze. He rested his hands on his knees to catch his breath. "Good, ya found Darric. Everythin' is ready. All goods moved an' such. We can head to the river anytime now."

Darric slid his hands down his face, leaving his fingers resting over his mouth, and continued kneeling by the base of his tree.

With both of us silent, Flint noticed my weapons jutting from the trunk. "What the hell?" He tugged at Luken's dagger.

Darric jolted upright and pushed his brother out of the way to jerk the blade free. He handed it to me without glancing in my direction, and I weakly sheathed it back against my ankle.

Flint giggled. "So, Aya, have ya figured out how he does *that* yet?" He pointed to the hole left in the bark.

I dropped my chin and shook my head as Darric leaned over me to yank my sword out of the branch. "All right. Let's go," he said bitterly and pushed the hilt into my hands.

———— ·⟨℘⟩· ————

Flint prattled by my side. I didn't hear a single word he said.

Not once did Darric look back at us. I felt strange and alone, worried the feeling I'd had while enraptured in his arms had been fleeting and unrealistic. The slowing, heavy beats of my heart were the only reminder that moments ago, he'd kissed me in a way I hadn't known existed.

I squeezed my eyes shut, attempting to restrain my erratic emotions. No lie I could tell myself would change the brutal fact that I was in love with him.

The Hovel appeared abandoned. With the fires extinguished, the food and pelts packed, and the fur doors removed and stored, everything seemed disconnected.

Darric went into his room to retrieve his haversack. I stood outside the cavern with Bromly and Flint, watching them tie cloaks around their shoulders that I'd never seen them wear.

With the absence of doors, I could see Darric eyeing my empty haversack. He looked up at me and leaned onto the bed frame, curling a finger towards himself.

I slid into his room and folded my arms over my chest, my stomach unrelentingly churning. "I know, don't overthink it," I said flatly.

He set his pack on the bed. "You could have told me my brother was trailing you. This is exactly why I apologized. I should have done that when I could explain. It was hellacious timing. All these weeks alone with you in the woods, and I choose ten minutes before we leave for Burge to capitulate."

I stared at my feet and raked my shoe over the floor.

He hooked a finger under my chin. "Look at me."

I raised only my eyes.

"I regret the time and place, not the action itself."

A long breath rushed out of my lungs, releasing worry from my core.

Darric's hand curled around the back of my neck, pulling me closer to him, as I ran my fingers up his chest and took handfuls of his shirt fabric into my fists.

"I meant everything I said. Am I insane for thinking that if you didn't know about my feelings for you, you might choose to stay in Burge instead of returning to the Hovel? You are trained. You're deadly. You don't need me anymore."

I tightened my grip on his clothes. "I'm always going to need you, Darric."

He smiled briefly, then yanked my hands from the fabric. "We can't do this—any of this—around Bromly and Flint."

I nodded reluctantly instead of asking why. My anxiety was warping my ability to form complete thoughts.

He thumbed the pout in my bottom lip and plucked my cloak off the wall. "We need to go. My brothers are waiting."

A carrot stuck out of Bromly's satchel. His pack weighed significantly more due to the vegetables he carried.

The journey held a mournful tone, yet light shone through the darkness. In the center of my chest, a fire had started—sparked by the man walking in front of me with his gray cloak swaying in the breeze. Each time Darric looked at me, he coyly smiled, and my cheeks flushed. Those hidden glances made leaving the Hovel easier.

I looked back to the cavern only once to remember it. The same way I had on horseback while riding away from Alamantia Palace. However, when I left Alamantia, I knew with certainty it would always be there no matter how far I ran.

The cavern looked far less entrancing from the center of the clearing. Without the warm glow of firelight illuminating the Hovel, it disappeared into the landscape as a foreboding hollow den. I would gravely miss the only place in Athera I would ever willingly call home.

We traveled to the lake at the edge of the valley. At the top of the ledge, the surrounding brush was newly cleared, and a large fallen tree created a bridge across the chasm that disappeared behind the falls.

Bromly mounted the log. Taking great care, he worked his way across the trunk in a sideways shuffle. Eventually he reached a mess of dying leaves still attached to the treetop and vanished behind the waterfall.

"I'll help you across." Flint laid his hand on my back, nudging me forwards.

I grabbed his arm to stop him from pushing me. "I don't need help."

Darric gave an amused chuckle, making his little brother wrinkle his nose in disgust.

I fluttered across the beam on my tiptoes and bounced into a small space where Bromly waited. He smiled, impressed. "I'd like to see you in action someday, Aya. Darric has never had a protégée before."

"I can't begin to explain the hours of balance training he put me through to perfect my equilibrium," I informed him.

"Oh, I can imagine," he said, growing more effervescent by the minute.

"You're excited to be leaving," I observed.

His eyes came to life with merriment. In a short time, he would have the woman he loved in his arms again. His radiating cheer was contagious, and I allowed his chipper mood to filter into me.

Across the falls, Flint straddled the log, scooting his bottom along the bark.

"He fell one year." Bromly laughed. "He won't cross on foot anymore."

When he came within reach, Bromly extended a helpful arm.

"I can do it myself." Flint tried to stand, stumbled, and hit his face on the rock.

Darric dropped from the bridge and landed beside me a second later.

Bromly led the group into a narrow stone passage cutting through the mountain. The dark, claustrophobic path touched our shoulders on both sides. A slick layer of wet moss lined the rock, and backwash from the falls seeped along the floor. Water dripped from the ceiling and down the walls, dampening my dress and filling the passage with the scent of mold and rotting foliage. The deeper we traveled into the mountain, the less the light from the opening helped guide our path.

The tunnel turned, and the bright outline of an uneven hole marked our exit.

"Don't fall, Aya," Bromly advised.

We filtered out of the passage and onto a shallow cliff outside the valley. An unimpressive waterfall trickled into a pool roughly one hundred feet below us, where the river disappeared into the evergreen forest and commenced its journey south.

Firmly attached to the surrounding rocks, a rope ladder cascaded down to touch the water, and resting along the pool's bank was a freshly repaired wooden barge. The rectangular boat curved upwards at the bow, and a simple short mast jutted from the center of the deck. A long bench built into the hull provided seating at the stern, next to the tiller. The *Burge traveling vessel* appeared to be just over twelve feet long by six feet wide and had a hull that made it appear more like a small ship than a barge. Oddly, I didn't see our cargo anywhere.

Darric and Bromly started hoisting the ladder up the ledge and rolling it into a bundle against the rock. The cat screeched an unpleasant chord and darted towards the rope ladder. Hooking her claws into the weave, she scampered down the remaining length. With the ladder growing shorter, she had no choice but to spastically toss her body towards the bank in an attempt to stay dry. Unsuccessful, she splashed into the shallows, crawled out of the mud, and shook her fur, puffing out the fuzz like a blooming burgundy dandelion.

The Hovel brothers erupted into laughter. I bit my lip, gazing over the edge to be sure she wasn't injured. The disgruntled feline perched on the stern, a look of detestation pulling all her dripping features downwards.

Bromly hollered in delight and leaped off the cliff. I yelped and covered my mouth. His descent took an eternity before he crashed into the water, making a colossal splash. I held my breath until he resurfaced.

"He's in a hurry this year," said Darric.

"He just flung himself over a cliff! And that's all you can say? He could have been hurt. What the hell has come over him?"

"He's in love," Flint sing-songed.

Darric stood next to me. "Hit the water with your feet, Aya. It hurts less."

"Hurry up!" Bromly called from the pool.

"You're not expecting me to jump down there?" I reeled with skepticism, discovering why the three had returned to the Hovel soaking wet every day.

My knees knocked together. The longer I peered over the edge, the dizzier I became.

"Priorities, Aya. You can face me dual wielding, but you can't jump off a little cliff?" Darric questioned.

I groaned. "I assumed we would be cutting through brush or climbing, not contemplating suicide."

"You can always stay here." He gave me a smug grin.

I narrowed my eyes at him. No more time to think. I filled my lungs to capacity and propelled myself off the ledge.

My legs sent a scream up my spine. The world flew by in a blur. The wind whipped at my face and dried my eyes. I couldn't see the water coming.

The rock-hard impact tingled through the souls of my shoes as the icy pond knocked the wind from my lungs. I swam for the surface and drew air back into my empty chest.

The weight of my dress made it impossible to stay afloat, and I furiously searched for the bank. Darric emerged beside me. He shook water from his head, and his unruly hair flared in haphazard directions.

"It's so cold." I shivered, clenching my jaw to stop my teeth from chattering.

"It's melting ice caps." He pulled me into his arms to ease my struggle. "Your lips are such a lovely shade of purple," he murmured.

The water didn't feel so cold in the warmth of his embrace. He pressed his nose into the back of my neck, and everything went fuzzy. I tried to prevent the fog. I didn't want to feel it anymore. I wanted to see him clearly and remember every detail in each moment he touched me.

"Why couldn't ya jus' leave the ladder?" Flint called, still waiting on the cliff.

"We don't leave the ladder because it makes our location obvious," Darric said to only me, his lips brushing my skin. "Flint is always the last to jump. He has absolutely no nerve."

Flint went rigid watching his older brother so close to me, and a baleful sneer warped his face. He backed three steps away from the ledge and sped forwards, launching himself into the air. He tried to dip his head into a graceful dive, but he overaccelerated. His limbs flailed like a rag doll. Unable to reorient himself, he hit the water headfirst with a loud slap and sank beneath the ripples.

"Shit!" Darric released me to swim to his brother's aid. Without him keeping me from sinking, I had no choice but to swim for the shore. Bromly frantically ran from the bank, sloshing through the shallows.

Flint's lifeless body bobbed on the surface, a trail of blood dripping out of his mouth. Small waves lapped over his torso as Bromly and Darric dragged his pale, limp form to shore. Tears welled in my eyes.

"He's not breathing." Darric turned Flint's face out of the mud.

Don't be dead—Don't be dead—Don't be dead.

"Breathe! Damnit, breathe!" Bromly hit him in the chest and slapped him, sending the blood in Flint's mouth spraying across his cheek.

"He's okay, right? He's going to be okay?" I blubbered.

Darric glanced at my distraught face with only his eyes, giving no reassurance.

"Do something!" I screamed.

He shoved Bromly off Flint's chest and wrapped his hand around his motionless brother's neck, searching for a pulse.

A huge smile grew across Flint's mouth. His front tooth was chipped, and his teeth were coated in blood. "I require a kiss from Aya to awaken." His eyes shot open, and he released a howl of hysterical laughter.

Darric tightened his grip on his brother's throat, raised him off the ground, and forcibly slammed him back into the dirt. "You stupid motherfucker!" he erupted. Flint yelped a pathetic squeak from the punch to his larynx.

Darric stormed to the cliff face and rested his hands on the stone, visibly trying to quell the trembling in his shoulders.

Bromly sank into the mud, removed his cap, and angrily wrung the fabric between his fingers.

"Oh, c'mon, it was funny." Flint choked between laughs. "The three of ya were frantic. It was great."

My cheeks burned with uncontrollable rage. "You! Unimaginable! Ass! Flint Keene!" I cried and kicked him in the ribs as hard as I could. "I thought you were dead!"

Flint grasped his side and rolled. "Damn, Aya, just 'cause I'm alive don't mean that fall didn't really hurt!" He wiped the side of his face, smearing blood onto his fingers. "Look. Blood."

"Do your worst, Aya." Darric leaned against the rock, unwilling to intervene.

"Kick him again," Bromly added scornfully.

I dug my nails into my scalp and ran from the shore before I committed murder. Landing on a large rock just inside the trees, I buried my face in my hands.

"Aya, it was a joke," Flint called, trying to sit up. The moment he stood he lost his balance, catching himself on the side of the barge. "My chest is burning," he admitted, taking a shallow breath, and winced.

Darric approached the barge. "It's probably a cracked rib, but whether Aya or the fall caused it is up for debate. We'll lay him in the bow. He'll be fine by the time we reach Burge." He leaned onto the hull and spoke directly to Flint. "I hope you're proud of yourself."

"So worried I was dead. Now so pissed," Flint grumbled, rubbing his tongue over his newly chipped tooth. "Admit it, Darric, if somethin' truly happened to me, you'd miss me."

"If you ever do something that stupid again just for a laugh, then I'm going to give myself the opportunity to find out," Darric berated. "Lucky for you that broken rib is going to be an ample punishment. Have fun trying to breathe over the next couple weeks. Maybe you'll find some fucking humor in that."

Flint groaned and whined as his brothers helped him into the barge.

Darric grabbed my waist and lifted me over the hull. I'd never been on a boat. Luken used to tell me stories of the Duvali fishing ships that lined the coast, but I suspected this barge paled in comparison.

I curiously looked around and finally asked, "Where is everything?"

"Inside the hull, below the floor," Darric answered. "Illegal cargo, remember?"

"That's amazingly brilliant." I stared at the deck, searching for signs of the stash, but there was no indication of anything.

Bromly removed a loose board to pull necessary supplies from under the floor: a metal frame that would hold a small fire above the wood planking, several pillows, and cotton blankets. Darric nailed linen to the top of the four-foot-tall mast and draped it over the bow, creating a tent that offered some privacy and a place to sleep. Once the floor inside the tent was covered with bedding, Flint curled into the soft pillows.

I leaned into the railing and waited as Darric and Bromly jumped onto the bank and untied the rope holding the barge to the shore. They gave the boat a huge shove and reboarded as it floated into deeper water.

Bromly relaxed on the floor, adding cut logs to the metal frame. Darric took the tiller and steered the barge towards the river. The vessel moved into the endless string of blue cutting through the lush mountain forest, taking me farther away from home than I'd ever been.

I smiled with excitement and glanced back at my stranger. He returned my joy with a wry smirk, and his beautiful steel-blue eyes gripped tighter around my falling heart.

Bromly's Appendices 1

"Aya." I wrapped my hands around this tiny woman's shoulders. She was exquisite and cared for, even if she was dirty from days of travel. Her puffy bottom lip was split but still a supple pink in color.

Her eyes rolled back into her heart-shaped face, and I shook her, hard. She went limp, melting into Darric's arms. "Aya!" I shouted. "Did they make you drink anything? Aya! Answer me! Damn it, Darric!" I released my grip and took a handful of Darric's shirt. "How could you do this?" This was heinous, even for him. My younger brother offered a quick end; he never let people suffer. It appalled him.

Darric stared at her wasting frame, cradling her in his arms like the most precious object he'd ever held. "I couldn't leave her there."

I blinked furiously, trying to comprehend the surreal way he looked at her. I had never seen him look at any woman as if he needed her. As if permanent anguish would consume him if she died in his arms in the middle of the cavern floor.

"We need to get her into the house," I said. For everyone's sake, I had to calm down and ignore the oddity of Darric's actions until we stabilized her.

Flint's neurotic green eyes darted in a mix of confusion and excitement.

Darric ran his arm under the girl's knees and lifted her from the ground, nothing but a light corpse of dead weight. The color was quickly vanishing from her face, creating a ghostlike haze over her skin. She was reacting to the poison at an astonishing rate. If we didn't work fast, she would be dead before nightfall.

I pulled the front door aside for Darric.

"Put her in my room!" Flint bounced eagerly, exuding astounding ignorance. This beautiful creature was dying, and he cared only to celebrate her arrival.

"Your room is decrepit. Darric doesn't sleep. She'll go in his," I blurted.

Darric had the same idea. He quickly moved to his room, his travel companion squeezed to his chest. He lowered her onto the mattress and laid two fingers on her neck, looking for a pulse. "Bromly, I need you to brew tea. It will help detox her."

"How ya gonna get her to drink it?" Flint asked, blocking the doorway.

I shuffled through the baskets above the workbench looking for tea bags, knocking over cups and spoons until I found five—critical for a strong dose. "Flint," I called as he lustfully gazed at our half-dead visitor.

"She's gorgeous," he said, ignoring me.

"Flint!" I yelled, snatching the kettle from under the table. "I need more water. This won't be enough." I emptied the remainder of the bucket into the pot.

"You go get it," he said and immersed himself back in the girl.

Darric busily unlaced her shoes and let the small boots fall to the floor; they would have fit a child.

"What 'bout her dress? We should take that off too," Flint suggested, his desirous eyes tripping over the girl's body. "I'll help."

"Go get the fucking water!" Darric roared. My heart rate spiked. I hated when he used that malevolent tone; in all these years I'd never become used to it.

Flint backed out of the doorframe with a huff. In no particular hurry, he snatched the bucket and disappeared from the Hovel.

I sank the kettle into the coals and dropped in the tea bags. The sparse water quickly began to simmer. "Tea's on," I announced and joined Darric in his room.

The girl had turned lily white except for the delicate skin around her eyes, which was a dark, morbid gray. Her unnaturally long almond curls were strewn across the bedding. No denying it; even in the first stage of death, she maintained every ounce of the unmeasurable beauty she'd held in life, from her thick lashes to her fading lips. My thoughts went to Hazel and what she would think upon learning a woman had stayed at the Hovel. "Do you need anything else? Your pack?"

Darric shook his head and leaned into the bed.

"It might be the wrong time to ask, but what the hell possessed you to bring some poisoned bandit girl here?"

He hung his head and squeezed the bridge of his nose. "I had the most colossal lapse of judgment of my entire life. I'm not ready to explain it to you."

"Brilliant." I groaned. "So, now what?"

"I haven't thought that far. I truthfully thought she would be dead before we arrived. I even tried sleeping in hopes I could end her with a sword so she wouldn't have to suffer the poison."

"That is sick." My upper lip quivered in disgust. "She has as good a chance of living as she does dying."

He squeezed his eyes shut, as if thinking of her dead caused him physical pain. "Are you going to berate me? Try to make me feel worse than I already do?"

"No, you'll be hard enough on yourself. I just hope you know what you're doing."

Darric moved her skirt to expose her bare ankles. From under the pillow, he removed a dagger in a luxurious black scabbard. He loosely wrapped the supple leather fastenings around her ankle, making sure not to cut off circulation.

"She's armed?" I questioned.

"She's armed," he repeated, bewildered, ". . . with a Hell Squad dagger from the Alpha's stock. It's identical to the one I used."

"How the fuck did she get that?" I asked, stunned.

He tugged the bottom of her dress over her feet and brought the fur covers up to her knees. "I don't know. Onyx Guard weapons are impossible for citizens to obtain. And the Alpha's stock is under lock and key." He squatted onto the balls of his feet and leaned his forearms onto the bed. "I'm in over my head this time. If this girl wakes up . . . I don't know what we are going to do. Everything will change."

"I wish you wouldn't do this right now—the cryptic hinting when you want to express what's on your mind but can't bring yourself to say it."

"I'm not expecting her to survive, but if she does, I'll need you to understand something." He lifted his eyes and looked over her face. "The day will come when I'll have to explain why I did this, and I need you to attempt to not be furious with me. Before you ask one hundred questions, just know, I won't be able to kill her like the others who have wandered here."

"So, she's staying?" I asked, amazed.

"She is staying," he murmured, "but I'll deny it."

I groaned. Her chest slowly rose and fell, long deep breaths that fought for life. "How long has she been with you?"

He slid away from the bed and propped himself against the wall. "A couple days. I don't know much about her. I didn't bother." He scoffed. "I wouldn't be in this mess if Flint didn't keep insisting I stop for the damn dried pork."

"I've got the water!" Flint burst into the Hovel. He dropped the bucket by the doorway, sloshing water onto the floor, and almost tripped over the fire. "She's still alive, right? Did I miss anythin'?" He shoved me out of the way to get a better look inside Darric's room.

I sighed and tended to the tea. When the first dose was ready, I filled a cup and blew vigorously over the liquid before bringing it into the bedroom. Darric slid his hand under Aya's head, lifted the dead weight, and poured a small amount into her mouth. Setting the cup on the nightstand, he massaged her neck until the medicinal brew eased down her throat.

It was time consuming and tedious, but Darric worked late into the night, refusing to leave her side. Eventually, Flint fell asleep on the floor. I threw him over my shoulder and dumped him on his bed to give Darric some peace from prying eyes, then slunk to my room and lay on top of the covers, staring at the dark ceiling.

Darric had never been one to care about rules or regulations. He lived by his own creed. But bringing a girl to the Hovel after she'd failed to adhere to her fate broke the rules he'd set for all of us.

When the sun rose over the valley and the Hovel quieted into a ringing silence, I caught the last private murmurs of his distraught state. He incoherently mumbled to himself, reeling in anguish that she was going to die.

In the past, I'd witnessed him kill without mercy, carefully concealing his emotions under the thick blanket of secrecy he'd learned from the Onyx Guard. He never mourned. Never wavered in his steel strength. But the pain he displayed over this girl made him seem broken. Who was she?

Lost in his turmoil, he didn't notice me creeping around the doorframe. He ran a finger over her icy hand, analyzing her like a beautiful unsolvable puzzle. She took a deep breath, stronger than the last, and seemed to benefit from his touch.

"Don't die," he whispered, taking her hand in his and dipping his forehead to rest it upon their interlocked fingers. I took a step back but couldn't pull myself away. "You can't die. Please, hold on. Minutes at a time if you can." His lips brushed one of the many lacerations marring her delicate skin. "Are you already going to force me to live without you? Please, stay with me."

My jaw fell.

I dropped onto my bed and rubbed my hands into my beard, then massaged my ears to ensure they were working properly. I must have misheard him. There was no other logical explanation. The concept of Darric Ursygh falling in love . . . well, that was as impossible as the closure of the Riving.

For information on upcoming releases visit
www.AnnaPatrickPaige.com
or follow on social media.
www.facebook.com/annapatrickpaigebooks
www.facebook.com/groups/theGlitterandGoreBasement
instagram @Anna Patrick Paige
twitter @annapatpaige